OPEN INVITATION

Open Invitation

—— JASMINE HAYNES ——

HEAT
NEW YORK, NEW YORK

THE BERKLEY PUBLISHING GROUP
Published by the Penguin Group
Penguin Group (USA) Inc.
375 Hudson Street, New York, New York 10014, USA
Penguin Group (Canada), 90 Eglinton Avenue East, Suite 700, Toronto, Ontario M4P 2Y3, Canada
(a division of Pearson Penguin Canada Inc.)
Penguin Books Ltd., 80 Strand, London WC2R 0RL, England
Penguin Group Ireland, 25 St. Stephen's Green, Dublin 2, Ireland (a division of Penguin Books Ltd.)
Penguin Group (Australia), 250 Camberwell Road, Camberwell, Victoria 3124, Australia
(a division of Pearson Australia Group Pty. Ltd.)
Penguin Books India Pvt. Ltd., 11 Community Centre, Panchsheel Park, New Delhi—110 017, India
Penguin Group (NZ), Cnr. Airborne and Rosedale Roads, Albany, Auckland 1310, New Zealand
(a division of Pearson New Zealand Ltd.)
Penguin Books (South Africa) (Pty.) Ltd., 24 Sturdee Avenue, Rosebank, Johannesburg 2196,
South Africa

Penguin Books Ltd., Registered Offices: 80 Strand, London WC2R 0RL, England

This book is an original publication of The Berkley Publishing Group.

This is a work of fiction. Names, characters, places, and incidents either are the product of the author's imagination or are used fictitiously, and any resemblance to actual persons, living or dead, business establishments, events, or locales is entirely coincidental. The publisher does not have any control over and does not assume any responsibility for author or third-party websites or their content.

OPEN INVITATION

First edition: December 2006

Heat trade paperback ISBN: 0-425-21360-9

An application to register this book for cataloging has been submitted to the Library of Congress.

PRINTED IN THE UNITED STATES OF AMERICA

10   9   8   7   6   5   4   3   2   1

To Linda Simi
For always listening, and actually hearing, too!

Special thanks to
Jenn Cummings, Terri Schaefer, Rose Lerma,
Lucienne Diver, and Christine Zika.

CONTENTS

Invitation to Seduction

PROLOGUE

THE ECHO OF her moans faded through the open window into the summer night. The tremors of her self-induced orgasm dissipated. Hot, she pushed the covers aside, then rolled and hugged her knees. Her belly ached as if she were starving, and a giant-sized fist squeezed her heart.

Lately, she'd taken to moaning loudly and thrashing on the bed in the hopes that her husband would get so turned on he'd have to join her. Instead, he upped the volume on the TV. She'd made the mistake of suggesting they turn one of the guest rooms into a den so they could use the living room for entertaining. They didn't entertain, so the room never got used, and now she had surround sound pounding through the wall that adjoined their bedroom.

She could count on one hand the number of times he'd made love to her in the last five years. She clearly remembered the last time. Halloween, after they'd run out of candy and turned off all the lights so the kids wouldn't knock. Nine months ago. My God, she could have had a baby in that time. Not that she wanted to become a mother at the age of thirty-nine.

No, she wanted him to make love to her more than once in nine months.

So what had happened to them? He'd never been as sexual as she was, but in a slow degradation of their intimacy, lovemaking had dwindled to practically nothing. Three years ago, she'd suggested he see a doctor. For her, the specter of impotency was more palatable than believing he'd stopped wanting *her*. As delicately as she thought she'd broached the subject, that had been one of the worst arguments in their fifteen-year marriage. He'd reacted as if she'd accused him of murder, he'd refused to get help, and he wouldn't even acknowledge there was a problem.

Right or wrong, she'd taken the path of least resistance and never mentioned impotency again. But she couldn't help feeling that if he truly loved her, he wouldn't be so unwilling to at least participate in finding a solution.

She couldn't breathe over the pain that seized her throat, her chest, every muscle, every corpuscle. She didn't crave only sex. She wanted the passion, the fire, that overwhelming high when a man groaned, then whispered, "I'm going to die if I don't get inside you right this minute."

Without that kind of passion, *she* wanted to die.

The worst thing was, she couldn't tell anyone. Her friends would look at her as if she'd lost her mind. *So, why haven't you left him? Why are you still there? Where are your guts? Leave him! Or at least take a lover.*

Her guts were lying on the floor in a puddle beside the bed, ripped out by the TV's unbearable volume in the next room.

He wasn't a bad man. He didn't beat her, he did the dishes every night, he managed not to pee all over the toilet seat, and most of the time he left the lid down. He could make her laugh until her sides hurt, and he knew something about everything, not the know-it-all kind of thing, just smart and well-read. He made her coffee in the morning and called her from work every day. He stopped on the way home for the milk she'd forgotten to pick up, and he never complained if all she had time to prepare was Hamburger Helper. When she was freaking out over something at work, he soothed her frayed nerves. He was a good man.

Together, they'd worked hard so that next year she would be able to retire to focus on her stained glass work. She now had a contractor who recommended her custom windows to his upscale remodel clients. She'd opened her own business checking account, and she'd been in the black for months. Their future looked bright. Financial freedom was just around the corner.

But what good was a flourishing business when you barely had the will to get out of bed in the morning? What good did it do to think about changing your life when you were terrified that no one else would want you either? That you'd end up alone.

Old.

And unwanted.

ONE

"SO, WHAT ARE you wearing tomorrow night?"

Sackcloth. "I haven't decided yet."

Debbie Carter hadn't decided on her attire for tomorrow night's bachelorette party because she hadn't decided if she was going. She wasn't sure she could take all the happiness, the giddiness, and the sexual innuendo. Well, where they were going, there might be more than sexual innuendo. A lot more. She was too damn tired to withstand it all. *Not now, please, not now.*

Stacy, her friend and manicurist for years, shook Debbie's fingers. "Relax, will ya? Bad day at work?"

Bad day, bad year. Right now, the most she could manage was a topic shift. "Don't you think it's kind of strange that Virginia's having her bachelorette party at a sex club?"

Stacy rolled her eyes. "She's hit the big four-oh, and she's getting married for the fourth time. What do you expect, a nice little girlie get-together that her grandmother could attend?"

"I'm not sure about this. Tell me what goes on at these places."

A wicked grin curved Stacy's lips. "That's what we're going to find out. Did you tell your husband where we're going?"

She'd thought about mentioning their destination, wondering if the idea would get his motor running. She'd chickened out for fear that it wouldn't. "No. Men are sworn to secrecy about what happens at bachelor parties, and women should do the same."

"Jeez, everyone knows what goes on at bachelor parties. Some little hottie with big tits jumps out of a cake and goes down on the groom."

"Do they?" Debbie leaned forward. "How do you know?"

Stacy winked. "With inducement, someone always tells."

Debbie knew what inducement Stacy had used. Forty-five, with a body and face that looked ten years younger, she didn't hide the fact that she was a woman at her sexual peak. With her red-gold hair, D-cup breasts, and a sexy laugh that turned men's heads, Stacy attracted the opposite sex like honey. Debbie admired her for it, though she avoided looking in the mirror when Stacy was standing next to her. Not because of the hair or the breasts or the full lips. No, it was the sparkle in her friend's green eyes. That was what men wanted. They looked at the body, listened to the seductive laughter, but they approached because Stacy was so . . . alive. No one gave a damn about her age.

Next to her, Debbie felt ten years older instead of five years younger.

"Come to my house first. I've got an outfit for you."

"You know, I really think I'm going to skip this one." She wasn't good at mingling. Not in her current frame of mind.

"No." Stacy scowled. "You are *not* skipping this."

Debbie tilted her head at the sharp tone. "I'm not sure I can handle it."

Stacy's fingers tightened on hers. "You deserve this. And I'm going to make sure you have it."

Her sudden intensity made Debbie's heart race. "Have what?"

Looking down, Stacy seemed to realize she'd stopped filing Debbie's nails. She started once more, accidentally getting too close to the cuticle and filing the skin away. Debbie winced.

"Sorry." Stacy dabbed the spot of blood with antiseptic. "I just think you need to have a little girl fun. We'll have something to talk about for the next few months. Please come."

It was strange the way Stacy now talked to her fingers, and Debbie was convinced something odd had been in her tone, but the party had been planned for weeks. There would be just the three of them. Stacy, Debbie, and Virginia. More than ten years ago, they'd met at the company they'd all worked for in various departments. Though moving on to new jobs, they'd kept up the friendship, getting together every couple of months for dinner and girl talk. Which inevitably, with Stacy at the table, turned to sex talk. Increasingly, Debbie had found herself unable to join in the fun.

Which was pathetic. She had to stop feeling so damn sorry for herself. If she wasn't careful, the inscription on her tombstone would read, "She pitied herself to death."

"You don't have to do anything, Deb. I know you're married. But you're not dead."

Not physically, but deep inside, something *felt* dead.

"There's no harm in looking. It's a girl's night out."

Girl's night out. Just for fun. Something they could shock themselves with later. A taste of the wild side. It couldn't hurt her husband. He didn't really care anyway. In fact, he'd be glad she wasn't scrutinizing him across the dinner table, wondering if tonight would be the night.

It was only one night. Maybe, as Stacy said, she deserved it. And dammit, she *needed* to enjoy herself and end the excessive pity party she'd been engaging in lately. "All right, I'll go. What time do you want me at your place?"

"Seven. Aren't you even going to ask me about the outfit?"

"No. I'm giving you carte blanche."

Stacy sat back, regarding her, once again forgetting to file. "Wow. That's trusting."

Actually, it was scary as hell. Stacy had an awesome—and somewhat revealing—wardrobe.

Patting her hand, Stacy went on, "Well, don't worry, I won't give you something that doesn't fit your boobs. So tell me, how's everything going with your contractor?"

"Oh my God. Stephen knows tons of people interested in my windows. I've done over sixteen pieces. Really big stuff, not sun catchers. Thank you so much for putting him in touch with me." Debbie felt her enthusiasm rise and her spirits lift. The only thing that gave her joy these days was working a beautiful piece of stained glass. That was truly the only time she felt in control of her life. Stephen, though they'd never met face-to-face, only e-mailed, had done a lot to help her feel that way. "By the end of the year, if this keeps up, I'll be able to quit work."

Stacy did a final buff. "That's great. I'm so happy for you. I'll pick out your polish while you go wash your hands."

"Don't choose anything too outrageous."

Stacy smiled, another wicked grin.

"IT'S A VERITABLE mansion." Virginia, seated in the backseat, rolled down her window. For the outing, she'd worn a peach silk suit, the skirt covering her to her knees. Next to Stacy, and Debbie in her sexy borrowed skirt and blouse, Virginia looked like a maiden aunt. Yet this place had been her choice, though Debbie thought The Sex Club was way out of character for Virginia.

Set amid a grove of eucalyptus at the end of a long, sloping drive, with the moon providing the only illumination, the house looked like something out of a Vincent Price movie. A hulking behemoth over three stories high, with dormer windows at presumably the attic level. No lights filled any of the windows. No valet parking attendants swarmed about the wide stone porch. Not a single living soul moved; not even a curtain flickered.

"It's so quiet," Virginia said, "it's almost creepy."

Stacy huffed. "It's private. And exclusive. What did you expect, floodlights and a marching band?"

Debbie didn't find the mansion creepy. Excitement rippled through her at the sight of it. The Sex Club's mystery made her blood pump faster and her nipples harden. Moisture gathered between her thighs. The darkness beckoned, promised secrecy, seduction, and fantasy fulfillment. *Just* fantasy, she didn't have to *do* anything. Observe, pretend for a little while. Jaywalk over to the wild side for a night. The clingy black top and skirt Stacy had loaned her, the high heels and stockings with garter belt, even the truly outrageous shade of vermillion Stacy had painted on her nails, all fit her blossoming mood. She'd walked out of her home with the promise to herself that something spectacular was going to happen. Something that would make her feel alive. This was a night for magic and a house that invited it.

Some gorgeous man was going to seduce her with nothing more than a look. Of course, she wouldn't act on it, but she would believe, for one night, that she was gorgeous, sexy, and desirable. She wanted to add to her store of fantasies that could be put to good use when she was going mad for an orgasm.

Stacy maneuvered the car into the parking garage, which turned out to be under the house, pulled into a spot, and turned off the engine. Porsches, Jags, and BMWs dominated in the underground lot. Sex appeared to be for the rich, at least here.

"Virginia, the invitations, please." Stacy waggled her fingers, her French manicure gleaming in the shaft of overhead light falling through the windshield.

Virginia pulled the stack of cream-colored envelopes from her purse. Stacy took them with a flourish. "Now, ladies, here are the rules. It's invitation *only* the first time. After that, women are allowed without it. Or, sometimes a woman might be sent an invitation by a very special someone." She arched a brow and smiled, which made Debbie think Stacy'd been honored with a special invite at one time or another.

"But men," Stacy went on, "*always* have to have an invitation or they don't get in. That excludes horn-dog frat boys who don't know a clitoris from a hole in the wall and aren't willing to spend the time to learn. We don't use real names. We do use condoms. They have bowls of them all over the place. Like candy dishes. We say no to whatever we don't want, and we say yes to whatever we do. If somebody bugs you, you tell an attendant, and the offending party bites the dust. Got it?"

With all the talk about clitorises and condoms, Debbie glanced back at Virginia. She was getting married tomorrow in Las Vegas. Was she out simply for a night of titillation before settling down? Or did she plan on something more? Titillation, Debbie decided, or Virginia would have chosen a more provocative outfit than the peach suit.

Stacy flipped through the gold-labeled envelopes in her lap. "This one's mine. Serena." She put a hand to her sequined chest. "I look like a Serena, don't you think?" *Serena* could do anything she wanted, she had that kind of feminine power.

She handed the second invitation to Virginia. "Regina."

Virginia wrinkled her nose. "I was going to say something about that earlier. It reminds me a little of vagina."

Stacy smiled. "Depends on how you say it when you introduce yourself, darling." Then she got to the last envelope.

Debbie held her breath.

"Desiree."

Debbie held the invitation lightly in her fingers, the name embossed in gold. *Desiree. Desire.* "I like it," she whispered. "So this is the name we give if anyone asks?"

Stacy gave her the once-over. "Everyone's going to ask. No real names, remember."

Debbie traced the raised lettering. "This place must cost a fortune to get into. You haven't asked for any money."

"The first time, you're a guest." Stacy held her gaze.

"The first time?"

"Almost everyone comes back."

Debbie felt the challenge in the statement. For a moment, she got the distinct impression that Stacy knew her entire marital history, even the months and years between lovemaking. She'd given herself away somehow, though she couldn't remember even hinting at her problem.

Stacy turned in her seat. "Now, we can stick together or we split off. But we'll meet back in the lobby at midnight." She checked her thin gold watch. "That gives us three hours."

Virginia just smiled, a secretive smile Debbie could swear she'd never seen before.

Stacy yanked on her door handle. "Well, ladies, let's see where the night leads us."

LEANING AGAINST A column at the top of the stairs, Stephen Knight recognized Debbie the moment she entered. Her Web site picture didn't do her justice. Her blond hair, teased lightly around her face, curled about her shoulders. Her black stretch top clung to her breasts, large enough to fill a man's hands, small enough to maintain their perkiness. She turned to the side, revealing peaked nipples, yet her hand shook as she handed over the invitation. Her ass begged to be touched in that form-fitting skirt, and sheer black stockings molded to her toned calves. In those heels, her height was perfect for a quick fuck against the wall.

Except that she was so much more than a quick fuck.

This place would give her the shock of her life. He wanted to watch every moment of her journey, to drink in the scent of her arousal, the musky aroma of wet woman. He wanted to see the darkening of her eyes and watch the tip of her tongue sneak out to lick her dry lips. She'd drink champagne; the stuff flowed freely at the club. The taste of it, the bubbles tickling her throat as she swallowed and the headiness as the sparkling wine seeped into her bloodstream, would drive her arousal higher.

Then he'd reveal himself to her. He would touch her if she allowed, kiss those lips, skim his fingers over her nipples, then cup her bottom in his hands. If not tonight, another night. He'd wait as many nights as he had to.

There were things he knew from her e-mails, her enthusiasm over the custom stained glass orders he'd steered her way. Her creative mind, her sense of color and form, her ability to read people, to figure out what they wanted when they didn't even know themselves, her sensitivity. And her need for praise. He could sense her self-respect grow when he marveled at her work, almost as if she didn't believe the piece was good until he told her. They'd only worked together online a few months, but he'd learned to read her moods. He detected when she was down, more often of late, the tone of her e-mails more curt, sometimes wistful, and in the last weeks, almost despondent. He read her unhappiness between the lines of everything she wrote to him, even though their e-mails couldn't be called personal. At first, she'd politely asked how he was, chatted about work, a new project she'd envisioned, then their business. Lately, he'd sensed her creativity drying up along with her ability to make small talk. She no longer responded to his compliments about her talent, as if she'd completely lost the belief in herself he'd helped her build over the last few months.

There were, of course, the more personal things Stacy told him. Because her friend was tight-lipped about her emotions, Stacy learned more from what Debbie didn't say rather than from what she did, especially her sudden silences when the talk at their girlfriend get-togethers turned to sex and men.

It didn't take a brain surgeon to figure out that Debbie Carter badly needed some loving. It didn't take her manicurist to tell him that Debbie's husband wasn't up to the task. He was probably out porking his secretary instead of making love to the beautiful woman occupying the opposite side of his bed.

If he was having an affair, her husband was a goddamn idiot, and he didn't deserve the gorgeous lady he was married to.

Stephen intended to show her that, while proving to her that she was beautiful, desirable, and everything he'd ever wanted.

TWO

MARBLE COVERED THE lobby floor, which was like the formal entry hall of a grand home, complete with a ceiling chandelier, Greek columns, and a T-bone stairway with a huge mirror on the middle landing. The lobby was empty except for their hostess, though music floated softly on the air. Debbie had expected a much more sordid atmosphere. This was . . . classy.

A waiter appeared with a tray of champagne flutes.

The rules buzzed in her head as she sipped champagne. Don't touch unless invited. Don't accept unless you want to. And the condom command several times over. Black-suited male attendants located themselves at strategic positions. If anything got out of control, they would take care of the problem. *"Feel free to explore all the rooms, stop where you want, partake as you wish."*

Like a tour guide at Hearst Castle, their hostess drew them a verbal map. On the first floor to the right, through double doors that had been soundproofed with rubber molding, were the viewing rooms. Performance art. Debbie had heard of such a thing, but she didn't think this would be anything like what she'd seen on PBS. To the left, through an ornate set of doors was a grand ballroom. It wasn't in use tonight.

On the second floor, well, every kind of sexual vice you could think of. Couples, women on women, BDSM, orgies. Their guide's smile never wavered as she described the outrageous activities, and Debbie had to stifle an inappropriate giggle. The private rooms occupied the third level, some of them decorated in a theme, complete with costumes. Though Debbie figured the costumes didn't stay on for long.

The hostess smiled. "Now you're free to move about at will. The ladies' lounge is right through there." She pointed to an unobtrusive door that Debbie had mistaken for a coat closet.

"Regina," Stacy said as soon as the woman left them, "your choice, since it's your party. Where to first?"

Virginia tapped her lip. "Orgy Galore."

Stacy grabbed her hand. "Good choice. We're off, ladies."

Debbie trailed behind as they climbed the stairs. The music was only slightly louder in the wide, second floor hall. Wall sconces provided a muted illumination. Here, people milled about, sipping champagne, talking, laughing, and moving from room to room. The women were dressed in anything from cocktail dresses and long gowns to sexy, tight clothing like Debbie wore. Male attire ran the gamut from tuxedos to jeans.

Exiting a door, a couple leaned against the wall for a long kiss, the man's hands stealing inside the woman's unbuttoned blouse. Debbie stared as he openly massaged her breast. "You know, I think I'm going to wander by myself."

Virginia stopped in the middle of the hall. "Are you sure?"

Debbie felt the soft strains of the music inside her, a forties standard. She didn't want to share this night with her friends. This night was hers alone. She backed away. "I'm going that way. I'll see you at midnight." Like Cinderella.

*   *   *

STACY CAUGHT HIS eye, giving him a brief nod in Debbie's direction. Stacy had secured his invitation and given him his instructions. He was to follow Debbie, take care of her, and show her a good time. Stacy was good at issuing orders, but she'd relinquished all control to him the day she'd given him Debbie's Web address, told him of her friend's magnificent artwork, and suggested he recommend her windows to his clients.

Whatever happened now was between him and Debbie.

DEBBIE STOPPED AT the fourth doorway just short of entering and gripped the jamb to steady herself. So much going on around her: sex, the sounds of sex, the scent of it. She sipped her champagne to calm herself, but the bubbles went straight to her head. She put a hand to the rapid rise and fall of her chest.

A couple bumped her arm as they entered the room. The man's eyes fell to the swell of flesh above Debbie's low-cut neckline. Then, raising his gaze to hers, he smiled and licked his lips.

Moisture rushed between her legs. God, he found her desirable. It was magic, momentous, maybe even the "something spectacular" she'd been thinking of earlier.

The man's broad shoulders disappeared beyond the door. She knew she'd follow. Not for him. But for herself.

Straightening, she entered.

Sconces lined the walls as they did in the hall, leaving much of the room dimly lit. An abundance of comfortable sofas, chaises, overstuffed chairs, and ottomans consumed the room. Every available seat was occupied.

At first glance, the sight was tame, a civilized gathering of well-dressed yuppies. Social drinking, small talk, laughter, and the soft beat of yet another standard tune. Except that man over on the sofa had his hand up his companion's skirt. As Debbie watched, the woman spread her legs slightly and put her hands on top of his, guiding him. And over there, on a chaise, a woman in a long gown pulled down a man's zipper and removed his cock. He set his drink on a nearby table, then laced his hands behind his head as she stroked his penis, crooned to it, then took him in her mouth. For what seemed like forever, Debbie couldn't tear her eyes from the sight of that erect cock sliding in and out of the woman's shiny red lips.

My God, sex was everywhere if you just looked. In the soft light of a sconce, a brunette rocked herself gently on a male lap. He bunched her lemon-yellow dress in his fists and revealed his cock sliding in, sliding out. The penetration mesmerized Debbie. Her eyes trailed his fingers as he stroked up the back of that lemon dress. She met his gaze. He was the man who had passed her in the doorway. The one who had licked his lips. He stared at Debbie as he fucked the other woman. The heat in his eyes said she could have the honors next, if she chose.

"Excuse me." A woman pushed past her, forcing her farther into the room. The blonde's nipples peeked above the line of her dress, which was short enough to reveal her pubic hair.

Moving aside, Debbie leaned against a table, traded her empty glass of champagne for a full one, then drank as if she were parched. Maybe ditching the others had been a mistake.

She wasn't a prude. A prude didn't give herself orgasms. But this shocked her. Titillated her. Her panties were damp, her lace bra chafed her nipples, and she had the insane need to touch herself. To touch someone.

What made her heart ache, in addition to all her other bodily parts, was the fact that the majority of men in the room were not young studs. They were her age. Her husband's age.

They were living, breathing, horny proof that something was rotten in her marriage. Her vision blurred, and she sucked in air, almost choking on the sudden tightening in her throat.

Stop pitying yourself.

Deliberately stuffing down the maudlin thoughts, she reached for her glass and brushed warm fingers.

HE CAUGHT THE flute before it fell. Debbie's expression was a mixture of shock and excitement. As he'd imagined, her arousal scented the air around her, a subtle, sensual aroma that made his balls tighten and his cock jump. He wanted to linger, to talk, to touch his lips to her beautiful mouth. But rushing the moment might destroy it. He wanted her past the point of fear, riding the edge of arousal where she was consumed by what she saw, creamy on the inside, unable to utter a word, where even taking a breath was enough to bring her to orgasm.

"Your champagne?" He handed her the glass, letting his fingers touch hers briefly in the exchange.

"Thank you."

She wet her lips with the tip of her tongue, blue eyes wide, the dilated pupils attesting to her surprise and innocence amid the decadence in the room. He wanted to bury his cock inside her. She was gorgeous, the kind of woman capable of tying a man's gut into knots.

He backed away, holding her gaze until he could disappear into the shadowed hallway. He wanted her, Lord, how he wanted her. Still, he was a patient man. He didn't fear that she would turn to someone else in one of the rooms she explored. She wasn't ready for that.

No, when she finally decided she needed a man, he'd make sure she came to him.

GOD. THAT VOICE. It caressed her lips, her breasts, then reached between her legs. She watched until the man vanished among the hall rovers. She'd longed to touch his hair, run her fingers through the silver strands. He'd dressed more casually than most, a plain, dark, button-down shirt with black jeans. His tanned face didn't come from any sunlamp but from hard work outdoors. His fingers as they touched hers were rough with calluses. How good they'd feel against her clitoris.

She closed her eyes and pressed her thighs together. What was he doing here? She'd come for the titillation factor and to fantasize about letting herself go. What would a man with that handsome face and honed body need here? Was he married?

The word brought her back to herself. He might not be, but she was. Married to a man who hadn't made love to her in ages. Dammit, she deserved to feast her eyes on every little detail, had a right to see how the other half lived. A person yearns for what they lack, and with each successive night lying lonely in her marriage bed, the kinkier her fantasies had become.

Tonight was for *her*.

She pushed away from the table she'd leaned against and met a man's gaze head-on. The man who had invited her to have sex with a lick of his lips. *Not you,* she whispered in her mind. In her wildest fantasies, sex with multiple partners or in front of an audience, there had always been a bond with one man, one soul. She didn't have to be touching him or even looking at him. He was just there, watching her, wanting her, loving her.

The guy with his dick between yellow-clad thighs wasn't him.

She did, however, lift her glass in the air, tipping it in salute. Then she left the room. God, she felt alive. Tilting her head back, she drew in a deep breath of air laden with the musky intoxication of sex. Voices murmured along the hallway, the high pitch of laughter, the barely discernible moan of sexual release. Activity had picked up. Obviously their little group had arrived much earlier than most.

Passing another doorway, she glanced in and found herself compelled by the sights inside. Again, she entered to stand just inside the door to watch. Vibrators. Dildos. They were being fitted to every orifice, the gender of the user notwithstanding. Some worked the toys alone, but one couple in particular grabbed her attention. The male took the lead, stuffing the biggest vibrator she'd ever seen inside his partner's vagina. Pumping it, twirling it, making her moan then scream with it.

Debbie's skin felt suddenly flushed, hot, sweaty. God. Yes. She'd love that. It was so damn exciting that she could feel her nipples rasp against her clingy top.

Then she saw Virginia and Stacy chatting in the corner, watching the activity. She slipped out the door before they saw her. It might be Virginia's party, but it was Debbie's night.

Music beat against the soles of her feet. She longed to shed her high heels and let the rhythmic throb travel up her legs to her moist pussy. On the first level below was the wing for performance art, closed off by double doors and rubber stoppers.

Performance art definitely sounded interesting. She'd come to watch, to spin her fantasies, and beyond those doors, heaven awaited her. Heaven for a sex-starved almost-forty-year-old.

Weaving through the growing throng, she headed for the stairs. That's when she saw him a short distance down the hall. The silver-haired man. *Her* silver-haired man. She stopped, one hand on a newel post. He leaned against the wall, hands in his pockets. Some floozy with bleached hair sloshed the champagne in her glass as she waved her hand about. Clearly he wasn't listening. Nor was he looking at the woman's impressive chest.

His gaze stroked Debbie from her hair to her thighs and everywhere in between. Her knees turned to jelly, and she tightened her grip on the post. His eyes seduced her, set her skin on fire.

Her husband's eyes had never burned for her like that. Desire had nothing to do with age, because this man was older than her husband, perhaps close to fifty. He didn't hide his years with hair dye. Nor did she hide hers with caked-on makeup. Even in the dim lighting of the room down the hall, he would have seen the wrinkles at her eyes, the lines on her forehead.

Yet he'd looked a second time. He didn't stop looking when she caught him. A corner of his mouth lifted, then he blew a kiss in her direction. Oh my God, he was flirting. With *her*.

She laughed. Flirting? In a sex club? Where all you had to do to get laid was crawl onto a lap and pull down your panties? But that's how his kiss felt. Flirty. Innocent. It was all the more sexy for its very lack of explicitness.

The kiss tempted her to approach. Instead, she tipped her head, smiled shyly, and continued down the stairs as if her legs weren't about to collapse. As if her panties weren't wet.

The lobby, which she'd thought immense upon arriving, was now packed to the gills. She squeezed through, lifting another glass of champagne from a passing waiter. Hugging the glass to her chest to avoid spilling, she made it to the double doors on the left. They gave easily with a slight push.

Rock music drummed against her ears, and a strobe flashed at the end of the hall, disorienting her. The doors closed behind her with an audible vacuum-packed whoosh. The walls were painted black and littered with small round mirrors that reflected the strobe's flash. Light spilled into the hallway from numerous open doorways. A woman, her dress a neon orange in the strange lighting, exited one chamber and entered another across the hall.

Debbie peeked through the entrance. Fabric-covered partitions, like the ones forming her cubicle at work, had been set up all around to construct smaller octagonal rooms. Plexiglas filled the cutouts on each of the eight sides, creating long, narrow windows. The neon woman stopped, squinted through the Plexi, then moved on. Others enjoyed the sights, too, couples giggling like teenagers, men alone, women alone. What was inside those partitions? She almost stepped in, would have except that a shout rose from the room at the end of the hall. The strobe room. Debbie had to see what was going on in there.

The vacuum doors opened and closed, sending a gust of air

rushing up her skirt. She didn't have to turn to know he was behind her in the hallway. He'd followed. Stalking her. In another place, she'd have been frightened. Here, she wanted it.

She pushed through the crowded corridor, once more nestling the glass of champagne between her breasts. The cool liquid sloshed into her bra. Perhaps he'd offer to lick her skin clean.

Not that she'd let him, despite the hot buzz in her clit.

The room at the end, with its throbbing music, flashing lights, and surging voices, called to her. She squeezed through the crowded opening and slid along the wall. The show was in progress center stage, mattresses strewn about the floor with couples reclining and watching. Touching. She wondered how often they changed the sheets, then thrust the thought aside. It wasn't as if she was going to use one.

In the intermittent beat of the lights, a woman onstage slid down her partner's torso. Debbie didn't have a doubt as to where she was headed. Was it perverted to so love the feel of a man's cock in her mouth, the salty taste, the smooth texture of a fully aroused male organ? If it was, Debbie was going to hell for sure. She clenched her fists against the intense desire to join the woman on that stage. Her body wanted the sensations, her mouth wanted the taste. So badly, she ached.

Lips opening, the woman stroked with her tongue, then took his cock all the way in. Debbie's breath increased and her throat went dry as she savored the show. Her palms flat to the wall, she braced herself, squeezed her thighs together, willing the orgasm to build inside her. Her own juices drenched her panties. On a floor mattress, a woman spread her legs and touched herself. So close to doing that herself, Debbie dragged in a deep breath of air that smelled and tasted of hot, sweaty sex. Oh God, she wanted that cock. She wanted that come in her mouth. She wanted an orgasm brought on by someone else's touch.

The need was a physical ache behind her eyelids, in her chest, between her thighs. She tore her gaze away before she completely lost control.

And met *his* gaze. He stood by the opposite doorjamb, not more than five paces from her. Watching her, not the sex onstage. He tracked the rapid rise and fall of her breasts, the spasmodic clenching of her fingers. In a burst of light, she could see the hard ridge of his cock outlined against his jeans.

She realized she'd smashed her glass against the wall when she'd put her hands there to steady herself. Thankfully, she hadn't cut herself, but something wet trickled down her calf. Not her own moisture, but the cool lick of champagne.

She knew if she didn't leave right that minute, she'd drag her stalker onto one of those mattresses and beg for his cock in her mouth. Or worse, she'd beg him to fuck her.

He made a move as she bolted out the door. The hallway was a throng of hot bodies. She pushed and shoved, but she knew she'd never make it to the lobby before he was on her. Instead, she ducked into the room she'd seen earlier, the one with the octagonal cubicles, and hurried around the partitions to the back, praying the man hadn't seen her.

She clung to the edge of a long window opening and stared sightlessly into the small room created by the dividers. Her body still throbbed to that incessant beat, and her breath hurt her throat as she panted. Closing her eyes, she leaned her forehead against one of the Plexiglas cutouts.

She willed away the image of him filling her. She'd only wanted a little fun; she wasn't an adulterer. For God's sake, she didn't even know him. But that look had called to her starving soul.

"Get a grip," she whispered, using Stacy's words. Stacy. And Virginia. She glanced at her watch. Eleven thirty. She wasn't sure she could survive the next half hour without doing something reprehensible.

Wrong. She'd survived all these years without going outside her marriage. She'd been strong, despite the debilitating needs. She *was* strong. She could re-create this fantasy when she needed to. She didn't have to be consumed by her passions now.

Opening her eyes, she looked into the small cubicle, willed herself to watch dispassionately. Yet another mattress filled the octagonal room, covered with a silky black sheet and stacked with pillows. Muted lights illuminated the bed. Reclining on the cushions lay a nude woman. Debbie glanced at the other cubicles, at the faces glued to the Plexi, like a fifty-cent peep show where guys jacked off while they watched. She leaned back, checked the glass. It was clean, thank God.

The woman on the bed thrashed her head back and forth as her hand moved between her legs, fully enjoying her own touch. Her hips moved, lifting as she dug her heels into the sheet, striving to reach her peak. Then she relaxed, though the flick of her fingers continued. The scene went on and on, the rise, then backing off to savor. Debbie knew so well how the act worked. Bring yourself to the brink, but don't plunge over. Don't let yourself come until your body became a mind of its own, and you couldn't stop the orgasm if you tried. Those were the best ones.

What would touching herself be like with eyes on her?

Her clitoris began to throb once more. She clutched the edge of the small window. Is that why she'd gotten so turned on watching the woman on that stage? Because she actually wanted to *be* on that stage? Wanted all those people watching her?

"You like it, don't you?"

She jerked, but he held her firmly in place, his hands at her hips, his body pushing her against the divider. His scent, some spicy aftershave, intoxicated her.

"Would you like to be there, on that bed, knowing everyone was watching you get yourself off?" he whispered. His voice, deep, husky with desire, shivered along her spine.

She knew, horribly, that she would. She wouldn't be able to hold off the orgasm knowing all those eyes were on her, drinking in her moans, perhaps even touching themselves.

"I'd go mad watching you."

His breath caressed her hair, her ear, forcing a shudder she knew he could feel.

"I'd have to stroke my cock. I wouldn't be able to hold back. Oh Jesus."

He rubbed his erection in the crease of her butt. Her body, moving of its own volition, pushed back into him. The woman on the bed arched into her fingers, moving faster, her moans filtering through the fabric walls.

"Do you know how beautiful it is watching a woman touch herself? I want to watch you. I want to see your fingers dipping in all that hot cream. I need to see the pleasure on your face, hear you cry out. I'd kill for that." His tongue traced the shell of her ear. She trembled. "Tell me your name."

"Desiree." Using the name was so easy, so simple. This close to him, she *was* Desiree. She *was* desire.

"Christ, what you do to me, Desiree. You'd bring a man to his knees for a touch of your hand on his cock. You've been driving me crazy all night. I'm going to see you in my dreams. Only you. With your fingers buried deep in your pussy."

His words brought her to the edge. She held onto sanity with only one small part of her brain. She forgot even that as his hands tugged her skirt up.

Then he touched her, palmed her mound.

"You're wet. And hot." He took in a deep lungful of air. "You smell so good. I want to make you feel good. As good as she feels. Better."

Outside her panties, he eased a finger along her slit, the friction of silk and his heat almost unbearable.

"If we were alone," he whispered, "I'd taste you. I'd make you come over and over against my tongue. I'd savor every drop."

She was going to come. Oh Jesus, oh God, he was going to make her come with a soft slide, a little circle. She gulped air and moved with him as he worked his cock against her backside.

She wanted his touch, wanted to come, wanted to turn and take him in any way she could.

"Come for me. I need to feel you come so bad, my guts ache."

She rocked against his hand, trapped it between her thighs, rode him. She was so close, she couldn't breathe. The woman on the bed screamed and rolled, hugging her hand between her legs as she climaxed.

For the first time, Debbie saw her face.

Virginia. Oh my God, the woman was Virginia.

THREE

DEBBIE WAS IN shock. That's why she couldn't talk. That's why she was sitting next to Stacy in the front seat of the car with her fingernails tearing holes in the vinyl door grip.

Nothing better to rip you out of the moment than realizing your friend was masturbating right in front of you. In public. And you were letting a man touch you under your skirt.

While her head had been rudely jerked back to reality, Debbie's body wouldn't follow suit. It ached in delicate places. Pressing her thighs together made the sensation worse. She'd wanted that orgasm, wanted so badly to come by someone else's hand besides her own. Though there was more than the physical. She'd needed his words, his passion. He'd followed *her*, touched *her*. In a sea of willing women, he'd chosen *her*.

She'd run before she'd let him take her to the stars.

Stacy glanced at her. "So. What'd you think, Debbie?"

Debbie stared out the window. "It was interesting."

"Interesting?" Stacy snorted. "Where'd you go?"

"Just the rooms on the second floor." She couldn't say she'd been down to the viewing rooms. Virginia hadn't said a word as they'd piled into the car. She and her fiancé were flying to Las Vegas in the morning for a quiet wedding, no frills, no attendants. Virginia's last fling had been with herself, and Debbie wasn't about to let on that she'd seen.

Stacy gave her a long look.

"Keep your eyes on the road, please."

"You hid out in the ladies' room, didn't you, that's why you disappeared so fast?" Disgust laced her friend's voice.

She didn't even wonder why Stacy would suggest such a thing. Debbie had been hiding out for years. Not tonight, but over the last few years of her marriage. She sneaked off to bed to ease her pain, both physical and mental, and was too ashamed to tell even her best friends what was bothering her.

She'd at first been appalled upon realizing that Virginia had exposed herself to the salacious gazes of a bunch of horny men. But on second thought, at least Virginia had courage. Debbie had skulked around in the shadows, on the fringes. Wanting and needy, but running away just the same.

Yeah, some Desiree she turned out to be. She deserved Stacy's disgust. She'd employed the same tactics tonight that she did in her marriage. Retreat and hope they follow.

Except her husband didn't follow. And she let him get away with it.

"Yeah, I was in the ladies' room all night."

She had to do something about her marriage before she went stark raving mad.

The only question was, *what*?

A COOL BREEZE blew through the open bedroom window. Her husband snored softly. In a scrap of moonlight, Debbie could see the book he'd been reading lying in the middle of the bed. There was always a book or something else between them.

Her panties were still damp. She was wet. She had been most of the night. She knew she should feel guilty about what she'd done tonight. But she didn't. She'd let the guilt come tomorrow.

Right now she needed that orgasm she'd denied herself.

She backed out of the bedroom, softly closing the door, then went into the den, shutting that door, too. She kicked off the high heels and laid back on the couch. With sinuous movements, as if someone watched her, she raised the tight skirt and peeled off her panties. The garter belt and stockings remained.

"I need to see the pleasure on your face, hear you cry out."

Her fantasy man's voice echoed through her. She spread her legs and dipped a finger in her pussy. Wet. Hot. Needy.

"I want to see your fingers dipping in all that hot cream."

She willed herself back to that room at the club, felt the vibration of his voice inside her, his finger sliding across her. Circling her clitoris, she reached up to squeeze her breast, then pinched her nipple. She pushed her head back into the couch cushion and moaned.

"I'm going to see you in my dreams. Only you. With your fingers buried deep in your pussy."

In her fantasies, he watched as she touched herself. Hot eyes, hard cock. Only for her. Her hips bucked. She'd never been so wet, a trickle of dew dripping down along the crease of her bottom. She swirled in her moisture, her clitoris a hard knot aching for release. She imagined him standing before her, his cock in his hand, stroking, faster, his hair a moonlit silver, the heat in his eyes unquenchable. She put one foot on the floor, spreading herself for his view, fitting the rhythm of her fingers to the image in her head. Oh, better yet, she would have him use that huge vibrator on her, like the man she'd seen in that upstairs room. Yes, yes. Pumping her with it, harder, faster, deeper. Heat blossomed in her clitoris and streamed out to every part of her body. Her hips rocked. Her pussy burned.

"Come for me. I need to feel you come so bad, my guts ache."

She burst wide open in a flash of blinding light and searing heat between her legs. She didn't know if she cried out and for that long moment, she didn't care. She rode the climax with his words filling her to the brim.

HIS CELL PHONE rang just as Stephen threw his keys on the hall table. He answered, knowing who it was without asking. "It's none of your business, Stacy."

"I don't want details. I only want to know if Debbie enjoyed herself."

She had. For a moment. Until something had frightened her, he couldn't say what. "You need to talk to her, not me. I told you whatever happens stays between Debbie and me."

"Call her Desiree."

"That's not her name."

Once, a long time ago, he'd thought about sleeping with Stacy. Until he'd figured out she was all hard edges. He'd always preferred a softer woman. Like Debbie.

Silence a moment. "You care about her, don't you?" Stacy sounded almost wistful.

It pissed him off that she was planning something in that sneaky little brain of hers. "You're not her fairy godmother. You can't wave your magic wand and make her life perfect."

"I sent her you, and she thinks she can quit her job at the end of the year."

"Don't take credit for her talent. That's what'll allow her to turn everything around. All you did was network for her."

"You're being mean, Stephen."

"Why did you call? I'm not a dirty detail kind of guy."

"I want to know if you're seeing her again. That's all. No details."

"We do all our business through e-mail."

"No, I mean . . . *seeing* her, like you did tonight."

He suddenly didn't want Stacy probing Debbie for any of those elusive details. "I won't be seeing her again like that." She'd run. He'd lost. Maybe they'd both lost.

"You will if you go to the club."

"She's not going there again."

"I slipped the card into the purse she borrowed. She'll find it tomorrow when she cleans it out before she returns it. I give her three days before she simply has to go again."

"The club wasn't her gig." It wasn't his either. If Stacy hadn't conned him into going, ostensibly to watch out for Debbie, he wouldn't have gone within miles of the place. Though he had to admit there was something about all that rampant sex. In his younger days? Maybe. Now, closing in on the big five-oh, sex wasn't just about . . . sex. It was about the relationship, about finding someone who shared your passion, about not wanting to face the rest of your life alone. You didn't find the right woman to share your life with at a sex club.

"Stephen. She needs you. That bastard is cheating on her; I know it, I feel it. She needs you to rescue her from that terrible marriage."

He was damn tired of this conversation. He'd been listening to different renditions for weeks now. "If he is, she's got to deal with it. I can't rescue her. I'm hanging up now, Stacy."

"But—"

He didn't say good-bye before he punched the End button. Leaving a trail of clothes, he made it to the bathroom, took care of the necessities, then crawled into bed.

He couldn't sleep. When he closed his eyes, he smelled the heady musk of Debbie's arousal. He wasn't into touching another man's wife. But he couldn't help wanting her. He'd lived a long time, searching for perfection, *his* perfection. He'd never married, always thinking that he'd meet her just around the corner. When he finally did, she wasn't free.

In the past few months, he'd looked forward to her e-mails far more than he should have. And yes, at night, he'd imagined her face in his hands, her lips receiving his kiss, her mouth taking his cock. Tonight, feeling her body tremble in his arms had catapulted him into full-blown obsession.

The sane part of his brain dictated that he set up a meeting, tell her his feelings, and see how she reacted. The crazy half, which also comprised his lower head, said she needed to be as obsessed as he was. He needed to seduce her. He had to bind her with his passion.

He'd spend a fortune to make sure he was at The Sex Club every night, hoping Stacy was right, that Debbie would have to go back. She'd have to go back for *him*.

SHE'D DRESSED LIKE a tart, watched people having sex, and let a man she'd never seen before put his hand between her legs. Then she'd given herself an orgasm, the likes of which she'd never known, with his words in her head. Debbie stared at the embossed card lying on her worktable in the garage. Someone, most likely Stacy, had sneaked it into her purse last night.

Debbie took a steadying breath and picked up the soldering iron. A couple of blotchy spots needed smoothing, and then the piece would be ready for the patina. The carousel horse was her most ambitious work to date, with over a hundred pieces, some of them no bigger than her thumbnail. She'd promised Stephen she'd have it to him by Friday. It would be there early.

"I'd go mad watching you. I'd have to stroke my cock."

She closed her eyes. The words shouldn't be important, but they were. The emotional high was like a drug spreading through her veins.

Had she committed adultery? She'd let a man who wasn't her husband touch her. Even if his hand hadn't been in her panties. Then she'd given herself an orgasm just by imagining his voice. Oh my God. Adultery or not, it was wrong.

"How's it going?"

She almost dropped the soldering iron onto the glass, a bolt of fear and guilt jolting through her body. Her husband stood with one foot in and one foot out of the kitchen door. For a panicky moment, she thought he might come into the garage for a look at what she was doing. Then he'd see the card. She grabbed it and shoved it into her back pocket.

Guilty, guilty, guilty flashed like a neon sign above her head. Taking a deep breath, she put the soldering iron in its holder and wiped her palms on her jeans. Then she wondered what she was worried about. She could tell him any lie she wanted, and he wouldn't question her. He wouldn't want to know.

That hurt worse than anything else. He was good to her in so many ways. Why not in the one she needed?

He came to the table, leaning down to study her work. "You know, I admire your diligence and persistence. You never give up. I'm proud of that. I'm proud of *you*."

"Thanks. That's really sweet." *Don't be nice to me, please, don't be nice.* It made the guilt worse.

"Well, have fun. I'm going to do a little gardening." He backed off, then gathered a few tools and his gloves. Gardening was one of the few things he seemed to enjoy these days.

Once, a few months ago, when she'd been needy and on the edge, she'd told him she couldn't survive if he didn't have passion for her. He'd asked why that one thing was so important. Why the only thing he couldn't give her should make her feel as if nothing else in their life together was good enough.

She didn't have an answer. It just was.

He'd never been unfaithful. He'd encouraged her to pursue her dreams. She couldn't consider retiring from her job if he hadn't supported everything she'd wanted to do with her life. She gripped the edge of her worktable until her fingers ached.

"You'd bring a man to his knees for a touch of your hand on his cock."

That was what she wanted. Passion. Her husband didn't have it for her anymore. Though he did have lots of excuses. He was busy at work and tired when he came home. He was getting older, and his libido was fading. He had a headache. He was getting a cold. He hadn't slept well the night before. Over the years, he'd offered her a dozen choices. A dozen excuses. Of course, they were all about him, never attaching blame to her, and never ever saying, "Hey honey, I'm having trouble getting it up these days." How could she fix a problem he wouldn't admit to?

She turned off the soldering iron and pulled the card out of her pocket. Staring at it, she remembered the touch of a special man's hands. Closing her eyes, she tipped her head back. A moan bubbled in her throat. She forced the small sound down.

Grabbing the card, she went inside to e-mail Stephen to let him know she'd ship the horse this afternoon. In her office, her foot tapping impatiently, she booted up the computer. Slow, slow, far too slow. It gave her a moment to set the card on her desk and stare at the gold lettering.

"Do you know how beautiful it is watching a woman touch herself?"

No, she didn't, but, with an intensity born of her restless emotions, she wanted her mystery man to watch her. She wanted him to take his cock in his hands because *she* turned him on. Her pulse beat at the juncture of her thighs. Her clitoris throbbed.

The computer beeped, and she realized she'd been lost in the memory of *his* voice. God. It was something she *couldn't* have. She ripped the card into pieces and threw it in the trash.

Stephen had sent her an e-mail asking how she was and if she'd enjoyed her night out with the girls. She'd told him about the bachelorette party. What on earth would he think of her if she told him the truth? *Yes, Stephen, I had a wonderful time watching women suck men's cocks and my friend masturbate behind a Plexiglas window. And there was this man . . .*

She replied to him, saying only that she'd had a nice time and would be shipping out the carousel horse that afternoon.

The glass was for a child's playroom. She'd used lead for basic strength and jewels made of a hard plastic for decoration on the saddle. She hoped he'd be pleased with the results. Someday, she'd find the courage to ask him to take her to one of the houses he was working on so she could see the installation. She had yet to see her work in place. Which was kind of crazy.

"Jewels," he answered a few minutes later. "Great idea. Can't wait to see it. So where'd you go last night?"

Stephen was always chatty. She'd figured out he did it to put her at ease. Telling her a little about himself and asking questions about her so that she didn't worry so much over his reaction to a new piece she'd sent him. If he'd been strictly business, she'd have been a mess waiting for his e-mail after she'd made a shipment.

"A club," she typed, and waited for his reply.

"Dancing?"

"I don't dance."

"Why not?"

Why not? Her husband hadn't danced with her since her brother's wedding over eight years ago.

"My husband's self-conscious. He hates dancing." The words sounded like a complaint, but in a way, it was almost cleansing. Not that she'd ever complained to Stephen about her marriage.

He didn't reply for awhile. She'd almost given up. Then he wrote, "But do YOU like to dance?"

This was probably the most personal conversation they'd had. Her stomach fluttered. "Yes, I like to dance."

She waited, a hand over her mouth as she stared at the screen. Stephen was a nice guy, funny, articulate, smart. He complimented her, made her laugh when she felt a little down. From things he'd said—a couple of months ago he'd mentioned his class reunion—she figured he was close to fifty. He wasn't married, though she didn't know if he had been, and she didn't think he had kids because he never talked about any.

Her heart beat faster when his address popped up. There were times she found she'd spent an hour e-mailing with him, and the messages hadn't all been business. More like conversation.

She had to admit, too, that late at night, something he'd said would come back to her. Make her smile. She'd imagine what he looked like, what his voice sounded like. And yes, she'd put his name to a fantasy or two.

The reality was, she'd had orgasms imagining Stephen was going down on her. There, the truth.

Then were only talking about dancing. He didn't translate the conversation into something sexual. She did. Yet her hand trembled as she reached for the mouse to open his message. Maybe she was still on overload from last night.

"Then you should dance whenever you want to. You can dance with girlfriends, you know."

She laughed to herself, her tension easing, then wrote, "That isn't done."

He dashed her a reply. "Why not?"

"You ask *why* too much." Though she hadn't noticed him doing that before. "Women aren't supposed to dance with women."

"We're not talking slow dancing here. Women dance together all the time. Haven't you been watching at those clubs you go to with your friends?"

She sucked in a breath. She'd been watching, that's for sure. Only it wasn't dancing. Did he think she was some party animal?

"I don't always go to clubs."

"I wasn't criticizing."

She was overreacting. The admission, if only to herself, that she'd fantasized about Stephen made her nervous. "I don't want you to think I'm always running around with my friends."

"I don't think that at all. You deserve to enjoy yourself."

He sounded like Stacy. Yet after the things she'd done last night, she didn't know what to say or how to reply. Cupping her face, she massaged her temples. What was the big deal? Stephen was just being nice.

"I enjoy seeing my friends. We've known each other a long time." There, that was noncommittal enough.

"Are you okay?"

She wasn't used to intuitive men. For a moment, she wanted to scream, *No, everything is NOT okay. I think I'm becoming a manic-depressive because I'm flipping moods every two seconds.*

God. "Everything's fine, Stephen. I'd better run if I'm going to get that piece out today. Have a good one. Bye."

Her hands shook. Now she couldn't even e-mail Stephen without losing it.

FOUR

STEPHEN STARED AT her last e-mail on his monitor. *Shit, shit, shit.*
He'd pushed too hard. But Christ, what kind of man wouldn't
dance with his wife—a wife who liked to dance—because he was
self-conscious? She'd told him other things, little details she'd revealed without realizing that they drew a picture Stephen saw
clearly. The guy was a self-centered prick who didn't like her
friends, wouldn't attend parties she was invited to, groused about
the family barbecues at her brother's, and hadn't taken her on vacation in years.

He wanted to hate the man.

Stephen would savor a dance with her. He'd hold her tight,
swaying gently, as he planted kisses in her hair, against her ear, and
took nibbles of those luscious lips. Just holding her. He closed his
eyes and knew he wanted to do far more than dance. He wanted to
love her, show her with his body how beautiful she was. Everything
she missed out on, he would make sure she had.

How the hell had he managed to fall so hard for her with nothing more than e-mails between them? It wasn't logical to feel he knew her so well. People pretended, people lied. He wasn't usually so trusting, nor did he take everything at face value. Except with her. He couldn't say why. He only knew that he did.

Yet wanting a married woman this badly could only end in Shitsville.

DEBBIE HAD GOTTEN through the weekend alternately scared, hurt, guilty, and angry, the full spectrum of emotions except the good ones. The invitation came on Tuesday, waiting for her on the kitchen table. She didn't open her husband's mail, and he didn't open hers.

"What'd ya get?" he asked, standing by the sink.

No return address, a simple computer-generated mailing label. She could feel another envelope on the inside. She slit the top, revealing her made-up sex club name in beautiful gold script on the second envelope.

Her stomach turned over. How did they know where she lived? "Oh, it's nothing. One of those stockbroker invitations."

"You wanna go?" He didn't ask why the note had been addressed to her when the accounts were in both their names.

"No, they're boring." Her mind whirled. She put a hand on the table to steady herself.

In her office, she shut the door and dialed the phone.

Stacy picked up as if she'd been sitting beside it. "Hey."

"Did you send me something?"

"Like what?"

Debbie stared at the thing in her hand as if it were a spider crawling across her palm. "An invitation."

Stacy needed no further explanation. "Ah, an invitation to seduction." She could almost hear Stacy's smile. "No, I didn't send it. Are you going?"

"How did they get my address? You didn't give it to them, did you?" They knew where she lived, the nebulous *they*. Spies who knew everything about you.

"Of course not. Did you give it to someone?"

"Get real." She paced as far as the phone cord would allow.

"How about your phone number? They might have done that reverse directory thing."

"I didn't give anyone anything." Except that she'd given a stranger a touch of her crotch. Oh my God. Could he have followed her home? "This is scary."

"Only if you let it be."

"Stacy. This was supposed to be a secret. No one was supposed to know." Her voice and her pulse rose with every word.

"Calm down."

"I can't."

"It's just an invitation. Don't start worrying unless something happens."

"I could get attacked." Her husband could find out.

Stacy snorted. "Maybe someone wants you to come back."

"Well, I'm not going." Friday night had been a mistake.

"Then throw the invitation away. Pretend you never got it. Ignore it." Stacy's sigh sounded over the phone line. "If you really want to."

"I'm ripping it into a million little pieces." She heard something outside the door. A soft footfall receding down the hall? "I gotta go. I'll bring your stuff by this week. I took them to the dry cleaner."

"You should keep the outfit," Stacy said softly. "Maybe you'll need it."

No. Not again. Yet, instead of shoving the invitation down the garbage disposal as she should have, she tucked it in the back of her desk drawer.

*　*　*

"GOT THE CAROUSEL horse. You're fantastic." *Talented. Desirable. I need you. I'm going crazy waiting for you.*

Stephen hit Send, wondering if she'd gotten the invitation, and if so, what she'd done with it. One thing for sure, she hadn't used it. He'd gone to the club every night this week. Without her, the unbridled sexual activity didn't do a thing for him. And the wait was killing him.

Stacy had called, saying Debbie was freaked about the invitation. He'd admitted nothing. His strategy had been simple. Let Debbie know she was wanted, that someone was willing to pay for her to come again. Instead, he'd frightened the hell out of her. Her e-mails since had been short, sentences clipped, no pronouns, too many acronyms. She usually spelled everything out. She couldn't know he'd sent the invitation, but somehow, his rash act had made her turn in on herself.

Her answer to his e-mail, when it came half an hour later, was once again short. "Glad you liked the horse."

Come and see your beautiful work when it's installed. His fingertips itched to type the words. Instead, he picked an innocuous statement. "You're very talented."

"Thank you."

Goddamn it, talk to me. "Have a good night."

"Thanks. You, too."

He wanted to slam his fist through the monitor. He'd fucked up. Still, he headed out to the club. He'd go until he had no hope left.

DEBBIE HAD MADE it through a week and a half subsisting on caffeine and fear of that damn invitation, but she'd survived on the sound of a stranger's voice in her head.

"Do you know how beautiful it is watching a woman touch herself?"

Moisture creamed her thighs at the memory even as a spectacular television explosion shook the bedroom wall.

Think about how scary it is that he knows your address.

The frightening thought didn't drive out the passionate ones. Her nipples tightened, ached, and begged for a touch.

"I'd go mad watching you. I'd have to stroke my cock."

She wanted him to watch her. She wanted to spread herself for his eyes, wanted to feel his gaze on all the intimate, moist, aching parts of her body. She wanted him to fuck her with that vibrator.

Would her husband really worry if another man took care of her needs? Maybe, maybe not, but going to the club was wrong; it was adultery. But it also might be the only thing that kept her sane. In a way, it was like closing the bedroom door and bringing herself to orgasm, but with help from someone else's hand.

A voice sneaked through her mind. *You're rationalizing.*

Yet her marriage couldn't continue the way it was. *She* couldn't continue. The Sex Club could give her what she needed. The slut Nazis weren't after her. *He'd* sent the invitation. He wanted her to come back. To finish what they'd started. To watch her touch herself, to taste her, to make her come.

The next orgasm she had would be with him.

HIS CELL PHONE chirped. Stephen punched the button.

"She's going tonight," Stacy said.

He should have told her it didn't matter to him or that he didn't want to talk about it. He was past the point of caring what Stacy was up to. "How do you know?"

"She broke a nail and stopped by after work to fix it."

"Maybe she just wanted her nail fixed."

"Not Debbie. She's frugal. She comes in every three weeks when she should do every two, and she waits until her appointment to have something fixed. Which is next week. But tonight, she needs her nail fixed. And I know that husband of hers sure as hell doesn't have anything big planned."

Her manicurist would understand the subtle nuances. Friday

night. No work tomorrow. It had taken almost two weeks for her to make her decision, and he'd died a million times. She hadn't even answered his e-mails for days, and he'd lusted after a word from her. Christ, he had it bad.

"Talk to you later," was all he said to Stacy.

"Treat her right."

He would treat her like the goddess she was.

STACY PUT THE phone down and blew on her nails. Perfect. Absolutely perfect. Mission accomplished. A little nudge here, a little shove there. She was so very good at getting people to do what they really wanted.

DEBBIE STAYED IN the bathroom for hours. Her hair would not do what Stacy had done to it that Friday two weeks ago. In frustration, she simply ruffled it up with her fingers. Perfect.

Stephen had e-mailed her a couple of times, and she still felt guilty that she hadn't replied. But darn it, she'd felt as if something would slip through in her words. Somehow, she'd reveal the things she planned to do tonight, and she didn't want to contemplate how his opinion of her would change.

Funny, insane even, she was more worried about Stephen's opinion than she was of her husband's. But her mind was made up. Her body had readied itself. She couldn't turn back now for anything.

She replaced her usual light makeup with darker shades and deeper tones. Lining her lips, she stood back for the effect. Pretty damn good. The black bra showed beneath her filmy, see-through blouse. She wasn't used to revealing her underwear, but they did it on *Sex and the City* all the time. The short, pleated skirt had been part of a Halloween costume a couple of years ago. She'd attended a party as a cheerleader. Tonight, she left the matching panties on the hanger.

The stilettos? Well, every woman had a pair in the back of the closet. Last Friday, she'd borrowed a pair of Stacy's. She hadn't worn hers in . . . forever.

Looking in the full-length mirror on the door, she decided she liked her efforts. Slutty and schoolgirlish all at the same time. She left the blouse untucked and unbuttoned to the center of her breasts. When she moved, the darkened aureoles of her nipples displayed themselves above the lacy bra.

With one last look, she clicked off the bathroom light and went in search of her husband. She found him in the den, the remote in one hand as he flicked through the on-screen guide.

"I'm not sure when I'll be home. So don't wait up."

"Okay. Have fun." He looked up. He could have asked her right then not to go. Instead, all he said was, "You look nice."

She looked a lot of things. Nice wasn't one of them. "Thanks. I'll see you later."

The last thing he said as she walked out the door was, "Drive carefully."

She had the invitation. She had her lipstick, her license, and a few dollars. Condoms awaited her at the club, candy jars filled with them. Yes, she would drive her mystery man very carefully. Drive him insane.

STEPHEN SCENTED HER before he saw her. She was hotter than he remembered, than he could have imagined. Her honeyed arousal filled the air like exotic perfume. Gone was the hesitancy, the deer-in-the-headlights look. Her fingers didn't tremble as she handed over the invitation, nor as she took a champagne glass from an offered tray.

Debbie was home in her bed. Desiree had come out to play.

He watched her through the throng. Lips the shade of deep red wine, she sipped the sparkling libation, looking over the crowd as if searching. He hovered by a back wall, in shadow. She turned, the light outlining her sweet, tight nipples, the gauzy, transparent material of her blouse hiding nothing.

A walking advertisement for fucking, the clothing she'd chosen attracted several pairs of eyes, male and female. Her gaze flowed right over them. She wasn't here for them. His cock hardened. She would look but not touch, not until she found *him*.

Her backside swayed gently, a hint of creamy flesh showing, as she climbed the stairs to the second floor. An image formed in his mind of his fingers trailing the crease of her buttocks straight to her pussy. He knew he'd find her already wet. Pulling away from the wall, he followed her.

He could have tracked her scent, but all he had to do was trail the turn of heads. A man squeezed his partner's breast, his gaze glued to Desiree's bare thighs. The animals were out tonight, and they all recognized a tasty morsel.

She stayed a moment at the edge of a doorway, then another, moving to the end of the hall. Starting back along the other side, she stopped, searched, and came closer to him. Gliding in those high heels, she raised a hand to stroke the line of her throat, then the upper swell of breast just inside her blouse.

So unconsciously sexy, he was sure she had no idea the effect that slow caress had on him, on the men, on women not averse to same-sex pleasures. He melted into an alcove as she approached then passed by. Dragging in a breath, her light scent tickling the back of his throat, he leaned against the paneling. His body couldn't take much more of her inadvertent teasing.

Pulling himself together, he stepped out once more. She was at the other end of the hall, making her turn like a runway model. A guy put his hand out, not quite touching, a question in his upturned palm. She sidestepped, shaking her head.

Stephen backed off and headed down the stairs. He knew where she'd go next. He'd be waiting for her. And she'd be his.

At least for tonight.

FIVE

SEX PERFUMED THE air, hot, sweaty, musky. The walls seemed to ooze with the scent of come. The darkness hid the peak of her nipples and the flush heating her skin. Strobe lights flashed at the far end of the performance hall, beckoning. She knew he was here, had felt his eyes on her even as she'd searched for him. He wanted to fuck her. He'd wanted to the other night, but he'd watched instead, like a hunter stalking his prey. Tonight, she'd let him do it. Oh God, yes.

Moisture coated her bare thighs. She'd ditched her bra and panties in the car. All she wore now was the short skirt, her see-through blouse, and the heels that screamed, *Fuck me.*

She headed down the hall, following the beat of the strobe, ignoring the doorways on either side of her. The focal point of the large room she entered was the stage outfitted with a bed and three performers. The spectacle had barely begun, the woman still dressed and the two men stripped to their pants. With each flash of the strobe, the actress lost an article of clothing, first the red blouse, then the black skirt. All that remained were wisps of lace at her breasts and thighs. One of the men leaned into her, his lips to one breast, his fingers to the other. Another flash revealed the second man between her thighs.

Debbie stood in the back, behind the low rail that encircled the room. It created a wide aisle for people to move about or to stand and watch, both the stage and the acts on the mattresses strewn about the floor. Full and ready, she clasped the brass rail, her grip almost painful. She struggled to catch her breath as Man Number Two put his mouth to the woman's mound and sucked. She couldn't see the finer movements of his tongue, but she felt them deep inside, as if he were licking *her* clitoris.

Her previous trip, she'd come for the titillation, the kinky excitement. Tonight was altogether different. Stronger. More powerful. This time she knew she would have him.

The obsession had begun, taken hold of her like a fist tight around her innards. She didn't care at all about the man that lay asleep and snoring at home in his bed. Her bed.

She smelled him before he touched her. A light, spicy tang, barely there. Still, his scent tantalized her, reminded her of that last time, his soft caress between her thighs. The promise. He knew she'd be back for that. She'd returned for so much more.

She concentrated on the threesome. The two males turned the woman, brought her to her hands and knees, her mouth milking one cock, her pussy sucking in the other. The man rammed home, muscles flexing with each thrust.

Her pussy contracted. She squeezed her thighs together, intensifying the pressure on her clitoris.

A hand slid beneath her skirt, *his* hand along her inner thigh. With a fingertip, he traced her center, barely dipping into her folds. She almost came. He cupped her, then ran his hands over her hips, her butt. He trailed two fingers up the crease between her cheeks, then down to the joining of her thighs. Lips against her hair, he whispered, "Open up."

She did, spreading her legs for him. She thought he'd enter her with his fingers, but he gathered cream and skimmed forward to her clitoris. Circling, he caressed her. She looked down at her hands on the rail, her knuckles white, black, white, black in the throb of light. She moaned, joining the other voices. Cries of pleasure pounded against her ears, and the incessant stroke of his finger on her clit brought her to the edge of madness.

"I'm going to fuck you now. I can't wait. Bend over."

He pushed at the top of her spine. She shoved her ass at him, begging without words. God, she wanted this, needed it.

After a brief moment as he donned a condom, the tip of his cock breached her vagina, and she shoved back, taking him. Pain shot through her body. She was wet, but tight and unused to a man inside her. Putting a hand to her hip, he started a rhythm that eradicated the ache. And he never let up on her clit.

She fought to keep her eyes open, needing to absorb the sexual feeding frenzy on the floor, on the stage, the rawness of fucking, and the feel of his hard cock deep inside her.

Faster, his cock, his fingers, her breath, her racing heart. She climbed, lost sight of the room and all sense of time as he pounded her. Someone was screaming, and the strobe hammered against her closed eyelids. Fire swept through her, from her nipples to her clitoris to uncharted territory at the center of her womb. Then it consumed her, as if she'd shot straight into the flames of a burning sun.

He was still inside her when she came back to herself, his cock pulsing. His ragged breath sawed in her ear. He held her flush against his body, trapping her to him with an arm beneath her breasts, the other across her abdomen. Held her as if he couldn't let her go.

Then he whispered to her. "I want to bury my face in your pussy. I want to make you come until you think you're going to die. I want to fall asleep with my cock inside you."

* * *

SHE FELT SO right in his arms. His cock still throbbed deep inside her. She smelled so damn good as he buried his face in her hair. Fruity. Something citrus. He pushed aside her hair and kissed her neck.

"Let's get out of here," Stephen whispered. He didn't want to share anymore. He wanted her to see him, to talk to him. When he took her again, he wanted no one else's eyes on them.

Her body tensed against his. "No, I have to go home."

Not yet, God, not yet. "It's early." He rotated his hips lightly against her backside, then pushed deep, needing to remind her that he was still inside her. His balls tightened, and his cock hardened. She moaned and dug her fingernails into his arm beneath her breasts. "Don't go," he whispered.

She leaned her head back on his shoulder, letting out a long sigh. "I'll stay. For a little while."

He pulled out and zipped himself one-handed. Shit, he had to get rid of the condom. How the hell could he keep her with him? The moment he let go, she'd bolt.

Smoothing her skirt down over her sweet ass, he turned her, then took her hand. "Come on."

He pushed through the mass of bodies, keeping her hand securely in his. Their clasped hands felt so goddamn right. The light in the lobby almost blinded him as he shouldered open the double doors.

Setting her in a corner, he rubbed her arms. "I'll only be a minute." He wanted to beg but commanded instead. "Don't go."

Lip gloss glistened on her mouth. He had yet to take those lips, to taste her. Bending his head, he cupped her face in his palms. Touching his lips to hers, he licked the seam, urging her to open to him without words. She parted, stroking his tongue with hers. Her champagne taste sizzled between them.

"Stay right here," he murmured once more, holding her gaze with his, waiting for her promise, demanding it.

"All right."

He left her with a last glance over his shoulder, his heart in his eyes, if she chose to look, and a lump in his throat.

NOW WOULD BE the time to escape. But she wouldn't leave.

Her lips still tingled with his kiss. The sheer fabric of her blouse tantalized her nipples. She needed his touch on them. She wanted more. More kisses, his tongue in her mouth, his arms around her, his cock inside her, and his come filling her.

She needed to hear him whisper all those beautiful things to her over and over. *"I want to fall asleep with my cock inside you."* She needed so much more of the sensations.

She closed her eyes and sagged against the wall. She craved the zest of his semen in her mouth, the feel of his cock between her lips, his hands in her hair, a groan torn from his throat. And those words that wrapped around her frozen heart.

"Hey, you look a little lost over here all by yourself."

She jerked and opened her eyes. A man hovered. Close, but not too close. Tall, blond, and wide, like a linebacker or a bull rider, he braced himself against the wall. He didn't touch her, yet his enticing cologne surrounded her.

"I'm here with somebody else," she said.

"But he's left you alone, hasn't he." Not a question, but a flat statement. As if he assumed her "date" was enjoying himself upstairs with someone else.

"He'll be right back." She hoped.

The man smiled and traced a finger along her nose without actually touching. "He'd be an idiot if he isn't. He shouldn't leave you alone. Some shark will definitely hit on you."

"Are you a shark?"

He bared his teeth and crinkled attractive blue eyes. "I saw you standing over here, your eyes closed, looking like you needed to be kissed, and you turned me into one."

Somehow her need had been written on her face. He was probably in his mid-thirties, with a low voice that caressed. Lines at his mouth suggested he laughed. A lot. He smelled good, and he looked good . . .

"He will be back," she said, glancing once more at the door.

"Call me selfish, but I hope he won't be."

If he'd been more overt, more unattractive, or less sure of himself, she wouldn't have been flattered. But he did flatter her. She smiled slightly, liking the attention.

He pushed away from the wall and held out his hand. "Let's make a run for it, before he returns."

She looked from his hand to his charming eyes. "No thanks."

He cocked his head. One corner of his mouth lifted as he assessed her. "I don't mind a threesome. Not if it's with you."

"I mind." Her date, if he could be called that in this place, stood just beyond the big guy's shoulder. He wasn't as tall or as wide, but his tone of voice more than made up for it.

Still smiling, the blond man turned. "You shouldn't leave her out here by herself."

She looked at the man who had taken her so thoroughly, so intimately, and wondered if he knew she wouldn't have gone with anyone else, no matter how long he left her. She might have run, but she wouldn't have taken another man's hand.

Face expressionless except for a dark glint in his eyes, he stood with his feet slightly apart, his hands at his sides. Like a gunslinger ready to do battle. For her. Finally, looking at her, he said, "She isn't alone anymore."

With those words, she knew he referred to so much more than this moment, this night. She stepped forward to take his hand.

The blond man smiled and said, "Lucky man." Then he melted into the swimming pool of bodies and disappeared.

Squeezing her hand and letting his gaze follow the crowd, her lover murmured, "Yeah, I am lucky." Then he looked down at her. "He made you feel good, didn't he?"

She dipped her head so he couldn't see the truth, but he lifted her chin until she was forced to meet his eyes. "It's okay you felt that way. You're beautiful, and I'm not the only one who wants you." He cupped her throat. "Every man here does." He turned, pulling her beneath his arm, then bent to her ear. "See how they look at you."

"I don't think I see the same thing you do."

"Over there. That one." He pointed to a man near the bottom of the stairs, a curvy brunette at his side. "He's not seeing her, he's looking at you. Watch his eyes."

She did. Turned half toward her, the man let his gaze slide from her short skirt to her breasts in the see-through blouse.

He eased her in front of him, his hands coming to rest on her shoulders. "Look at them all, see them watch you."

Her breath caught in her throat. She saw several men's gazes on her. Eyeing her, salivating over her. She leaned into him, felt the hard press of his penis at the small of her back.

"But you're mine," he whispered into her ear.

She shivered. Yes, she was his. Yet she reveled in the desire of all those men. Her nipples hardened. She moistened between her legs. Then she pushed back against his erection, rubbed him, letting him know that the others didn't matter beyond this moment of titillation.

He nipped her lobe, then said, "Let's get out of here. I want to be alone with you."

He turned her once more, took her hand again, then leaned in to rub his nose against hers. The caress was so sweet, so familiar, and he was so *there*.

He grazed her knuckles with a kiss. There was something about a man looking in your eyes when he touched you. Her heart beat faster. "Where are we going?"

He pivoted, pulling her along with him. "It's a surprise."

With a moment's hesitation, she let him step ahead of her.

He felt the slight lag and stopped while the crowd flowed around them. "I'm not taking you to my place. You don't need to be frightened."

He didn't frighten her. Not right now. But she didn't know him. She'd let him fuck her, but she didn't know him at all, or what he might be capable of. There was also the issue that had troubled her. "You sent me the invitation, didn't you?"

His lack of answer confirmed her educated guess.

She drew in a breath, then let it out slowly. "How did you know my address?"

He tipped his head back and swallowed, his eyes a shade darker when his gaze met hers again. "Don't be afraid of me."

"Did you follow me home that night?"

Again, no response. She didn't want to be afraid of him.

He tugged on her hand, pulling her close so that his voice was the only thing she could concentrate on. "I want you. For tonight, if that's all I can have. Then I'll leave you alone." He rubbed his face in her hair. "If that's what you want."

The damage, if any at all, was already done. Right now, she wanted to believe him.

He waited, her hand held to his chest, over his heart.

The viewing hall doors flapped open with a burst of laughter and music. Someone bumped her arm. She stood in the middle of a crowded lobby, naked under her skirt and her breasts covered only by a thin, see-through blouse. Sex upstairs, sex downstairs, sex everywhere around them, yet his dark gaze on her wasn't about sex at all. It was passion, it was fire, it was what she'd been longing for, dreaming of, fantasizing about. In his eyes, she saw the invitation to seduction. And more.

"I'll go with you." Wherever he wanted to take her.

HE'D BORROWED A friend's car. Not that he figured she'd leave with him, but he didn't want the truck, with its company logo, sitting in the underground parking for her to see. Now, Stephen damned the bucket seats. He wanted her next to him.

Her scent filled the car. Citrus and sex. More than the hand brake sat between them. She hadn't said a word since he'd closed the passenger-side door. He sat tongue-tied, his guts twisted into knots, like a first date at sixteen.

For a moment, when she'd stood there looking into his eyes, waiting, wanting, he'd wanted to tell her the truth. He wanted to say she'd given him the address herself, months ago, so he could mail the commission checks. But he couldn't kill the fantasy, not yet, just as he couldn't let her go home. So he'd said nothing, let her draw her own conclusions, and hoped to hell they didn't scare the shit out of her.

She'd regretted her decision the moment they entered the garage. He'd felt her doubt in her withdrawal, her hand slipping from his, her distance growing in inches and in silence.

He didn't take her far, only a fifteen-minute drive from the club to the reservoir. The park closed at dusk. He pulled over just short of the gate. The moon glimmered across smooth water, and when he opened the door, warm summer air caressed his face the way he wanted her to stroke him. He stood, waiting for the soft snick of her door latch to tell him she followed.

The grass leading down to the water's edge had been clipped recently. The sharp tang of its fresh shave rose up from the ground. He wanted to make love to her here. In the moonlight. Amid the stars and the sweet night air.

"It's beautiful," she said, as she came to stand beside him. Close, but not close enough.

He stuck his hands in his pockets to resist the urge to pull her beneath his arm. "I like it at night when no one's around."

"It's quiet."

Crickets chirped in the woods behind them. An owl hooted. He knew she meant the quiet without voices. Nature didn't disturb the peace; people did. "The afternoon wind dies down so the water's still."

He turned slightly to look at her in profile. She hugged her arms to her breasts, covering the sheerness of her blouse. Her hair, artfully messy, framed her face. She had an elegant nose, aristocratic, with the slightest of upturns. Full lips, defined chin, and the smooth lines of her throat leading down to the hollow. He wanted to taste the scented skin there.

I love you.

He wouldn't say the words, not now, probably not ever. Yet he could acknowledge the emotion to himself. She was beautiful. Talented, passionate, thoughtful, and caring. Everything he'd ever wanted, all the things he'd never found. Not in one woman.

And she was here with him.

He opened the car door, put the key in the ignition, and rolled down the window. Turning on the radio, a soft, meandering jazz melody floated out into the night. A lover's song.

As he stood and closed the door, the music wafted softly on the air. He held out his hand. "Dance with me."

He could give her that at least, a dance.

With the moon in her hair and the crickets adding their unique voice to the ensemble, she came into his arms. "I'm not very good," she whispered against his chest.

"You're perfect." He held her close in the moonlight.

The song ended; another began. He didn't let her go.

"What's your name?" She leaned back, looking at him. "I don't know what to call you."

Over her head, he stared across the water. Yet another lie between them. He was so damn tired of lying, but he didn't know another way. Not at this point. "Call me whatever you like."

She snuggled closer, put a hand up to play with the ends of his hair. "I think I'll call you Stephen."

His heart seized in his chest, and he couldn't breathe for several seconds. He put his face to the sky and forced in two great gulps of air. When he could speak again, he said, "Yeah, Stephen would be fine."

SIX

WHY DID HIS arms around her shoulders and the gentle caress of his breath at her ear feel as sweetly passionate as his body filling hers? Why did his voice make her tremble when he asked her to dance with him as easily as when he told her he'd make her come over and over against his tongue?

"Stephen?" She liked saying the name. She'd feel weird tomorrow when she e-mailed the real Stephen, but for now, she liked the seductive feel of his name on her lips.

"Hmm?" He rested his cheek against her ear. His voice vibrated inside her.

"I like this as much as I like it when you make me come."

He rubbed his cock against her. "So do I."

She kissed his throat. "You make me feel . . . passionate."

He cupped her face and tipped her head back. "You are passionate. You're alive with it. You should have a man making love to you all night long."

She searched his eyes. With the moon behind him, they were black as night. She thought maybe he could see into her soul. "I would like that more than anything." She couldn't tell him the depth with which she needed that loving.

He moved her in their slow dance. One finger slid over the wedding and engagement rings she wore. "Tell me about this."

Her heart pounded. "I'm married."

He touched his lips lightly to hers. "I know that."

"Does it matter?" Burying her face against his neck, she drew in the spice of his aftershave. Inside, her stomach flipped, waiting for his answer.

It took forever. "Not for tonight. But tell me anyway."

How could she tell him she was feeling used up and washed up? That going to the club had been the desperate act of a pitiful woman who needed a man to get it up for her. Yet she felt she could and whispered, "He doesn't want me anymore."

His arm tightened across her back. "Then he's an idiot." He rocked her. "Is it possible he's having an affair?"

She almost laughed. It was better than crying. "No, I don't think so." If only it were that simple, but she didn't use the *unmentionable* word. She'd betrayed her marriage tonight, but calling her husband impotent seemed almost worse.

Stephen didn't say anything. Silence beat against her ears. She looked up to gauge his reaction but could read nothing in his expression. "I'm not lying to myself."

He pushed her head to his shoulder, then stroked her back. "I don't really know."

She gulped a breath. Her eyes suddenly ached. "I really don't want to talk about this anymore."

"If he doesn't make love to you, it isn't because of you. It's him."

That was exactly what her husband always said. Now she was the one who didn't answer.

He stepped back. Her body screamed at the loss of his heat.

"Look at me."

God, he was beautiful. His hair frosted with moonlight, the strong face, the hard body. Intensity radiated from him.

"You are the most desirable woman I have ever known."

She closed her eyes and drank in his words as if they were water and sun to a wilting flower.

"I wanted you the first moment we—" He stopped. "From the first moment I saw you."

She was so damn weak and pathetic for needing to hear him say how much he hungered for her.

He kissed her eyelids, feathering down to her lips. Rising on her toes, she wrapped her arms around his neck and opened her mouth to him. She touched her tongue to his, sucking him. He nipped then licked her lower lip.

"I want to make love with you again," he murmured.

She knew what they'd done hadn't been making love. This time, she willed it to be different. "I want to taste you. I want you in my mouth, Stephen."

His fingers tensed, and something fierce glittered in his eyes, then he took her with a soul-deep kiss that stole her breath and set her ablaze.

"I need you so damn badly," he whispered against her lips.

"Will you let me swallow?"

"*Let* you?" He laughed, choking it off when she cupped him through his jeans. She reveled in his throaty growl.

"You don't have to ask. I'm already begging." He put his hand over hers, using her palm to stroke the hard ridge.

She pulled at his belt buckle. He helped her loosen it. The rasp of his zipper filled the night. He sucked in a breath as she reached inside his briefs. Warm, velvety smooth. And hard. For her.

"Tell me what you want." She needed his command, needed to fulfill his desires exactly as he described them.

"Reach down and squeeze my balls."

They were hard and tight. She rubbed, molded. He put his head back and drew in a deep breath.

"Make a fist around my cock and stroke me."

She wrapped him in her hand and worked to his tip. Back down, then up once more. With her thumb, she smeared a drop of precome over his crown, delving into the small slit.

He stretched, then arched into her, raking his fingers through his hair. "Suck me. I want your mouth on me. Jesus H. Christ, I need it now."

She licked his neck as she pushed at the waistband of his jeans, sliding them over his hips. She dropped to her knees. Cold concrete and gravel bit into her flesh. She didn't care. He had the most beautiful cock she'd ever seen, not huge, but perfect. Another droplet of come glistened. Holding him with one hand, the other on his thigh, she licked the tiny jewel.

"You're gorgeous." He tangled his fingers in her hair, pulling the locks aside so that he could watch her.

"Blow me, baby," he whispered, as if it were a sweet nothing.

To her, it was. She slid her tongue along his slit, then blew on the light film of moisture. "Is that what you want?"

He hissed through his teeth. "I want you to suck me. Fuck me with your mouth."

She looked up and smiled. "All right."

She took him until her lips kissed her own hand fisted around him.

"Christ." His body heaved, his cock pushing her limits.

She sucked hard, drawing another bead of come. Salty, hot, all male, the taste of him spiraled her own desire higher. She worked the tip with her lips. Then taking him fully, she stroked him with her tongue and mouth. With a feral groan, he twisted his fingers in her hair and rocked his hips. Removing the hand she'd kept at his base, she grabbed his thigh, squeezing.

Then she took him deep, to the back of her throat.

"Jesus, you make me crazy." He held her head in his hands and fucked her mouth, his muscles bunching beneath her touch.

She'd never felt so needed. She'd never wanted a man's come so much. He pulsed in her mouth, his breath a harsh pant. With a gut-deep cry, he filled her, his semen pumping down her throat. She swallowed every burst, savoring it, working him for more. When his orgasm subsided, she didn't let him go. He was still hard, still delicious. She stroked him lovingly with her tongue.

"I died and went to heaven, right?" His fingers running through her hair, massaging her head, he held her close. "That was so fucking incredible."

She ran her tongue from base to tip, then let him fall from her lips. She tipped back to meet his gaze. "You taste good."

He rubbed his thumb across her lips. "Let me taste, too."

"You want to kiss me?" Her heart tattooed in her chest. Even way back when, that had been taboo with her husband.

"What you just did was so damn beautiful, I wanna share."

Tugging his jeans up with one hand, he pulled her to her feet with the other, then held her arm as her legs wobbled. She brushed the dirt from her knees.

"Don't you want to kiss me?" He held her still, only inches away, his gaze roaming her face.

"More than anything." She licked the seam of his lips and knew he could taste himself even with that small swipe.

"I want," he whispered, "more." He ran a hand up her arm, then cupped her nape. The glitter in his eyes was need.

She knew the feeling so well, the pulse-pounding, gut-wrenching need to touch and be touched, to have and to hold, to share every facet of lovemaking, the very essence and flavor of it. "I think I'll die if I don't have more of you."

His groan vibrated up from deep inside as he took her mouth. With lips, tongue, teeth, he tasted and claimed her depths.

Finally, his breath harsh, he gathered her to him, leaned back against the car, and held on tight. Hard again, his cock nudged her stomach through the opening of his jeans. "You don't know how good that is, knowing you've taken me with your mouth, then tasting what you tasted."

"Was that making love, Stephen?"

"God, yes. Can't you tell?"

She stuck her hands up the back of his shirt. "I thought . . ." She held her breath, squeezed her eyes shut. "I thought maybe it was just fucking."

He rocked her. "Call it whatever you want. Fucking, screwing, making love. The name doesn't matter. It's the feeling inside that defines it."

The feeling had been beautiful; passion and heat and want. She hadn't had that in so long. "I want you inside me, Stephen."

His arms tightened, and he lifted her off the ground for a moment. Setting her down again, he exhaled, a long pent-up sigh. "You don't know how long I've waited to hear you say that."

A day, a week, two weeks? It seemed like a lifetime to her, too. "Now. In the backseat."

Stephen pulled back, held her head in his hands, and rubbed the tip of Debbie's nose with his. "No. I want you out there by the lake. In the moonlight."

He wouldn't let her climb into the backseat. Debbie wasn't a backseat kind of woman. He wanted her by the water's edge, under the stars, with the scent of freshly cut grass around them.

He'd beg her to say his name over and over. He wasn't an e-mail address. Or someone who believed in her work. He was the man she chose as her lover, even if she didn't know it.

His belt still unbuckled and his pants unzipped, warm air stroked the tip of his cock. He took her hand, walking slowly, wary of her heels sinking into the earth.

"What if someone sees us?"

She'd given him one helluva blow job against the side of the car.

Someone could have seen that, too. Yet he knew what she meant. She hadn't been the one exposed. "Don't worry. I come here by myself a lot late at night. No one's ever around."

"Why do you come here alone?"

To think. About her. About what he wanted in his life. And what he could actually have. "Just thinking."

They stopped a few feet from the water, where the grass would be dry except for the dew. She stared at the opposite shore, and he was almost sure she was debating whether to ask more questions.

In the end, she didn't ask anything. He ached with her choice, though at least he wouldn't have to lie. He sat, pulled her down, then flopped onto his back to gaze at the stars.

She curled her body into his. "What do you see up there?"

Her. In his bed. At his kitchen table. In the morning light. "Stars. I see millions of stars."

"Make me see stars, Stephen."

When she said his name, he'd do anything for her. "Get on top of me."

She straddled his hips, her movement tugging at his open zipper. Settling her skirt around her, she slid her hands up his chest, leaning down to rub her breasts against him. The tip of his cock touched her warm, wet pussy.

"You feel so good," he whispered. So fucking good that his body ached. He'd never had this before in his life.

She moved her hips a fraction, teasing him, bathing him with her juices. "You feel good, too."

"Undo your blouse for me."

She sat up, adjusted. He slipped deeper between her folds, nudging her clit. She sucked in a breath, gathered her hair in her hands, and did a slow, sinuous stretch. His cock pulsed as she moaned softly.

Her nipples peaked against the sheer material. With a sultry look, she loosened the button at her cleavage. Then the next. Then all of them until a strip of flesh showed from throat to abdomen. He tugged on the bottom, pulling the opening apart. The edges clung to her nipples a moment, then slid free.

"Your breasts are so beautiful." Small, yet perfectly shaped, perfectly pert.

"Do you want me to touch them, Stephen?"

He almost grabbed her hips to shove himself inside her. Despite the orgasm he'd had in her mouth, he was sure he'd come the next time she said his name. "Please."

"So polite." She cupped her breasts, held them out to him.

This was the way he wanted her, sure of herself, her beauty, her passion, his attraction. "I'll probably come before I ever get inside you, but I want to see you play with your nipples."

She smiled, a seductive, knowing smile.

He never wanted her to lose that sense of power. "Please, baby, do it, you're driving me crazy."

Licking first one index finger, then the other, she dropped her hands back to her breasts and circled each nipple. Tipping her head back, she rubbed with her palms.

"Does it feel good?"

She bit her lip, moaned, then said, "Yes, Stephen. When I close my eyes, it's as if you're doing it."

His cock felt like solid steel. He wanted to bring her pleasure so badly that his whole body ached with the need. Waiting another moment to have her would be the death of him.

He reached up to cover her hands. "Let me inside you."

She took a shaky breath. "Yes."

God, say my name again. "I've got a condom in my front pocket. Take it out."

She rose up on her knees, her skirt falling over him, but he missed the sweet, warm contact. Moving back, she fished out the condom packet. "Here. You put it on."

A flush blossomed on her cheeks. Christ, she was freaking embarrassed. She pulled off to kneel beside him as he struggled to get his pants over his hips, then tore open the wrapping.

The job done, he took her hand and wrapped her fingers around his cock. "Feel how much I want you."

She squeezed but didn't stroke him the way he wanted. Maybe she was afraid of dislodging the condom.

"Come here." He pulled her down for a kiss, stealing inside for a touch of her tongue. "You taste so damn sweet."

She trailed a finger down his cheek, then kissed him with a light caress. "You don't have to keep complimenting me. I'm going to fuck you anyway."

Something inside him went numb. Pain sat on the back of his eyeballs. He put his forehead to hers. "Then please fuck me, because I can't stand this anymore."

Couldn't stand the doubts that slipped in so easily with one wrong word between them.

Putting her arms around him, she pulled him over her. "I want to feel you on top of me. I haven't felt a man's weight in more years than I can count."

He moved between her legs, bracing himself on one elbow as he slid a hand beneath her skirt and found her warmth.

"Get inside me. Then I want you on me, all of you. Don't hold anything back."

He wasn't gentle or tender. He wasn't the way he wanted to be, but he gave her what she asked for. She was wet, and when he plunged deep, her body took him more easily than the first time. Pulling her legs to his hips, she locked her feet behind him.

"Now, Stephen. All your weight. Please."

God, finally. What's in a name, just a name? It meant everything. He settled on her, forcing the air from her lungs. Her breath ruffled his hair like a sigh. "Is that the way?"

"Yes." She closed her eyes, wrapped her arms around his neck, and clung to him. "That . . . feels . . . so . . . good."

He couldn't stay like that for long. Even now, her chest heaving against him, she struggled for breath. He could give her a moment more. A moment more to enjoy the rapture on her face.

Then he put a forearm on the grass, reached down to grab her butt, and went as deep as he could. Talk about bliss. So tight, she felt like a warm hand milking him. She lifted her hips, angling higher for his next thrust.

Stroking himself with her body, he tipped her face in his hand. "Look at me. I want you to see me."

She opened her eyes, giving him what he wanted. The window into her soul. He found a rhythm, not so fast that he came too quickly but enough to start her on that sweet climb to oblivion. She bit her bottom lip. A soft moan slipped from her.

"Look at me when you come. Don't close your eyes."

"I won't." She took a breath. "I promise." Wriggling beneath him, she clutched his ass, trying to force him to a faster pace. Instead, he circled his hips, rubbing her clitoris with his body as his cock hit high and deep.

She started to pant. "Oh God, Stephen. I've never come like this. Not this way. With someone inside me." She tossed her head. "Oh God, don't stop. Please don't stop."

He held her, forcing her to look at him. "I won't ever stop, I swear." Never stop wanting her, never stop loving her.

With a strong, steady pump, he stoked her fire. Her hands roamed from his hair to his arms to his back. He wanted her crazy. He wanted her to remember how he felt inside her, to dream about him at night. A moan welled up from deep inside her. Her pussy pulsated around him. She bit her lip, then opened her mouth on a long, low cry.

She never broke eye contact.

When she cried out his name, he came with a long, blinding, star-studded release.

SEVEN

IT WAS FOUR o'clock in the morning. Her clothes were grass-stained, her heels covered with dirt, and she smelled like come. But she wouldn't wash off Stephen's scent. Instead, she threw everything into the back of the closet and crawled into bed.

"You're pretty late," her husband murmured.

"I was a little drunk. The girls and I stopped at a coffee shop until I felt like I could drive."

"You should have called. I was worried."

"I'm sorry." She should have felt something. Shame. Guilt. Fear.

"Well, good night."

"Yeah. Good night."

The only indication that anything bothered him was the length of time before he started snoring. She clocked it at fifteen minutes. He usually fell asleep right away.

She was heading toward a bad end. Adulterers always did. She didn't care. She had never experienced more passion, more intensity. No man had ever wanted her as Stephen did.

His lust wouldn't last forever. No man's ever did.

Still, he was hers for now. She put a hand to her face and smelled him. His scent settled like a blanket, soft, warm, and gentle. She could still feel his weight, his hardness inside.

She'd given herself this one night as a gift. Now she knew she'd have to go back. Again and again. Until he tired of her.

DEBBIE SLEPT UNTIL ten o'clock, an unheard-of hour, even for a Saturday morning. Her shower erased all trace of Stephen's scent. All that remained was a tenderness between her legs.

Her husband was cleaning out the garage. She could have worked on her glass, but she couldn't face him after last night. Strangely, sharing the same work space seemed infinitely worse than being in the same bed.

She headed down the hall to her office. She had to e-mail the real Stephen. Somehow, the act of giving her mystery lover that name morphed them into the same person. Stephen's caring and kindness matched with a lover's fire and passion.

She tapped off a brief answer to his inquiry about the next project she'd planned.

He came back quickly. "Hope you had a good evening."

Last night had been exhilarating, terrifying. If she could, she'd do it all over again. "It was nice, thanks. And yours?"

"I enjoyed my evening very much. Thanks for asking."

They sounded too damn polite. She wanted to type as if he were the man she'd taken inside her body. She ached to share, no matter how big a mistake that would be.

"I did something important. It made me a new woman." She almost hit Send, then deleted the line.

Saying anything at all was like opening up to your best friend. You plan on telling them one small thing, then the rest gushed like a flood. Which is why she wouldn't let Stacy steer her toward talking about The Sex Club at all.

Except that with e-mail, you could always think before you sent. You could pour your heart out, then hit Delete. She couldn't count the number of times she'd done that with Stephen over the past several months.

What did she really want to tell him now?

I want to change my life. I want the Stephen of last night and the Stephen of today to be the same man.

They weren't the same man, could never be the same man.

Still, there couldn't be any harm in asking Stephen a little bit more about himself.

STEPHEN HELD HIS head in his hands waiting for the beep announcing her next e-mail.

"What are you passionate about, Stephen?"

Her. Right now, that was the only answer he could find. She consumed his waking thoughts, his dreams, and his nightmares.

Yet he wrote the only other thing he could point a finger to. "My work."

He wasn't an architect. He didn't design. He executed someone else's vision. Still, he brought the lines and angles on a piece of paper, even a three-dimensional CAD, to life. He made a dispassionate model into a home, a refuge where the cares of the world could fall away, even down to the streams of sunlight that fell through the trees onto a back deck or patio. He didn't do malls or office buildings or apartments. He specialized in home remodels. Though they'd discussed his work at length, especially as to how her windows fit into the finished picture in his mind, he'd never described what he did in terms of passion.

He typed another line before he hit Send. "I'm passionate about giving people the perfect sanctuary in which to recharge their batteries after life has beaten the hell out of them."

She replied in little more than a series of heartbeats. "That's the most beautiful thing I've ever heard."

And something that very few people would understand. Her perceptiveness awed him, though somehow he'd known that she felt the same way. "What are you passionate about?" he typed.

"I'm passionate about . . . passion. In everything I do, everything I want, everything I think, everything I feel."

She'd taken him with that level of passion. Right down to the full weight of his body pressing the very air from her lungs.

Before he could reply, she sent him another message. "I want passion, Stephen, I want it so badly it hurts. I want it more than one time in my life. I want it over and over."

Once again, he felt her anguish as she'd whispered that her husband didn't want her anymore. In the space of a few seconds between messages, she'd taken the discussion from the abstract to the deeply personal. She couldn't know what she did to him. He had the terrifying thought she might actually tell him about last night, and he didn't know what the hell he'd say. He'd never considered that she'd turn him into her confidant.

Yet a part of him wanted to know every detail, what she'd felt in his arms, what she wanted, what she needed.

If he urged, would she tell him the truth?

Christ, would he be able to handle her inner thoughts if she let them all come pouring out? Hell, no. He had too damn much at stake.

His fingers trembled over the innocuous words he typed, words that didn't exactly invite any confidences. "I'm sure you'll have a good life, Debbie."

He felt like he'd waited forever when the beep finally came.

"You're right. Sorry for dumping on you."

He read her regret, and God forgive him for his relief. "You didn't dump on me." He bent his head, closed his eyes a moment, and after a deep breath, resumed his typing. "I've another client interested in some glasswork. She's got a panel of three windows overlooking her atrium. Got any ideas?"

With her reply of, "Let me meditate on it, Stephen," the intimate moment was lost.

He needed to create another to fill its place.

EIGHT

THIS TIME, SHE was waiting for his invitation.

It came on Monday. Her husband had left the envelope lying on the kitchen table, separate from the bills and grocery flyers. What if she'd told him the envelope was an invitation from a man she'd met at a sex club? Would he ask her not to go or cover his ears like one of those monkeys? Hear no evil, see no evil. She'd crawled into the house at four o'clock in the morning smelling of another man's come, and he hadn't gotten mad. Was that denial or lack of caring?

She turned the envelope over in her hand. Her skin tingled as if an electric current raced from her head to her toes. She ripped the envelope sideways. The invitation slid out. Raising it, she drew a deep breath. *His* aftershave still lingered. On the inside, he'd written "Friday" in capital letters. The wait would kill her, but she had oh so many plans to make.

As her alter ego, Desiree, she called ahead and reserved a private room at the club. She started thinking of herself as Desiree sometime on Tuesday, and Desiree ordered a sex toy as well. Wednesday, she had her hair highlighted, something she hadn't done in ages, and her nails done Thursday, choosing Chili Pepper Red. Though Stacy had tried, Debbie wasn't ready to talk. On Friday during her lunch hour, Debbie bought black stockings, a lacy red thong, and matching bra and garter belt.

Soaking for an hour in a scented tub, she prepared her body for seduction. Once she'd dressed, the panties caressed her pussy, and the bra sensitized her nipples. She was hot and ready before she even closed the front door.

Driving away from the house, she didn't care what her husband thought. No guilt, no shame, only a slight anticipatory rush of moisture between her legs. She focused only on the night to come, a man's kisses, his touch, and his cock deep inside her. Such was the nature of obsession. Only the goal had importance, only what she wanted.

Desiree was obsessed.

STEPHEN WAITED FOR her at the head of the stairs, no hiding, no following this time. He wanted everyone to know she was his from the moment she stepped through the door.

His heart skipped several beats when she entered. It skipped another as she handed her invitation to the hostess and accepted a small item that she deftly slipped into her bra. Snaring a glass of champagne, she turned to search for him. Her gaze locked with his, then her lips curved in a sweet, sensual smile that hardened his cock and captured his heart.

Her red jacket, unzipped to well below her breasts, revealed a slender column of tantalizing flesh. He ached to run his tongue from the edge of that zipper to the hollow of her throat. The slit in her long black skirt rose to the top of her stocking, giving him a glimpse of skin as she raised a spike-heeled shoe to the first step.

She was the perfect combination of lady and whore. Class and elegance wrapped in a seductive package.

People flowed around her, coming up, going down, touching her with their eyes, undressing her, wanting her. She blinked, a slow, sultry dip of her lashes, then raised her champagne to her lips. First a sip, then the tip of her tongue licked a drop from the edge of the glass. Just as she'd savored a bead of come from the head of his cock. She glided toward him, every movement, every glance seduced him, tied him in knots.

She stopped a stair below him, her chin raised, her breasts beckoning, a heated pulse at her throat. Her gaze traveled to the hard ridge filling out his jeans. She licked her lips, then trailed a finger along his cock from base to crown. If she'd stroked him with her tongue, he'd have come with a single caress.

"I have plans for you, Stephen."

He was sure he'd explode before she executed them. This was the way he wanted her, sure of her allure, sure of his desire. There wasn't a thing he wouldn't do for her.

He held out his hand. She placed hers in his palm, then rose that last step to stand beside him.

"Tell me about them," he murmured.

She smiled, that same delicious, sensual curve of her mouth. "I'd rather show you."

"Even better."

She pivoted, pulled his hand close, almost tucking it into the crease of her gorgeous ass, and led him up the stairs to the third floor and the private rooms.

He let his fingers caress her backside as she swayed against him. At the top of the stairs, she set her half-empty champagne glass on a table. He tugged gently, then leaned down to whisper in her ear. "You look so fuckable, you're driving me insane."

She nestled to his chest. "I want you insane. Totally."

She dashed a quick kiss across his lips, tempting him to grab her for a longer taste. Pushing him back, she ran a hand down his arm, trailing electricity. "I can't decide whether to go in alone and get everything ready. Or to let you watch."

"Let me watch."

She whirled, leaning back, tugging on his hand, trusting that he wouldn't let her fall. She laughed like a playful child. Any number of personalities lived inside her. He wanted to plumb her depths, discover each one.

"Do you like red?"

"Yes." He loved her red jacket, the red bra he'd glimpsed, her lipstick, the polish on her fingers.

Like the pied piper, she led him down the hall. "I asked for the red room. It sounded very bordelloish."

Which meant she wanted to play the whore. Every man wants his woman to be a whore for him. Wants her to give him every dirty, nasty, hot, and delicious act. Though few men had the confidence to admit the truth. There was always the thought that if she acted the whore for him, she'd do it for someone else.

He wanted Desiree the whore. Desiree the laughing child. Desiree the sensuous, mysterious woman. Desiree with his heart in the palm of her hand. He wanted all of her. "Yeah. I think red will do just fine."

She glanced at each of the doors, finding the one she wanted near the end of the hall. Reaching into her bra, slowly, touching herself, touching him with her gaze as she did so, she pulled out the small item the hostess had given her. A gold filigreed key. Unlocking the door and throwing it open, she gasped on the threshold. "It's outrageously tacky."

He closed the gap between them, their bodies touching full length, and glanced past her shoulder. Deep shades of red everywhere, silk wall hangings, the curtains surrounding the bed, the spread shot through with black threads. The gilt furniture looked like something Marie Antoinette would have sat on. Which certainly fit the bordello theme.

He pushed inside, closed the door, and leaned against it. She turned in circles, the heels of her shoes sinking into the plush carpeting. Then she put her hands to her mouth, giggling. "It's terrible, isn't it?"

"It's perfect. I can fuck you on the floor, on the bed, or against the wall in perfect comfort." He eyed the chairs. "But I think the furniture would break."

"I hope not." She laughed, then plucked at a lapel. "My jacket clashes. It's orange-red instead of blue-red like everything else." Then she smiled. "Guess that means I'd better take it off." She slowly unzipped, watching him, then slid the garment down her arms and threw it across a corner chair.

A red lace bra and all that dazzling flesh. He'd taken one step toward her when she held out her hand.

"No. You can't touch me yet." She pointed at a dainty sofa. "Sit there."

A bottle of champagne iced in a bucket beside the delicate piece of furniture. Next to that sat a small round table with two champagne flutes. He popped the cork, filled the glasses, beckoning her closer with one as he sat. She took it, tapping the edge to his, then sipped the sparkling liquid.

"Do you know how close I am to throwing you on that bed and fucking the hell out of you?" He returned his glass to the small table and reached for her.

She sucked in a breath, her nipples burgeoning against the lace. He wanted to give her everything, the words, the passion, the fire she craved. "You have to wait."

"I don't think I can."

She leaned forward, her hand on the sofa's arm, eyes glittering like the bubbles in her champagne glass. "I promise you'll like what I've got planned."

He would cherish whatever she chose to give. He'd die for every touch. Running a hand inside the slit of her skirt, he palmed her damp panties. "I think you're going to like it just as much."

"Take them off," she whispered.

He slipped a finger under the elastic and slid the panties down slowly. They clung to her pussy for a moment before coming free. When he reached her ankles, his mouth close to her apex, he blew on her.

She clutched his shoulder. "Oh God, Stephen."

His gut clenched with need. "Step out of them."

She lifted first one foot, then the other. He slipped the delicate lace into his back pocket. "Souvenir," he whispered, when she tipped her head.

So close, so sweet-smelling. He wanted to taste her flesh, the swell of her breasts, the gentle curve of her belly, her inner thigh, the back of her knee. He waited, letting her lead.

She swallowed half the champagne, then set the glass next to his on the table. Straddling him, she settled onto his lap. He eased back against the sofa, his hands on her hips.

"I want to kiss you, Stephen."

"You can do anything you want to me."

She cupped the back of his head and put her lips to his. He let her control, let her taste him, let her deepen the kiss. His fingers flexed against her hips as she took him with her mouth. Soft, gentle, wet, and warm. She nibbled his lower lip, sucked his tongue, then fully opened to him, inviting him in. She gave him the sweetest, hottest kiss he'd ever known. Her fingers played his face, her breasts caressed him, and her thighs hugged him. She kissed with every part of her body.

He didn't know how much more he could stand.

She pulled back. His lips followed hers until forced to part from her. Rising up, she lifted her long skirt over her hips, allowing room to straddle him completely. Hot arousal scented the air. His. Hers.

She licked her lips, held his gaze. "I want to touch myself for you, Stephen. I want you to watch."

He gripped her thighs, squeezed, his fingers flirting with the tops of her stockings. "Jesus, God, please."

I WANT TO touch myself for you, Stephen.

The thought made her heart race with self-consciousness. His hot, dark eyes and hoarse voice were the reward. Debbie had planned this. Desiree wanted to execute the plan. If she didn't, she'd never forgive herself.

She cupped her breasts, traced the nipples through the bra, then pushed the lace aside and circled each nipple with the tip of her finger.

"Lick your finger and make them wet." His low, rough command coated her pussy with cream.

She trailed a finger down her abdomen and dipped in for the moisture, then rubbed it into her nipple.

His hips bucked, and his fingers dug into her ass.

She undid the bra and tossed it aside. Leaning forward, she cupped his head and put her nipple to his mouth. "Taste me."

His lips closed around her, suckled. Fire raced down to her clitoris, and she closed her eyes, tipped her head back. Then she pushed him. "That's enough." It wasn't, by far, but she wanted to tease him, drive him wild. In the process, she'd tease herself as well. "No more touching by anyone but me."

He leaned in for one more quick swipe, sending another jolt of electricity between her legs. "Then do it, now. Put your hot little finger in your pussy and make yourself come before I die."

"Don't rush me. We have to build up to it."

He groaned and squeezed her backside. His need was what she wanted. She let it drive her higher until her body hummed.

"Please, baby."

She palmed herself for him, moisture drenching her hand. Stephen breathed deeply, his eyes closing as he sampled her aroma. Then he raised his lids once more to drink her in.

"I'm so wet, Stephen. That's what you do to me." She parted the folds and teased her clitoris. A sigh fell from her lips, and her body arched. "It feels so good with you watching."

She needed his eyes on her, his gaze everything. Her hips seemed to move on their own, pushing against him. She circled her clit, tormenting it to a hard bead. She raised herself, riding her fingers as if they were a cock deep inside her.

He held her butt, helped her find that perfect rhythm. "I've never seen anything so beautiful." Then he stopped her. "I want you on the bed without the skirt."

He held her gaze. And she wanted everything he wanted.

"Yes, on the bed," she whispered.

She was sure she would have fallen if he hadn't helped her to stand. He reached behind and unzipped her skirt, letting it drop. He told her to lift her feet by tapping behind one knee, then the other, then tossed the garment aside. He kissed her belly, then licked along the garter belt. She shivered. Then he rose and pushed her toward the bed.

She slipped off her high heels. Wearing only garter and stockings, and with him clothed, she should have felt vulnerable. Instead, she felt sexy and decadent. She climbed onto the bed, lifting her ass. He squeezed a globe. Then she rolled over and lay on her back.

"Oh my God. There's a mirror up there."

He glanced up. "So there is." Rolling to his side, he propped himself on an elbow, and together they looked at her in the mirror. He pulled her leg toward him, heightening her wanton display. Caressing her thigh, he gazed up into the mirror. "Now we can both watch. Touch yourself. Put your hand right here."

In the reflection, she saw him place her hand between her legs, his covering hers, forcing her to draw light circles on her sensitized flesh. "You're so damn beautiful."

Though his voice was in her ear, the mirror distanced them. A man dressed in black, his hair silver. A woman in lingerie, her breasts and pussy bared to him. His big, tanned hand guiding her smaller, lighter-toned fingers looked so right together. Two halves of a whole, neither complete without the other.

He sucked her earlobe. "Make yourself come, baby."

A pulse throbbed at her throat. The warmth of his hand left hers, and in the mirror, the woman rubbed her glistening pussy. She wet her lips with her tongue and fought to keep her eyes open as heat and tension built. Stephen nuzzled her hair. Her hips danced in the mirror, rising to rock against her fingers.

"Who do you imagine when you're alone in your bed and your body's aching?" His murmur wafted across her face.

"You." She gulped in a breath. "It's you touching me."

"Say my name."

"I imagine you, Stephen. Your tongue. Your cock inside me." She strained off the bed. "Oh God, I want you so badly."

He rose to his knees and peeled off his shirt. Unzipping his jeans, he pushed them past his hips and took his cock in his hand. "Do you know what your little noises do to me?"

The skin of his cock stretched tight at the tip. "Little sighs and tiny moans, I hear them at night when I'm in bed." He stroked his erection. "I have to take out my cock. You make me come even when you're not there. You drive me crazy." He leaned down, bracing himself on one hand, and matched her rhythm. "Do you know how long I've waited to watch you? I've dreamed this a million times. I've ached to see you just like this for real."

His voice wrapped around her as his hand wrapped around his cock. He worked her with the words. She panted, dizzied by his speed in the mirror, watching her body writhe on the bed.

And then she remembered her surprise. "Stephen, wait, wait, I need you to do something for me." She had to have this, needed it for her store of memories.

He dropped his pace down to a gentle stroke.

"I asked them to put a vibrator in the side table drawer." Heat bloomed on her cheeks, yet she didn't know how she could be embarrassed after all they'd done. "I want you to use it on me."

For a moment, he didn't move; then he grinned. "You astound me."

When he retrieved it, she saw it wasn't as big as the one she'd watched, but she didn't care. It would be perfect.

"Stephen, fuck me with it," she whispered, her heat rising again just at the sight of it in his hand. "Please fuck me. Make me come. Please."

He came down by her side, his cock caressing her thigh, and pulled her legs wide. "You're so wet, I don't think you even need this thing lubed." He turned it onto a low buzz and tested the humming tip against her clitoris.

She jumped. "More."

It was like a thousand tongues beating at her, and her passions rose so quickly, she almost came right then. "Inside, put it inside. Oh God. Now."

He fondled her, toying with her as he parted her folds and slipped the vibrator inside. In, out, in, out, he went a little deeper each time. She started to pant and raised her gaze to the mirror above them. It was so utterly decadent and beautiful. Her leg over his hip, his silver hair, her pussy spread for him, the white base of the vibrator in his tanned hand, working in and out of her. So full, so good. She closed her eyes and pushed her hips up to take more. And he fucked her with it, fucked her long and hard and so damn good.

Then he put his tongue to her clit. Nothing. Ever. Nothing to compare. A cock taking her, a tongue bringing her.

She screamed his name, and her body gushed and came apart at the seams. His voice flowed over her like warm, wet come, urging her on, filling her up. She buried her face against the coverlet, the material tantalizing to her skin, her blood pounding through her veins.

"Oh my God." Her breath was fast, and she didn't feel quite in her own body.

Setting the vibrator aside, he lay beside her, trailing fingers up and down her thigh, leaving a path of sparks. "I have never been a party to something so utterly gorgeous." He kissed her lips lightly. "Thank you."

"No. Thank *you*."

He rolled to his back and took her hand, raising it to his lips to suck her taste from her fingers, then he clasped it to his chest. "Do you see what I see?"

She saw him, pants below his hips, cock hard and high, chest dusted with hair, and black eyes willing her to see what he wanted her to see. She looked at her own body, nipples a rosy pink, still tight, thighs parted wantonly. The curls at her apex darker, damp, a streak of moisture across her hip. The stockings and garter belt made it that much more sexy. Her belly quivered.

Then she drank in the sight of him. Crinkly hair sprouted at the base of his cock. A tan line bisected his belly, the crown of his penis crossing it. Dark hair sprinkled with gray covered his chest and flat, brown nipples tempted her tongue.

Before she could move to take one in her mouth, he stroked through her curls. "A woman's glory. Her power." He found her clitoris and rubbed it to throbbing heat. "Do you feel it?"

Sensation streaked through her limbs. "Yes."

He slid one finger inside and pumped as he had with the vibrator. "Do you want me inside you?"

His touch rushed her to the edge as if she hadn't orgasmed only minutes before. "God, yes."

He stopped long enough to whisper a harsh demand. "Say my name. Beg me."

"Make love to me, Stephen. Please. Make me come again."

He pulled back to shove off his clothes and put on a condom. She wanted to feel every inch of him with every part of her body. Belly to belly, he pulled her tight, trapping his cock between them, rocking gently. He closed his eyes, groaned, then finally, he rose and braced himself with one hand.

"Take me inside you," he whispered.

She parted her legs, reached between them and held him, using him to stroke herself. "Just to get you all nice and wet."

His eyes gleamed. "Do anything you want."

She closed her eyes, fitted him to her. Then she wrapped her arms around his neck. "I want you inside. All the way. As high as you'll go." She pulled herself up to press her breasts to his chest. "In one thrust."

He settled on her, gathered her butt in his hands, then slammed into her. She gasped, wrapped her arms around him, and held him that way for a moment. Savoring the feel. It was so much better than silicon.

"Now fuck me, Stephen."

He moved inside her.

"Faster," she urged. "Harder."

He rose to his elbows, increasing the pace, the friction. She raised her legs to his waist. With one hand behind her knee, he forced her higher, his penetration deeper. She felt him touch her womb. His body pummeled her, thrust her across the bed until her head hit the pillows. She braced against the headboard.

"You feel so damn good." Sweat beaded on his forehead.

"Fuck me, Stephen. Fuck me." She chanted the act, his name, over and over.

He lowered his head like a ram and took her with the mindless ferocity of an animal. Their slick flesh slapped and rubbed as he angled and arched. With each thrust, rough hair and hard flesh pounded her clitoris. On the inside, he captured a sweet spot she hadn't known existed.

"Jesus, God." His throat corded. "Fuck. Oh God. I—" He squeezed his eyes shut. "Shit. Ah shit." Then he threw back his head and howled.

She came as he pulsed inside her. Came as he cried out. Came as he lost total control. She clung to him in the storm of sensation and kept on clinging when the tempest was over. His warm flesh stuck to her, their bodies fused. He breathed hard against her shoulder, his head buried in her hair. He trembled against her, inside her, all around her.

Nothing had ever felt so perfect.

She didn't care about the wrongness in what she was doing, didn't care about the consequences. That's what addicts did. Told themselves they were in control. She wasn't, but she would take everything she could get for as long as Stephen offered it.

NINE

IT HAD BEEN a week since Stephen last held her, a week in which pieces of his soul died. Their e-mails weren't enough, leaving a gaping hole in his chest. In the garish bordello room, buried deep inside her, he'd almost shouted out his love. Every day since, the need to tell her grew stronger, more obsessive. He didn't want a quick fuck, not even a long night of fucking if he couldn't wake up beside her in the morning. Every morning. He couldn't sneak off to meet her. He wouldn't share her.

Yet he'd sent another invitation.

Tonight, The Sex Club was too damn crowded. Stephen had tried to get a private room, but they were all booked. Jesus. It was like ordering a motel room, and the feeling in his gut was just as seedy. Too many people wandered the halls tonight, and the club reeked of sweat, cloying perfume, and dirty sex. This wasn't how he wanted their night to be.

He tugged her into an alcove, pulling the green curtain, then leaned back against the wall and brought her into his arms. Her citrus scent burned away the stink of the club.

She put her hand to his cheek. "What's wrong, Stephen?"

"I want to be alone with you." He breathed her in, willing the ache in his chest to subside.

"We're alone in here." She touched her sweet lips to his.

He crushed her against him. This time, she'd dressed as Debbie, the woman he dreamed of, in a camel-colored skirt and black jacket with a white blouse beneath. He ran his hands under the jacket, taking her warmth inside him. Her kiss turned him inside out, dragging a low moan up from his belly. He felt the desperation in it. If this was all he had, making love in this darkened alcove, he would make it the best for her.

"Let me taste you," he whispered.

"God, yes. Please, Stephen, I've waited so long for that."

Backing her up against the wall, he inched her skirt to her waist and slowly, very slowly, got down on his knees. Beneath the Debbie skirt, she was purely Desiree, naked and beautiful.

Tiny droplets glistened on her curls. Her hips tilted toward him, begging, her lips plump with arousal. He drew his tongue along the slit, pointing at the top and hitting her clit. He felt her body's light jerk. Then he spread her, opening her fully, and licked gently along the crest. Her fingers tangled in his hair, and her soft moan was like music. He drank from her, her taste sweet and tart like fruit. She dragged one calf up his arm and draped her leg across his back as he bent to her.

He sucked her clitoris until her juices bathed his lips. He caressed every pleasure spot he could reach until her moans became one long sound that wrapped around his gonads, until she filled his mouth with a sweet gush of cream, and her moans filled his soul. He lapped gently as the shudders in her body subsided. He stayed on his knees before her until his cock ached so badly he had to stroke himself to ease the pain.

He would never ease the ache in his heart.

"That was beautiful," Debbie whispered. Nothing had ever been so beautiful or made her feel so complete. She tugged on Stephen's ears until he looked at her. "Come here."

He rose, her skirt falling between them. His lips shimmered with her come, then he rubbed them against hers. "You came so hard I drank you up. Taste it."

Looking into the deep pool of his eyes, she kissed his mouth. Her taste laced with his. The hard ridge of his arousal rocked against her belly. She wanted more of him. "Make love to me. I want you inside me."

Something flickered in his gaze. In the dark behind the velvet curtain, only a sliver of light to see by, it was hard to discern. Earlier he'd vibrated with raw tension, not sexual, anxious, out of character. There'd been too many people in the halls. It hadn't been like the other times. Or maybe it was and something inside her, something between *them*, had changed. She wanted, needed, maybe too much. Maybe he sensed how her emotions about him were becoming tangled. Maybe the end of it all was nearer than she thought.

"Please, Stephen. Now. Make love to me." The aching whisper hurt her throat. As did the mechanics of watching him don the condom. A symbol of what stood between them.

Then he cupped her face in his hands, his eyes roaming every inch of her features. Finally he put his mouth to hers in a kiss that stole her breath, stole her heart. Dipping his knees, he matched his height to hers and took her tongue with his.

He tasted of her juices and something indefinably him, sweet, caring, loving. If it was an illusion, she wanted it, needed it. His kiss said everything he didn't say with words. She was more than a fuck at a sex club. She was wanted as much as she wanted him, needed by him. His hands traveled her hips, caressed her buttocks, encompassing all of her. Then the slide of her skirt up her legs. When he traced her folds with his finger, she moaned into his mouth.

Pulling her legs to his waist, he hoisted her above him and looked up. "Christ, I want you so goddamn much."

It was there in his eyes. For this moment, she was all he wanted. Tomorrow didn't matter. She wrapped her arms around him and pulled him into her body.

Nothing had ever felt like this, the steel glide of his cock inside her, higher, deeper. The slide of his hips as he rotated and found that perfect spot. He thrust, and she clung. Heat and pleasure rose along with a hard knot of almost painful need.

He threw back his head and drove deep inside her. "God, I love you." His breath shot out, and he dropped his gaze to hers, piercing, wild. "I'm so fucking in love with you."

She tightened her legs at his waist, crushed him in her arms, and whispered, "I love you, Stephen."

Then she let her desires burst in a riot of color and stars and passion. He rode the starburst with her, shooting her higher, taking everything.

She would hug those precious words close and live with them the rest of her life. They were all she might ever have.

"COME HOME WITH me." Shit. Why the hell did he open his goddamn mouth when he knew the demand would ruin the night? She'd said she loved him. It was all he should have needed.

She stirred, snuggled closer. "You know I can't do that."

"I want to fall asleep with you in my arms. With my cock inside you." Fuck, fuck, fuck. Why couldn't he shut up?

"Next time we'll get a private room, then we can sleep for awhile." She kissed his throat, then settled into him once more.

Next time? Fuck next time. He wanted her in *his* bed, not in some goddamn bordello room. He closed his eyes against the rising pain. She'd meet him again if he asked. She'd shower him with her passion, say his name, tell him she loved him. But she would always leave the bed before he was ready to let her go.

He loved her with everything in him, wanted her, needed her, knew he just might die without her.

But he wouldn't do this again.

There was a time and a place for the truth. The Sex Club wasn't it. Tonight wasn't it. Or maybe it was just a way to avoid his day of reckoning, to save the memory of this one last night without ripping it all to hell.

But he would reveal himself. The next invitation she received would be from the real Stephen. He could only hope she didn't hate him for making her choose. And that he wouldn't hate her if she didn't choose him.

"YOU CAME IN late again last night." Her husband leaned against the bathroom doorjamb, arms folded across his chest. She hadn't heard him enter.

"Yes." She smoothed face cream into her skin. "I haven't seen Virginia since she got married."

"Does her new husband mind she stays out until three?"

Her heart stuttered. God, she hadn't even called Virginia when she got back from her honeymoon. Debbie gave a telltale pause in her morning routine. "He knows her well enough by now." Though she doubted he knew that the weekend of her wedding Virginia had masturbated for a room full of men.

"Do you really think this is good for you, Debbie?"

Suddenly they weren't talking about late nights with her friends. This was the closest he'd come to questioning her, the biggest threat he'd made to the status quo. She tipped her head, looking at him for the first time in . . . weeks. New lines had etched themselves in the flesh beneath his eyes. Sadness leached the color from his irises. He looked older. Tired. Unhappy.

Guilt clogged her throat. Shame closed her eyes. For a moment. Then she looked at him once more. *Are you going to make love to me with Stephen's passion?* If he asked her to give up Stephen, he was asking too much and giving nothing in return.

He simply didn't have that much passion in him.

"I think it's fine," she answered. "I can always make up for the lack of sleep another time."

She would never make up for a lack of Stephen in her life. After last night, she didn't think she could live without him. Yet all she could do was wait for the next invitation from a man who'd said he loved her, a man whose real name she didn't know.

THERE WAS NO *next* invitation.

Stephen had said he loved her. Everyone said that when they came. It didn't mean anything. He couldn't love her because he didn't know her. She couldn't love him either. But she was living a fantasy, and in fantasy, you closed your eyes and pretended it was real.

Debbie so very badly wanted to pretend it was real.

Six days later, she couldn't pretend anymore. She'd fallen into hell. On Thursday, in desperation, she'd called Stacy, telling her she needed a polish change. What she'd really needed was a talk, Stacy's no-nonsense attitude to shake some sense into her. She should have told Stacy weeks ago, before she made the cataclysmic mistake of accepting that first invitation. But then, she hadn't truly wanted to hear whatever Stacy said. Now, everything was different.

Do I bore him already?

She'd known rejection would come eventually. All men tired of the same old thing. She just hadn't imagined it would be so quickly. Especially not after he'd said he loved her. *"I'm so fucking in love with you."* They had to be more than mere words.

Now, it was obvious they were nothing more than orgasm talk. Oh God, how that thought made her ache inside.

"What's wrong, sweetie?" Stacy tugged on her hand.

I screwed up. "I did a pretty stupid thing."

Stacy stopped filing. "What?"

"I went back to the club."

"You know, I thought you might go back." She shook Debbie's fingers a little, signaling her to relax.

Debbie couldn't do that. "I went back for one man." She took a deep breath. "I saw him there that first night."

Stacy continued filing, waiting.

"I think I'm a little obsessed with him." Her chest tightened. Tears ached at the back of her eyes.

Stacy pursed her lips, then picked up her clippers to cut away a stubborn hangnail. "Obsession doesn't have to be a bad thing, you know. Maybe you enjoy the feeling."

"He stopped sending me invitations. I don't think he wants to see me again." Debbie yelped as Stacy filed away skin.

"God, I'm so sorry. I did that before, too, didn't I?"

This one was worse. Blood welled along her nail. Stacy dabbed at it with the alcohol, cooing as if Debbie were a baby.

"It's okay."

The bleeding didn't stop no matter how much pressure Stacy applied. Just like the pain in Debbie's heart. She'd wanted Stacy to bandage the wound with kind words, maybe even a few lies, but the pain wasn't going away. She was such a fool to think a fuck from a guy she didn't even know would stitch the gaping wound that had festered around her heart for years.

"WHAT THE HELL do you think you're doing?"

Stephen almost hung up on Stacy, but he couldn't. The need to know what Debbie had told her drove him, controlling his actions. "What did she say?"

"She's a mess. I thought she was going to start blubbering right there in the salon."

He shouldn't have felt so pleased. "What's bothering her?"

"Why didn't you send her another invitation?"

"I did. A different kind." An invitation to meet him at the house where he'd installed her carousel horse. "She hasn't answered yet." She hadn't answered his e-mails since Tuesday, the day before he found the courage to ask for what he wanted.

"You were supposed to make her life better, not miserable."

"I'm sorry she's miserable. But she's married. A fling with some nameless guy isn't going to solve her problems." The statement contained the only emotion he'd given away to Stacy in the whole godforsaken mess he'd let this turn into.

"Well, you can't give her three times and expect *that* to build her confidence enough to make some serious decisions."

He couldn't let Debbie tear his heart out either. To Stacy's credit, she didn't know his emotions were involved. To her, this was all about Debbie. He couldn't let Stacy know his feelings. Jesus, the woman would start trying to fix him, too.

"It's wrong, Stacy. I can't do that to her anymore. It was a temporary fix for a much larger problem."

"What exactly is going on with her?"

Maybe that was what Stacy wanted all along, to find out the truth. Stacy was a fixer. Give her a problem, and she'd find ten solutions. She flopped around helplessly like a fish out of water if she didn't know how to *fix* something for someone. With Debbie, she hadn't even understood the issue.

The riddle wasn't about another woman in her husband's life. It was about her total loss of faith in her own desirability. Three *months* wouldn't give it back to her. He could not be her drug of choice that helped her stay in a dead marriage.

"Keep at her until she tells you, Stacy. Because I'm not."

He hung up, then checked his e-mail. Debbie still hadn't replied. His heart lay bleeding on the office floor.

MEET STEPHEN? DEBBIE shuddered. In her current state, she'd probably start begging. *My nameless lover dumped me, and I need you to take his place.* How pathetic she'd become. She'd been sitting on his e-mail for over two days without replying

Now it was Friday evening, and she had to say *something*. Debbie stared at the unanswered e-mail for a full minute. A minute could be such a long time. Long enough for a woman to realize that she was almost forty years old, and she'd lived without passion for most of that time. She would live without it again. She would work with Stephen on the stained glass. She would breathe life into her business. She would go on.

"Sorry it took so long for me to get back to you, Stephen. When do you want to get together?"

She didn't expect an immediate reply, but she got it.

"Tomorrow. 10 a.m. Do you need directions?"

"No, I remember. See you there." She hesitated, then added, "It will be nice to finally meet you."

He hadn't said a word about the days between e-mails. He probably didn't think a thing of it. After all, she was the one who'd been having histrionics. A man fucked her, a man walked away. That's what men did when they didn't want a woman anymore. Except her husband . . . though God only knew why.

Her fantasy Stephen hadn't owed her a thing. Neither did the real one. In truth, it was the other way around.

---------------------------------- TEN ----------------------------------

THE FAMILY HAD chosen to move out during the remodel. Most couldn't afford to do so. Most couldn't afford the extensive changes this couple had wanted. Stephen had damn near rebuilt the entire house, everything except the outer structure, though that, too, had been altered, pushing out a wall in the kitchen, adding a bay window in the living room, and a sunroom in the back.

The playroom was in the front of the house. Debbie would see the horse as she drove up. He'd left the front door open. Pacing the new hardwood floor, he ran his fingers through his hair. He'd been jumpy all morning, looking at his watch every minute, snapping at his secretary when she'd beeped him.

Shit. He'd certainly woven the proverbial tangled web.

Outside, a car pulled up, an engine died, then a door slammed. He imagined her on the front walk, her eyes shaded to look up at the horse where he'd installed it in a circular frame above the main playroom window. It would be even more impressive inside. He climbed the stairs to the second floor. He wanted her to see the piece in all its glory before she saw the truth.

"Hello?"

Her voice wrapped around him. He closed his eyes, drank the sound in, then called, "Come upstairs."

He entered the playroom, standing to the left of the door so that she would see the glasswork first, before seeing him. He couldn't take that moment from her, that first long glance at a piece of her heart filling the room with light, sun sparkling through the jewels in the saddle.

Soft footfalls on the hall carpet. Then she entered the room, staring at the gleaming carousel horse dancing in the sunlight almost as if it were real.

Her blond hair shimmered with highlights, her blouse hugged her breasts, and the flowing skirt played with her calves. She'd brushed her cheeks with a hint of blush and tinted her lips with rose. The sight of her stole his breath as she'd stolen his heart.

"Do you like seeing it up there, Debbie?"

She didn't answer him. Tipping her head, her breasts rose with a deep breath, then she turned to him where he clung to the wall like a shadow.

Eyes softened with sadness or pain, she stared for a moment. "What are you doing here?"

His lips went numb. His throat felt paralyzed. He waited for her to figure the truth out on her own, to realize that the man she e-mailed and the man she'd made love with were one and the same. He recognized the instant she came to that conclusion. Her spine stiffened, adding an inch to her height, and her blue eyes turned the shade of a stormy sky.

"Did you know it was me at the club?" she asked softly.

"Yes."

"Why did you let me call you Stephen?"

Because he needed her to so badly it had blinded him to anything else. "It's my real name."

She looked away and chewed on the inside of her cheek. "You shouldn't have let me call you that."

He felt her thoughts as if they pounded inside his head. She'd called him Stephen, and in so doing, told him things she never meant for him to know. She'd revealed her fantasies. About *him*. He'd been there long before the mythical Stephen. Though she never let a word slip, she'd dreamed about him.

Until this minute, he'd never realized how sacred a fantasy was. He'd broken her trust. "I'm sorry."

"I have to go."

She turned quickly, but not fast enough to hit the doorway before he did. He blocked her, both arms on opposite doorjambs. "Let me explain." Except that all the explanations he'd planned couldn't cover what he'd actually done to her. "I was an idiot, Debbie." Far more than her husband had ever been.

"Let me out."

"Say my name." *Please.* If she called him by his name, he'd know he still had a chance.

She turned once more, hugged her purse to her chest and walked to the window. The morning sun beat through the panes of glass. By the time it moved round, the room would be baking.

She must have felt the same thing. "Shutters would be nice in here. White ones."

He didn't want to talk about the goddamn shutters. He knew she wasn't ready for anything else, but he'd started down this path, and he owed her an explanation.

"Let me tell you why."

"I don't need to know," she said, still facing the window.

He crossed the carpet to her. Her body was so close, her back against his chest, her heat jumping across the small distance he left between them. Her scent wrapped around him like a blanket he wanted to curl into. As badly as he needed to, he didn't touch her.

"I wanted you to feel better. You were so sad. I couldn't stand it." He put a hand up, letting her hair brush his palm.

"You didn't even know me."

Look at me. Let me show you how wrong you are with my eyes and my lips. "I knew you. I don't think you even know how many little details were in everything you wrote to me."

She stiffened, tension in every line of her body. "And you fucked me so I wouldn't be sad?"

He closed his eyes, taking the knife thrust straight through his heart. "That isn't what I meant."

She turned then, backed away, anger finally setting her muscles in motion. "Then why don't you tell me exactly what you thought you were doing?"

"Ask me anything you want to know." The only thing he had left to give her was the truth.

"Why were you there that first night?"

Because he was already half in love with a woman he'd never met. A woman he *had* to meet. "I wanted to make sure you didn't get hurt." Though he'd certainly failed there.

Her eyes glittered with unshed tears. "Did Stacy know all about this?"

"She knew I'd be there."

"What on earth was she thinking? What was her plan?" She started to pace, agitated jerky steps.

"I have no idea what was in her mind." He hadn't wanted to know anything beyond the fact that bringing Debbie to the club gave him exactly what he wanted.

"Then what was in *your* mind?"

"I wanted to see you." He paused, struggled for the truth. Without honesty now, they didn't have a chance. "I wanted to see you that first time without your husband between us."

She became a flurry of action then, throwing her purse to the floor, her arms out, then up, finally turning on him with a haunted look in her eyes. "What the hell is that supposed to mean? You wanted to fuck me, and you figured I'd be more open to it at a sex club?" She paced in front of him. "That if I showed up there, it would prove I was some sort of amoral whore who would do anything you told her to?" She stopped long enough to stick her finger in his face. "I did prove that, didn't I? I let you fuck me from behind with everyone watching. I sucked your cock and swallowed. I masturbated for you. Oh, and let's not forget when you fucked me with the vibrator. But maybe there was something else you wanted." Pacing back and forth, back and forth, she seemed oblivious to her movements. "Maybe you wanted to watch me get fucked by three guys at once, you know, one in every orifice. Would that turn you on? What did Stacy tell you about me?" She screamed the last at him.

He couldn't breathe. He could barely manage to watch her anger, her pain. Couldn't forgive himself for having done that to her. Yet he wanted to shake her until she listened to him. "Stacy didn't tell me a goddamn thing. Everything I knew, you told me yourself in so many different ways. This was never about what I wanted. It was about what I could give you."

"You're such a fucking liar." Then she threw herself at him, pounding her fists against his chest, his shoulders, his arms. "I told you everything about myself. Everything. And you were just using me for some sick reason I don't understand. You probably told her my husband didn't want me anymore." Panting, her words choppy and broken, she rained blows down him. He took every one, dying inside. "And you laughed with her. I know you did." Then she beat at him wildly. "Are you fucking her, too? Did you fuck me so the two of you could laugh about me later?"

He wrapped his arms around her, dragging her to the floor. Leaning back against the wall, one leg twisted beneath him, he pulled her onto his lap. He let her hit him over and over until it seemed she couldn't lift her arms to hit him again, until all she could do was cry against him.

"I'm so sorry," he whispered. "Jesus, I'm so sorry." He rocked her as she sobbed, cradled her to his chest.

Running his hands up and down her back, stroking her hair, he whispered, "There's nothing between Stacy and me. Never."

She took two gulps of air against his chest, then fisted her hand in his shirt.

"We only wanted to help you. *I* wanted to help you."

She shuddered and screwed more of his shirt in her fist.

He forced himself to go on, to answer her every accusation. "I never used you to get my sexual kicks. I only wanted to give you pleasure, to make you see how special you are. To me. You know that. You *feel* that. I know you do."

Still she didn't answer.

The heat in the room continued to rise, and he realized she was right about the shutters. He'd recommended low-e windows, but the Thomases had been afraid the coating would cut some of the light. He should have thought about shutters. He should have thought about so many things where Debbie was concerned. Instead, he'd thought with his cock and his heart. He deserved to have the one chopped off and the other ripped to shreds.

Her crying gentled to a few muffled sniffles and a couple of hiccups. His leg cramped beneath him, but he couldn't have let go of her for anything.

"I never wanted to hurt you like this."

She didn't lift her head, her breath fanning his damp shirt front. "What did you want, Stephen?"

His name on her lips should have warmed him. Instead, it chilled his blood. *I wanted you to love me.* He'd told her he loved her. The sentiment had seemed so right and been so easy to say when he was buried deep inside her. Just as it had been easy for her to say, then pretend they were only emotions of the moment. Now, those words burned his throat and eyes.

He held her, kissed the top of her head, buried his face in her hair, and drank in her scent. Fruity, tangy, feminine. "I wanted to be with you. I wanted to make love to you."

"Are you saying you wanted to have an affair with me?"

He tightened his arms around her. "No. That's not what I wanted."

"Then what is it you do want?" Whispering the words, she looked up at him, her cheeks tear-streaked, smudges of mascara beneath her eyes.

His heart swelled, and his vision blurred. He tipped his head back to hide his eyes from her. "You. With me all night long. In the morning. The afternoon. Every day. For the rest of my life."

She held her breath, then softly exhaled against his chest. "You want me to leave my husband?"

He could tell nothing from the tone of her voice, but he couldn't hide behind a half truth. "Yes." He gulped air as if his body thirsted for it. "I'm in love with you."

She was silent for so long, he wanted to howl like a wounded animal. He felt the sun on his face, searing his flesh, burning through his lids to his eyeballs. Keeping his hands lax lest he shook her until she answered, his head ached with the concentration that feat required. A strong man would have looked at her, studying each emotion as it played across her face. A strong man would have searched for answers in the depths of her eyes before she ever said the words.

With her, he'd lost his strength. He could only hold on to his last shred of hope if he didn't look at her.

Finally, when the synapses in his brain were about to misfire, she pushed upright, away from him. "I can't do that, Stephen. I can't leave my husband for you."

Her words sucked the air from his lungs. Each word carved a slice off his heart until there was nothing left. For the last few weeks, he'd tasted heaven.

Today, he knew he'd landed in hell.

EVEN AFTER LONG minutes of silence, Debbie didn't know what to say. *I'm sorry. You're rushing me. You don't even know me. A month from now, maybe a year, you'll be tired of me.*

She had a life. It wasn't perfect by any means, but if she wasn't married, she might very well end up alone. Out of the frying pan and into the fire, as the old saying went. She wasn't sure she could stand that either. She'd rather die than be totally alone as age crept up.

Needing distance, she crawled off his lap and stood. "We never even met until today. You don't really know anything about me." *I don't know anything about you except that you've lied to me for the last month.* She was past the sobbing of minutes before, past the rage, but she wasn't past his lies.

"I know you, Debbie," he said, rising to his feet. Crossing to the window, he stared out. "Regardless of what you think."

His voice sounded so . . . dead. She ached for him, she really did. She'd been angry, and for a moment, she'd hated. Hated him for tricking her, for making her believe that fantasy could be reality, then ripping the rug out from under her. He'd sent her an e-mail asking to meet her instead of sending her an invitation. He hadn't rejected her the way she'd thought. And now, after that storm of emotion, she felt curiously light. Almost relaxed. Numb? Maybe. Most importantly, she was grounded. She hadn't been for more than a month, not since the night she'd met him.

She saw now what she hadn't wanted to see then. He was searching. He was probably a perpetual searcher, never finding what he was looking for, and moving on to the next search.

"How old are you, Stephen?"

Though his hair was almost completely silver in the sunlight, he still didn't have the number of lines that many men his age had. "Fifty this year."

Just as she'd thought. Maybe he was looking for a younger woman. She wouldn't be *young* for much longer. She couldn't bear another man turning from her. She'd rather lose him now. "I know you think that we've revealed so much in our e-mails. And we have. But people can . . . edit what they say. They edit their feelings so that you won't have a bad opinion of them."

He turned his head, viewing her through only one eye. "Is that what you did? Edit yourself right out of every e-mail you sent me?

Did you edit yourself when you held me in your arms and told me you loved me?"

Her heart rose to her throat. "I wanted the fantasy."

He turned back to the window and whatever was so fascinating out there. "So you lied."

"No. It's what I felt at that moment." She believed he'd felt it, too. Still, she was old enough to know lust and love were two different things. No matter what he thought he felt.

"You think my saying 'I love you' was just some orgasmic release?"

Yes. If she said that, though, he'd only deny it. He'd even believe it was true love.

"I'm not your husband," he said, facing her, forcing her to see the stark pain in his eyes and riding the lines of his face.

"I know that."

His eyes were dark, intense, unfathomable. "Do you even know what I mean?"

"No," she admitted.

"I'm not going to lose my desire for you. I'm not going to stop loving you. I'm not going to get tired of you."

"Stephen—"

He cut her off. "Not after a year. Not after fifty years. Not even the day I die."

She drew in a breath, drawing his words deep inside her. They were the words of her fantasies. She wanted them to be true so badly she felt tears rise once more.

"Have you ever been married, Stephen?"

"No. That doesn't change how I feel about you."

"Everything dies, Stephen. Desire and passion can't live forever. Feelings change as you change, as you grow older. I've been married fifteen years, Stephen, and I—"

"Stop saying my fucking name like that." After the outburst, he faced the window, his jaw clenching.

"I'm trying to get you to see."

"You're the one who doesn't see. For *some* people, desire dies. But not for everyone." He shoved his hands in his pockets. "Leave him. Be with me. I'll show you it's true."

What if it wasn't? What if five years from now he was the one turning the volume up on the TV? She couldn't stand that. If she'd thought she was dying now, that would kill her. At least now, she didn't have a dream to watch die. She had security and . . . she closed her eyes. She had something she'd been living with a long time. She'd proven that, as much as it hurt, she *could* live without a man's passion.

Stephen was the unknown. He offered, but he couldn't guarantee.

"I can't," she whispered.

He laughed, a harsh sound, rolled his head on his neck, then straightened and looked at her. "So you're going to drive off to The Sex Club when you need to get laid. Or better yet, fuck yourself all alone in your bed while you fantasize."

Her nose tingled, her eyes pricked, and she bit her lip to stop the trembling.

He was at her side in the time it took to blink away the tears, but he didn't touch her. "I'm sorry. That was shitty. You don't deserve that."

"I'm not going back there. It was a mistake to go in the first place."

He touched her then, a finger trailing down her arm until he grasped her hand in his. "It wasn't a mistake."

She couldn't look away as he raised their clasped hands to his lips.

"Why did you call me Stephen?" His words were nothing more than a breath.

She swallowed and closed her eyes so that she couldn't see the need riding his face. "I don't know."

He tugged on her fingers. "You do know. Tell me."

"I wanted a fantasy." She opened her eyes. "And you happened to be it for the moment."

"You're lying."

"I was just needy because it had been so long since someone touched me." It wasn't admitting anything she hadn't already admitted to him at the club.

"It was because you felt something even through all our e-mails. Just the way I felt something." He stepped closer, his body flush with hers, the tips of her breasts to his chest. "Long before you ever saw me, you knew me. And I knew you."

"No. It was make-believe." But her heart was racing.

His fingers tunneled beneath her hair and curled around her nape. "It was real." He kissed every tear track along her cheeks. She couldn't breathe. Her hands fisted in his shirt, holding herself upright. Then he took her lips, and she opened. She couldn't help herself. She wanted, God, how she wanted.

"You touched yourself," he whispered against her mouth, "and you wanted it to be me. No one else. You called me Stephen at the club because I was the one you needed."

"No."

"Yes." He took possession of her mouth once more, before she could utter another denial. "You still need me," he murmured. "And I need you."

He branded her with his lips. He tasted of mint and spice and man, and yes, he was everything she wanted.

He backed her up to the wall. "Say it," he whispered. "Say you need *me*."

Then he was all over her, demanding capitulation with his kiss, devouring her, sucking away her will. A hand on her breast, possessing her nipple, sending lightning strikes deep inside. His cock hard against her, pushing her thighs apart, finding that special, soft, needy spot and rubbing it to an ache. Then he held her chin in his hand and forced her to look at him.

"Make love with me."

She wanted it more that anything, yet it was so damn wrong for her. She had a husband. She couldn't be with Stephen. She shoved at him. "No. I can't do this."

He stood before her, his breath harsh, his eyes dark, compelling, and she knew if she let him, he'd carry her away. And she wouldn't know up from down or right from wrong. This couldn't go on between them. She'd been able to fool herself into accepting what she'd been doing when it was at The Sex Club, but this was something else entirely.

She made a move for the door, almost making it before he grabbed her arm. This time he crowded her face-first up against the wall, pressed his body to her backside, and pulled up one side of her skirt until he caressed her hip.

His breath heated her nape, his cool aftershave and hot male scent swirling around her. "No one else will ever touch you the way I can."

He forced a hand between her body and the wall and stroked her to total wetness. His fingers slipped beneath the elastic edge of her panties, then he plunged deep into her, the heel of his hand massaging her clitoris. His touch drove her to the edge, his words wrapped around her heart. He sucked on her neck and raised her skirt to her waist, then a moment later, after the rasp of his zipper, she felt the warm, hard slide of his cock against her backside.

"It's just sex," she whispered, as if the words would keep her safe.

He tore off her panties, the flimsy material giving way easily, then hitched her back into him, his knees spreading her legs. "It's more than sex, godammit. It's us. Together." He bunched her hair in his fist and pulled her head back. "I'm like a drug in your veins. I make you crazy. You'll never get enough of me."

He ripped her blouse open, the buttons flying, then wrenched her bra up over her breasts until she spilled into his hands. "You can keep your back to me while I make love to you, but you are going to face how much you need me."

A moan rose up from up her throat, and God yes, she did need him.

His fingers and his cock caressed her. "Say no," he whispered. "All you have to do is tell me to stop, and I will."

She had a chance to put an end to it. To stop herself. But she couldn't seem to force that one word *no* past her lips.

"You can't say it. I know you can't. You don't even want to." He rocked against her, caressing her rear cleft with his cock and her clitoris with his work-roughened fingertips. "I want you without a condom. With nothing between us."

The moment she left the house, she'd regret letting this happen. But he was right. He was her drug, and she wouldn't stop him now. She braced against the wall, pushed back and rotated her hips against him, begging without words.

He buried his face in the hair at her nape, parted her for his entry, and bent his knees. She cried out with the first thrust. Hot, hard flesh, like silk, individual ridges and textures caressing her, stretching her. One hand on her hip, his arm wrapped below her breasts, he carried her along with his need, heat, friction, on her skin wherever he touched her, deep inside where he claimed her. He wasn't gentle, he was consuming, his body pounding, his cock reaching straight up to her heart. She braced herself against the wall and met each stroke.

Colors kaleidoscoped across her eyelids. She harbored every sensation, the roughness of his chin against her neck, the sweet smell of his skin, the musky scent of his sex, and the throb of his cock inside her. He dropped his hand to her clitoris, swirled her own moisture over the hard nub, and she was lost.

Her body spasmed around him, heat rose, shimmered like hot sun on concrete, then slammed down to their joining, and she screamed. When the hot flood of his semen filled her, she came again.

It was riotous, explosive, elemental. But she'd been right, the moment her head cleared, she hated her weakness for him.

* * *

HE WAS WRAPPED around her, and her scent played havoc with his mind. Aftershocks twitched through his limbs, and his breath stirred harshly against her hair.

Then she slipped away, the loss of her body warmth chilling him straight through to his bones. Reaching for her mangled panties, she stared at the torn material, then crumpled it in her fist. And he knew he'd lost her.

"Don't walk away from what we have, Debbie." He zipped his jeans, buckled, watching her distance herself with every rustle of their separate pieces of clothing.

"I'm married." She didn't look at him but down at the missing buttons on her blouse. There were two left, just enough to hold it together.

"And I love you. Walk away from *him*." The bastard had left her emotionally a long time ago. Stephen held his breath. His head pounded.

If she'd continued to stare at the carpet, fiddled with her blouse, or employed any other delaying tactic, he would have had a chance. Instead, she snared his gaze. "No."

That was it. Flat. Final.

She crossed to where she'd flung her purse, its contents spilling, and shoved everything back inside.

"I think you're afraid, and you're using your marriage vows as an excuse not to fix what's wrong with your life."

"Don't be cruel, Stephen."

He felt cruel. He felt angry. He felt abandoned.

Before he could bring an apology he didn't mean to his lips, she closed the distance between them and put her hand on his chest. "I don't want to fight. All those times with you made me feel like a desirable woman. I'm grateful for that."

He wanted to howl. She was fucking *grateful*? Rather than rail at her, he held her fingers to his heart. "It doesn't have to end."

"Yes, it does."

Then she was gone. Only a wisp of her scent remained and the warm impression of her hand on his heart.

Holding her, he'd told her the truth. He needed her now. He would need her for the rest of his life.

And he would go on loving her until he died.

ELEVEN

IN THE THREE weeks since she'd seen Stephen, life had returned to normal. Minus her daily e-mails to him. Though she wasn't sure what normal was anymore. That day in the house, she'd been so angry, so hurt, almost feeling violated in some weird way. Those emotions had died away. She was left now with the knowledge that he was a kind, caring, and passionate man. He had changed her in some indefinable way. He'd been her weakness, yes, but he'd somehow given her a strength she hadn't had before.

At work, she didn't take the blame so easily. Instead of keeping her mouth shut in meetings, she gave her opinions, threw her ideas on the table. The more she expressed herself, the easier it got. Even her boss started coming to her to solicit her view on issues.

When she looked at her stained glass, she didn't need to be told she'd done a good job. She could see the beauty in what she'd created. Though she couldn't have explained that to a soul, she could feel adrenaline in her veins and a strange sort of giddiness.

She no longer worked endlessly on a piece. She simply knew when it was done.

Stephen's voice in her head said, "That's perfect."

Late at night, alone in the bedroom, wanting to touch herself but never quite being able to, the TV blared, and anger replaced the pain that had torn her apart for so many years. Why couldn't her husband *try*? Why couldn't he go to a doctor and ask for a little pill? That's all she wanted. The effort.

Her husband had stolen even her ability to masturbate, even that minuscule relief.

Or had she lost that to Stephen, knowing that nothing could replace his touch, not even her own?

After the anger died, her thoughts remained on Stephen. How he made her feel that she was his total focus. Of all the things he'd done for her, all the ways he'd touched her. The one she kept playing over and over in her mind was the night he'd danced with her. Of course, she'd told him that in a weak moment, but he'd catered to her fantasy, given her what she needed. How many other things had she revealed without knowing it? With all those e-mails she'd written, then deleted, how much of her heart and soul had still slipped through?

Maybe he did know her better than she'd ever thought.

And his next to last words to her still haunted. Was she really using her marriage vows as an excuse not to fix what was wrong with her life?

STACY DIDN'T ASK her about Stephen. Debbie didn't tell her anything. Not until her third nail visit. Stephen had neither called nor e-mailed. But he'd given her several referrals. Each time she met with a client, she felt closer to him, as if he were some angel sitting on her shoulder. Her knight in shining armor. That sense made her feel strong enough to finally ask Stacy the questions that burned in her.

"Tell me about Stephen. About the club."

Stacy didn't look at her, but her hands stilled, the file held aloft for several heartbeats. "What do you mean?"

"You introduced me to him. Then you had him come to the club for Virginia's party. He said you knew he'd be there, but I think you asked him to come." She didn't ask if Stacy had slept with him. Stephen told her they hadn't. She believed him. In fact, she believed everything he'd said, even that he thought he'd never tire of her. Still, she had to understand Stacy's role in the whole debacle. "I want to know why."

Stacy set her file down. The hand holding Debbie's trembled. "I care about you. I knew something was wrong."

Somehow, despite their years of friendship, Debbie felt betrayed. "Did you two talk it over and decide what I needed?"

"No. He wouldn't talk about you. I kept asking, but he would never tell me anything. His refusal made me think he cared. I told him we were going to the club. I'm not even sure anymore if he said he'd be there or I asked him. But I wanted him to meet you that way. In that place."

"I don't understand. It was so . . ." She searched for the right word. "Extreme. You already had him helping me find clients. Why'd you have to do the rest?"

Stacy's grip tightened on her fingers, and her gaze locked with Debbie's. "Because you needed someone to want you. I knew he did, even if he never said so outright. The club was the only place you would let anything happen between the two of you."

"I've never told you anything about my marriage. Why did you think . . . ?" She trailed off. Stephen had read between the lines of her e-mails. Stacy had read between her words.

"Everything. You stopped having your hair highlighted. I think you would have stopped doing your nails, too, if you'd been going to someone other than me. You didn't seem to care about anything anymore. Not even the stained glass until I put you in touch with Stephen. You used to wear pretty things, you used to like dressing sexy. You used to talk about your husband all the time. But you stopped. I thought he was having an affair." She picked up the file again, buffing the same nails she'd already finished. "And I thought you should have one of your own."

It was nice to be cared about. But . . . "I don't like being manipulated, Stacy. I don't like you deciding what was wrong, then picking out the solution for me."

"But I've always been that way."

"Yeah, you have." Debbie gazed at the rows of bright polish on the shelf over Stacy's shoulder. "I didn't have an affair with Stephen." What they'd done was so much more and so much less. "And we don't talk anymore. It's better that way."

For the first time she admitted to herself how much she truly missed him, his banter, his praise, his touch. How much he occupied her thoughts. Not just her nighttime fantasies, but her waking hours, every day, at lunch, during her commute, or soaking in the bathtub with a glass of wine. Any time her mind had free time to wander, it wandered straight to Stephen.

Stacy pulled on her fingers. "I'm not sorry I did it. I know you think I should be, but you wouldn't talk to me about what was going on, and I had to do something." She tipped her head, moisture suddenly collecting along the lower rim of her eyes. "Why didn't you tell me? We're friends. I could have helped, even if all I did was listen." Stacy sniffled and bent over her filing.

Debbie took her friend's hand in both of hers and squeezed. "I'm sorry. I should have let you help me. He isn't having an affair. He just doesn't want to make love with me anymore. He's having impotency problems, and he won't even go to the doctor. It was all too embarrassing and humiliating and painful to talk about. Even with you."

"Has it gotten any better? Because you seem different now."

Yeah. She felt different. "No. It hasn't changed. But *I* have to decide what to do about it. On my own."

"Just get him Viagra."

You had to *want* to take Viagra. Her husband wasn't even interested in *going* to the doctor, letting alone asking for a pill. The thought didn't hurt as much as it used to.

Stacy covered her mouth and gasped. "Oops, sorry, I wasn't supposed to tell you what to do."

"It's all right. You know, if you don't start filing, you're going to be late for your next client."

"You're my last. I thought maybe we could go out for dinner. We don't have to talk about . . . stuff. We don't even have to talk about Stephen. Even though I'm dying to know all. I haven't talked to him in weeks." She gasped again. "Not that he'd tell me anything. He *never* told me anything, I swear."

The sniffling Stacy was gone, replaced once more by the lively, optimistic, and out-there woman.

Debbie was glad. "You know, I love you. You might stick your nose where it doesn't belong, but your heart's always in the right place." She met her friend's penetrating gaze. "But I don't want to talk about this again. So don't ask, okay?"

Stacy widened her eyes and nodded solemnly. "I swear I won't."

"Then I'd love to have dinner."

Regardless of whether she talked about it with Stacy or not, she was going to have to figure out how to fix her marriage.

If it could be fixed.

She wanted a passionate *marriage*, not a series of interludes that she had to keep repeating as if she were addicted. And she wouldn't settle for security; she wanted it all. Passion and fire. Stephen had taught her that she deserved those things.

And if her marriage couldn't be fixed, then she'd find another way to take back her life.

DEBBIE LOOKED AT her husband across the kitchen table, the scent of the tangy sweet and sour sauce tingling in her nose, the red pepper flakes bursting in her mouth. At dinner last night with Stacy, she'd decided what she had to.

"That was good, honey, thanks." He licked his fork and smiled.

"You're welcome." Stir-fry was easy. She just hadn't bothered to put herself out in too many months to count.

He pushed the plate away and sat back. He was a good man. Always polite, always kind, always appreciating the little things she did. But there were tired lines beneath his eyes that hadn't been there a couple of years ago. He didn't smile or laugh as often as he used to.

"Did you have a good day?" she asked.

"It was fine." He always said he was fine, and thus prevented any real discussion between them.

"I love you," she said.

"I love you, too," was the automatic reply.

She would *not* let this go, not this time. She'd already determined she wouldn't immediately jump into the impotency thing. If she did, she'd never get through to him. She broached the issue in the only other way she could. "Are you ever going to want me again?"

"I want you. Don't be silly."

She put her fork down. He ate faster than she did, and her plate was still a quarter full, but she wasn't hungry anymore. "You always say that. But you don't act on it."

"I know. And I'm sorry. I'll get better. I promise."

He always said that, too. The situation didn't get better. "We have to make a change. This isn't working the way it is."

He leaned forward, elbows on the table, fingers massaging his temples. "I'm tired. This isn't a good time."

There was never a good time. Before, that had angered her. Now, she saw how much he really meant it. Could his problem be mental as well as physical? He was so tired of . . . something. His career? A lack of life purpose? A feeling that he'd gone to work every day for the last twenty years and hadn't accomplished anything important? Maybe it was his pride in her stained glass work that made her think that. He'd often said he wished he had something that meant as much to him as her glasswork did to her.

"Want to tell me what's wrong?" she asked, hoping to draw him out, even as she knew that was next to impossible.

He closed his eyes, sat there rubbing his temples in circles. "Not really."

"Maybe I can help."

He looked at her, seemed to study her for several minutes. "I don't think so. It's just some midlife crisis thing. Don't worry. I'll be better in a little while."

Midlife crisis? He'd been this way for over five years, and he wasn't even forty yet. "You're not happy, are you?"

He gave a small laugh, something halfway between self-deprecating and a snort. "I'm too tired to think about it."

"We need to think *and* talk about it. I want us to start making love again. Maybe we should have a goal. Like once a week."

He scrubbed his hands down his face. "Why is sex so important to you?"

How many times had she heard that question? She struggled to answer with something different, something that might reach him. "Without it, we're just roommates. It's not a marriage."

"I don't know how you can say that. I do everything for you. I go to work every day. I come home every night. We've got financial security. What more do you want?"

"Passion."

"Why?"

"Because without it, I don't feel vital. It makes me feel strong. And alive. A part of something. Instead of just going through the motions."

"Doesn't it mean anything that I love you?"

"It means a lot." But in some ways, it was a phrase he used to appease her. She drew in a breath, held it. She'd exposed herself to

Stephen, but she'd never tried with her husband. If they were going to have a marriage, then she had to give him the same things she gave to Stephen. "Why don't you come into the bedroom while I'm masturbating? I'd do it for you, if you wanted me to. I think about you watching me, and it turns me on."

Once the words were out, her fingers tingled and her heart raced. She even saw spots before her eyes. She'd never admitted aloud to him the things she did alone in their bedroom.

He dropped his hands to the table, folding his arms, and looked out the window at the garden. "I didn't know you were."

"Be honest," she whispered.

He looked at her then, really looked, his gaze traveling over her forehead, her cheeks, her lips, then up to her eyes. "I just can't do it. I don't know why. I just can't."

"You have to figure out why." She hesitated, wondering if this was the right moment. Between them, though, there would never be that *right* moment. It simply had to be said. "Why don't you see a doctor? I know I asked you before, and you didn't think it was necessary, but *I* think it's important."

He sucked in a deep breath, rolled his lips inward, then let the air rush out between them. "I'm too tired to bother."

Tears pricked her eyes. Even after all the anger, the sadness, the despair, those words still had the power to tear her heart out. Maybe if he'd exploded like the last time, it wouldn't hurt so badly.

They sat in silence. The clock ticked on the wall. The oven's temperature gauge clicked back on. She'd warmed the plates but forgotten to turn it off when she took them out.

"I do love you," he said.

"And I'll always love you."

He turned to study the garden once more. "I'm sorry I can't change."

The problem was that he wasn't willing to. He wasn't even willing to consider the possibility that he had a solvable physical problem. She knew he never would be. She pushed the pain she felt aside. "It's not your fault. We could have gone on if I didn't feel that I need more."

Stephen had given her that something *more* she'd been looking for, even if for such a short time. But this wasn't about Stephen. It wasn't about the club or the things he'd done to her and for her. This was only about her marriage. She'd known it wasn't working long before Stephen.

She put her hand over her husband's, squeezed until he looked at her. "I don't blame you. If I could help you, I would. Only I can't. You have to work it out for yourself. I hope you do, but I'll still love you even if you don't."

He looked at her a long moment. "But you're not going to be here, are you?"

"No. I can't wait anymore. I really wish I could."

He closed his eyes. "I don't know where we went wrong. I'm so sorry. I knew you needed more, and I should have—"

She stopped him with a finger over his lips. "Almost every screwup takes two to make it happen. You're a good man. Maybe this change will help you figure out what *you* need."

She couldn't stay. She'd lost faith, lost hope, in him, in their marriage. The brutal truth was, she didn't *want* to wait anymore. She wanted to take charge of her life again.

"God, we're so fucking civilized, aren't we?" He laughed, a short, sad little sound, though Debbie thought she detected a thread of relief that it was all finally over.

"Yeah," she said. "We always were civilized. Maybe that was the problem."

This time when she went to bed, she covered her mouth with her hands and cried all the tears she hadn't cried in front of him. Tears for all the special moments they'd had, and all those that would never come. She would miss him. She wished she could hate him. It might have lessened her own pain. But she couldn't blame him for what had gone missing in his life. He honestly didn't know how to fix it. She was afraid he never would.

But she knew her wants. Passion and fire. Finally, after so many years, she'd chosen that over the safety of her marriage.

Outside the bedroom, the volume rose on the TV.

THERE COULDN'T HAVE been a more amicable divorce on the planet. Yet there were still myriad details to handle. Debbie bought out her husband's half of the house. It would mean she couldn't quit work for a long, long time. That made her like most people. Then, there were the cars and the big-screen TV and the stuff they'd accumulated over the years. There were all the new things, too, that she had to buy to replace the necessities he took.

She cried half the time and was almost overcome with paralyzing fear the rest. Almost.

The only rays of sunshine were the clients Stephen continued to send her way and the praise they passed on. She praised him in return. It almost felt like they were communicating. She kept his e-mail address, his home address, his cell phone number. Late at night, alone not only in her bed but in the whole house, the urge to call him beat like a drum in her head.

She had things to do, emotions to reconcile. She couldn't call Stephen until she did. Until she was free of her former life and all the doubts that had consumed her for so long.

She couldn't call him until she could tell him she believed he wouldn't tire of her. Even the day she held her divorce papers in her hand, she still couldn't say that. She'd begun to believe she never would be able to.

TWELVE

STEPHEN SHUFFLED THROUGH the stack of mail. Bills, flyers, a magazine. And one cream-colored envelope with no return address.

Like the invitations he'd sent her. His fingers trembled, and his heart hammered.

He'd kept his promise and hadn't contacted her in eight months. His only news of her came through clients and the occasional phone call from Stacy. When Stacy told him about the pending divorce, he'd gone to the club in desperation and hope. He'd left after a fruitless search, not really expecting her to be there in the first place.

He carelessly ripped at the envelope. Sinking to his knees in the front hall, he opened the enclosed card.

"Friday." In capital letters, just as he'd written it all those months ago. His heart raced and his palms turned sweaty. She'd given him a time, too. "7:00 p.m."

He had two days to prepare, two days in which to go crazy.

Two days until he discovered whether he would rise from the hell he'd been living in or was doomed to stay there forever.

THE FRONT HALL was empty except for the usual hostess and a waiter with a tray of filled champagne glasses. Shaky on the inside, his fingers numb, Stephen could barely manage to take the invitation from his inside jacket pocket, let alone hold a glass without spilling the contents.

"We're so glad you could join us." The hostess smiled. "Your lady is in the blue room, if you'd like to go up."

His lady. God, yes. He needed her to be his.

"Third floor," the woman prodded when he failed to move. "Fifth door on the right. Just knock."

To ease his tension, he counted the steps as he climbed. Earlier, he'd ransacked his closet, finally deciding on the tux he hadn't worn since a friend's wedding ten years ago. The weight of the jacket and accoutrements stiffened his muscles. His knees creaked with each riser. He'd aged ten years in the last eight months, another five on the drive over.

He told himself she wouldn't send the invitation if she planned only one night. Debbie wouldn't tease, then walk away.

At the fifth door on the right, he straightened his tie, adjusted the cummerbund, and smoothed down the jacket.

After a deep breath, he knocked.

He'd been expecting her, and his heart dropped to his knees when a white-coated waiter opened the door. The man smiled and waved him in with a flourish.

She was seated at a small round table set with crystal and silver. The soft lighting from the wall sconces sparkled in her hair but left her face in shadows. Then she rose and took his breath away. A short, black dress draped her curves, the neck plunging to her breasts. Moving to him, she revealed a creamy expanse of thigh he'd dreamed about kissing.

Debbie stepped into the pool of light from the chandelier and held out her hand. "Stephen, I'm so glad you came."

He took that hand, raised it to his lips, placed a lingering kiss, drawing in the scent of citrus lotion and woman. She was as beautiful as he remembered, the same and yet different. Her blue eyes glittered. The shade of gloss, richer, deeper, plumped lips that had already been luscious. Her skin glowed. Though she'd worn fuckme heels for him before, she seemed taller now, and her breasts swelled, almost overflowing the lace cups that tempted at the edge of the dress's deep vee.

For the first time, he was seeing the true Desiree she'd kept hidden inside. The sure, strong, confident woman he'd wanted to set free. She'd set herself free without his help.

"Aren't you going to say something, Stephen?"

I love you. I want you. I need you. Don't let this be the only night. "It's good to see you. You look gorgeous."

She smiled, genuine and pleasure-filled. "Thank you." She traced a hand down his lapel, caressed the boutonniere. "You look beautiful." She waved a hand at the table behind them. "Would you like a glass of champagne first? Eduardo will pour. I ordered dinner for seven thirty."

He wanted only her. But she'd planned this for him, and he would take everything, jealously hoarding each surprise. Eduardo popped the cork, then poured expertly, keeping the foam to a minimum. After handing them each a glass, he retreated to a corner. The wine sizzled in Stephen's throat as he downed half.

He came back to himself as she touched his arm. "Do you like the room?"

For the first time, he took in the plush layout. To one end, the table and two chairs were placed intimately side by side. Beyond sat a settee big enough for two. He imagined her on her knees between his legs, her mouth on him. He'd imagined her often in the last eight months, but without hope, his crazy sexual thoughts brought more pain than pleasure. The really pathetic thing was that he'd kept the pair of panties he'd stuffed in his back pocket that long-ago night at the club.

She turned slightly, pulling him with her. As in the red room, everything followed the blue theme. Silk hangings graced the walls, candles burned in silver candelabras, and a pure blue spread covered the huge, high bed. Missing though, was the mirror on the ceiling.

Leaning in, her breath warm at his throat, she whispered, "We don't need the mirror. I can see everything I want to see in your eyes when you look at me."

He closed his eyes, his heart aching, breaking, and soaring all at once. She would see the desire, but would she understand the rest? He was too damned scared to ask.

She stroked his arm. "I'm glad you're here, Stephen."

Her touch inflamed, yet strangely, calmed him as well. Debbie, even wearing her Desiree persona, had never been a cruel woman. After what had occurred between them in the Thomases' house, she wouldn't play with him.

"Eduardo, perhaps we could start our salads now. Stephen's hungry, I think."

"Yes, ma'am. Right away." Then he disappeared through a door Stephen had missed.

She led him to the table. He held out a chair, seated her, then took his own next to hers. Her thigh brushed his. He ached to touch her. His cock throbbed, hardening in his trousers.

Setting her glass down, she leaned on her elbows and laced her fingers. The scoop of her dress fell forward, revealing the swell of her breasts and hard nipples straining against the sheer cup of her bra. His hand lifted as if it weren't even a part of him, and his finger trailed across a stiff peak.

She drew in a breath. Her pupils dilated until her eyes seemed as deep as the midnight of her dress. "I suppose you're wondering why I asked you here tonight."

He remained silent, afraid his voice would crack.

"Besides wanting you to fuck me because it's been so long."

The word slapped his face. "I don't want to fuck you."

She put his hand on her thigh, guided him to the top of her leg. The tiniest of panties hugged the rise of her hip.

"Don't you?" she whispered. "Didn't you once tell me that fucking and making love were the same thing? You said it was the feeling inside that counted."

He remembered. He hadn't thought she believed him.

He slipped his hand between her thighs, his finger resting against her warm, damp panties. She was ready for him. He'd never stopped being ready for her.

The door opened. Eduardo rolled in a trolley with a bowl and condiments, then prepared their salad. Stephen kept his hand where it was, buried beneath her skirt like a stamp of ownership.

"Thank you," she murmured as the waiter placed the freshly prepared salad in front of her, then centered Stephen's plate. Eduardo's eyes dropped to her thighs briefly before he exited.

Stephen ate with his left hand so that he didn't lose contact. She shifted, opening her legs, then cupped his hand to her pussy. Running her fingers through her hair, she closed her eyes and arched, rocking against his hand. "Oh, Stephen, you don't know how long I've dreamed about this."

He'd been dreaming about her, praying for this moment, for eight long months. Watching her, feeling her cream further dampen her panties, he decided he didn't care what she wanted from him. One night or a lifetime, he'd take whatever she gave.

"I'm sorry," she said on a mere breath, opening sultry eyes to look at him. "I meant to wait until after dinner. I wanted to make this special."

Everything about her was special.

And he couldn't wait another second. "Screw dinner. I want you now." Pulling his hand from her legs, he drew her onto his lap, forcing her to straddle him. The dress rose, revealing black minuscule panties. He put his lips to her sweet throat, whispering, "I want to make love to you until you scream."

Hands in his hair, she held him to her, guiding his face to her breasts. "Touch me, Stephen. Please touch me."

She trembled against his mouth as he pushed aside the sheer bra and took her nipple, sucking the bud into a tight marble. She moaned, twisted his hair in her fingers. He shoved her dress higher, giving her room to open herself fully to him. His cock thrust against his pants, thrust against her. Then he palmed her pussy. She rewarded him with a throaty groan.

He struggled with the elastic on her panties. He couldn't get them off without letting her go, and that he wasn't willing to do. Nor did he want the tiny scrap of lace between them. He groped the side of his salad plate, found the knife edge, grabbed the handle, then pushed her back against the table.

She didn't ask him what he was going to do, but trusted that he wouldn't hurt her.

The elastic popped as he cut each side. Throwing the knife to the floor, he peeled the fabric away. She was so sweet, so hot, her curls glistening with a wealth of dew.

"Make me come, Stephen," she whispered. "I haven't come since the last time you touched me."

He stilled with his hands high on her thighs and met her deeply blue gaze. "You didn't even do it yourself?"

She took his face in her hands. "Touching myself wouldn't be any good without you there to watch. I wanted to wait."

For him. The unspoken words stole around him. She'd always planned to come back. She'd taken care of business, and she'd come back to him with her freedom.

"Every time I had to stroke myself, I made myself believe it was you touching me," he whispered, "your lips sucking me, your tongue driving me crazy, and your mouth drinking my come."

He wasn't sure whether he took her lips or she took him, but he tasted her for the first time in all those long months. Her flavor, sweet with champagne, burst in his mouth. She licked his lips, took his tongue, wrapped her arms around his neck, and devoured him as if her need could never be quenched.

Then she slowly let him go, putting her forehead to his, her mouth only a breath away. "I should tell you everything. I meant to. Before we did this."

"Tell me when you come against my hand."

He clasped her to him, one arm low over her hips, holding her tight, and put his hand between her legs. He slipped two fingers between her folds, sliding first up inside her, then back to the sweet little button. He loved her with his touch. She gasped and threw her head back.

"Oh God. Oh Stephen." She panted as he took charge of her clitoris, circling the nub, then dipping into her slick cream.

The door opened. Eduardo had the trolley halfway through before he looked up. Then he stopped. Stephen knew he should have removed his hand from her body, but he couldn't, not now, not when she was so close to being his. His fingers moved faster, pressed harder. She writhed in his lap.

His gaze challenged the young man. Stephen closed his eyes as he heard the soft snick of the door, then he shoved two fingers deep inside her, and whispered, "Tell me, tell me now."

"Oh God, Stephen, I love you so much." She screamed then, something that might have been his name once more. Her pussy milked his fingers as she came hard and long, hugging him tightly as if he were a life preserver.

When she let him go, all that remained of Eduardo was the trolley with their dinner beneath silver lids.

Her arms still around him, she sagged against his chest, her breath puffing across his neck. "I love you, Stephen," was almost another wisp of air.

He heard, held onto the words, tied her to him with their magnitude. "I never stopped loving you."

She settled closer against him, letting his rigid cock rest between her thighs, only the material of his tuxedo pants separating them.

"Did you finally accept that I was telling you the truth, that I'll never stop loving you or wanting you?"

She eased back, stroked his face. "No, Stephen, I didn't."

He felt as if the air had been sucked from the room. She would leave now. She didn't believe. It was over. Again.

"After I left my husband, I wanted to call you. I have no idea how many times I picked up the phone, then put it down. I kept thinking, what if it doesn't work? But I finally figured something out. There are no guarantees. You might get tired of me." She raised a brow. "I might get tired of you. I don't think so, but you never know. The point is, I don't know what's going to happen." She touched her lips lightly to his. "The only thing I do know is that if I walk away from the way I feel about you because I'm afraid that I'll get hurt down the road, then I'll be walking away from the chance of having it all, too. Passion, fire, love, desire." She put her cheek to his. "Friendship. Someone who believes in me. Someone who thinks I've got talent. Someone who whacks off in the middle of the night just thinking about me." She rubbed noses. "Do you know how much all those things mean to me?"

"Yes, I do. As much as they mean to me."

She kissed his eyes. Her own widened in surprise at the trace of moisture on her lips.

He held her face the way she'd held his. Forced her to look into his soul. "I love you. I want to fuck you every night and every morning, for the rest of my life. Even when I'm ninety. And through it all, I'll always be your best friend."

"Stephen. I've changed my mind. I don't want you to make love to me here."

"Where then?"

"Can you wait until you take me home? I want you to make love to me in your bed. So that we can fall asleep with your cock inside me."

He laughed, the sound almost hurting his throat. He hadn't laughed in eight months. "I'll walk stooped over if I have to."

He helped her rise. She made a small sound when she saw the trolley. "Oh my God, when did he bring that?"

"Right when you were about to come."

Her face flamed. After everything they'd done, she could still blush. Another thing he loved and cherished about her.

He took her hand. "I think it was the most beautiful thing he'd ever seen in his life." Tugging on her fingers, he forced her to look at him. "I only hope he carries that picture with him until he recognizes it in his own soul mate. When he does, he'll know in every part of his being that he'll feel that way forever." He stroked her cheek. "The way I know."

He kissed her palm. "Do you believe me?"

She searched his face for an eternity. Then she smiled and whispered, "Yes, Stephen, I do."

Invitation to Pleasure

ONE

YESTERDAY, SHE WAS Virginia Hansen, three-time loser at love. Tomorrow, she'd be Mrs. Brett Branoff, wife to a handsome, intelligent man. But tonight, at The Sex Club, she was Regina, a sexy, desirable woman who could have her pick of men.

She knew she was desired by more than one man tonight. She could feel it. Beneath her tailored silk suit, her body spoke to her. One couldn't wander The Sex Club without feeling the heat, without succumbing to its allure. The demure lines of her suit only enhanced the appeal, contrasting with the sexy lace garter and stockings under the sober facade.

Many eyes had touched her tonight. Many more would. Later. She'd come to The Sex Club tonight to shock and titillate herself. And she'd definitely done that so far. For now, though, Virginia and Stacy were taking a respite in one of the club's bars.

Music drifted over them from the dance floor. Tables ringed the dance floor, love seats and chairs on the outside flanking the walls.

Stools lined a mahogany bar outfitted with every libation imaginable. The music wasn't loud enough to make conversation impossible, and candles burned on each table, scenting the air with a light cinnamon perfume.

"You know, it's not like what I expected," Virginia mused. Sure there was rampant sexual activity, and the scent of pheromones heating the air. "It's sort of tame, in a way. I mean, the champagne, the mood lighting, and everyone's dressed so—" she shrugged trying to find the right word "—nicely." It was inadequate, but she'd seen ball gowns, cocktail dresses, tuxedos, suits. Even those attired less modestly, women in tight skirts or low-necked outfits, were nonetheless . . . neat. She leaned forward. "I mean, where are the nipple rings and black lipstick and spiked hair?"

Stacy rolled her eyes. "That is *so* stereotypical."

"Maybe. But I really thought it would be more kinky, more crass and crude, you know, whips and chains, lots of leather, mesh, studs, risqué outfits, but this is classy."

"That's because of Jud McCord. He caters to more refined tastes, to an affluent community. It's the contrast that turns on his clientele, the cocktail party surroundings, with the kink layered beneath." Stacy smiled. "And believe me, there's a lot of kink going on."

Virginia had seen plenty of that, too. She and Stacy had observed in several rooms, including Orgy Galore and The Massage Parlor. The name of the game there was to find a unique way to employ a vibrator, by yourself or with a partner. There'd definitely been unique uses. Virginia wasn't sure she was dexterous enough to try them all.

"People come here looking to let go of their inhibitions," Stacy went on. "It's about sensuality as much as it is about sex. I don't want to feel as if I'm coming to some dirty back alley dungeon and playing with a bunch of creeps."

"Well, I'm still not sure I like the idea of Debbie wandering around by herself."

Stacy flapped a hand. "She's fine. Don't worry about her. Jud has rules, and all she has to do is call a passing waiter and any problems are nipped in the bud. Trust me, she's a big girl, and she can handle herself."

They were all big girls. Virginia had turned forty almost six months ago, and Stacy had just hit forty-five. Debbie was only a year younger than Virginia.

Debbie. She'd seemed a little downcast at their last couple of dinners, and tonight she'd disappeared into the crowd soon after they'd arrived. Something was up with that woman. "Is she okay? I've been worried about her."

Stacy glanced at her champagne glass, twirled it by the stem. "I'm sure she'll work out whatever's bothering her." She added nothing else.

That's what Virginia liked the most about Stacy. The three of them, Stacy, Debbie, and Virginia, had known each other for years, having at one time worked for the same corporation. They kept in touch even as their lives moved on, and still got together regularly. But Stacy, privy to all their secrets laid bare over a good manicure, never revealed what was talked about. Virginia knew Debbie wasn't happy, but Stacy never breathed a word of what Debbie was going through. Virginia was glad, since it meant her own secrets were safe with Stacy. She didn't care for anyone else, not even Debbie, to know how debilitating it had been stumbling through divorce court three times.

"You can call off the wedding, you know."

That's what she liked the least. Stacy always knew when Virginia had a bad thought and zeroed right in on the cause.

"I have no intention of calling it off." Brett was perfect for her fourth, and last, trip down the aisle. "He's considerate and respectful." With hair as dark as midnight and a strong, aristocratic face, Brett was handsome, but more importantly, he exuded the strong qualities she'd been searching for in a man. "And I like him, believe it or not."

"You talk about him like he's a warm coat you can take out of the closet when there's a chill."

"What's wrong with that?"

"Everything. Let's talk about your criteria for marrying him."

"The most important was that I *knew* him before I jumped into the relationship." Brett's company had become a supplier of Virginia's firm eighteen months ago. She'd worked with him for a year before they even started dating. She'd ferreted out the man he was instead of jumping in headfirst with her eyes closed. This time she was not letting lust impair her judgment. "He is the most ethical businessman I've ever encountered."

Stacy snorted. "Observing how he directs his business affairs has nothing to do with how he'll act in a marriage."

"You're wrong on that one, Stace. How a man conducts himself in a stressful business meeting shows exactly what kind of person he is." Brett was commanding, his temper never rose, even when one of the VPs harangued him. He had all the answers, and the ability to bring calm to a heated exchange. If she were honest, his handling of volatile situations had actually turned her on.

"It's one element, sure. But you approached the whole relationship like you were conducting a job interview."

"You're exaggerating."

"Oh no, I'm not. Look at what you did." Stacy raised a hand and started keeping count on her fingers. "Five dates at fancy restaurants, each discuss your previous marriages on the sixth date, sex after the seventh date, introduce him to your friends at the three-month mark, then get engaged. It's like an old-fashioned arranged marriage except that *you* did the arranging."

"I just don't want any big surprises."

"You can't choose a husband based on a checklist." Stacy mimicked writing on the table. "Must be stable, check, sensible, check, handsome, check, ambitious, check, civilized, check, a good companion, check, decent bank balance, check."

"I never asked what his bank balance was, and it's not his wealth I care about." She wasn't simply being materialistic.

"No, you want security. And I understand that completely."

She wanted a partner, not a man who became a boy the moment life threw a few curves. In her experience, when the going got tough, the so-called tough started to whine. She wanted someone to *share* problems with, a helpmate, not a hanger-on who drained her energy reserves and her savings.

"But where's all the emotional high in that little checklist of yours, Virginia?"

Virginia shook her head. "That's what I *don't* want." She had the highs, only to have them snowed under by the lows.

"Look, I know you haven't had the best luck in men."

"The best *luck*?" She blew out a disgusted breath. "Thanks for putting it so diplomatically, but I freely admit I used bad judgment." She'd jumped into marriage before she really knew the man she was marrying. Not just once, but three damn times.

"Everyone makes mistakes," Stacy said sagely.

Virginia wasn't about to go into the whole thing again. Stacy had seen her through two of the divorces. "The important thing is that Brett wants the same things I want." Peace and companionship. He'd had an unpredictable marriage to a volatile wife, and that was putting it mildly.

"But you can't give up fantastic sex because it wasn't on your freaking checklist."

The sex *wasn't* bad. It might not be earth-shattering, but it was good enough. Brett made love the same way he entered a business meeting, civilized and controlled. She had to admit, in his bed she was a bit controlled herself. He wanted calm and serene, and that's what she gave him. It was almost frightening to think of giving more. She might actually start *expecting* more, and that would make her vulnerable. In this marriage, she was not going to allow a speck of vulnerability.

But Stacy didn't let the issue drop. "Six months, a year from now, you're going to start wanting more. For God's sake, Virginia, you chose to spend your last night of freedom at a sex club fulfilling your final fantasies. Don't tell me you can live with boring, comfortable lovemaking for the rest of your life."

Once Stacy started talking about her escapades at The Sex Club, Virginia couldn't get the place out of her mind. It was true, she wanted a last fantasy before settling down with Brett. She just hadn't realized Stacy would use that to needle her.

Stacy's glance fell across the room, her attention suddenly diverted, which pleased Virginia no end, since the discussion had taken an uncomfortable turn. Following Stacy's gaze, she spotted a tuxedo-clad gentleman heading to their table. "Who's that?"

"Jud McCord."

Ah, the legendary owner of The Sex Club, who catered to fantasy and affluence. Tall, with flecks of gray shot through his dark hair, he was positively yummy. Not that Virginia wanted a yummy man tonight. No, she had other plans for herself.

He leaned one hand on the back of Stacy's chair, his body bracketing hers, his gaze on her. "Ladies, I hope you're having a good time."

"As always. This is bachelorette number one, Virginia."

He smiled, all white teeth and gleaming eyes, except that the gleam seemed a whole lot brighter when he was looking at Stacy. "Congratulations on your upcoming nuptials."

Virginia felt a blush rise to her cheeks. What must the man think that she was at a sex club the night before her marriage? But then he owned the place, and he'd certainly seen and heard a lot worse. "Thank you."

He smiled, then turned the gleam back on Stacy, and the wattage went up. "Duty calls. Have fun. Talk to you later?"

"Sure."

They both stared at his retreating figure, and what a figure that was. "He's melt-in-your-mouth hot," Virginia whispered. "Have you . . ." She let her voice trail off.

Still watching him, Stacy shook her head. "No. Some friendships aren't worth screwing up simply for a good," she tipped her head at Virginia, "screw."

As much as Stacy loved her matchmaking, she steadfastly maintained she wasn't the monogamous type. Yet Virginia sensed a little sizzle between the two.

"That's the last thing I'll say on the subject," Stacy backtracked as if Jud McCord had never interrupted the conversation, "except this. In your quest for stability and companionship, I think you're selling yourself short. And maybe you're selling Brett short." Stacy smiled, a sultry, almost knowing smile. "I'm not sure you know him as well as you think you do. I'd be willing to bet that man has hidden depths."

"What on earth gives you that idea? Just a minute ago you said I was settling for something less than what I really need."

"Well then—" Stacy spread her hands "—make the most of what you are getting. Despite his sophisticated, urbane facade, there's something compelling in his eyes. Like a banked fire just waiting to rage out of control."

"Give me a break. You couldn't possibly have seen that." She'd brought Brett to one of Stacy's cocktail parties. The conversation had been polite and superficial. Stacy was imagining things.

Yet Stacy gave her a long look rife with meaning. "You'll never know unless you give it a shot." Then she dropped her voice to a seductive whisper. "Let him surprise you, Virginia. Let him make you burn."

Virginia's belly crimped. She did want to burn. But she had innumerable burn scars, and the risk of a repeat wasn't worth it. She'd let her sexual needs dictate her actions in the past and ended up with disaster on her hands. No, she was happy with the relationship she'd established with Brett. "I'm not—"

Stacy zipped her lip. "That's all I'm going to say. Now go enjoy the club. I know you've got plans."

When they'd first decided on this sojourn, Virginia had taken the club's number from Stacy and made her own arrangements, though she hadn't told Stacy what they were. Nor had her friend asked, respecting her privacy, at least on *that* subject.

Stacy glanced at her watch. "You've only got until midnight." Which was the time they'd agreed to meet back in the lobby. "Go before Debbie shows up." Stacy glanced over Virginia's shoulder. "*If* she shows up."

"What about you?"

"I'm enjoying the sights right here." Stacy looked pointedly at the dance floor where a woman was sandwiched between two men, her dress around her waist, one guy taking her while the other held her aloft.

Virginia's pussy contracted. Beneath her peach suit, her silk panties dampened. If she wasn't careful, she'd drench her skirt. Watching sex turned her on. Didn't the idea of watching turn most people on, even if they didn't admit it? Tonight, she'd watched enough to feel desire thrumming through her body like a vibrator on high speed.

It was time to stop watching and put her plan into action.

It was time to burn, to use Stacy's terminology. Her last time, and Virginia was damn well going to make the most of it.

FOLLOWING HER WITHOUT being detected was easy. There'd been that dicey moment when her friend had turned his way, catching him off guard, but he'd ducked into an alcove, and after that, it had been clear sailing. They didn't examine faces but bodies and positions, walking slowly, glancing in doorways, rarely looking back as if each new sight was more intriguing than the last.

He'd realized, at some point in the evening, that she wasn't going to turn around. As if she sensed his desire and lured him in by pretending she wasn't aware. He moved in closer.

Her choice of attire might have seemed circumspect to the casual observer, but the well-cut suit molded to her breasts tight enough to reveal the bead of her nipples in profile. The knee-length skirt formed to her backside, outlining each firm cheek as she walked, hugging her contours, drawing attention to the delicate play of feminine muscle. She strolled languidly, as if she expected men to see the hot-blooded woman hidden beneath the elegant suit and neat knot of blond hair piled atop her head.

His cock knew. He'd been hard almost from the moment he'd stepped inside the club, from the moment he saw her.

His greatest chance of discovery now was when she started down the stairs, alone, her friend left behind in the bar. He hung back in the shadows of the landing in case she noticed a flicker of movement out of the corner of her eye.

But again, she didn't turn.

She disappeared through the swing doors off the lobby. The viewing rooms. She enjoyed watching. He'd likely find her in the arena.

He took the stairs quickly, his cock throbbing. Striding through the doors, he closed his eyes briefly as music assaulted him, the strobe light beating against his eyelids as it flashed up and down the hall from the room at the end. The arena. Where she could watch the stage show. Perhaps it would be a one-woman, three-man act, each filling a different orifice at the same time. She'd like that. Her pussy would be dripping. He could have her then. Bury himself in her. Make her scream when she came.

Opening his eyes, a flash of peach and a silk-covered leg disappeared into a room on the left. So she wasn't going to the arena. It didn't matter. He would have her. Here. Where her passions were at their peak.

VIRGINIA FELT HIM, almost smelled him. A uniquely male scent oozing from his pores. Salty like an ocean breeze and hot like sweaty, sun-heated skin. The scent of a man just before he came in a woman's mouth.

She couldn't say how long he'd been behind her. She hadn't noticed him as she'd prowled the rooms with Stacy. But he was closer now, bolder in his perusal. She didn't look. She had no desire to actually see him. It was like pulling alongside a sexy Jaguar XK-8 only to find it was driven by a sixty-year-old woman or a pockmarked man with his paunch hitting the steering wheel. The fantasy was so much better.

And tonight was all about fantasy. After all, she'd have to live on this one night for the rest of her life. Better to imagine him as hot as his scent.

Though she'd planned her evening at the club long before tonight, her anticipation peaked when she'd felt him behind her. He wanted her, his intent spiking the air. He'd do anything to have her, only her. No one else would do.

Blossoming under his all-important, consuming desire, she led him exactly where she wanted him to go.

Into the viewing area. A large room filled with octagonal cubicles, a small window cut into each side of the cloth-covered dividers. The long, rectangular cuts allowed only one person to view, or a couple standing close. Overhead lights illuminated the cubicles and kept the halls between in relative darkness. It gave a feeling of privacy to the onlooker while the eight sides allowed the bed inside to be viewed from all angles.

The cubicle occupants, be they couples, threesomes, or loners, were there to be seen. Seen but not touched by their audience. There were strict rules about not entering.

To be seen but not touched. Virginia was getting married tomorrow. Despite what Stacy might think, she wasn't here to commit prewedding adultery. That wasn't Virginia's idea at all.

She'd reserved her own cubicle in the back of the room. Threading her way through the maze, she didn't stop to watch the activity. She had her own impressive show to contemplate. In the dim hall lighting, she passed a man jerking off, eyes intent on the spectacle inside.

That's what she wanted. A man so beyond himself with desire

for her that he took his cock out and set his rhythm to hers. Right now, she wanted to feel her mysterious follower's desperation as he watched her. Desperate for her.

Desire bubbled through her veins as she stepped inside her cubicle. She'd called for black silk sheets and a mountain of pillows. Scented candles burned on a small table. She bent to remove her pumps. She couldn't see through the windows, the smoked glass and the lights centered on the bed making the view virtually one-way. If she tried, she could make out an outline, but Virginia didn't try. She wanted fantasy. She wanted to pretend a man watched her without her knowledge. She would perform in abandoned ecstasy, without inhibition.

She laid her suit jacket over the back of a cloth-draped chair one might find in a boudoir. Her nipples were hard points against her lacy camisole. Lifting her skirt to her knees and raising a leg to the chair seat, she rolled off one stocking, then the other, letting them drift down to settle on top of her jacket. Then she reached beneath her skirt to lingeringly touch the damp crotch of her thong before slipping it down her legs and tossing it to the carpet. Unzipping her skirt, she shimmied it over her hips, then let that, too, drop crumpled to the floor.

A gaze caressed her bare backside. She imagined *him* touching her flesh, running a finger down her cleft. She bit her lip, then reached for the hem of her camisole and swiped it over her head. Her hair fell loose with the action, pulled from its knot to fall about her shoulders.

The room was warm but not hot. Still, a slight sheen of perspiration speckled her skin. Salty. She imagined his tongue licking it off.

Virginia always imagined a lover while she masturbated. A faceless lover who did whatever she asked, who made her come with his tongue against her clit and his fingers in her pussy.

This time, *he* was out there watching. There were eyes at every window, gazes on every part of her body, but the thought of *his* stare let loose a bead of moisture between her thighs. She reached down, smoothing it away with the pad of her finger, glazing across her pubic hair, then lifted her hand to her mouth and sucked.

The bed. She needed to spread herself for him, show him the pink folds of her pussy, the hard nub of her clitoris.

She sank into the cushions, the black sheet soft and silky against her bottom. She started with her breasts, holding them aloft, plumping them, then pinched the tight nipples until they stung. Caressing her belly, she wriggled on the bed, shifting restlessly. Bringing her feet up, she let her knees fall wide, exposing herself directly to the window right in front of the bed. Her fingers slid through all the moisture, first inside, then back up to her clitoris. She stroked herself slowly with long caresses that started in her vagina and ended at the top of her slit, sweeping her clitoris over and over. Beneath the steady beat of the arena's music, she thought she could hear him breathe. Did he have his cock out already? Or would he wait, letting the sight of her build his anticipation, his desperation, until he would come with only one stroke of his hand. Imagining his loss of control, she plundered her clit to a quick high, almost to the point of orgasm. Another moment, and she would have come, but that was far too soon.

She rolled onto her stomach, rising to her hands and knees, pointing her ass to the window. She spread her legs, then dipped her hand low and back, to the outer edges of her anus. Returning to her pussy, she shoved two fingers inside and rode her hand. So good, so hot. It would drive him insane with need.

She should have asked for a vibrator to use on herself, but the thought hadn't occurred to her, not even in the Massage Parlor. It did now, and her juices soaked her fingers.

She didn't know how long she played with herself, how many positions she went through, or how many times she came close to orgasm, barely managing to pull back at the last instant. Her body thrummed, vibrated, and bucked on its own against her hand. She drenched the bed. Her ears rang.

She dragged her finger over her clit, intending to hold herself just beyond orgasm for as long as she could, but it was the last time. Her body took over, going off by itself, out of her control. Orgasm rocketed through her womb, slamming into her heart, and shaking her limbs with its intensity. The screams of abandon filling her ears were her own.

HIS COCK WAS on fire, and his balls ached with an unbearable need he couldn't quench. But he didn't touch himself. When he came, he wanted her to be watching.

For now, all he could do was clench a fist on the window's sill and drink in the sight of her gorgeous pussy, the scent of her sweet come, the echo of her passion ringing in his ears.

She'd fucked herself in every imaginable position. Her juices on the bed, coating her thighs, shimmering on her fingers.

He'd seen a lot of things, done a lot of things, but this was new. This was an abandon he'd never before witnessed, never before worshipped. She played her body like a maestro. She knew how to bring herself to the brink and not go off, how to keep herself rising and falling until the inevitable orgasm shot her into the heavens. He'd thought about taking her, shoving his cock deep inside her as she knelt before him on the bed. She'd teased every man in the room with that ass as she'd fucked herself with her fingers. Rules be damned, he'd almost gone in there and taken her. Earlier in the evening he might have done just that without a second thought.

The last half hour had changed his strategy. There was so much more beneath her elegant business suit than he'd imagined. So much passion he'd never dreamed she possessed. He would have *that* woman. He would give her unimaginable pleasure.

And that would take a foolproof plan to get her to reveal her inner self completely to him.

Brett Branoff eased back from the window, fading into the shadows along the wall, and left the room. When he'd decided to

follow her, it was to find out why his serene, ladylike, not particularly sexual fiancé had chosen The Sex Club as the party place for
her final unmarried night, a fact he'd inadvertently stumbled upon.
He wasn't a jealous man in the main, but he had to admit to a certain inexplicable tension riding him until he realized her rendezvous
was with herself. Now, he wanted to learn more about Virginia's
deepest desires. She liked to watch. More, she liked to *be* watched,
something that appealed to his sexual nature. He'd unearthed
something so much more intriguing than he'd ever expected.

Tomorrow, he would make Virginia Hansen his wife.

Then he'd find a way to release the woman he'd discovered at
The Sex Club.

TWO

"THAT WAS GOOD." After last night's trip to the club, Brett wanted more from Virginia. He'd actually expected it. More involvement. More passion.

Beside him, Virginia sipped her champagne. "Very good."

Brett propped his feet on the balustrade, his robe falling open over his legs, and rested his glass on his stomach. Sitting side by side on patio chairs, his forearm brushed Virginia's as he settled. They'd turned out the lights and before them, the Las Vegas strip glowed across the skyline, illuminating the night. With the sunset long gone, the hot summer air had cooled to comfortable. Traffic noise and the cacophony of a million voices on the street drifted up to the penthouse terrace, muted by distance. They'd been married six hours ago, enjoyed a sumptuous dinner at a refined restaurant, then returned to the room where a chilled bottle of Dom Perignon had awaited them. After which they'd made love for the first time as man and wife.

Brett waited for her to say more. She didn't. Wrapped in her fluffy hotel robe, Virginia had curled her feet beneath her on the balcony chair, her champagne flute tucked to her chest, a faraway look in her eye as she gazed across the Las Vegas glitz.

The look signified her level of participation in their lovemaking. He didn't touch her on the inside. He wasn't sure why last night had changed his own level of participation, but it had. He'd made her come, but he hadn't made her scream the way she had on the black silk sheets in the club.

Making her scream had become his new goal. But hell if he knew how to accomplish that. He'd rubbed her, gone down on her, thrust deeply in her body. She'd remained . . . uninvolved. As if sex were a duty to be performed, not a pleasure to be savored.

Truly, before last night, he'd been satisfied with that. Virginia never displayed an inordinate amount of emotion. It was one of the reasons he asked her to marry him. He craved her serenity. He'd had emotional overload in his previous marriage. Life with Virginia as his wife promised calm seas ahead.

Last night had given him a taste of something different, and he wanted it again.

"So, what are your plans?" he asked.

After several seconds, she turned, as if it took her a moment to realize he expected an answer. "For tomorrow?"

"For our life."

She tipped her head, her gaze traveling his face, the glow of red, green, and blue neon reflected in her eyes. "Well, this week, I'll finish cleaning out my apartment and moving the rest of my things over."

She'd spent the night occasionally and left her stamp on his condo with a few personal items, but they hadn't lived together. "Then what?"

She tipped her head the other way, as if she were seeing him for the first time and couldn't figure out who he was. "You mean like when am I going to plan our first dinner party?"

She'd make an exceptional hostess. In her professional life, she was executive assistant to the CEO of a major customer for his company. Which meant she managed her boss's life with the same aplomb he expected she'd manage his. Another reason he'd married her. She'd be an asset to his career and his social life, which were one and the same. Since his divorce three years ago, he never did anything without a business goal in mind.

Until now. "I was referring to something more global. Such as, are you going to quit your job?"

She stared at him. After making love, she'd gone into the bathroom and repaired her makeup, fixing the hair and face she wore for the outside world. Her lipstick was perfect; even the sips of champagne hadn't removed it. "I thought we discussed this, Brett, and we decided I'd keep my job. I don't know what I'd do with myself all day if I wasn't working."

Well, she could take care of him. He'd never been taken care of by a woman. With his ex-wife, he'd done the caretaking. He'd spent a lot of energy trying to manage her moods. In addition to her serenity, her competence, her single-mindedness and her efficiency, Virginia didn't have moods. Thank God.

"I didn't expect that you'd quit. I just want you to know you can if you like. It's up to you. You can do whatever you like, Virginia. I want this marriage to bring you a sense of freedom you've never had before. Marriage doesn't mean a loss of freedom for either of us. I want you to indulge yourself in any way you choose." Beneath the robe, his cock stirred to life with thoughts of how he'd like her to indulge herself.

"Well, thank you, Brett. It's nice to have choices. Still, I don't want to give up my job."

Virginia drew much of her self-esteem from her work, just as he did. Perhaps if his ex-wife had kept her job, she wouldn't have been so unhappy. But then, she'd married him so she wouldn't have to work. Virginia had married him for the same reason he'd married her, because they complemented each other.

He sipped his champagne in a silent toast to that. "Good, now

that's settled, how about doing something wild and crazy to celebrate our wedding?"

She smiled. "I wouldn't have suspected you were a wild and
crazy man."

"Ah, I still have secrets then."

"What did you have in mind? We did the elegant dinner. Did
you want to go to the roller coaster at the top of that hotel? I can't
remember the name of it."

"Actually I thought we should make love again. I don't believe
we've done that twice in one night."

Virginia laughed, with no undertones or hidden meanings, just
pure amusement. "Oh my, you truly are wild. I'm shocked."

He set his champagne glass on the small table next to him. "Let
me show you how much more wild I can get." He dropped his feet
to the terrace floor, unbelted his robe, and pulled the lapels apart.
His cock had risen to half mast in anticipation.

She gasped. "Brett. Someone might see you."

Where was the woman who'd stripped off her clothes and masturbated for strangers? He would bring her out in the open.

"It's dark, and we're on the top floor." He wrapped his hand
around his cock and pumped slowly a couple of times. "Of course,
someone might be using binoculars."

Bracing his feet, he pushed his chair back so that he could see
her profile better. So that he could gauge her reactions. Her head
followed his movement, her eyes riveted on his cock.

A tiny drop of come oozed under her gaze, and his partial erection flared.

"You like this, Virginia?" He hoped to stir her more erotic incli-
nations.

Her lips parted, revealing the tip of her tongue. "It's kinky."

He closed his fist around the crest of cock, gathering the moisture in his palm, then sliding back down. She'd gotten a helluva lot
kinkier last night. "Is that good or bad?"

"It's . . . surprising."

He wanted her to grab his cock and take over. Perhaps to crawl between his knees and suck him. Better yet, to part her own robe and touch herself.

She did none of those things. She merely stared. Her robe was too thick to judge the state of her nipples, and over the noise of the traffic below, he couldn't discern an alteration in her breath rate.

Maybe she needed The Sex Club to set herself loose.

"Let's both indulge ourselves, Virginia."

She almost seemed to drag her gaze from the slow pump of his hand to his eyes. "What do you want me to do?"

Don't ask, just do. "Whatever you want. Total freedom, remember?"

"But, I don't . . ." She didn't finish.

All right, she needed a little help releasing herself in front of him. Perhaps that was the club's secret. Anonymity. She'd never have to see those men again. She didn't have to get up beside them in the morning or brush her teeth at the other sink in the bathroom.

"Stand between my legs."

She rose, holding the folds of her robe tight around her. He spread his legs to accommodate her.

"Open your robe and pull it apart. Let your fingers trail your nipples as you do."

She parted the upper lapels first, her fingers grazing her breasts. In the glow of the city lights, he could see they'd risen to hard nubs. Untying the robe and pulling the sash loose, the terry cloth fell open to reveal her slightly rounded belly and blond bush two shades darker than her hair.

She stopped, having done what he told her to and no more.

Okay, he was getting her unspoken message. She'd obey his instructions, but she wouldn't take the initiative. He could work with that.

"Get down on your knees."

The decking was pebbled and might bruise or scrape her knees. He let go of his cock long enough to lean forward and tuck the bottom of her robe protectively beneath her flesh.

"Put your hands here." Brett guided her to his thighs, then once more started the slow masturbation of his cock.

"This is weird, Brett."

He was a seemingly different man. Virginia had watched men whack off before. She'd bent her head at the moment of climax and received their come in her mouth. It had been very sexy, very exciting.

With Brett, the act of watching was scary. Dangerous. Their relationship wasn't supposed to be sexy or exciting. Yet she couldn't take her eyes off his hand, his cock. He had a unique technique, twirling slightly so that he stimulated up, down, and around, caressing the crown of his cock, coating his palm with beads of precome, then retreating only to start the whole sensual rhythm over. Each time the head of his cock popped through his closed fist, it was a little darker, the skin stretched a tad tighter, the length a taste longer.

She wanted to open her mouth and follow the pied piper of his pumping fist with her lips.

"Do you like it, Virginia?"

"I don't know what to say." He kept asking her questions, kept telling her to do things. But what beat at her more than desire was fear.

"Indulge yourself, sweetheart."

She'd indulged herself last night, her last unwedded night.

And she had the sick feeling that Brett knew all about it.

"Touch yourself while I'm doing this."

Her heart seized, then started beating erratically.

Their sex was conventional. They performed oral sex briefly as foreplay, then finished in the usual way. They rarely varied position. He'd never stroked himself while she watched, never asked her to do the same.

So why now?

She licked her lips. His pace increased, the sweep of his hand hypnotic. Up, down, around. Her fingers tightened on the taut flesh of his thighs. She bent slightly. Closer, closer. A drop of moisture broke through and creamed the top of her legs.

"Indulge yourself."

What was he trying to tell her? That visiting a sex club was okay? That she could take other men? That he wanted to take other women? Or was he trying to lull her into admitting aloud what she'd done so he could slam her down?

Fear and desire were a potent mix. His hooded gaze and the purpled crown of his cock beckoned. Almost as if it didn't belong to her, her hand slid across her belly to the thatch of hair above her pussy.

"That's it, let me watch you."

She stopped, her fingers suddenly numb. A week ago, when she'd been in the bathroom, she'd asked him to answer her ringing cell phone, hoping it was a call she'd been waiting for. She'd forgotten that right next to it in her purse were the invitations to The Sex Club.

Later, she'd told herself that he hadn't noticed, let alone found time to take one out, open it, read it, and put it back in exactly the same spot.

His eyes glittered, dark and mysterious despite the Las Vegas glory and the full moon.

The enigma of his gaze tantalized, mystified, and released a gush of heat and wet. His whole body moved with the rhythmic stroke of his hand, faster, his hips rising to the slap of his fist, his thighs gripping her, the muscles of his chest rippling.

Then he threw back his head, groaned into the night and came all over her breasts and throat. After his final spurt of semen, he collapsed in the chair, his eyes closed.

His warm, salty come dribbled down her chest to her belly. She raised a hand, sliding two fingers through his essence, circling first one nipple, then the other.

It felt so good, so right, yet worrisome. She didn't want to have emotions about Brett. She'd had enough turbulent emotion to last a lifetime. And she'd made a lot of disastrous decisions based upon it. She didn't want that this time, not with him.

Brett opened his eyes, locking gazes with her.

He took her breath away. She'd always thought him handsome, but naked, slouched in the chair, his hand still idly stroking his cock, he was magnificent.

He smiled, soft, lazy, content, his head resting on the back of the chair. "That was good."

"I thought you wanted to make love." It sounded like a complaint, though she didn't mean it that way.

He raised a hand to stroke a finger down her arm. "That *was* making love."

"But I didn't participate."

He smiled that slow, lazy smile again. "You watched. Sometimes that's all the participation necessary."

A kernel of fear soaked up all the saliva in her throat and expanded like a sponge. He did know. He had to know. What did he want? What did it all mean for a marriage over which she thought she'd have perfect control?

"What are you thinking?"

She almost laughed. Women were supposed to say that, not men. But she didn't answer. She had to figure this out first. Revelation was such a common thing yet sometimes a big mistake. She didn't know if she could trust this new and almost predatory Brett.

Instead of pushing, Brett leaned forward. His mouth only inches from hers, his eyes never letting her go, he slid his fingers down her throat, her chest, across her belly, and straight into her pussy. His come hadn't cooled, the sensation an exquisite warmth.

She closed her eyes.

His lips touched her hair, his tongue rimmed her ear, then he whispered, "You haven't said a word for over a minute."

"I'm stunned."

"You're wet, too." He fingered her clit, two passes, bottom to top and back again, then he stopped. "You could have come when I did."

She wanted to now. He'd started stroking again, circles, light caresses.

"Rub it in."

His come. She put the flat of her hand to her chest and smoothed his cream over her skin.

"Why didn't you?"

She understood exactly what he meant. Why hadn't she touched herself when he asked her to? "I'm a little tired, I guess. A long day."

She felt him smile against her cheek.

"Poor baby. Let me have the pleasure of doing the work."

And work he did, nudging her knees apart, filling her with two fingers, then drawing out to worry the hard bead of her clitoris again. Back and forth, from her clit to her pussy, then farther still to that sensitive spot of flesh just before her anus. He pressed. She dug her nails into his thighs.

Slick, hot, and unbearably close to orgasm, she hung on to her last vestige of control. His gaze was dark and fathomless. Unreadable. Almost detached. He was so obviously directing, trying to bend her to his will rather than giving in to her feminine power.

She couldn't let go as she had last night by herself. Instead, she took the orgasm, closed her eyes to savor the purely physical explosion from the bud of her clitoris out to her extremities, but she trapped the primal scream in her throat.

Stacy had been right. There were depths to Brett she hadn't dreamed existed. Yet she had to figure out what it all meant to her careful arrangements before she succumbed to temptation.

HE'D GIVEN HER all the gentle reassurance and acceptance he could, yet she hadn't screamed. She hadn't even cried out. But she'd marked his thighs with the half-moon slices of her nails.

Brett figured it was a start.

Virginia shifted in the bed beside him and settled once more. She fell into an endearingly soft snore he could barely hear over his own breath. They'd taken a shower, then tumbled into bed. He'd thought about making love to her again, there against the tile wall of the shower. He'd thought about it and decided against it. She needed time to assimilate the changes she sensed in him.

He could have taken the direct approach and told her he'd found those envelopes in her purse, that he'd been curious enough to spend a rather extraordinary amount of money to secure his own invitation just to see what she was up to.

He was neither a jealous nor a possessive man. God forbid, he'd had enough of that from his ex-wife. He'd meant it tonight when he'd told Virginia she had the freedom to indulge herself in any way she wished. He didn't own Virginia or her body. His offer, therefore, didn't preclude finding pleasure by another man's hand, though he had to acknowledge that stab of relief at the club when he realized Virginia wasn't meeting a lover. Her party of one was far more to his liking.

He could have told her all that. Maybe he should have.

But somehow he knew that wouldn't release her passions any more than his fingers buried deep in her pussy had made her scream. Her teeth had sunk into her lip just as her inner muscles had clamped around him. Trapping everything inside.

Three marriages had somehow made her fearful of releasing her sexuality. Even with him. Exactly why hadn't come out in their discussions. He knew she'd married too quickly, allowing herself to be blinded by lust or some such thing, but he hadn't asked for details just as he hadn't offered the embarrassing minutiae of his own breakup. But he wanted that feeling he'd discovered at The Sex Club. He'd been on the edge, full of combustible needs. And he wanted her to feel the very same thing. Maybe the excitement of the place had been an integral part of Virginia's experience.

Maybe he'd tried too hard, concentrating on making her

scream instead of just going with the flow. Delving beneath her serene facade would take something more than his simple command to indulge herself. It would take a slow, steady onslaught of overwhelming sensual encounters until she realized he meant exactly what he said.

THREE

"THEY DON'T GO with your furniture." Virginia crossed her arms and studied the china figurines she'd unwrapped.

Brett mimicked her stance. "They look fine."

Black-lacquered coffee and end tables enhanced Brett's camel-colored leather sofa and chairs. Which fit well with his state-of-the-art entertainment center. "They're too . . . frilly."

"I like the contrast. The feminine versus the masculine. Yin and yang, you know."

She made a face at him. "They don't work in here."

"Then we'll buy new furniture."

"You can't buy all new furniture to match my knickknacks."

"They're probably worth more than the furniture."

He was right. Her parents had collected the figurines over years, and many of them were antiques. A few china pieces were the only reminders she had left of them now. Within a year of each other,

her mother had succumbed to cancer and her father to a heart attack when Virginia was in her twenties.

Brett bumped her hip with his. "Which do you like best?"

"The ballerina."

He fingered the delicate figure on point. "Why this one?"

"My father gave my mom the pair on her fiftieth birthday. You should have seen her face." Remembering her mother's happy tears, Virginia smiled. "The tutu's made of real lace dipped in porcelain. They just don't make things like that these days."

Brett looked in the now-empty box she'd had all the figurines packed in. "Where's the other ballerina? You said it was a pair."

Damn. She hadn't even realized she'd said that. And instead of a good memory, it gave rise to a bad one that still had the ability to start a slow-burning anger in her belly.

"It was stolen." She started shuffling all the wrapping paper back in the box, her movements crisp and irritated.

"That's too bad. Did they steal anything else?"

She sighed and kept throwing the papers in the box. "All right, it wasn't stolen per se. My third husband sold it." Trying to hide his stock market losses, he'd taken it without her knowledge. As if she wouldn't notice. Bastard. He would have disposed of more if she hadn't seen the ballerina was missing. In an already floundering marriage, that was the last straw.

Brett stilled her hand. "I'm sorry."

She had the feeling he understood exactly what had happened. Though they'd discussed their breakups, they'd done so in more general terms, not specifics. Virginia hadn't believed in going into the whole "he did this and then he did that" routine.

Brett crumpled a piece of wrapping and threw it in the box. "Was the tutu dipped in lace, too?"

She looked at him, wrinkling her brow at the odd question. "Yes. But it was blue, and the ballerina was doing a pirouette."

"Well, I'm sorry it's gone." He tipped her chin. "Nothing else will go missing. And they all belong in this room. Okay?"

She felt her tension ease. What's done is done. She'd divorced the bastard, and this time she'd married a different kind of man. An extraordinarily considerate man. She'd taken the week off after the wedding to move, putting things she didn't need in storage, including most of her furniture. She didn't have much she couldn't part with, most of it being new since the divorce three years ago. She treated a divorce as a beginning, getting rid of the old and bringing in the new, furniture included. Still, she'd keep it in storage until she and Brett settled in. They might want to switch a few things out later.

Brett had been good about letting her rearrange his condo to fit what she brought with her. Mainly her home office equipment. And her figurines.

"You're sweet," she said with a smile.

"Yeah. That's what they all tell me."

"I mean it."

Her belongings were just part of it. Brett had been great about everything. His usual workday was seven to seven, but this week he'd come home early to help her. He'd taken Friday off to help clean her apartment, and he hadn't once suggested they get a cleaning service, which he could well have afforded.

She had to clean up her own mess, as if doing so set her new marriage on a different path than her previous ones.

Brett had indulged her.

Which made her think of their wedding night. *"Indulge yourself."* Today was the one-week anniversary, and Brett planned something special. A surprise, he'd told her this morning.

"Is that the last of your boxes?"

She nodded, pretending to still consider the proper placement of the figurines.

They hadn't made love in the week since their wedding night, which was par for the course in their relationship. He hadn't mentioned indulgence again. It was as if the whole conversation and everything they'd done out on the terrace had never happened. She'd managed to convince herself that she'd imagined the similarities between what he'd done and her escapade at the club. He didn't know. He would have said something by now, a week later, if he had. She hadn't brought it up either, just as she hadn't asked exactly what he meant by indulgence.

Before they'd married, she hadn't given much thought to Brett's extracurricular activities. She'd figured what she didn't know wouldn't hurt her. She wasn't in love with him, he wasn't in love with her. If he needed a little excitement outside the marriage, what did it matter as long as he didn't flaunt it in front of their acquaintances and friends? That was the problem. The humiliation factor, everyone knowing your personal business. Been there, done that.

"Earth to Virginia?"

She popped back to the here and now. "Sorry, I was just thinking about moving the lady in the chair over there and the ballerina here."

His mouth quirked as if he knew that wasn't even close to her thoughts. "I said it's time for you to get ready for our evening out."

She glanced at her watch. It was after seven. "Oh. Sure. Where are we going?"

He wagged a finger in her face. "It's a surprise."

"At least tell me whether it's casual or dressy."

"I'll lay out your clothes for you while you're showering."

Hmm, this was interesting. She felt a flash of heat between her legs thinking about Brett's big hands sifting through her underwear.

HE'D PURCHASED UNDERGARMENTS as delicate as the lace on her china figurines. A black garter belt and thigh-high stockings.

Imagining himself peeling the stockings off with his teeth, his cock hardened in his trousers. Brett adjusted slightly to accommodate the new length. It was the bra that tightened his balls to an ache. It had affected him even in the lingerie shop. As he'd held the lacy confection in his hand, the sudden bulge tenting his slacks had been a bit embarrassing.

He couldn't wait to see Virginia in it.

Just as he'd planned the evening's details, he'd thought long and hard about what she should wear over the sexy lingerie. Something short, tight, and slinky?

Virginia was elegant, classy, far above the hooker look. He'd purchased her attire accordingly.

The shower had stopped five minutes ago. Everything was laid out on the bed in readiness for her. Brett sat in the chair to wait.

After what seemed like an eternity but was probably only another five minutes, the bathroom door opened, and she stepped out amid a cloud of steam and perfumed lotion. A towel draped her from the swell of her breasts to the tops of her thighs.

Scenting her like a lion with his mate in heat, Brett wondered if he could actually wait to have her until they returned from The Sex Club.

"AREN'T YOU GOING to take a shower and get dressed?"

Brett sat in the overstuffed chair next to the closet. He shook his head slowly, his eyes an enigmatic bottomless blue.

Then he pointed to the bed. "I bought you something new to wear for tonight."

What looked like a classic black cocktail dress lay across the foot of the bed, a pile of lacy underthings next to it.

"You didn't have to do that."

"I wanted to."

Brett had never been one for buying her things, sticking to birthdays and holidays, which was how she liked it. Receiving expensive gifts would have made her uncomfortable, as if she was a woman who could be bought by high-priced trinkets. She'd never married for money, and she didn't want anyone to think she was the kind of woman who did. Especially not Brett.

But this showed real effort. He must have checked her size, right down to the dainty strappy sandals on the carpet.

"It's beautiful." The dress was black velvet, soft beneath her fingers. She was touched.

Then she thought she was having an attack her heart pounded so hard. Her breath choked off in her throat.

An envelope lay on top of all the pretty lingerie. A cream-colored envelope with curlicue font spelling out the name Regina.

"I was there." He was beside her, a warm presence.

She turned. "Brett, I—"

He covered her lips with his fingers. "You don't need to explain. Just indulge yourself."

She searched his eyes for something. A spark of spite. Condemnation. There was only the same warmth as when he'd told her to put her parents' china wherever she wanted. And beneath that, a flare of heat equal to that when he'd opened his robe on the terrace and began stroking his cock.

He leaned forward, sucked her lower lip into his mouth, then kissed her hard. Finally he whispered, "Think of it as an invitation to pleasure. Get dressed. I'll be waiting for you."

Then he backed away. She was still staring at the envelope when she heard the front door of the condo close.

She'd gone to a sex club, for God's sake, and he actually encouraged her to go again. He'd bought beautiful clothes for her to wear, and he'd said he'd be waiting for her.

Virginia was suddenly dying to explore a few more of Brett's hidden depths.

THE DRESS WAS sexy yet elegant. A scooped cowl neck draped her bosom, revealing nothing unless she leaned too far forward, yet gave the promise of what lay beneath the velvet. Sexy and decadent. Only Brett would know about the lace-trimmed openings of the bra through which her nipples fit perfectly. The subtle shift of the holes with her every movement made her feel as if a warm mouth sucked at her constantly.

He'd provided a garter belt and stockings but no panties. Her pussy was bare beneath the elegant velvet dress, wet before she even stepped through the doors of The Sex Club.

Brett had created a fantasy for her. How sweet. Maybe a little strange, but somehow the atmosphere at the club bothered her less than his seduction on the terrace. He was giving her a kinky fantasy, nothing more.

Being later in the evening than she and the girls had arrived last week, and also perhaps because it was Saturday night, she had to wait in line to submit her invitation. A waiter, dressed in a black tuxedo, offered her champagne to sip as the line moved forward. Tonight, everyone dressed as if they were attending a black-and-white ball.

Virginia smiled to herself, wondering how the men were going to find their way beneath the long ball gowns. Her dress was cocktail short, the full skirt resting midthigh. Brett wouldn't have any trouble finding the tops of her stockings.

Her turn, but when she handed over the envelope, she was given another in return and told to open it as she stood at the bottom of the stairs.

Formal skirts brushed her legs as she set her champagne on a table and moved aside to see what Brett instructed. A hand lightly caressed her bottom, but when she turned, a sea of faces floated by. Anyone could have touched her.

A key fell out of the envelope into her hand, and the accompanying note was written in Brett's neat script.

"Up the stairs to the third floor, turn right, and enter the fourth room on the left."

The third floor. The private rooms. Stacy had told her about them.

She floated up the stairs with the crowd. Unlike last Friday night, she didn't notice anyone having sex in the halls or the alcoves, just couples in their fancy dress.

Unable to contain her curiosity, she tapped a woman on the shoulder. "Is there a party I didn't hear about?"

The woman laughed beneath heavy makeup applied to hide her age, which had to be over fifty. Her skin was a tad too yellow against the whiteness of her dress. "Oh my dear, it's the Swingers Ball. Every dance, you have to partner with someone new, and it can't be the person you came with."

Virginia raised a brow. "You just dance?"

"Now that's a foolish question, dear. This *is* a particular kind of club, you know." She brushed a hand down her abdomen to the skirt of her ball gown. A slit had been fashioned up the center almost to her pubic hair.

"Of course." Virginia kept a straight face. "Silly of me."

"And there's a prize at the end of the ball. It goes to the couple who . . ." She paused, smiled, then winked at Virginia. "To the couple who enjoyed the most partners. After every . . . dance you collect your partner's card." It sounded like some sort of tag team wrestling match. "Don't you think it's a divine idea?"

The woman delved into her evening bag and pulled out a gold card holder filled with turquoise cards, the number sixty-three printed on them. The stack must have been at least thirty deep.

"The couple with the most cards at the end of the night wins a Hawaiian vacation."

For that much activity, the couple deserved a six-month trip around the world. The candy dishes filled with condoms, which were all over the club, would certainly need refilling often.

Virginia realized now why the line in the lobby had been so long. Everyone was getting their numbered cards.

Did Brett have a set of cards for her upstairs?

She hoped not. The Swingers Ball seemed so . . . impersonal. She'd be one of at least sixty-three, and probably double that num-

ber by the feel of the crowd. That certainly wouldn't make a
woman feel special. How could a man have a chance to want any
one woman desperately if he had to work his way through every female in sight?

No, no, no. The Swingers Ball wasn't for her. And obviously
not for Brett either. He'd ordered a private room.

And she needed to get up to it right now.

"Good luck." Despite the peculiar circumstances, she smiled as
politely as possible at her informant. Then she climbed the second
flight of stairs and left the crowd behind, though the voices, the
merriment, and the strains of a waltz drifted up from below as she
reached the third floor.

Suddenly, she couldn't wait to see what Brett had planned just
for her indulgence. Oddly, knowing what would occur in the ballroom enhanced her surprise private party.

She fumbled at the door, got the key in, then rushed into . . . an
empty room.

Where was Brett?

The room was done in soft gold tones. A king-size bed stood on
a pedestal in the middle, with two steps up. On the left, four steps
up, was a sunken tub, steam wafting off its surface. The mirror behind it tilted slightly to reveal a froth of bubbles. A bucket held an
uncorked bottle of champagne, and on the table beside it, a glass
had already been filled. Cheese and fruit graced a crystal platter
along with strawberries dipped in chocolate. All within reach of
the bath.

On the corner of the porcelain tub sat another envelope. Step-
ping up, she saw that this time the note had an instruction on the
outside.

"Indulge yourself, take your pleasure, then open the envelope
when you're done with your bath."

She tingled with anticipation. Turning back to the room, she
noticed the mirror along one wall. It reflected the bed and beyond
that, the tub. The room and the mirror were designed to produce

the maximum view. Someone was behind that mirror, which she was sure was two-way. Maybe more than one someone.

Brett was giving her what she'd had last Friday all over again. But this time with more luxury.

Her heart beat faster. He'd chosen what he thought would most tantalize her. His actions the night of their wedding now made perfect sense.

Brett had masturbated for her. He'd asked her to do the same. Instead of freaking out like a normal husband would over the knowledge that she'd performed for a crowd at a sex club, Brett condoned and encouraged with his every action. The man had a delicious streak of kinkiness she could never have imagined.

Virginia suddenly wanted to drive him wild, and she'd do it by driving herself wild.

First, a striptease. Her back to the mirror, she unzipped the dress slowly, exposing herself to her audience inch by inch. A chair sat by the door ready to receive her cast-off clothing. She tossed the dress, then stretched her arms over her head, naked but for the lacy underthings he'd bought her.

Then she turned. God, she looked hot. She saw what he saw, her nipples tight beads burgeoning from the black lace bra, the blond thatch between her thighs, the tops of the stockings flirting with her curls, and the garter belt high on her hips.

She palmed her breasts, plumping them for the mirror, then stuck one finger in her mouth. Circling first one nipple, then the other, the peaks ached. Moisture coated her inner thighs, and her clitoris throbbed. She slid a hand over her belly to her mound but didn't slip inside to caress herself.

He'd indicated she should take a bath first. Then there was another note to read.

She lifted one foot to the bed frame, spreading her legs a little wider than necessary, then removed her shoe and unclipped the stocking. Sliding her hand between her legs, barely brushing her clitoris, she rolled down the stocking. After a long, slow caress the length of her legs, she tossed the stocking across the room, missing the chair. She repeated the procedure, this time rubbing her clitoris a little before removing the stocking. Then the garter went the way of the silk and velvet. Finally, she turned back to the mirror, pinched each nipple, then undid the bra, tossed it aside, and stood naked a moment.

Her bath awaited her, and if she preened for the mirror much longer, the water would cool. She hated a lukewarm bath.

She'd worn her hair down for tonight, but she wound it on top of her head and secured it with clips she found in a little dish. She smiled to herself. Whoever had prepared the room thought of everything. Once she was beneath the water, soothing bath salts tenderized her skin, and they'd even provided a bath pillow to cradle her head. A sip of champagne sizzled on her tongue, and the chocolate strawberries dazzled her taste buds. The cheese was light and tangy like Swiss but with more subtlety.

The thought of Brett on the other side of that window heated her in a way the tub of steaming water and bath bubbles couldn't.

Brett alone in an empty room watching her. For tonight, she didn't need other men. It was enough that he'd brought her here. It was enough that he would enjoy her performance. This was pure sex, pure pleasure.

Sinking down until the bubbles covered her to her throat, she let her knees fall apart and stroked a hand between her legs.

Show time.

FOUR

WITH A COCK the size of the Washington Monument and just as hard, Brett salivated over his wife in the steaming water. The mirror next to the tub was angled to give a tantalizing view.

And Virginia tantalized him in every way. The bubbles obscured her actions, but her expression gave away exactly what her hands did below the surface. She'd closed her eyes, and the ripples of her pleasure lapped against the sides of the tub.

He wanted to taste the champagne and treats on her tongue. He wanted to savor the confection between her legs. He wanted to suck the cherried buds of her nipples through the slinky bra.

She was like the lady of the manor performing her evening ablutions. A hot bath, sparkling champagne, and a little play to help her sleep. She fluttered under the water, preparing herself but not coming. He felt like a kid in a candy store waiting for the patron in front of him who just could not make up his mind.

The wait made her actions all the more sexy. She arched,

moaned softly—the room was wired for sound—then relaxed again, lifting an arm to snag another piece of cheese and a champagne chaser. Is that how women masturbated when no one was watching, stretching it out, rising to a heated level, then backing off to relax and sip champagne, only to start all over again?

He'd never asked, never even wondered about it. It hadn't mattered. Playing his share of sex games, he'd also done his share of watching a woman make herself come, but what did they do when they didn't have an audience? Yes, Virginia knew the mirror was two-way, but still, this was different from her prewedding sojourn. Perhaps she was already so hot and wet that night after wandering the halls of the club that she'd gone at herself in a frenzy, even if she had been able to hold off her orgasm for an extraordinary amount of time.

He gripped the window frame as her hips arched and rose from the water, bubbles popping, her fingers working. The mirror revealed the bliss on her face, her lashes fanned below her eyes, her teeth worrying her lower lip.

She moaned again, but she didn't scream, and he knew she hadn't come. No matter how languid she appeared, she was well aware of him behind the window, well aware of his reaction.

Just as before, he didn't take his cock out of his pants. For now, it was all about her pleasure. He watched and waited, his balls tightening all the while.

He'd thought of parading her through the party throng. He'd even changed into a tuxedo for the occasion. The club had a locker room, perhaps for those who wanted to wash off the night's revelry or change their debauched clothing. But doing what everyone else was doing didn't appeal. In the end, he'd gone with his original plan. A private room, a private show.

Then she rose from amid the dying bubbles. Water streamed down her body as she poured soap into her hand. He'd made sure the attendants left her favorite scent. She washed, her hand delving into her mound. In the mirror behind her, he watched her fingers peek from between her legs, then she soaped her ass, spreading her cheeks, teasing. Pinching soaped nipples, she caressed beneath her breasts, her throat, arching her neck.

She was dazzling. He'd always appreciated her beauty, her elegance. Now he craved the passion he'd seen beneath the surface the night he'd followed her here.

Drying off, she stepped from the tub, then finally, finally, she opened his second instruction. And smiled.

She dropped the towel, left her champagne behind, and mounted the bed, tugging her hair loose at the same time. The pins she'd used to secure it flew in all directions.

If she'd been alone, she probably would have climbed under the covers, snuggling into the warmth. Instead, she crawled across the mattress on her hands and knees, her eyes on herself in what to her was a mirror. Then she swung her legs around, pulled a pillow beneath her head, and lay back.

Her gorgeous bush faced him, showing him a hint of warm, wet pink. He wanted, needed to bury his face in her. A door, disguised to look like another wall panel, was set to one side of the window. He could enter her room any time.

She spread her legs and wiggled her ass on the bed. In the note, he'd told her to indulge herself on the bed in any way she liked. She wanted to tease. He passed a hand over his erection, squeezing through the cloth. It wasn't enough to relieve the ache. But he didn't pull out his cock. He didn't open the door.

She slid her middle finger into her pussy, over her clit. Her heels planted in the coverlet, she suddenly plunged deep, arching her hips off the bed. She fucked herself with two fingers as he died with desire.

Then she settled once more, stroking her clit with a slow hand. He couldn't say how long she touched herself, how many times she plunged, squirmed, circled. It went on forever until he thought he'd go mad. Until he wanted to grab the only chair and throw it through the glass so that he could get at her.

Her gasps filled his small compartment. Her moans echoed all around. His heart raced, the sound pounding in his ears, and his breath timed itself to her rhythm. And when she finally let loose and orgasmed all over her fingers, he almost came with her as she screamed out her delight.

Primitive instinct urged him to rip the door off its hinges and have her. To bring her more pleasure than she'd known just moments before. He almost gave in to the force.

His intent to wait until they got home was dying a fiery demise. He was sure he didn't retain enough control over his impulses to make it far past the front doors of The Sex Club.

IF THAT DIDN'T make Brett come in his pants, nothing would. She'd climaxed imagining him jerking off in his hand, unable to stop himself, overcome by the sight of her. Wanting her desperately.

Virginia lay on the bed recovering her breath. Her spread legs faced the mirror. Her hot, wet pussy lay open and exposed.

A shiver traveled her arms and legs. Goose bumps rose. She hadn't married Brett because he wanted her desperately. She didn't want him desperately either.

What they'd done tonight was about kinky pleasures, not messy emotions. And that's the way she wanted to keep it. Fantasy. Sexy games. Nothing more.

She rolled to her stomach and languidly rose to her knees, this time exposing her ass. Since they were playing sex games, she would enjoy every minute of it.

Virginia followed her last set of instructions, dressing as slowly as she'd undressed, petting and stroking for the mirror. As he required, she stood for a time clothed only in garter, stockings, and the tantalizing brassiere with its tight nipple holes. The light flush of her climax still suffused her skin, and her clitoris throbbed delicately as she contemplated whatever else Brett had planned for the night.

Finally, dressed, she exited the room. The lacy underthings caressed her as she took the stairs to the second level.

She'd never seen so many couples engaged in sex. It was beyond even her first foray to the club. On the floor in the middle of the hallway, for God's sake, a man mounted his partner, taking her with deep strokes. Against the banister, the wall, on the stairs, more couples. She negotiated the carpeting as if it were a minefield, careful not to step on anyone's dress.

It was almost amusing, yet the scent of perspiration, perfume, and sex laced the air with an aura of decadence and abandon. The hot and heavy atmosphere stole her breath and increased the throb between her legs.

Her so-called friend, Lady Number Sixty-three, was laid out on the lobby table illuminated by the overhead chandelier. Her white dress creased as she wrapped her legs around the hips of a mid-fifties gentleman. Though gentle was hardly the word to describe the rough pounding of his body into hers. The lady suddenly threw back her head, her listing hairdo hanging off the other side of the table, and wailed through her orgasm. Watching from the bottom step of the wide staircase, Virginia knew the man came, almost on the heels of the woman's climax, by his series of grunts and the jerk of his hips.

Virginia's nipples peaked through the holes in her bra, hard and aching. She was as wet as she'd been in her private room.

Watching was beyond titillating. It was a force in itself, beating at her, ratcheting up her need. Her hand dropped to the front of her dress. She caressed herself through the fabric. The desire to lie down on the stairs and spread herself for a man, any man, was almost irresistible.

No, not any man. Not tonight. She turned, searching, wanting, needing unbearably, but Brett was nowhere in sight.

Sixty-three's gentleman pulled out of her, the withdrawal of his penis audible, amplified by the tall ceiling. He removed a condom, tossed it in a conveniently available receptacle, then tucked his cock back in his tuxedo pants. After which, he helped his partner off the table, straightening her ball gown politely.

Then they exchanged cards.

It was the most bizarre thing Virginia had ever seen.

Lady Sixty-three turned, her face glowing with satisfaction, her eyelids heavy, sultry. Then she saw Virginia.

"Oh my dear, how many have you had?" Her gray-haired yet extremely distinguished gentleman kissed her ear. She waggled her fingers at him, and he headed for the stairs in hot pursuit of another card, eyeing Virginia as he went. She turned away.

If Brett's instructions had told her to get a card herself, she probably would have done it. She was in such a mood, such a need. But that wasn't part of his plan.

She answered her newfound friend. "I'm afraid that wasn't my goal for the night."

What was her goal? To feel sexy, hot, and wanted. Brett had given her that. But she needed more, more, more.

The lady fanned her cards. "I'm up to twenty-four," she announced proudly as if she were collecting donations for stamping out breast cancer.

Twenty-four. It boggled the mind. What was that, a different man every five minutes? How did they all manage to come that many times? "That's wonderful. Congratulations."

Virginia wanted a man inside her. Now. If Brett didn't plan to take her in their own bed, she'd beg. Hot, wet, and needy, she'd promise him anything.

"The night is oh so young." Then the woman grimaced. "Sadie has twenty-five, that bitch." She beamed. "So I'm off. I saw the most delicious man before the party started, and I simply must find him. I love tall, dark, and exquisitely handsome." Her eyes widened at something, or someone, on the stairs above Virginia. The lady fluttered her eyelashes. "Ooh, speak of the devil, there he is."

Virginia knew without looking. She felt Mr. Tall Dark and Handsome's gaze on the curve of her ass. Brett. "He's mine."

"We'll see about that, sweetie." Without the slightest animosity lacing her tone, Virginia's companion waggled her fingers. "Toodle-oo."

Virginia felt as hot and desired as the night before her wedding. There was something about Brett's focused attention that beat against her flesh without her even needing to turn.

She crossed the hall to the front door, her body moving with a delicate sway, a seductive invitation.

He would follow. He couldn't help himself. Lady Sixty-three didn't stand a chance. Virginia's pussy, unconfined by panties, dampened further, coating her thighs. She felt his desire as if he'd already buried his cock deep inside her.

She took the outside stairs down into the garage, her heels clicking on the cement, echoing in the otherwise empty parking lot. All the activity was at the Swingers Ball, and as her friendly informant had said, the night was still oh so young.

She missed his footsteps behind her as she fumbled inside her small purse for her keys, over the beep of her alarm, and the pound of her heart in her ears. His body suddenly covered hers as he reached for her keys and purse, retrieving both from her grasp and tossing them on the roof of her car.

Without a word, he dipped inside her dress and pinched her nipples, first one, then the other, to hardened peaks through the holes in her bra.

"I've been wanting to do that all night," he murmured.

She swelled against his palm. He stroked in circles, testing the outer rim of the holes with a finger. She pushed back against his cock, rubbing herself against him.

"Ah, I see you want something, too." He abandoned her breasts to reach beneath her dress, raising the hem to expose her garter and hot pussy. His heat caressed her bare ass as his hands slid from her waist to her hips, then he divided his attention, stroking down the crease of her butt and coming at her from the front as well. A rough finger slipped into her pussy. His champagne-laden breath ruffled the hairs at her nape.

"Please," she whispered, begging with just that one word.

He stroked her clit, widening her stance with his leg between hers. "Please what?" He nipped her neck, then laved with his tongue. "Do you want me to fuck you now, Virginia, right here? With your little dress hiked up around your waist?"

Her breath seemed trapped in her throat, and her pulse beat in all her erogenous zones. "Yes." It was all she could manage.

He pushed her forward against the car. "I want you so badly I'm going to come on your ass if I don't get inside you right now."

His words filled her up, consumed her. She couldn't wait for home. She couldn't even wait to open the door of her car and drag him inside. "Fuck me, Brett. Please."

He hitched her hips against his, cock already out, hot, hard, questing. She wriggled against him, rising slightly on her toes to ease his entrance.

She gasped with the first taste of his tip against her open pussy. She pushed, he drove, and his cock slid deep. She closed her eyes against the intense pleasure, the smoothness of his fill, the moisture between them.

His hands clutched her hips, fingers biting into her flesh with his need. "Wider." He slipped a hand over her behind, spreading her cheeks, pushing deep. "Let me in. All the way."

She felt as if he'd reached to her womb and beyond.

"Christ, you've got the sweetest-feeling pussy." He groaned, his hands slippery on her backside, his voice laced with a harsh need that set her on fire. "So fucking good. So fucking hot. Better than any fuck I've ever known in my life."

He pounded into her even as his words lifted her to a place she'd never been, more than desire, more than mere sex with the entire Swingers Ball. The rough, crass language said so much more than any sweet romantic compliments ever could. She braced herself against the car and rode him. Her clit throbbed, screaming for attention, his, hers, it didn't matter. But the sensation on the inside was even better, the clench of her pussy, the slickness, the heat of his cock, the just-right spot he hit with each thrust.

"Heavens, they're fucking like rabbits."

Virginia heard the voices and didn't care.

"Are they allowed to do that down here in the garage?"

"It's a sex club, Marta, they can do it wherever they want."

She was aware of Brett's hands pushing her dress higher, of the slight shift of his body away from her, his cock pulling out almost to the tip, but not quite leaving her, not quite able to give up the heat of her pussy. He slammed home again and again, anchoring her at the waist with her dress held high, revealing their union to greedy eyes.

"Look at the size of his cock. Fuck me like that, Sven."

"I'm not that big, my sweet, I don't think I can."

"It's not the size, darling, it's the way he's fucking her, like he can't get enough of her."

"Like she's the only woman in the world?"

Silence, then the woman's awed whisper, "Yeah. Like that."

"The only woman in the world." Virginia almost came. It was how Brett made her feel. In this moment, she was the *only* one who could satisfy him.

"I'm not sure I can duplicate that quite the same way." Sven's voice held a note of reverence for Brett's performance.

"Then let me have him after he's done with her."

She'd scratch the witch's eyes out if she so much as tried to touch Brett. But she couldn't stand it anymore, the feel of his cock inside her and the couple's envious eyes on them. She shoved her hand between her legs. His incessant thrusts forced her finger over her clit, back and forth, harder. She panted.

"Do you want to fuck her, Sven?"

"Try it, and you die, Sven."

Brett's words washed over her, the rasp of his breath, the tremble of his muscles each time he hit home. Then his fingers joined hers on her clitoris. The voices dimmed, there was only his cock, his hand, his voice, telling her how much he loved fucking her. The moan in her throat rose to a cry as the world splintered. She climaxed from the inside out, her ears ringing and her pussy drinking his come as he filled her.

She no longer heard Sven and Marta. She wasn't sure if they'd left or were doing it on the concrete. She was only truly aware of the feel of Brett's cock slipping from her, the stroke of his hands as he lowered her dress, and the gentle caress of his lips against her nape.

He held her against him, his arm across her waist as he opened her car door. Her legs wobbled, and her knees threatened to collapse. He lowered her to the seat, tucked her feet into the car, and handed over her keys and purse.

"Can you drive?"

She took a deep breath and nodded. "In a minute." Long minutes, in which she regained the senses she'd lost.

His eyes as he bent inside the car were darker than a stormy ocean. He grasped her chin and pulled her close for a sizzling open-mouthed kiss, his tongue taking her as deeply as his cock had moments ago. She wanted him all over again.

Then he was gone, leaving behind only the spice of their sex and the soft snick of her car door beside her. She gripped the steering wheel as an orgasmic aftershock rippled through her. Eyes closed, she dragged in a breath.

God. Never like that. Never. Not with anyone. No one but Brett. And not even with him before this night.

It felt almost once-in-a-lifetime.

HE'D NEVER EXPERIENCED the like. But he knew he could have it with Virginia over and over again. He *could* have it.

They could.

Brett followed Virginia home. She hadn't seemed quite in her own body in the garage, but she'd driven safely, as if the effects of the club wore off once they were out in the night air.

"The only woman in the world." That's exactly what she'd been to him. With a multitude to choose from at the Swingers Ball, she was the only one.

He liked the feeling.

And he'd made her scream this time. He'd taken her out of herself. He'd forced her to succumb to their mutual desire. When she went off in his arms, his cock buried deep inside, he had the best orgasm of his life. Yes, the best. Incomparable.

Was it just her? Or was it Sven and Marta, the Swingers Ball, The Sex Club, all of that combined?

Brett couldn't say. But hell, he didn't care. If it took a sex club as a backdrop, then it would be a regular haunt. He *would* make Virginia scream. Every time.

He allowed her time to park and enter the condo. He sat a moment, the lot's lamps illuminating the hood of his car but leaving the interior in darkness.

She'd gone off with his whispered threat to Sven. She'd hit her peak with that stamp of ownership, possession, and need. Brett knew he'd found the key to unlocking her passion. Virginia needed witnesses to her power as a woman. He'd give her that as much as she wanted.

Inside, the condo was dark except for a stream of light from the bedroom. Her shoes lay on the carpet in the upstairs hall, her purse, a few feet closer to the bedroom door. He entered to find her sitting at her vanity removing her makeup with a cotton ball.

The scent of his loving rose off her like a sultry perfume.

She threw the cotton in the trash can, then swiveled on her vanity stool. Something shimmered in her eyes, and her lips were plump from small nervous bites. "Brett, I—"

He covered her mouth with his fingers.

"Don't say anything." Her stroked her lower lip with the pad of his index finger. "Wait for the next invitation."

She blinked, her lashes long and full even without the benefit of her mascara. "But—"

"There's life as Mr. and Mrs. Brett Branoff. And then there's a whole different life at The Sex Club."

"You mean—"

He shook his head. "When the time comes, just do what the note tells you to do, Virginia."

He intended to see just how far he could get her to go and just how good he could make it for her.

BESIDE HER, BRETT breathed softly, rhythmically.

Virginia couldn't fall asleep. Her body hummed, erotic images played across her mind, and her flesh buzzed with the electricity of the club.

Stacy was so right. There was so much more to her husband than she'd ever thought possible. He'd conceived of a double life for the two of them. A place to play out their fantasies. A separate life that existed only at The Sex Club was like having a secret lover.

She'd follow the instructions in the next invitation to the letter. In fact, she wouldn't be able to resist.

And she wouldn't think about how she was starting to feel far too much emotion in a marriage that was supposed to be comfortable, convenient, and controlled.

FIVE

"IS THE STEAK good?" Virginia grimaced at her own polite conversation. It had been three weeks since their visit to the club, and she was starting to think she'd imagined the man Brett had been out in the parking garage.

"I want you so badly I'm going to come on your ass if I don't get inside you right now."

Despite the things he'd said then, maybe it hadn't been as exciting for him as she'd made it out to be, because at home, their lovemaking was as predictable as usual.

"It's perfect," Brett said, spearing another piece of filet mignon. He smiled. "You're an excellent cook."

He complimented her, asked about her day, laughed with her over an amusing anecdote. They watched TV together, a movie, a PBS presentation, or sometimes a sitcom. At least when they weren't attending one of his frequent business engagements.

But was he ever going to take her to the club again? She couldn't bring it up. Part of the allure was having him do the asking. Yet the club obviously did something for them that they couldn't achieve at home. In their own bed, Brett just wasn't *wild* for her the way he'd been that night. She had to admit that lack of ardor made her a little inhibited, too.

"You do realize you're asking for more than what you originally bargained for."

So what? She was only asking for it at the club. What was wrong with that?

"How was your day?" she asked, shutting out the sound of her annoying internal argument.

"The usual. I vanquished a banker, screwed a supplier, and secured an exorbitant contract the customer was overpaying for."

"You're such a liar, Brett."

He was an honest businessman, a fair employer, and a shrewd negotiator who made sure both parties to an agreement came out on top. With Brett Branoff, you got the highest quality and the best deal. Virginia admired his ethics.

But dammit, she wanted his next wicked surprise.

His eyes crinkled at the corners. "Really, my day was fine. Thanks for asking. Garrett's coming into town next week. Do you have time to arrange another party?"

Oh yes, she had time for another party, a Sex Club party. She'd have him on his knees . . . except he wasn't talking about *that* kind of party. "Yes. Fine. No problem."

In the last three weeks, they'd experienced a grueling social schedule. When would it slow down? Brett's business life included regular socializing, but he also wanted to introduce his new wife to his associates, which meant more engagements than usual. Virginia loved her day job, but she wondered how she'd keep up if the pace continued. Thank goodness for the few nights they did spend at home in front of the TV. Though one trip to The Sex Club would definitely have gone a long way in recharging her batteries.

She was starting to hear sexual innuendo in every exchange they had. Brett usually called her at work during the day. His voice over the phone set her skin alight. Husky, intimate, even when all he asked was if she wanted to go out to eat. Everything he said, no matter how innocent, made her think of sex.

"What's for dinner, Virginia?" She'd have visions of laying herself out on the dining room table for him to feast upon, his tongue delving deep into her pussy, teasing her clitoris. *"What do you want to watch tonight?"* Brett, stroking that gorgeous cock of his, fingering her to multiple orgasms, then coming hard on her clit, his heat sending her over the edge again . . .

God. She was driving herself mad with her fantasies.

"Is everything all right, Virginia?"

"What?" She blinked, clearing the images, but her panties were drenched. "Sorry, what did you say?"

His lips rose, growing slowly into a smile. "You're not paying attention to me. I'm hurt."

She patted his hand. "What can I do to make it up to you?" *"Beg me to suck your cock deep into my mouth and swallow every last drop of come. Tell me you'll go insane if I don't suck you right this minute."*

But he wouldn't. He'd only displayed that kind of fervor at the club.

He propped his chin in his hand. "I get to choose the show we watch tonight."

Oh, she'd give him a show, all right. If he asked. "And what would you like to watch?" She'd let him hear the sexual innuendo this time.

He sat back. "The history channel has a great documentary on World War II."

Bastard. Waiting for the next invitation was killing her. Her skin felt tightly stretched over her bones.

"You're distracted tonight. I'll do the dishes while you go upstairs and take a bath. Then we'll watch the show. Okay?"

"You're too good to me." She smiled sweetly when what she

wanted was for him to beg to join her in the bath where his soapy fingers could caress her overheated clitoris or aim the detachable showerhead right on her pussy.

"Off you go, then." He started gathering dirty plates.

Brett had offered to hire a cook and a full-time maid. Maybe later she'd like that, but for the time being, she wanted them to settle into their married routine. Besides, she enjoyed cooking for him when they were at home for dinner. She was, however, not stupid enough to let him get rid of the housecleaner they had come in twice a week.

"Don't put the scraps down the garbage disposal. It gets clogged."

He eyed her. "I'm forty-three, Virginia. I know how to do everything exactly the way a woman wants it done."

She bit her lip. It wasn't her dishes she wanted doing. But if she asked for it, that would spoil everything for her. Brett had to be dying to do it, or it just wasn't enough. Which was the whole problem they had in the bedroom.

Since when had she started thinking their bedroom activity was a problem? What had Stacy said? *"Six months, a year from now, you're going to start wanting more."* Virginia hadn't even lasted a month.

She left Brett to the dirty dishes. A bath, an intimate massage, a little release of tension, just a small orgasm. If he walked in on her, maybe that would set the wild man free . . .

A blue chiffon outfit was laid out on the bed, a small beaded purse attached to the belt. A pair of matching high-heeled pumps sat on the carpet. Over the heart of the dress lay a cream-colored envelope and a single strand of pearls.

He knew she didn't like gifts, but in some odd way, the pearls were part of the night, part of the seduction. Beside the dress, she found a note scribbled with his familiar writing.

"Just the dress, the pearls, and the shoes, nothing else."

Her hands started to tremble, and her heart beat so fast it drowned out the sound of running water down in the kitchen.

Finally. Thank God.

HE WANTED HER crazy. So hot, wet, and needy that she'd do anything he told her to. Beg, suck, scream, everything.

In three weeks, Brett had fallen in love with the comfort and serenity Virginia brought to his life. It was more than pleasant to come home to a woman who wasn't alternately a raging lunatic, a tearful mess, or filled with manic happiness before the inevitable crash. Virginia gave his life gentle stability. He found himself telling her about his business day and thereby easing some of his pressures. She was the perfect hostess, the perfect decoration on his arm, the perfect companion for sitting in front of the TV or reading. Virginia was the perfect wife.

Yet when he made love with her, it felt like she was simply expecting . . . more. More what? He'd told her they would have a separate, exciting life at the club, but that didn't preclude hot sex in the privacy of their own home. He was a man who prided himself on always being able to predict exactly what his customers needed and supplying it to them in a mutually agreeable deal. Virginia, though, continued to baffle him in the bedroom.

They'd had an extremely busy schedule since the wedding, his suppliers and customers clamoring to meet the new Mrs. Branoff. He'd wanted to show her off as the jewel she was. But he'd been compelled to fit in a Sex Club tryst tonight. Whatever it was Virginia needed to let herself loose, she'd found it in the decadence of The Sex Club.

There, he would touch her, taste her, savor her, and make them both come so hard, it would turn their sex life inside out.

* * *

AS BEFORE, VIRGINIA was handed an envelope containing instructions when she turned over her invitation to the club's hostess. She
shivered, wondering what Brett had planned for her, but she
climbed to the second floor before opening it. People jostled her,
someone offered a bowl of condoms, and the scent of sex wafted on
the air.

The mirror at the top of the stairs reflected the blue chiffon. The
pearls at her throat glimmered in the flickering light of the wall
sconces. She'd piled her hair up in a neat twist, and her lips were a
modest shade of pink. She looked like a prissy society matron. Except for the spaghetti strap that had fallen off one shoulder. That
one detail said it all. She was a woman, neat on the outside and
melted chocolate on the inside. Virginia ripped open the envelope.

"Visit three rooms of your choice. I'll be watching you."

Was she to indulge herself in the three rooms? With another
man? By herself? Would she find *him* in one of those rooms doing
another woman? A sick feeling swept through her midriff. Not even
a month ago, she'd told herself she wouldn't let the notion bother
her. Now, she prayed that wasn't what he'd planned for their evening. No, he wouldn't do that. Visiting the rooms was part of the
game, the titillation. Brett wanted her to watch other people,
wanted her achingly hot and bothered by the time he revealed himself. She wouldn't allow her thoughts to get in the way of their mutual pleasure.

She tucked the note into the beaded purse at her waist. He had
thought of everything, even a place to stash her license and car key.
Three rooms to visit. Then he was hers.

She turned left down the hall, strolling past the orgy room. Been
there, seen that. Because she couldn't go around, she stepped over
the feet of a woman on her knees performing oral sex in the middle
of the hallway. The man's groans filled the air, and Virginia's chiffon suddenly felt scratchy, rubbing her nipples to peaks and making
her feel . . . hot and bothered.

Something ahead tooted, like a train whistle. The Train Depot.

She dodged a couple making out, her skirt brushing the male back-side. She was sure he liked it, the faint touch of strangers passing by, the electricity pulsing around them, the knowledge that every-one could see his tongue down his partner's throat and her hand in the open zipper of his pants.

The train whistled at Virginia once more, and she glanced through a gap in the onlookers. Inside, only two walls were mir-rored and half the ceiling. A plywood mock-up of a train depot filled an entire wall, complete with painted figures dressed in Victo-rian clothing. She found herself sucked inside the room by the press of bodies. An oral train was taking off just as she was pressed onto the makeshift "depot" platform. Naked bodies squirmed on the floor. A woman on her back, a man on his elbows and knees, his face buried in her pussy, his legs splayed over another woman as she sucked his cock, and between her thighs a female head bobbing. On and on it went in a human train pulling ten cars. Bright cloth-ing, naked flesh, private parts exposed.

Virginia plastered herself to the painted wall. The room was close and filled with the aroma of come and arousal, but what set her skin humming was that within all the scents, she smelled him, Brett, musky, hot, salty. Like the taste of his come on her tongue. She couldn't see him, yet she knew he was watching her.

In front of the mirror, another train started, this one with full penetration. It gathered speed with gusto, a cock in a vagina, a woman with a dildo strapped to her waist impaling the man in front of her. It was fascinating in a horrifying way.

A beckoning hand emerged from the oral train. God only knew who it belonged to in the mass of writhing bodies. Virginia plunged for the door. While she was moist from the underside of her breasts to between her legs, she didn't do trains.

In the hallway, she caught her breath. The crowd grew thinner the farther into the depths of the huge mansion she went, as if the guests got mired in the first rooms they came to. She wondered if peeking into a room counted as one of the three she was supposed to visit. She opened a closed door—no one said closed doors were taboo—saw all men. Yes, the peek counted. Air wafted over her as she shut the door, and with it came Brett's unique scent again, brushing the back of her neck. He was there behind her. Following. Dogging her every step.

And she remembered the night of her bachelorette party. Brett hadn't just been at The Sex Club that night, he'd followed her from room to room. He was the man she'd sensed behind her. That night, she'd performed for him. Why she hadn't realized it before, she couldn't say. Maybe she'd been afraid to contemplate the consequences.

Just as she hadn't turned to find her watcher that night, Virginia didn't turn now. Titillation wasn't in The Train Depot. It was behind her in the man who stalked her. It was in the scent of sex that shuddered from his pores. That was the moment her body came fully to life, the moment her nipples ached for his mouth, her clitoris throbbed for the rough swipe of his tongue, and her core dripped for his possession.

One more room to visit, and he was hers to do with as she wished. Virginia turned abruptly into the next door she came to. No one clogged the entry, and at first it appeared to be nothing more than a workout room. Then she saw the workout they were giving each other. One man, one woman. She was spread above his face, clutching the bar above her for support. He lay on his back on a bench. The weights lay immobile as he gripped her buttocks and held her to his mouth.

Her legs trembling, Virginia closed her eyes and imagined imitating the position with Brett. She could almost feel his tongue enter her, the lap and suck of his mouth, the clench of her thigh muscles as she steadied herself for his intimate foray. She clung to the wall to hold herself upright, the woman's keening wails echoing in the room.

Her hand restlessly stroked her abdomen, the need to lift her skirt and caress herself humming through her blood. This was what

Brett wanted, her need so unbearable that she'd do anything. The best, however, was yet to come. When Brett finally revealed himself in the throng of strangers.

She stumbled from the room, her eyes darting through the guests heading her way. People were moving on, looking for new excitement. When would Brett come to her and extinguish the fire burning in her? Her mind spilled over with the image of him shoving her dress to her waist and taking her in the middle of the hallway with the crowd all around them. She wanted it, badly. Her feet were unsteady in the high heels. Her legs didn't seem to work the way she wanted them to, and her vision blurred around the fringes.

Someone bumped her, and she fell against the wall, bringing her hand up to the hardwood paneling to catch herself. She was at the edge of an alcove, and for a moment she thought about ducking in just to catch her breath.

Through a gap in the alcove's curtain, she saw a couple kissing as if they were the only two people in the world. He cupped her face with a sort of worship, his knees dipping as he took her mouth. The woman's black jacket and camel-colored skirt were circumspect enough for work, yet the scene was anything but. His hands slid down to lift the hem. When he finally touched her between her legs, she moaned, deeply, overcome.

"Christ, I want you so goddamn much."

Only a couple of feet beyond the alcove, Virginia heard more than desire in his voice, more than need for a mere physical joining. She heard his soul in his words.

He lifted the woman and pulled her legs to his waist. Bracing her against the wall, he entered her with a reverent thrust Virginia felt all the way to her womb.

Virginia wanted that feeling, that emotion, a man that needed her that badly. She wanted Brett to need her that badly. With the sliver of light through the curtain, she couldn't see the woman's face, only the man's, filled with something so profound it could only be called love, making the tableau all the more potent. For a moment she *was* that woman and the recipient of all his desire. His words flowed over her, inside her, took her as he took his lover, over and over.

"God, I love you. I'm so fucking in love with you."

After the purely sexual heat in the workout room, those beautiful words were her undoing. Virginia leaned back against the wall, closed her eyes, and pressed her thighs together as an orgasm rolled over her and dragged her under.

BRETT WATCHED AS Virginia came without a touch. It was the most humbling sight he'd ever experienced. He hadn't caused it, wasn't a part of it. Yet he exulted in having found a woman so passionate that her body could take over her mind so completely.

He'd never wanted a woman so badly in his life. Every room she visited, each expression on her face, the subtle, tantalizing changes in her scent and her body, had driven him higher. His cock pounded as if it were an entity all on its own. Demanding. Compelling. Unstoppable.

What had she felt as she watched the couple behind the curtain? He sensed it was far more than a sex act for her, yet he didn't comprehend the *more* of it. He'd thought she needed witnesses to her feminine power, but this was something else entirely. He vowed he would figure it out. That's what this night was all about. Discovering what made Virginia come undone.

Ten feet and a gaggle of guests separated them. Even as he watched, a man approached her. Brett growled low in his throat. Without feeling his feet move, he grabbed the guy's hand just as it reached for Virginia's tight nipple.

"She's mine."

"Sorry, old boy. Thought she was a free agent." The man, somewhere in his mid-thirties, looked pointedly at Brett's white grip on his hand. Brett dropped it as if it were a searing ember. He realized with a little extra pressure, his grip on the man would break bones.

Virginia finally opened her eyes just as her wannabe partner backed away, keeping a wary gaze on Brett.

"Brett?" She blinked twice as if to regain her faculties.

"He was going to touch you without your permission." Yeah, that was his mission, to make sure she was touched only when she wanted to be.

He wanted her now, like this, still dazed from what she'd seen, her body in control rather than her mind. Her pupils were dilated while her lids were slumberous. He wanted to put his lips to the flushed skin of her shoulders, drag her bodice down to give her nipples up to his touch. He wanted to drive his cock so far up inside her that she came with the first thrust.

"Do *I* have your permission?" He held out his hand, waiting.

She trustingly put her hand in his. "Yes."

He needed no more encouragement. He pulled her flush up against his side and wrapped her beneath his arm. She stumbled, he held tight. At the next alcove, he swept aside the curtain. A woman squeaked. Stifling his irritation, he shrugged his shoulders in apology.

He led Virginia to another recess. This time he only moved aside a corner. Occupied. Again. He checked two more curtains.

Need boiled over. "I can't find an empty one, dammit."

"It doesn't matter," Virginia soothed.

"It goddamn matters." He realized how out of control he sounded, like a wild man, and he didn't care. "The next one, don't worry."

At the far end of the hall, he found what he wanted and dragged Virginia inside, yanking the curtain closed behind them. Bending his knees, he skimmed both hands beneath her skirt, slid two fingers inside her with unerring accuracy, then buried his face at her throat. Breathing her in, deeply, he savored the feel of her pussy even as a spurt of frustration burrowed beneath his ribs at the fact that he wasn't the one who'd made her wet.

He pushed her against the paneling. "Do you know how badly I want you?"

He felt her shake her head.

Though still working her beneath the dress, he pulled back. "I could have—" He stopped. He could have what? Killed the guy for touching her? It was extreme, but that's exactly what he wanted to give Virginia. Extreme emotion, a fantasy to fuel their pleasure. "I could have killed him."

Her body soaked his fingers, and her muscles did a rhythmic give and take around them. The musky scent of desire permeated the small alcove. His cock and balls screamed in response.

She leaned in to stroke her tongue over his bottom lip, and he knew he'd said exactly the right thing. Yet the kiss was too gentle, too sweet, when what he needed was to pound her into the wall and consume her totally.

He pulled in a long breath of air, clearing his head, then gradually withdrew from her pussy. He wanted this coupling to be more than a rutting, but he feared he was past that point.

"I'm going to fuck the hell out of you, Virginia."

She cupped his cheeks. "I'd like that."

Like? He'd make sure she more than *liked* it. He pulled her flush against him. "Tell me to fuck you hard. Beg me." He wanted her need to match his.

"Please, Brett, now." Her voice shuddered through a deep breath that set his balls on fire. "I can't wait."

And he lost any modicum of control he had. He didn't recall each separate action, only that finally, finally, her legs were around his waist, and his cock was deep and high. He wanted her so damn badly, his legs trembled and his hands shook.

And yet it wasn't enough. "More. Take me. All of me. Fuck me out of my mind."

Her arms around his neck, she took him, engulfed him, owned

him, whispering, urging him to harder thrusts, faster plunges until he could think only of staying inside her forever. She contracted around him, squeezed, and cried out her pleasure. Pure sensation rocketed from his balls to his cock, stretching out to his limbs and springing back as he exploded within her.

He lost his mind to her, and instead of consuming Virginia with his fire, she consumed him.

SIX

VIRGINIA HAD FALLEN completely into the fantasy her husband created. He'd taken her with fierce desire, then left her, only moments before, with a tender kiss. Her mind and body still reeled under the impact. Brett made her feel as special as that woman in the alcove. He'd touched her with a trembling need that made her come with mind-altering power.

"Do you know how badly I want you?"

Badly enough to threaten a man's life if he touched her. Just as he'd threatened Sven down in the parking garage. Not that Brett meant it; it was part of the illusion of The Sex Club. A great big bite of the pleasure. Virginia had gone up in smoke.

Smoothing her skirt another time, she pushed aside the curtain. A silvered-haired, fiftyish man in black tails awaited her, a tray of champagne empties balanced on his hand.

"I'm to escort you to the bar to meet your gentleman." The

waiter bowed elegantly without losing a single glass on his tray. "If that is your choice."

"Yes, it is." Marrying Brett had been the perfect choice. He knew how to give her the ultimate pleasure and indulge her fantasies. He knew exactly what she wanted to hear.

Her attendant swept a hand out before him. "Then please, follow me this way."

Virginia floated down the hall, the guests parting as if she were in some protective bubble. She paused at the threshold of the salon. A month ago, the night before her wedding, she'd sat in this very bar with Stacy and discussed Brett.

He sure had proven Stacy correct. Brett gave Virginia stability at home and pleasure beyond her wildest dreams at the club. She no longer gave a damn that they somehow failed to create sparks at home. If The Sex Club made his banked fire rage out of control, she'd come here as often as she could.

The waiter left her the moment they both saw Brett.

On the other end of the sofa on which Brett sat, a woman spread her legs and fondled herself. He didn't look, his eyes only for Virginia. Nor did he glance at what so fascinated the lady, a couple engaged in fellatio in the next chair.

Virginia stopped before her husband, the sounds of sex all around them, drifting on the air like a sultry breeze.

"Thirsty?" He handed her a glass of wine.

It was sweet, a tiny bit tart, a dessert wine, and it tantalized her taste buds as much as the taste of him.

"Sit." He indicated his lap with a pat of his hands on his thighs. Despite the power of the orgasm he had in the alcove, his suit pants were full.

Straddling him, she slid forward until he was cradled amid the folds of chiffon. His heart beat against her palm as she settled herself. She tipped the wine. "Do you want some?"

He sipped, but a drop dribbled down his chin because she

hadn't aimed correctly. Virginia bent to lick it up, tasting the sweetness of wine and the salt of his skin, his beard's shadow rough
against her tongue.

"Tell me what you liked the best."

She smiled. "Besides what you did to me in the alcove?"

His gaze unreadable, he ran two hands up each of her thighs beneath the dress. "You were slick before I even touched you. You owe
me every detail of the experience."

She had been wet, though her miniorgasm in the hall had been
nothing compared to the one Brett had wrenched from her. Yet she
wanted to tease him a little. "You said you'd be following. Where
did I go?"

He raised an eyebrow at her test. "The Train Depot first."

"Then do you think it was the train that turned me on?"

She tucked the wineglass against her shoulder as he cupped the
back of her neck and pulled her forward until his lips touched hers.
"Definitely not the train," he whispered.

"It was like watching," she laughed, "a train wreck."

Brett chuckled, then slid his thumbs higher until they rested at
the joining of her legs. "Funny lady." He tongued the pearls at her
throat. "Thank you for wearing my gift."

Virginia shoved her fingers through his hair, pushing his head
back so that he was forced to meet her gaze. "I do love the pearls,
but—"

Brett brushed her lips with his to stop her. "I *will* give you
things, Virginia, and not just for times like these."

"I didn't marry you for your money or for presents."

Which was exactly why he wanted to give her gifts, because she
didn't expect anything. He was in the process of acquiring a very
special gift for her, but it would take a few more days before he
could give her *that* surprise.

"But tonight was special," she finished.

God, yes, it was. The knife edge of want he'd been riding had
been appeased. Though still semihard, he could actually carry on a

sane conversation. He wanted to know the progression of her desire tonight, to isolate each step up the ladder. She liked that he'd been ready to do violence to have her, but the word *like* just wasn't good enough. He wanted her drugged with passion, as she had been standing outside that alcove. He would determine exactly what had driven her to that point.

"Tell me about The Male Room."

She smiled. "It wasn't like any mailroom I've ever seen." Then she crinkled her nose. "I peeked, so that counted."

She'd closed the door so quickly that Brett knew she couldn't have taken full stock of the activities. For a man, there was something uniquely erotic about watching two women together, the gentle caresses, the total immersion in the other's pleasure. He didn't think the thought process worked the same for a woman watching men. Certainly not for Virginia.

He ran a finger along the edge of her pussy without delving to the heat and wet he knew he'd find within. "Yes, it counted. Tell me about the last room."

"It was an interesting workout technique."

He'd imagined taking her up against the wall as she shuddered and panted over the bench press exhibition.

He slipped between her folds, but only for a moment. "You're very wet. Again. Do I take it that excited you the most?" He was sure it hadn't been the crucial moment.

She bit her lip but didn't answer.

He leaned forward to whisper in her ear while his hand gently stroked along the seam of her pussy lips. "I watched you up against that wall while he ate her. Your fingers were clenched in your skirt. You wanted to touch yourself. Why didn't you?" He pulled back to see her reaction.

Her skin was flushed, and the straps of her gown had slipped off her shoulders. Her neat twist had loosened, and tendrils of golden hair caressed her nape. A sigh of breath fell from her parted lips just before she licked them. He wanted to make her come again, wanted to seduce the orgasm out of her with words and soft caresses instead of slamming her up against a wall.

Though that had been particularly satisfying.

"You thought about sitting with your sweet pussy above me."

As if she'd lost her voice, she answered him with nod.

He glided across her clitoris, then again, and finally in a slow circle around it. Her pussy contracted, a droplet of dew melting against his finger.

"Why is it different than before?"

She tilted her head. "Before?" she asked in a whisper.

"At home." He'd gone down on her, she'd enjoyed it, but she hadn't been like this.

"I don't know."

"You know, Virginia. And you will tell me." He rubbed her clit full on.

She gasped and closed her eyes. "This is fantasy. At home, you're—" She bit her lip. "It's not the same at home."

Her answer validated what he surmised. Virginia's pleasure spiked at the club. She needed the double life to excite her.

Entering her, one digit only, he tested her wetness and heat, then slid back out to take long swipes across the bead of her clit. Her nails dug into his suit jacket, and she leaned closer until his lips brushed the bare flesh above her bodice.

"The couple in the alcove made you the hottest."

"Yes." The single word hissed on her out breath.

Around them a hush had fallen as if everyone waited to see if they'd get another show. His hand worked beneath the chiffon, invisible to prying eyes, yet the flush on her skin and the gentle rock of her hips told their audience everything.

"Why?" *Tell me, and I'll give it to you.*

"It was so private," she murmured, "just the two of them."

"Liar," he whispered, "it was more than that."

She'd masturbated in a cubicle with eight windows. It wasn't privacy that turned her on. He also knew he was skating onto dangerous ice here, his cock rising to a needy ache again. He wanted the taste of her on his tongue, wanted to make her come screaming, to bury himself inside her all over again. But more than the swift power of release, he needed to know what had made Virginia come without a touch.

She started to pant, and he knew she was close. Another moment, she'd tip over the edge, and he wanted her to, needed her to gush all over his fingers, take her pleasure from him just as she took the pearls around her throat.

He clasped his arm around her back, hitched her closer, and nipped her throat. "Tell me, Virginia. Now."

She clung and rocked, her eyes squeezed tight.

"Tell me, dammit." He shoved two fingers in her and pumped.

Her words burst out as if he'd wrenched them from her. "I wanted—" She gulped a breath of air, then finished her thought. "I wanted someone to do that to me. Just like that."

And then she came, her grip so tight around his neck he saw spots. All he could do was hang on with both arms. Her hair fell over his hands and face, the fruity scent of shampoo mixing with the heady aroma of her come. She came so hard, he felt her tears at his ear and her warm breath blow through his hair.

He sat utterly still while his wife shuddered in his arms. Something inside him cracked wide open, and revelation slid deep into the fissure. He didn't want anyone else to make Virginia experience what she'd felt outside that alcove.

He wanted to be the only one.

VIRGINIA WAS TOO exhausted to adequately control her car. They paid an attendant to bring it in the morning. She stretched and curled up on the seat, then opened her eyes a slit to watch him drive. He was magnificent. He'd made her so damn hot in front of all those people. The tactile memories still rode her flesh. She'd lost her faculties, only barely keeping herself from blurting out that she wanted Brett to take her as the man in the alcove had taken his lover. Even in her aroused state, she couldn't put that pressure on Brett or her marriage, not even on herself. Not that it mattered what she actually said—his fingers had been buried so deep and she'd been so high, she couldn't recall her exact words—Brett had given her everything she needed. A fantasy beyond anything she could have imagined.

She closed her eyes and didn't remember another thing until they got home. He must have carried her from the car, because she came to herself already in the bedroom. Her juices and Brett's semen covered her thighs, and she knew she should take a shower. But she didn't care. She simply kicked off her shoes and let her clothing slither to the carpet. Finally, naked except for the pearls at her throat, she crawled beneath the sheets.

She was vaguely aware of Brett stroking her hair a moment, then he was gone. Drifting, drifting, she was almost asleep when she felt him crawl beneath the covers beside her.

He pulled her into his arms. Their bare flesh melded. She nuzzled against his throat.

"Thank you," she whispered. And knew no more except the pleasure of his arms.

"I WANTED SOMEONE to do that to me."

Someone? Anyone? Shit. Hours later, Brett's revelation had turned to jealousy. It was almost laughable. He'd never before doubted his technique, but facts were facts. He didn't make her scream at home. Only at the club. And she would have screamed for someone, *anyone* else, too. Fuck.

The lines were blurred. He'd told her they'd have two separate lives, the club, and life as Mr. and Mrs. Branoff. Only his damned emotions didn't stop when he drove away from the underground garage. They played with his mind. When he crawled naked into bed beside her, he couldn't stop himself from pulling her close. When he kissed her lips and heard her sleepy murmur, he didn't let her go, didn't roll to his side or turn his back.

For the first time, Virginia fell asleep in his arms, and it felt so damn good, he ached deep in his marrow.

Something had changed tonight, and he didn't know how or why. He wasn't a jealous or possessive man, but in the space of one evening, he'd become irrevocably obsessed with his wife.

He wasn't sure yet whether that was good. Or bad.

VIRGINIA WAS A marvel. Four days after their trip to The Sex Club, Brett observed her from his post just inside their living room archway. He'd given her short notice for the party that started out at five couples and ended up a group of twenty-one, yet not a last-minute change rattled her. She'd rearranged the furniture to allow for mingling, and through the arch into the dining room, the table was already set for dinner. The crystal sparkled, and the silver shone. A red wine spill on the white carpet was sopped up with a smile, and a canapé upended on the arm of the sofa was brushed aside. She was unflappable. Marrying her was the best decision of his life. She was everything he could ask for: smart, elegant, organized, and hot as Hades beneath the chic persona.

Only problem? He regretted his damn words of their wedding night: *"Indulge yourself."* He was a fucking idiot. His words had tacitly given her the freedom to take another man. He hadn't determined yet how to tell her he'd changed his mind without revealing he was now obsessed with her. He wasn't yet ready to put that realization into spoken words.

Virginia moved among their guests with the aplomb of royalty born to the duty. She'd donned the same peach silk suit she'd worn to The Sex Club the night before their wedding, and the pearls he'd given her on Friday. There were enticing memories in every article gracing her figure. His cock had been hard since the moment she'd stepped out of the bedroom, and it was goddamn embarrassing having to keep his suit jacket buttoned to hide it.

"I congratulate you."

A man his own age, Wilson Garrett had eyes like a hawk and the savvy of years spent making multimillion dollar deals. He was Brett's biggest customer. Prematurely gray hair gave him a distinguished air, but his gaze held the sharpness of a predator. He offered a glass of champagne, and Brett realized his own hands were empty.

He took the drink and didn't bother to pretend that Virginia wasn't the topic of their conversation. "Thank you. She's made me the happiest of men."

Wilson held his drink aloft in a toast. "We should all strive to bring such charming domesticity into our lives."

"You don't know the half of it," Brett murmured. What was she wearing beneath the skirt? He imagined her hot and wet and ready for anything the moment the door closed on their last guest. And then he realized the possible sexual connotation of his comment to Wilson. What the hell was he thinking? Well, that was obvious, but he needed to get control of himself.

The dinner party was about business, and business was what he would conduct. "Did you receive the quote for the BK17?"

"We're meeting tomorrow at ten to discuss it, remember?"

Shit. His wits were rapidly declining. "Of course."

"After meeting your lovely wife," Wilson's gaze never left Virginia, "I can understand how you might be . . . distracted."

Wilson didn't generally have an oily voice, but there was something definitely oily in his slight pause and the trail of his gaze over Virginia's form. As if he, too, were imagining what lay beneath the peach suit. Something itched between Brett's shoulder blades, and he had the overpowering urge to drag his best customer out into the marble entry and beat his face in.

He'd lost his mind. Wilson Garrett was a gentleman of the highest order.

Virginia herself saved him from making a complete spectacle.

"What are you two doing hiding over here? Business will have to wait until tomorrow."

Wilson set his drink down on a table, one of the extras Virginia had provided, and clasped her hand in both of his. "I was congratulating your husband on his latest merger."

Her eyebrow rose in a perfect arc, and she regarded him with a warm smile. "Which merger would that be?"

"Your marriage, of course. And I'm extremely envious."

"You're too kind," she murmured.

"I'm simply appreciating the change in your usually imperturbable husband."

Wilson didn't let go of her hand even as Virginia glanced briefly at Brett and back to Wilson. Then the two of them shared . . . a look. He could almost hear Virginia's breath pick up its pace, a pulse beat at her throat, and the sudden peak of her nipples showed clearly against the silk.

That bastard Wilson Garrett was hitting on his wife. And she liked it. Brett's hands clenched at his sides.

"Wilson, we need you to settle this argument."

The male voice barely penetrated the fog in Brett's mind, nor did Wilson's words seem particularly clear as he backed off to answer the summons. One half of Brett's brain applauded the interruption before he planted his fist in his best customer's nose, while the other half saw only Virginia's hardened nipples beneath the blanket of silk.

"Virginia. I need to talk to you."

"Of course, dear."

Dear? "Privately."

Then he took possession of her hand, the one Wilson Garrett seemed obsessed with, and pulled her into the hall. He wanted to shove her up against the wall, raise her stylish skirt, and ram himself inside her, showing her whose woman she was. He was thinking like an ass, and he didn't give a damn. He tugged her up the stairs, down the hall, and into their bedroom, closing the door behind them. Then he stalked her until she was forced back up against the wood. She grabbed the handle to steady herself.

Her eyes widened. "Brett, what's the matter?"

He undid his suit jacket, ripped it from his shoulders to toss behind him, then pressed her to the door with his body.

"I've been thinking about doing this all night." He shoved his hand down between the lapels of her jacket, tearing a button loose. "And I'm going to have what I want, Virginia." He took her nipple between his thumb and forefinger.

She hissed in reaction.

"I thought about dragging you down in the middle of the living room carpet and doing this in front of all of them." He bent and sucked the turgid point of her nipple into his mouth. She squirmed against him.

He pulled back, skimming his hands along her arms. "You'd have liked it, too." It would have shown Garrett exactly who she belonged to in no uncertain terms. He shook her lightly. "Tell me you would have liked it."

Her eyes searched his face. "There'd be consequences."

"Fuck the consequences." He leaned in, letting his breath bathe her skin. "You would have loved it."

Her nostrils flared, and he knew the answer. He'd tasted it in her hot, hard nipples. But she didn't capitulate; instead, she pushed at his shoulders. "We can't do this now."

"I'll have this *now*." He took her mouth and ate off her lipstick, then invaded with his tongue. She didn't fight, she simply allowed, and he couldn't stand her nonparticipation. He wanted her in the act completely.

"And I'll take *this*." He pulled up her skirt, hearing the pop of several stitches. And then his hand was between her legs, his fingers tracing the folds of her bare pussy. No panties. Ah God. She was hot, her thighs already wet with her juices.

"It's made me fucking crazy all night wondering what you were wearing under this skirt." He breathed against her lips. "I should have bent you over the sofa and fucked you from behind. My cock sliding deep inside you for everyone to see." He held her chin in his hand. "And you'd scream for every inch."

"Brett." Her pupils had dilated to the point of obscuring the blue of her eyes. This time, she didn't deny him completely. "We can't stay up here too long."

He buried his lips against her throat and sucked her skin. Hard. Enough to mark her. She was his, no one else's. "We'll stay as long as it takes for me to have what I want." He sucked off the last traces of her lipstick, marking her that way, too. "And it's going to take a very long sweet fucking time."

She put two hands to his face and forced him to look at her. "This *is* crazy, Brett."

"You don't know the half of it." Exactly what he'd said to that bastard Garrett. He dragged in a breath and slammed her up against the door. "Fuck me, Virginia. I'm gonna go nuts if you don't. And you really don't want to see what I'm capable of then."

SEVEN

BRETT HAD SUCH a look on his face. Need. Desperation. All for want of her. This was her fantasy, to be desired so badly, a man would risk anything. It was more than physical, it was an emotion that touched her core desires. Brett made her burn, set her skin on fire, lit an inferno in her belly.

He'd fantasized about taking her in front of their guests. It rang with primal need.

It was what she'd dreamed of as she'd donned thigh-high stockings, forsaking panties. An illusion she'd wanted to create, walking amid his guests as the perfect hostess yet a burning woman beneath the surface. When she'd dressed, it had been a game. When Wilson Garrett congratulated her on perturbing her imperturbable husband, it had become something much more. With one glance at Brett, she'd felt her body heat and her nipples peak to aching, needy points. Something dark, seething, and delicious had been in his gaze.

One little push, and he very well might have fucked her in front of their guests. *That* was how badly he wanted her. He was on the edge of control.

He shook her lightly, bending slightly so he could see her at eye level. "Now," he whispered, just a breath of air, "don't make me wait. Or I'll just take what I need."

What woman could resist this level of desire? *Just this once,* she told herself. With their party going on downstairs, it *was* crazy, extreme, even stupid. *Just this time, never again,* she promised. They were supposed to keep this kind of thing limited to The Sex Club. But she had to have it now, because he might never be like this again, not her controlled, imperturbable husband.

"Yes. Now."

That was all she said, and he turned into an animal. At the club, he'd taken her with the need of a man teased for a few hours. Tonight, he was a wild beast.

He grabbed her chin and took her mouth, devouring her with more than just his lips and tongue, devouring her with his unleashed passion. She clutched his arms and hung on for the incredible ride, barely able to keep up as he yanked her skirt above her hips. He was all over her, nipping her lip, biting her throat, squeezing her buttocks. Then he slipped down the crease of her ass to push one finger inside her wet core, the underside of his knuckle pressing the spot between her pussy and anus. He groaned as if it weren't enough for him, and came at her from the front with his other hand, sliding another finger inside and working her clitoris with his palm. The sensations burned her.

"Undo my pants."

She gasped as he hit an acutely receptive spot. "I can't when you're doing that."

"You can do whatever I want you to." He backed off her clit to caress between her buttocks, using her own moisture to slide a fraction inside and create a blaze with a slow, gentle massage. She didn't do rear entry, but somehow he made it incredibly sensual. "And do it now, Virginia."

She loved the command in his voice. Fumbling with his buckle and zipper, she pulled his cock out. He was already dripping for her, his crown purple with need. She bore down on his finger and stroked his cock at the same time, squeezing from his base and back up again. Brett groaned, and another droplet of come glazed his tip.

"You're killing me," he uttered in a deep growl. "Stop playing and spread your legs for me."

His eyes flashed, and he grinned, a teeth-baring, feral, I-will-consume-you grin. Every thought went out of her head as he lifted her, spread her legs to rub her pussy along his cock, and set off sparks in her clitoris. She locked her feet behind his butt. His head falling back in ecstasy, a low rumble pushed its way past his clenched teeth. She sucked in a breath at the sheer pleasure, the immense power in his need.

He bent his knees and rocked against her, sliding in her moisture. His hot, dark gaze on her turned her insides to butter.

"You make me fucking crazy." He slammed into her and closed his eyes, a deep groan rising from his belly.

He'd done a complete one eighty from the controlled seducer of their wedding night. Her mind reeled. If this was a fantasy he wanted to give her, she'd grab onto it with both hands and never let go.

"I'm going to make you come. Make you scream."

He thrust into her with a hard, high stroke, pumped fast and deep, and she lost her senses. The first orgasm rolled over her without a single preliminary warning. Her pussy contracted around him, drenched him with her desire, and he took her cries into his mouth.

He tucked his lips to her neck and demanded, "Again. Do it again."

"Please, please, please." He didn't have to tell her to beg. The plea simply fell from her lips.

He started a relentless rhythm, his cock stroking deep, his body rasping against her clitoris. She pushed back against the door, bracing herself for each thrust. Clutching her bottom, he used his fingers to spread her, taking his penetration deeper, higher. She tore at her jacket, pulling the lapels apart to pinch her nipples. A streak of lightning shot down to their joining, and she blasted off yet again just as she felt him throb and tighten inside her, filling her with his need, his desire, his very essence.

THEY WERE ON the carpet, a tangle of limbs, the skin of her thighs soft under the stroke of his fingers. Leaning with a shoulder against the door, Brett was still encased in her body, steeped in her scent, and his cock gave a final throb.

He'd lost his mind inside her. What the hell had he been thinking? Uncontrollable jealousy and need. Feeling, not thinking at all. But Jesus, it was so fucking good, he'd do it again in a heartbeat.

"Do you think anyone heard?" she whispered, her breath warm on his throat, her body snug where she'd collapsed atop him.

"I don't care." He'd pounded her against the door, the wood beating in the frame and shouted her name in that seemingly unending moment of pure frenzy. He'd felt her keen of pleasure pulsing in his gonads.

She pulled back and put a hand to her hair. "I must look a fright."

The neat knot had fallen, her blond locks frothing about her face and shoulders. Mascara smudges darkened the skin beneath her eyes. Her lips were a kissed-to-oblivion cherry despite the lack of lipstick, and a hickey marred the flesh of her throat. The tantalizing perfume of her sex hazed his mind. She looked so gorgeously loved and pleasured, her blue eyes a dark shade of midnight desire.

"You look perfect," he murmured. *Never more so.*

Would everyone know what they'd been doing? Hell, yes. Without a doubt, even if by some miracle the sounds of their lovemaking hadn't made it down the stairs. She looked utterly pleasured. He

would have used the word debauched, but there was nothing debauched about Virginia. She was a lady.

She eased back farther still, his cock falling from her body, and
he felt the loss in his chest.

"We need to change," she said but made no move to do so.

Her suit was wrinkled beyond redemption, and a button had
torn loose. Her nipples were still ripe buds begging for his lips. He
reached out, dragging his pinkies across the peaks as he pulled the
lapels of her suit closed.

She looked down. His pants bore the traces of her orgasms, and
dabs of her lipstick were stark against the white of his dress shirt.
For the life of him, he couldn't remember how it had gotten there.

She put a hand on his chest and leaned in. Her lips were sweet,
her tongue tracing his mouth, then delving inside.

"Thank you," she whispered against his lips.

He'd just dragged her up the stairs in full view of all his guests,
then fucked the hell out of her in a frenzy. And she was thanking
him? Warmth spread through his chest. He should be thanking her.
It had been beyond description.

She took his chin between her thumb and fingers. "But maybe
the club is a better place for that kind of thing than the middle of a
dinner party. There's so much more—" she paused, tipping her
head to one side, then the other "—freedom at The Sex Club. You
do want me to indulge myself without inhibition, don't you?"

What was she saying? That she didn't want sex at home, only at
the club? Or that she wanted the freedom to indulge herself with
any man she chose, and she'd get that at the club? That subtle exchange with Wilson Garrett leaped to his mind. He didn't give a
damn what she meant. Like hell he'd let Garrett or anyone else
touch her. Ever.

But in the only remaining sane brain cell he had, he knew his actions had compromised her reputation and his business principles.
His jealousy had taken a pleasant exchange involving his best cus-

tomer, Wilson Garrett, and turned it into something improper, imbuing the most polite of smiles with sexual innuendo.

He needed to work on retaining at least a modicum of control for the remainder of the evening. After all, there was business. And *then* there was pleasure.

NO ONE HAD noticed a thing. Virginia explained her change of attire, choosing a high-necked blouse that covered his mark, by saying she'd spilled red wine on her jacket. And no one batted an eyelash. Brett had changed also, into a suit of the same hue as the one he'd been wearing. And no one noticed.

Brett had brought the two halves of their double life together, and there hadn't been a single consequence. Best not to tempt the fates again, though. She didn't want to expect that kind of intensity at home, in case she didn't get it.

In a few minutes, she'd call her guests for dinner. Brett was now mingling, seemingly involved in important discussion with . . . Harris? She'd forgotten the man's name, but who could blame her? Brett had blown out a few of her fuses, and it would take time to recover. She smiled. Softly. Just a lifting of her lips that only she felt but no one else would see.

It was all so delicious, her body still warm and moist. She was pleased with herself. She was pleased with him. They'd gotten away with it, and the knowledge beat an exhilarating pulse between her legs. Still, they had The Sex Club. It was a more suitable place to indulge themselves.

She couldn't wait for his next invitation to pleasure.

TWO MORNINGS LATER, Brett stood in front of the mirror. He'd nicked himself shaving, a spot of blood welling on his chin.

Three facts. Number one: A marriage both he and Virginia intended to be safe, comfortable, and controlled now had control of him. And, after due consideration, he'd decided he liked it that way. A little jealousy on his part had driven Virginia to new heights. Hell, she'd let him fuck her in their bedroom with their guests downstairs. What more could he ask for?

Which brought him to fact two. He could ask for a lot. He wanted that uninhibited woman in his bed every night. And he didn't want her thinking she could wander off at The Sex Club and take anyone she wanted any time she wanted.

"I wanted someone to do that to me."

Fact number three. Virginia was going to learn that *someone* was him. She needed a lesson. And he was so going to enjoy giving it to her. He'd decided it would be a dual message. He'd show her how utterly desirable she was, wanted by a horde of men. By him most of all. Then he'd show her that she belonged to him. Him alone. And she'd never need another.

Christ. He knew in ways he sounded like his jealous, possessive ex-wife. Yet he was man enough to admit that calm serenity, and hot, hot sex made for a potent mixture he now craved. As long as he got Virginia to accept that she craved the erotic blend, too, jealousy on his part could do no harm. It was when goals were diametrically opposed that a problem arose.

Or was he just rationalizing the new rules he wanted to lay down for their marriage? He risked ruining a damn good thing if she said no.

He stared at his reflection in the mirror, then let a smile slowly rise. "She's not going to say no." He wouldn't let her.

"Did you say something, honey?" Virginia called from the bedroom.

"Just talking to myself, darling."

Darling, honey. They'd taken to pet names. She'd seemed none the worse for his debauchery the night of the party. Though she'd fallen asleep on the couch last night while they were watching TV. He'd tasked her with a grueling social schedule, not to mention that she still refused to give up her day job. So he'd let her sleep, though his cock and balls screamed for her touch.

He smiled once more into the mirror. Tonight, there would be no sleep for either of them.

She poked her head into the bathroom. "You're not even done shaving."

"I'm running late. Go on without me." He had plans to set in motion before he left for the office.

"You're bleeding."

"It's a scratch." He dabbed at the nick.

She grabbed the tissue from his hand before he even realized she entered the bathroom. "You silly man."

She finished the dabbing, then kissed him on the chin. Her perfume, neither floral nor fruity but something more exotic and musky, filled his head.

"See you tonight," she whispered, then left him with a tap-tap of her heels on the tile floor and the intoxication of her scent. The exchange between them, like sweet love play, flipped his heart over. He craved this new tenderness between them as much as he craved the heated, overpowering sexual encounters.

With Virginia, he wanted it all.

He followed to the head of the stairs, making sure she was gone, then headed back into the bedroom. Inside her closet, he rummaged. He found what he wanted, what made him hot, his cock hardening in his briefs, and laid the dress out on the bed. He located black shoes on the floor of her closet and set those out, too. Finally he scribbled a note, and topped it with an invitation he'd had since Friday.

Then he went to his office to make some calls and set his plan in motion.

Tonight at The Sex Club, he would give her what she wanted. Men that wanted her badly. Lots of men. But only one man would get the pleasure of having her. Her husband. And no one else.

* * *

BRETT HADN'T BEEN in the condo when Virginia got home from work. Instead, he'd left her an envelope, a note telling her to meet him at nine attired in the dress she'd worn on their first date. It was a simple black evening dress. She was surprised and touched he remembered. And hot beyond belief thinking about what he had planned for her this time.

She handed her invitation to the same efficient blond hostess who'd greeted them the night of her bachelorette party. "Ah. We've been expecting you. Your gentleman requests that you allow the contessa to attend you in your preparations."

This was different. And intriguing. The contessa, a woman of about her own age draped in yards of white, led Virginia to an antechamber off the main hall. The Sex Club had more hidden rooms than a Halloween funhouse. This one was outfitted like a lady's boudoir, with vanity, striped chairs, and a small dais in the middle. With a flourish of her hand, the contessa bade Virginia to stand on it.

Moving behind her, the lady tugged on the zipper of her dress. "First, we shall remove your clothing," she said with an old-world accent.

Warm air rushed down her back, then the woman's fingertips slid the fabric down her arms and over her hips. Virginia was naked beneath. Brett hadn't left her any underwear at all. Next, she was divested of her shoes. It was the oddest feeling being exposed by another woman. Sensual and erotic, yet devoid of desire.

With a whisper of slippers across the carpet, the woman approached the vanity, opening a flat velvet case to reveal the sparkle of diamonds. "He requests you wear his special gifts."

Virginia knew she'd been selfish in not allowing Brett to buy her presents. Gift-giving was as much for the giver as for the recipient. She wouldn't disappoint him again.

Standing behind her, the contessa fit a belly chain to her waist, its diamonds flashing in the room's lamps. The gold chain warmed against her skin. She'd never worn such a thing, but it made her feel sexy, decadent. Circling her, the woman went down on one knee and slipped on matching anklets. From a pocket in her voluminous white robe, she withdrew a small vial.

"Wet your fingers and pinch your nipples."

Virginia blinked. The lady waited, a slight curve to her crimson lips and a crinkle of her porcelain skin at the corner of her eyes.

With the contessa's gaze on her, Virginia slid one index finger in her mouth, then tweaked each nipple until they rose to peaks. Tipping the vial onto a finger, her attendant smoothed an exotic perfume, something musky and pagan, around each of Virginia's nipples and down between her breasts. They started to heat and extend, and she was again assailed by an almost uncomfortable rush of sensuality.

Taking Virginia's hand in hers, the woman tipped the vial once more. "Rub it on your woman parts." Even her language was old-fashioned, in keeping with the ceremonial atmosphere of . . . well, the anointing. That's how Virginia thought of it. She was being anointed for her lover.

Keeping her gaze warily on the lady, Virginia slipped her finger between her legs and caressed her clitoris, swabbing it with the exotic scent. There, too, she began to heat and pulse. "What is it?"

"The scent your gentleman wishes you to wear." Then, with a tap of her fingers, she bade Virginia to turn and see herself in the mirror.

"You are beautiful. Your gentleman will be very pleased."

It felt terribly erotic to be clothed only in Brett's gifts, her breasts and clitoris buzzing with the application of that secret potion, and the woman's eyes on her. Black velvet was then draped over her shoulders, a long cloak falling to within an inch of the carpet, and her hair loosened to cascade around her neck and shoulders. Lastly, the woman fitted a blindfold over her eyes.

When Virginia stepped down, the tiny gold bells on the anklets tinkled, and the carpet was soft against her bare feet.

"Perfect. We are ready." Low and melodic, the contessa's voice whispered against her hair.

With a gentle hand on Virginia's arm, the lady then led her from the room. Virginia felt the sudden hush of voices. The only sound was the shush of the contessa's slippers across the cold marble of the entry hall and the tinkling of the ankle bells. Her cloak was held away from her so she wouldn't trip on it as she climbed the stairs, and the rush of air told her she was exposed to the eyes of the hushed crowd. The blindfold heightened her other senses, revealing soft whispers, the exotic scent of perfume, the caress of velvet on her heated nipples, and the cool slide of diamonds against her skin. Her body trembled in anticipation, and her mind whirled on what Brett's surprise would be.

The man was a magician. *Her* magician.

EIGHT

VIRGINIA COUNTED EVERY turn, and the long parade ended after they'd climbed three flights. The contessa knocked, then her hand dropped from Virginia's arm, and her white robe rustled as she slipped away. The door opened, and Virginia scented him, part expensive cologne, part hungry male, and all Brett. There were other scents, too, the commingling of spices and mouthwatering ingredients, laced with a rash of feminine perfumes. Champagne sizzled, ice cubes chinked, voices murmured, and beneath it all lay the hum of sexual energy. A light laugh to her right, a sigh from the back, a low groan in a corner.

The blindfold added an exciting dimension. She felt him circle her, inhaling deeply. "You smell like hot nights, exotic flowers, and desire." He exhaled. "Perfect."

The oil she'd anointed herself with sizzled, her clitoris and nipples plump, extended, achy, and eager for his touch.

Brett reached beneath the cloak, took her hand, and drew her into the room. With the lack of echo, she assumed it was relatively small. Hardwood, then a thick rug beneath her feet, and after six steps he halted.

"Do you like my gifts?" he whispered against her ear with a tantalizing mixture of toothpaste, champagne, and heat.

"I love each piece. Thank you."

"I have another present. Its diamonds match the ones you're wearing." He smoothed her hair back over her shoulders, undid the cloak's tie at her neck, and let the velvet fall to the floor. Warm air caressed her naked body, and a low murmur rose in front of her. She couldn't distinguish voices or how many people, but just imagining hungry eyes on her brought a flow of moisture to her center and a rush of heat to her thighs.

Brett shaped something with the feel of leather around her throat, fastened it at her nape, then tested the fit with one finger. A choker or collar, tight but not too tight. He tugged lightly on the choker, his knuckles grazing her skin. The chink of metal on metal filled the room, then a weight pulled on the collar, and something cool and smooth fell between her breasts and across her abdomen. Next he encircled her lower arms with what felt like long metal cuffs. She had no doubt he was manacling her wrists. He stepped away, more sounds, clink, clank. Her mind spun trying to determine what he was doing.

"Does anything hurt?" he asked, returning once more to her side, his body's heat searing her even through his layers of clothing.

"No." It felt . . . incredibly erotic. The weight at her throat, the feel of warming metal caressing chest and belly and binding her wrists. She tested. She could move her hands only perhaps a foot apart, the attached chain or whatever it was, slithering across her breasts. The teasing heat on her nipples and clitoris had retreated, but stimulated, her body manufactured its own warmth now, its own erotic pulse beat.

Then he stepped behind her and tugged the tie on her blindfold, pulling it away from her eyes.

The intimate party gathered all around her resembled her dinner affair of two nights ago, with couples dressed in evening wear. Two waiters circled the room providing drinks and offering hors d'oeuvres. Side tables interspersed sofas and armchairs, with lamps giving off a warm illumination. The ubiquitous candy dishes of colored condoms were placed strategically.

Virginia counted five couples. Wedding rings graced the hands she could see. Three couples snuggled individually on the sofas, a woman sat on the edge of her husband's armchair, and a dark-haired man stood by a table, his arm curled beneath his blond wife's breasts as she nestled back against his chest. All mid-thirties to mid-forties, pretty and handsome in very ordinary ways, nothing spectacular but that the group as a whole dressed up nicely. The men, handsome and fit, were boldly assessing, while the women ranged from envious to hungry for the show.

Her husband had manacled her naked in the center of the room, wearing only a collar, a diamond belly chain, and matching anklets, not to mention the little bells that chimed every time she moved. He'd fastened six-inch-long gold arm bands above her wrists, the detailing in the metalwork breathtaking. The individual bracelets were attached by a chain of the same braided gold as the one at her throat. A leash of sorts, it ran from her choker, through a loop in the arm band chain to a sturdy brass post resembling an old-fashioned horse hitch.

Her body liquefied, dampening her thighs, and she trembled, delicious shivers running down her spine. What on earth did he have planned this time? She was weak-kneed with anticipation.

Brett's dark gaze surveyed her beaded nipples, the flush heating her skin, and the quickened pace of her breath, then he raised her confined hands to his lips. "Ladies and gentlemen, my wife, Regina." He used her club name.

Then he tipped a glass of champagne against her lips. "Drink," he urged. She sipped, then he swooped in to lick the sweetness from her mouth. His semikiss sent heat shimmering through her belly, and a tingle tangoed between her legs.

"More," he ordered, and this time she took two long swallows, the sparkling wine fizzling in her throat and immediately going to her head.

He took in her wide eyes and leaned close to whisper, "Enjoy. This is all for you." His finger trailed her bare arm as he pulled away, a half smile on his lips. Then he turned to his audience. "Gentlemen, consider your bids carefully. My wife is a prize like no other. And you only get one chance."

Bids? She was the prize? He couldn't possibly mean it. This wasn't the surprise she'd been anticipating, not at all. His face was unreadable, his voice calm and controlled. She looked at him. He wasn't the man who'd begged her to fuck him up in their bedroom. And he certainly wasn't the man she'd kissed good-bye on the cheek this morning.

"What about their wives?" Surely the wives would put a stop to it.

"That was one of the questions during my interview process. A wife who desired watching her husband fuck another woman."

He'd *interviewed* these people? Oh my God. "What were the other questions?" She was terrified to think.

"They had to get a hard-on looking at your photograph." One eyebrow rose. "Not a *naked* photograph, darling. But then none of them needed to see you naked." He tapped her nose and whispered, "All that passion you exude shows in the eyes." He pulled back and raised his voice. "I feel the bidding is going quite high to get a piece of your ass, my love."

"They're going to make bids to see who fucks me?" *Please don't do this to me.*

He grinned like a feral animal. "Yes."

"And you're going to watch?"

"Hell, yes."

Another thought punched her, one worse than the idea of Brett giving her to another man. "Do you get the winner's wife?"

"That part's up to you." He covered her mouth before she could answer. "Tell me—" he arched a brow "—later."

Now or later, she wasn't going to let him so much as touch another woman. And she didn't want any of his assembled bidders. She wanted only him.

"Why are you doing this?" She felt all her fear seeping through the question.

The night of the cocktail party had been glorious. She'd never felt so desired. How could he take it all away now?

Circling her, he came up behind, pulling her against him, the hard ridge of his cock nestling along her spine. Turning her face, he kissed her, openmouthed, then licked the seam of her lips before drawing back. "Trust me," he whispered.

Trust him to what? Provide the latest erotic thrill in a marriage that, for being so short in duration, had provided almost more thrills that she could cope with? She wasn't sure she could cope with this one. Yet . . .

"Trust me." He'd given her more in their short marriage than she'd ever expected. Ever hoped for. He'd amazed her, delighted her, made her tremble. And he hadn't once disappointed her. Each new surprise was infinitely better than the last. He seemed to know what she wanted, what she needed. Always. His demands were as much give as they were take. With this night, he sought to provide something she craved. She could only hope he understood what she *didn't* want as much as what she did.

"Trust me." And she realized those two words said *everything*. He did understand. Perfectly. With a slight curving of her mouth, she gave herself over to him completely.

He swiped his tongue along her cheek in a gesture of ownership. "Show the bidders your wares, darling." He cupped her breasts, plumping them for her spectators, flicking the nipples until they peaked, so hard it was almost painful yet wholly delicious.

Flattening his palm against her chest, he arched her, then slid a hand down her belly, skimming the chain at her waist, and delved into her pussy. She gasped, the scent of her own arousal rising, clouding her senses. Or perhaps intensifying them. His finger felt unbearably hot, extreme, overwhelming. She melted into the pleasure of his touch and all those eyes on her.

"You're wet. Spread your legs. Show them your hot pussy." With a knee, he parted her thighs and braced her against him. "I want them to see what a juicy piece you are. How much you love my touch." He circled her clit. Her legs trembled, and he held her up. "Open your eyes. Watch how you excite them."

His voice was coarsely demanding. She didn't even consider disobeying.

The dark-haired man slid his palm down the center of his wife's dress, caressing her between the legs in conscious or unconscious imitation of Brett's ministrations. The woman moaned, wound her arm back around his neck, and rotated her hips. On the couch, another man unzipped his pants and forced his companion's mouth to his cock.

Brett pushed a finger inside her, and Virginia rose on her toes to allow him the deepest penetration. Her vision swam, her head dizzied, the scent of sex and desire perfuming the very air she breathed. Like an aphrodisiac, it spiked her arousal higher. She started to pant.

"They see what a perfect fuck you're going to make." Then his hand was gone as he reached around to take the leash attached to her collar and forced her to the carpet. "Hands and knees," he murmured, his voice harsh with his own need. "Spread wide. I want them to see how creamy you are."

The manacles were too close to allow her to comfortably rest on her palms, so she leaned on her elbows, her ass high, her legs spread. Brett took advantage of her position to come at her from the rear and slip a finger along the folds of her pussy. The first contact with her clitoris shot a bolt of need straight up to her womb. She pushed back on him, trying to fuck his finger.

It was almost surreal. Efficient, poised Virginia Branoff, naked and spread doggie-style on the carpet, undulating as if she were begging to be fucked in front of a small crowd. She'd have laughed if she wasn't already on fire inside.

A stocky figure rose from a couch, pulling his cock free of his slacks. Slowly stroking, he advanced. Brett took one step back, only one. The man circled her. On the sofa he'd vacated, another man lay back and pulled a red-clad woman on top, raising her dress and impaling her in one swift movement.

"Does she suck?" the stocky guy asked. Virginia felt his gaze on her mouth as he pumped himself, faster, the tip of his cock engorged. If she could have raised her eyes to see his face, judge the handsomeness of it, she would have. But all she could see was that cock and the swift movements of his hand.

"She loves the taste of come in her mouth." Brett's voice, low, guttural. She wanted to taste his come right now. Pulling up on the chain, he forced her to look at him. "And she will do anything and everything the winner tells her to do."

Anything? Everything? "*Trust me.*" She bobbed her head.

Beside her, the potential bidder leaned down, closed his eyes, and drew in a long breath. "She smells good." Then he reached for a globe of her upturned ass.

"Don't make me have to break your fingers," Brett growled. He meant it, and Virginia nearly came with the harsh sound.

The man withdrew his hand in a snap. Someone gasped, a female, but Virginia couldn't tell which one.

Still stroking, his cock head now purpled and needy, he eyed Brett. "May we have a demonstration?"

"I'd be only too happy to oblige." Brett unzipped, set himself free, and raised Virginia by the leash until she could grab his thighs for support. His gaze was rich with need. He put a hand beneath her chin, stroking her with his thumb. "Take me," he whispered. A command, yet a plea.

The gentle tone drowned out all the other sounds around them. There was simply his voice, his hand on her, and his offering.

Then he cupped her head and fed his cock into her mouth. The first taste was like ambrosia, a heady mixture of salt and sweet. She let him slide back across her tongue, deep into the recesses of her mouth. Against the tip of his cock, she hummed her pleasure, and he jerked. She put her fingers to his testicles, squeezing lightly.

"Christ. She's going to make me come." And he pulled from her lips. Virginia turned her face, leaning against him, a streak of his juice wetting her cheek, his salty taste piquant on her tongue.

The bidder studied his watch. "Jesus. That was less than fifteen seconds." He pumped himself more ferociously.

Brett tucked his cock away, his slacks tenting over the enormous erection he sported. "She's worth every penny." That half smile creased his mouth again. "I know what I'm talking about." He looked down at her, stroking her temple with just the tip of his finger. "You will never find another to give you such ultimate satisfaction. You will never want another."

Despite his words filling the room, he spoke only to her. Her heart flared, her pulse jumped.

His fist pumping fast and hard, the man didn't even get that they'd just had a moment. "I want to come on her face." His eyes had begun to glaze. His breath rasped in his throat, his mouth open to grab a gulp of air.

"Nothing of yours touches her, not your hand, not your cock, and not your come. Do it on the floor," Brett demanded.

The man's eyes bulged slightly, then he threw his head back, and his semen spurted in an arc from his cock, splattering the hardwood at the edge of the expensive carpet. An attendant quickly cleaned it up.

After a deep sigh, the stocky, now-florid man glanced at Virginia as she nestled against Brett's thighs. "Don't worry," he murmured, "there's more where that came from. You'll savor every drop as much as I'm going to savor you."

She realized her original assessment of the crowd was correct. Though good-looking, the man was still ordinary. Thick blond hair, a solid chin, a passable nose, and decently defined muscles, he wasn't bad. Yet there wasn't one single outstanding feature.

She wanted men to desire her, to lust after her, to jerk off for want of her. Perspiration beaded on her forehead, and a flush swept her body, but with Brett's hand slowly stroking her hair, she closed her eyes and savored his caress far more than that man's come in her throat.

"Sit down," Brett said, and the guy returned to his place on the sofa.

Tugging once more on the chain leash, Brett helped her to her feet. Sliding a hand along her nape, he tangled his fingers in her hair and drew her head back. "Look."

The assembly was one writhing mass of sexual activity. A rigid cock sinking into a warm, fleshy woman. A dress raised, fingers flying. A beating fist eating the length of a hard dick. A face buried deep in the folds of a lady's pussy.

"That's what you do to them," Brett murmured at her ear. "You make them wild." His words, his breath in her hair, his hot body turned her inside out. "You are their desire, and tonight, one lucky man in this room will pay a fortune to have you."

He stepped back and raised his voice to the room. "Gentlemen, determine your bids. Tender your offer on the note provided, put it in the envelope, and seal it."

She couldn't believe she was doing this. *"Trust me."* Part of her knew he wouldn't force her to take the winner, but another piece wasn't so sure. He thrilled and terrified her at the same time. Maybe those dueling emotions were exactly the kick he wanted to give her. Raise her excitement by raising the stakes.

Brett held her close against him as order was restored and furious discussion within couples began. "I forgot to mention one small detail," he said for her ears alone, his words a mere breath, his gaze fathomless. "Whoever wins the bid has to then fight me for you. And it's going to be very bloody."

Her heart skipped a beat, another, then it soared. "You are such a Neanderthal." And she loved it. "And if one of those harpies tries to touch *you*, I'll rip her arm off."

He blinked, slow and sensual. "I love a bloodthirsty woman." Then he molded her hard against him, forcing her manacled hands against his chest, and delivered a deliciously hot, bruising kiss.

Brett let her go as the two waiters carried a narrow wooden table to the center of the room and set it down just in front of her hitching post. That moniker made her laugh. Where did her devilish man come up with these things?

A waiter collected the envelopes, then handed the stack to Brett. Virginia couldn't tell which bid had come from which man. And she didn't care. Brett could beat any of them at this game.

"By the way, my wife chooses the winning bid."

Voices raised. "Hey, I thought it was the *highest* bid," and "You can't keep changing the rules."

Brett smiled, teeth bared. "There's only one rule you need to abide by. And that is that *I* make all the rules."

He slit the first envelope and read. "Fifty thousand." Then he ripped the paper in half and tossed it over his shoulder. "Idiot."

The next one. "One hundred fifty thousand." He glanced up. "A little better." And placed it on the table. The third. "Seventy-five thousand." He shook his head. "Loser," and sent the card sailing across the room.

She wanted to laugh. She wanted to throw herself at him.

He slit another envelope and read. "Now this one I like." He held it out for her to see. Five hundred thousand dollars. Some man was willing to pay half a million dollars for her. It was mindblowing. Something squeezed her heart. The bid had to be from Brett. But what if it wasn't?

He opened the last, read, and made a sound like the bleep on a game show when the contestant screwed up the answer. "A paltry two hundred fifty thousand."

There was a commotion at the side door the waiters had been using. One of them entered carrying a box a foot and half tall.

"It appears we have one more bid," Brett told his audience.

She counted up the envelopes. Five. Which covered all the men in the room. Except for Brett.

There was a hush as the box was placed on the table.

"Regina."

Her heart was trapped in her throat. "You do it."

He lifted the lid off the base. And Virginia just stared. She couldn't believe it. There sat her mother's pirouetting ballerina. Her blue tutu made of porcelain-dipped lace seemed to twirl. The colors were still vibrant. And perfect. She looked real right down to the cherubic bud of her lips.

She put a trembling hand to her mouth. "How did you find it?"

"It's amazing what you can acquire when you're willing to spend as much time as it takes and pay whatever price is asked."

His careful consideration brought a lump to her throat and tears to her eyes. From the moment he'd asked her what the missing figurine looked like, he'd been planning to find it for her. He made her want to cry.

"The choice is now yours, Regina."

He'd stacked the deck. He knew exactly which she'd pick. A pity she wouldn't get to see him bloody anyone. She kind of liked the Neanderthal. But she loved Brett for being the man he was. A man with more hidden depths than she could ever have imagined. "You know which one."

"Say it."

"Your bid. The ballerina."

He tipped his head and gave her that adorable half smile. "It didn't cost five hundred thousand dollars."

"It's worth a lot more than that to me." And Brett knew it.

She handed him her gold braid leash. "And now, I have to do anything—" she sucked his bottom lip into her mouth, demonstrating just how well she sucked "—and everything—" she pulled his hand down between her legs demonstrating just how wet she was "—my winner demands."

NINE

"WOULD YOU REALLY have made me do one of those men?"

He tossed her velvet cape to the carpet and secured the end of the leash around a bedpost. "You'll never know, will you?"

He'd wanted to drag her to the plush Persian carpet in front of his assembled bidders and fuck the hell out of her with those avaricious eyes on them. His mind had been screaming, "Mine, mine, mine." It had taken all his control to lead her out, parade her through the halls of the club like the prize she was, and get her home.

His balls ached with the effort of holding back. But he'd needed to make love to her in their own bed, needed to push her to the limit in *their* bed. Without an audience. He wanted her to scream for him and him alone.

Next time, he'd let her scream at the club.

"Get on your hands and knees." Still fully clothed except for his suit jacket, he crawled across the bed like a prowling jungle cat. "You are such an exhibitionist, and I think you need punishing."

She smiled, a sultry, promising smile, then did as he bade. The short length of chain between her confined wrists forced her to her elbows rather than her hands, pushing her pert ass high. When she'd done that in front of his guests, he'd almost ripped open his pants and impaled her. Almost. The rules he'd set up with Jud Mc-Cord to avoid any potential illegality resulting from the auction were exacting, and he'd expended too much effort choreographing the affair to take his pleasure of her before the main event. He'd wanted her to see how much other men would pay to have her for one night. And then he wanted her to know he'd commit violence rather than let any of them have her. Yet even that sweet suck had been almost too much. No lie, ten seconds in her mouth had been almost too much.

Snugging up against her backside, he smoothed a hand along her side to cup one breast and possess a tight nipple. "Whose breasts are these?" he murmured.

"Mine," she whispered.

He pinched lightly. "Wrong answer. They're mine. And if I ever catch another man touching them, I'll tear his fingers off."

She drew in a quick breath.

Still crouched over her, he slid a hand up her thigh to the sweet wetness between her legs. "Whose pussy is this?"

"Mine."

He barely heard her answer, but the clenching of her muscles as he entered her with two fingers filled his cock to the breaking point. "You are so wrong. Again. It's mine. And I'll slice off the dick of anyone who tries to enter."

She wanted possession, she wanted jealousy, she wanted an all-consuming need for her. And Brett wasn't lying. The thought of another man taking her made him crazy.

He rolled her to her back and slid down her body until his mouth rested just above her fragrant, beckoning pussy. Taking her clit with his tongue, he swirled around the little button, then sucked it into his mouth. Her breath sighed from between her lips, the sounds of pleasure and need whispering across his skin. Then he raised his head to look at her. The bedside lamp illuminated her face and cast shadows across half her body.

"Who's clit is this?"

She gazed at him over the slopes and valleys of her body. "Now that's definitely got to be mine."

"I fear you need punishment—" he sucked her clit until she gasped "—to help you figure out the correct answers."

She drew her legs up and out, cradling him in the lee of her thighs. "What about touching myself?"

"If I catch you sneaking off into the bathroom for a little midnight pleasure or I walk in on you fucking yourself on our bed—" he gave a bared-toothed grin much the same as he had back there at The Sex Club "—there'll be hell to pay, Virginia."

Christ, he was already planning the scenario. Virginia with her hands between her legs. Or a monstrous vibrator inside her. And his punishment. Tying her up so he could eat her for hours and make her come a thousand times. He pushed her legs wider, exposing every inch of her bounty and went at her clitoris. Beneath the onslaught, she writhed and moaned and bucked against him. His heart beat so rapidly in his chest he thought it might burst.

"I'm going to fucking die if I don't get inside you."

Rising to kneel between her legs, Brett ripped at his tie, his shirt, the front of his slacks. His clothing flew across the bedroom. In the one light from the side of the bed, Virginia watched him, her gaze a physical stroke down his chest to his cock rising from the nest of hair between his thighs.

"Undo the chain," she begged.

"Break it. You damn well know you could have at any time tonight."

"I don't want you to ruin your lovely gifts."

"I don't fucking care. I'll buy you more. Break it."

She pulled, the links on the bracelets snapped, and she wrapped her fingers around his pulsing cock. His eyes felt like they'd roll back in his head at the supreme sensation of his flesh within her grasp.

"Fuck. I want you. Now." He came down hard on top of her, pushing the breath from her lungs. "You'll accept any gift I give you. You'll take my cock inside you whenever I want it there. You'll suck me until I scream. You'll make me come until I die. Got that?"

She nodded, her eyes wide, her lips plump.

"You are fucking mine, Virginia. Don't ever forget that." She was so slick and hot that his cock found her unerringly, and he entered her with one powerful thrust. She pushed her head back into the pillow, her thighs gripping him, her body pulling him deeper.

"I'm willing to take you to the club so you can look your fill." He withdrew, then powered deeply once more. "I'm willing to let others look at you. I might even let them watch me fuck you." He grabbed her hip and pushed her higher, forcing her body to take his next thrust all the way to her womb. "But I draw the line at letting anyone have so much as a taste of your sweet mouth." He nipped at her bottom lip and withdrew. "Don't make me have to hurt *someone*."

"I don't want anyone but you, Brett. Ever."

He went mad, pounding her hard into the mattress, making every inch of her body his. His pubic hair rasped against her, hitting her clitoris, and he found the perfect spot on the inside. His cock knew it. Her pussy clenched, clamped, worked him, and when she gathered a breath, he knew his moment was here. He slammed home inside her.

When she came, she screamed.

And it threw him over the edge into heaven, his hot sperm filling her core. Her cries staked her claim on him as much as his cock staked its claim inside her body.

*   *   *

SHE ACHED. IT was the most wonderful feeling she'd ever experienced in her life. Three marriages, and Virginia had never felt this before.

Brett wrapped his body around hers.

Nothing had ever felt this momentous. His need was no longer a fantasy she'd created. It was real.

"You screamed," he murmured against her hair.

"Yes, I believe I did."

"You can't know how long I've waited to hear that."

She nestled deeper against him. "Didn't I scream at the club a few times?"

"You've never screamed in our bed."

"I would have if I knew you wanted me to."

He nuzzled her nape. "That wouldn't have been the same. I wanted you to do it because you couldn't help yourself."

"Ah well, I couldn't help myself tonight. In fact, I didn't even realize I had until you mentioned it."

"Oh yeah, you screamed," he said with a supremely masculine sigh of satisfaction. "The neighbors will be calling in the morning to complain."

"I'll have to be more careful next time."

"Like hell. I'm going to make you scream even louder." His arm tightened across her abdomen. "I said you were free to indulge yourself in any way you chose, but I've changed my mind."

She laughed. "I wouldn't have figured that out on my own."

"Wench." He rocked his hips against her backside. He was hard again. "You're mine, Virginia, and I'm yours, and we don't share with anyone."

She felt his words and the meaning take her over. She didn't know how much of his auction tonight had been real and how much he'd stacked the deck. All the bids might very well have been his, and he would have won her no matter which she chose. She wouldn't ask because she didn't care. There was one thing she knew was real. His desire for her. Only her.

"Thank you," she whispered.

"For what?"

"For marrying me. For indulging me." For giving her tonight. For all the future nights. "For the ballerina."

"I hated that asshole who stole it from you."

She rolled in his arms, because she had to see his eyes. Despite the bedside lamp they hadn't bothered to turn off, his gaze was dark and unreadable. She wouldn't have it any other way. With that gaze, he would always be able to hide his next delicious adventure from her until he made it reality.

"When we got married, I thought I only wanted security."

"Oh, you did, did you?"

She nodded, her tangled hair brushing his face. "I wanted you, but I was afraid of ruining a comfortable relationship."

"Fuck comfortable. And calm and serene. It isn't good enough." He rubbed his nose to hers. "I want cataclysmic."

The odd thing was, he'd given her both. He would always be the controlled, savvy businessman. He would always be his customers' ethical supplier. But he would also be the wild man he'd hidden from her. He'd given her more than she could even contemplate wishing for. She hadn't thought it possible.

"Brett, at the risk of screwing up a good relationship—" she pursed her lips "—I think I love you."

He touched his lips to hers. "I fell in love with you the moment I saw you spread out on black sheets in a sex club with your fingers buried in your pussy."

"Oh my God." After everything, she still felt a flush spread over her body even as his words grabbed hold of her heart.

"It was the most beautiful sight I've ever beheld, and I knew right then I was going to have that woman in my bed." He pulled her hand down between them and wrapped her fingers around his cock. "Just thinking about it has made me hard again."

Less than ten minutes, and he wanted her again. Oh no, she

could never even have dreamed of getting *this* from her marriage. "And what do you expect me to do about it?"

"Make me scream," he whispered. "And if you're really good, I'll give you another surprise." He nipped her lip. "When you least expect it."

She couldn't wait.

Virginia Hansen might have been a three-time loser at love, but Mrs. Brett Branoff was the luckiest woman in the world.

Invitation to Passion

ONE

A LOT OF things had changed in the year since Virginia's wedding, but Stacy Parrish's taste in lovers wasn't one of them. She adored younger men, their taut muscles. They had so much more stamina than the older variety and came with ferocity. True, they were quick to jump to the main course, but they were also good at taking hints. Between them, these two lavished her body with attention. What better way to celebrate her upcoming forty-sixth birthday? The husky blond sucked her nipple, testing the tightness with a little bite. She cooed her appreciation. The dark-haired one worked his tongue up her legs, swiping the special pleasure spot behind her knee.

"You boys are doing such a good job," she murmured. Encouragement always garnered results. She even imagined that their future lovers would thank her for tutoring them in the art of pleasing a woman.

"Thank you, Serena." That was the name she'd chosen for her

visits to The Sex Club. It was best to keep her real life separate from her sojourns to The Sex Club. And just as she used a false name, the boys had dubbed themselves Erik (the Viking blond) and Caesar (the dark satyr).

Caesar nibbled his way up her thigh, pushing her legs apart, his fingers questing. She arched, opening her pussy to the lips within inches of bringing her gratification, and pushed her breast against Erik's teeth, wrenching a throaty growl from him.

At forty-six her maidenly inhibitions were long gone, and her body was a feast for the two luscious twenty-five-year-olds.

"Your tongue would feel so good on me right now." She didn't demand; it wasn't polite. As soon as Caesar's tongue found her clitoris, she oohed and aahed her approval. Maybe it was time for her to do a little multitasking. Reaching down, she took Erik's impressive cock in her hand. Drops of come slid along her palm just as a thick finger plunged deep inside her.

Improvising. Very good. As much as she enjoyed the youthful companions she chose, they were a relatively uninspired lot. She inevitably directed the action. One of these days, she was hoping for someone to surprise her with his ingenuity.

For now, she'd enjoy what she had. "Use your fingers, too." It was good to let them know that fingers and tongues together were as enjoyable as a thick cock. Caesar's blunt fingers filled her, while his tongue played her like an instrument.

She moaned, writhed, and squeezed the hard cock. Erik groaned and pumped in her fist, his mouth remaining locked to her breast. Sensation jolted from her nipple to her pussy.

Stacy opened her eyes to gaze at the tableau in the mirror above the bed. Her red hair fanned the satin pillow, the burgundy comforter in deep contrast to the tanned bodies draping her torso and thighs. One dark head wedged between her legs, the light one moving from one breast to the other. Her slightly parted lips glistened, her lipstick matching the bedspread's color. She pushed on Erik's shoulder, dislodging him just enough to see her fingers wrapped tightly around his mammoth cock, her manicured nails looking dangerous against his aroused flesh. The decadent scene shot her higher toward bliss, her body dripping with desire. Her first orgasm of the night rippled through her. It was good. But the next one could be so much better.

Still, she murmured her approval. "Have I told you yet how magnificent you are?"

"Yes, Serena," they said in unison.

Rolling, she came to her hands and knees, another mirror along the wall revealing the lithe length of her body. She held up a condom like a treat. "Anyone interested?"

Her obedient lovers moved quickly. Without even fighting about it, Erik positioned himself in front of her, holding his cock out like a reward. Caesar rose to his knees behind her, rolled on the condom, then spread her legs to tease her pussy with the head of his imposing member.

The mirror reflected the beauty of those two steel rods.

She licked her lips, then parted them, salivating over the sight of the tiny drop of come oozing from the slit of Erik's cock as he worked himself for her pleasure. Caesar's hands on her hips positioned her.

Then they both hit home, a delicious penis in her mouth, an equally delectable cock hitting high in her pussy with one thrust. Tilting her head slightly to better view the mirror, she watched the two perfect male tools sliding, in, out, in, out, a mastery of sexual choreography.

Perfect, boys, absolutely perfect. She'd tell them later.

Then she closed her eyes, giving herself up to the pleasure of total penetration. Salty precome coated her tongue. She took Erik in all the way, working the muscles of her throat in time with his groans. She rode Caesar's cock, slamming back against his hard pelvis, her rhythm flawless.

The echo of masculine groans and her feminine moans filled the room. The aphrodisiac scent of sex, male sweat, and her own light, seductive musk wafted around them. If she could bottle the fragrance, she'd make a million. If she could cage these superlative animals, she'd have heaven on earth.

She squeezed the ball sack dangling in front of her, feeling Erik's approaching orgasm. He pumped harder, faster, without restraint. She drank from him, urging him closer.

Caesar slid a hand down her belly and parted the lips of her sex, gliding in all her moisture. Her clitoris throbbed, begged. She panted. Caesar didn't need much tutoring at all. As he stroked her clit, his body stiffened, and his penis pulsed inside her, gathering steam for his impending explosion.

Then she had the most marvelous idea. She let the lovely instrument of pleasure drop from her lips and pried the hands from her hips. "I've just had a brainstorm."

Erik groaned. "You've gotta be kidding."

"No, boys, I'm not. This will be better." So much better for all of them. "Let's do a sandwich."

"You wanna eat at a time like this?"

Caesar shoved his partner's arm. "Don't be a fucking idiot. She means she wants to be in the middle."

Lord. They were young. She had to give them a little leeway because of their age. "In front of the mirror, boys."

They clambered from the bed, eager to please. Stacy enjoyed the power in getting them to stave off their own orgasm. In return, she'd give them something incredible.

The floor-to-ceiling mirror covered the center portion of the wall. She knew it was two-way, and she wondered if someone was watching tonight. No, she *knew* someone watched. A thrill quivered through her belly, weakening her limbs. God, she wanted to give the performance of her life. That's what sex was for her, each and every act being the ultimate performance.

She gave her profile to the mirror, then smiled. "You in front." She grabbed a condom, then took Erik by his cock and situated him facing her. She wiggled her butt for Caesar.

"Enter me at the last minute," she told him, handing him a tube of lubricant, "at the perfect moment."

"Yes, ma'am." Her lovely dark warrior nestled up against her ass, his cock, already dressed with a condom and now the lube, riding the base of her spine.

"Fuck me," she whispered, her gaze on the blue flames in her Viking's eyes. His condom was donned with the dexterity of frequent deployment, then she felt herself lifted from behind and supported by Caesar's rock-hard chest as she wrapped her legs around her Norseman's waist. He impaled her, holding her hips to pump like a madman. She raised her arms, looping them behind Caesar's neck. Each pound inside her body rammed her against the cock sitting just above her ass. Powerful legs framed her bottom, steadying her to receive while at the same time rocking his flesh between their bodies. He pinched her nipples, hard, almost painfully, and sent a surge of heat and lightning shooting down to her clit. Supported by strong arms, she followed the lightning strike, circling her fingers over her clitoris and building her body's tension even higher.

She started to pant and moan. Colors swirled behind her eyelids as her fingers multiplied all the sensations.

"Now," she cried. Just as her orgasm rose to the peak, rushing to each and every separate nerve ending, her dark lover entered her from the rear. She screamed, the pleasure-pain of double penetration unbearable. Then Erik slammed home into her pussy, deep, high, hard, one last time, and filled the room with his roar. Lights burst behind her lids, and she came in a miasma of blinding flashes.

She opened her eyes to the mirror, those beautiful young bodies tangled about her. She didn't even remember falling to the soft carpeting. Breathing deeply, she arched, relishing the delicious ache in her muscles. Then she collapsed back into the heap of bodies. Ah yes, they were spent, their limbs lax, their mouths open to drag in air.

Stroking her fingers through their luscious locks, she whispered, "You were both wonderful."

She lay there in the lee of their bodies for long, sated minutes, until their respective breaths eased back to normal. And that was long enough. The best way to end a rendezvous was at its height, before the rapture of orgasm completely faded.

"You know, boys, I'd like a moment by myself to recover."

As one, they rolled to their knees, glorious animals. Erik shook his shaggy mane. Caesar grabbed his cock to remove the used condom. They both disposed of the remains in the provided receptacles, then turned to the piles of shed clothing.

"Thanks, Serena."

"It was great, Serena."

She smiled at their good manners. "You're both going to make fantastic lovers for some very happy women." She hoped her small hints added to their future bliss.

Propping herself on her elbow, she watched in the mirror as lean yet well-muscled limbs disappeared into black slacks and white dress shirts, though the club didn't have a dress code, and clothing ranged from casual to ball-gown fancy. People came here for a variety of reasons, to have a diversity of needs met. Neither of these two hunky specimens would leave feeling used by what she'd done with them. Quite the opposite, she was sure. They were equals in what they'd all received from the encounter.

This was the way she liked it. A swift end to a friendly assignation. Everybody went away happy, and no messy emotions to deal with later on. In her twenties, she'd desperately desired love. Yet what she'd gotten was more heartache than joy. She'd searched for Mr. Right, only to learn he didn't exist, at least not for her. Thank God she'd discovered she didn't need him anyway.

She'd found her true calling in life, talking with women, getting them to open up. What she offered was more than a manicure. It was hearing them, learning, and yes, God, helping them. She never judged; she listened. Many found what they needed through the simple act of sharing. Others needed a little extra help, and she did whatever she could, in any way necessary. She'd supported herself, but even more, she *gave* to those women. She'd made lasting friends. That was what was important to her.

The door snicked shut as her "boys" departed, and she turned to her reflection, arching her neck and stroking a hand down her throat. She was agile and strong from her daily workouts, the skin of her face smooth from her regimen of moisturizers. But it was a fact of life. She was forty-six, and she wouldn't have this body or face forever. Which was why she made the most of what The Sex Club had to offer the two or three times a month she ventured here. She didn't want to leave any wild oats unsown, and that left myriad possibilities, like the sandwich she'd just partaken of. It had been good, very good. The boys had certainly been surprised and appreciative.

But sitting before the mirror in a now-empty room, the languidness of orgasm almost faded, she couldn't help wondering what was around the corner for her. She could only hope there were other, more exciting things waiting. Wilder oats to sow.

Pulling her knees to her chest, she stretched her arms out before her, releasing the kinks in her back, then perused her reflection once more.

Oh yes, no matter her age, she still had a few surprises out there for some lucky young sex club attendees. And maybe, if *she* was lucky, one or two of them would have a surprise for her.

SERENA WAS ALL delicious, hot woman. She loved performing. Judson McCord was equally entranced with watching her.

Some people came to his club for the titillation, never actually participating. Some needed much more. Jud subscribed to the belief that desires suppressed could become needs that burst out of control, causing great damage to others. So, he provided an exclusive, private resort to safely act out those needs, clean, no drugs, no fighting, no divulging of personal information, no stalking. He watched his facility like a hawk, and if a guest disobeyed the rules, they were out, for good.

Serena came to the club to watch and be watched. The last three times she'd ventured upstairs, Jud had been her voyeur. Once she'd been alone, once with a single partner, and then tonight.

She disposed of her cohorts in pleasure with a few gracious words. He revered her confidence, her belief in her own beauty and power. He admired the pure grace of her feminine lines as she lolled in front of the mirror. She was a woman who had come into her own, an Amazon, a true woman of the new millennium. And he wanted her. Badly. Not merely Serena, the fantasy on the other side of a mirror, but the real woman. Stacy Parrish.

She was aware he knew her real name. He'd learned it when she first started coming to his club almost upon its grand opening two years ago. At the time, though he found her attractive, he'd already decided he wouldn't indulge with guests. One didn't abuse the client-proprietor relationship, and when the need arose, he took his pleasures elsewhere.

But that didn't mean Jud avoided Stacy's company. Though she was often frankly admiring of him, she didn't flirt. She talked to him without pretense, her open smile more captivating than the seductive mien with which she graced other men.

She had a habit of lingering at the club after a tryst, observing, theorizing about what made people tick. Many times she shared her studies with him. The more she revealed about what she saw in others, the more he learned about her. She enjoyed life to the fullest, savoring great big bites. She was ballsy, smart, confident, droll, and perceptive, with a streak of caring and loyalty. If someone she cared about was in need, she dropped everything to help.

He considered himself lucky to be counted among her friends.

She had more facets than a diamond and shone brighter than a cache of jewels. He dreamed of burying his fingers in her hair, its red tones softened by streaks of blond, as it curled about her ears and nape. Her body was another treasure: long, firm legs and taut, voluptuous breasts, while her face was the equal of a Greek goddess. But she was so much more than her outer casing. Somewhere in the two years he'd enjoyed her company, his casual attraction had turned to desire. A few weeks ago, he'd treated himself to a little harmless voyeurism. And damn if his desire for her hadn't turned to a bit of an obsession. Now he was considering breaking his own rule not to mix business with pleasure. Hell, after tonight, he wasn't considering it. He'd already decided. He wanted her, and he was going have her.

Jud had experienced all manner of pleasures. In his younger, wilder days, there wasn't anything he wouldn't try as long as it held the slightest appeal. But a purely physical connection was like a drug. You got high, you came down, you walked away. He wasn't going to walk away from Stacy Parrish after a few nights. And he sure as hell wasn't going to share her. All that was left was to let *her* know that.

"Hope you enjoyed yourself, sweetheart," he whispered. Tonight was her last fling with anyone other than him for a long time to come.

There was no better time to put his plan into effect than tonight, when she came downstairs for her usual tête-à-tête. In her quest to live life to its fullest, Stacy chose muscle-bound youngsters who would fawn over her, her high more about their adulation than about her own pleasure. Brief encounters were like skimming the cream off the top of the milk. You savored the sweetness, but you never got to relish the long, deep swallow. Your cup always needed to be refilled.

It was time he showed her what she'd been missing.

TWO

THE CLUB SPORTED a couple of bars, each offering a respite from the frenetic activity. Though sex wasn't prohibited, it was more discreetly engaged in. The salon Stacy chose was relatively small, yet the mirrors on the walls and ceiling gave the room a larger feel. The tables were surrounded by leather stools, the bar itself shiny chrome with lights running along the glass top, illuminating it from beneath. It was beyond her how the surface seemed perpetually clear of smudges and spilled alcohol. That was a testament to the club, which was always immaculate, its marble floors gleaming, its private rooms pristine.

It was also a testament to the club's owner, Judson McCord, who was now behind the bar pouring champagne into a flute. The buzz of quiet conversation masked the tap of her stiletto heels as she wended through the mostly full tables. Her tight-fitting black cocktail dress riding high up her thighs, she climbed atop a stool, just as Jud pushed her champagne across the bar.

"Your drink, Serena, my love."

"You're such a charmer." Sparkling bubbles glistened in the peach-flavored cocktail. That was another thing about Jud; he knew what his guests preferred, and he provided, right down to meaningless endearments that nevertheless made a woman feel special.

"So, Derek flaked on you again?" Glancing in the mirror behind him, she smoothed the spaghetti straps of her dress, liking the way Jud's gaze followed her hands, even though she knew he had no interest in her.

He was a gorgeous specimen at six feet, his black tux molding to his muscled chest. He hadn't an ounce of flab. Though he had to be in his late forties, his hair was still dark, dusted only with a distinguished smattering of gray and a streak at his temples. She suspected his ancestry included Italian descent, his skin swarthy and his nose patrician. Laugh lines flirted at the corners of his eyes, and he had the most amazing lashes for a man, long and thick.

He put his hands flat on the bar. "Derek's got issues. So I make certain allowances."

She'd never understood that. Jud impressed her as a man who demanded perfection. "Why do you make allowances for him?"

She truly wanted to know. She'd been coming to the club for almost two years, and rather than sleep with Jud, she preferred to keep him as her confidant, a man she didn't have to impress, pacify, or tame. After a session, she liked to unwind in Jud's company. He was funny, insightful, and attentive. He could, however, be close-mouthed about things, and one of them was Derek, who'd started as a bartender about a year ago.

God. Jud wasn't gay, was he? It would explain why he'd never made a pass at her. No. No way. He was too . . . manly, too virile. Plus, she'd seen him eye the ladies, mostly younger women in their thirties. If, however, he nipped off for a quickie, Jud was the epitome of discretion. She'd never seen him partake of the club's many pleasures.

Jud wiped down the counter in front of her, buffing it dry, then tossed the rag under the bar. "I feel a certain kinship."

She propped her chin on her hand. "Kinship?"

"In Derek, I see a lot of myself when I was his age. He needs direction. A mentor. He's wild and undisciplined, but he'll go far if someone offers him a hand."

That was the most Jud had ever said regarding his own past. She felt a little thrill of victory that he'd given her this additional revelation into his character. "So, you were undisciplined and wild. Interesting."

He cocked a brow, and she saw the devil in that look.

"Very. Someday I'll tell you the story of my wild days."

She almost laughed. He owned and managed a sex club, for God's sake. How much more wild could it get? She was suddenly dying to know. "Come on, reveal all."

He smiled. He had a wicked grin that intoxicated most women. "Later. Tell me how you think I should handle Derek."

That floored her. Jud always listened, and they'd had many an interesting political, ethical, or moral discussion, but this was something else entirely. "You want my opinion?"

"I value your opinion highly. Derek's had troubles. A bad home life when he was a kid, drugs, run-ins with the cops. He's lost his belief in himself, not that anyone could ever tell him that. There's a fine line between offering him helpful advice and telling him what to do. He'd listen to the former and ignore the latter."

"And you were a lot like him, huh?"

One side of his mouth quirked. "Let's just say, if someone told me I needed to get my life in order, I'd have told him to take a flying leap. I thought I was controlling my life when in reality, life controlled me."

"And now it's the other way round?"

"Yes. Exactly. I make my own destiny."

There were dimensions to Jud she'd never fully explored. He'd been a bad boy, but he'd turned around to take life by its tail. Not that she'd ever doubted that about him for a minute. Someday, she'd love to hear more, but right now, she basked in the fact that he'd asked for her help. "Maybe it's time for a little tough love."

"As in get your shit together, or you'll lose this job?"

"Yeah. Or maybe just tell him that out in the real world there are no second chances. And here at the club, he's on his last chance with you."

Jud leaned in and chucked her under the chin. "Lady, we're of like minds. I'm glad you approve of my choice of action, because that's exactly what I plan to do."

"Right. Like you needed my approval."

He cocked his head and stared at her for a moment. She shivered under his suddenly intense gaze.

"You'd be surprised what I need."

Now, that was deliciously mysterious. And just a bit frightening. Jud was her friend, and asking the meaning of that statement might be moving into dangerous territory.

"Well, I'm glad I could assist, and I have to say I admire you for helping the kid out."

He winked, and the odd tension she'd felt melted away.

"Now, tell me about your evening. How were the young men?"

She let her lips curve as she thought of her encounter. "Very enjoyable, thank you." If she sometimes wished for a bit more of a surprise, it certainly didn't diminish the pleasure.

"Good. Your satisfaction is my greatest desire." He brushed her hand, shooting a tiny spark of electricity up her arm. "Excuse me while I fill this order." Then he moved down to attend to the waitress at the end of the bar.

He was such a gallant, always checking on her pleasure. He'd set strict rules for his club, affording his patrons a feeling of security. Men required an invitation, and the first time they had to be accompanied by an approved female guest. Though a stickler for his rules, Jud made exceptions for what he deemed a worthy cause. Brett, Virginia's husband, had been one such worthy cause, as if

Jud somehow knew how well that would turn out. Still, if anyone misbehaved, they were out for good, even women. In other ways, though, women were given a different treatment. Stacy had secured complimentary invitations for friends, like Debbie, she felt might benefit from the club's offerings. Ladies could also be awarded a standing invitation, meaning they could arrive at any time on any evening and join in anything they chose, free of charge. Few were granted, but Stacy had received her coveted standing invitation long ago.

Sipping her champagne, she glanced in the mirror behind the bar, perusing the guests reflected in the glass. Someone had been watching her tonight. Who could it have been? Though she liked *not* knowing, it was always delicious to speculate. She surveyed the men at the tables but failed to make eye contact. Maybe her voyeur was shy, observing her only when she wasn't looking. What about him, the thin, lanky-looking one? He seemed like a watcher. Light hit his glasses, disguising his eyes and any intimate knowledge that might have been in his glance. She let her gaze move on to another table.

Hmm. Her two studs were back in the bar, stopping at a table occupied by two older women dressed in stylish suits, one in navy blue, the other in a bright shade of fuchsia. As Stacy's lovers took the empty barstools, the two women smiled in unison, their lips hopeful, their gazes needy.

Those young studs would make their wildest dreams come true, and really, Stacy felt happy for them. The club was all about female empowerment, about rejuvenating a woman's lost spark of desirability brought on by ignorant husbands and busy lives. A woman needed to be wanted, to feel special, incomparable in a man's eyes. These women deserved to feel like that. All women did. It was a God-given right.

Of course, it was an illusion. But who cared? The two ladies didn't. Stacy didn't.

Though it was a bit of slam that *her* two young men were prowling for fresh meat so soon. That was the problem with sex: it was like Chinese food; it tasted good at the time, but ten minutes after eating it, you were hungry again.

A warm hand caressed her bare arm. "They *didn't* please you, so you tossed them back into the sea. Tell me what they did to disappoint you. I'll revoke their club privileges."

"No, they were fine, Jud. I was just . . . tired, I guess." She smiled. She certainly wasn't going to tell him she was a bit disappointed to find Erik and Caesar in the bar. "I preferred coming down here for one of your special champagne cocktails."

He looked her over with a penetrating gaze. The lights shining up from the bar cast a shadow across his cheekbones, making his brown eyes seem deeper. He pinned her with that dark look as easily as he held her with his hand on her arm.

"They aren't what you need." His voice was barely more than a husky whisper, and tingles sped along her nerve endings.

"And what do I need?"

"You need a real man. A man who knows his way around the subtle nuances of every feminine curve. A man who has all the time in the world to lavish a woman's body with attention. A man who knows how to excite with a look."

Good Lord. That's exactly what Jud was doing to her. Her skin felt flushed, her nipples tight and achy, her body hot and wet. With just his gaze on her lips and his fingers on her arm. He made her forget all about her boys making time on the other side of the bar. But this was Jud. Their friendship was sacrosanct. The club was about sex, but the time she spent with Jud was something else. At the moment, she couldn't define what that was, only what it wasn't. It wasn't supposed to be about wanting him to drag her up to one of the private rooms and make her come until she was delirious.

"I told you they were fine." The faintest tremor flowed through her voice.

He didn't let her go. "They're too young. They don't have a

clue. They might be able to fuck the hell out of you, but they'll never touch you the way you should be touched."

Stacy was shocked into silence. Jud rarely employed gutter talk. He was too refined. Yet the words sent another tremor through her she was sure he could feel.

"You need a real man, not a boy playing at being a man, someone who knows how to provide the very thing a woman doesn't even know she needs."

He sounded like the kid in *The Sound of Music* who claimed his girlfriend needed someone older and wiser. Jud was older, and oddly, he exuded an aura of wisdom. He was a mentor, as his dealings with Derek indicated, having experienced wild times and learned from them.

Still, she'd found that some older men were pathetic, used-up has-beens who could only get a younger woman by dangling the scent of money. Or lying. Yet, she'd given older men a chance, more than once. She still remembered the "nice" man who'd insulted her and her friend within the first fifteen minutes after their arrival at a downtown bar. First, he'd informed her he didn't like her language (she'd used the word *screw*), she was rude to the waitress (not), and her friend needed to lose weight (get out!). Older men could be very judgmental.

Not that Jud was any of those things. He was the farthest thing from a has-been. Used-up? Oh no, he had quite a few more washings left before his stitches fell out. And judgmental? Jud lived by the motto, judge not lest you be judged. Jud was an anything-goes-as-long-as-no-one-gets-hurt kind of man.

But she wasn't in the market for a sexual lesson.

"I know exactly what I need," she said, refuting his claim.

"Do you?" He tilted his head, his long lashes effectively hiding his expression.

"I want fun with no entanglements." Monogamy was good for some of her friends, very good, in fact, but the idea of it didn't do a thing for her. "I want to leave what happens at the club behind and go home to my business and my life." Which truly was more important than any surprise she might wish for.

"I beg to differ. I think there's a lot more you need."

"Really? Why don't you tell me?" She felt a certain coolness enter her voice, as if he'd stepped over some invisible line between them. She didn't like being under his microscope.

Before he could answer, a blonde wriggled onto the barstool next to Stacy's.

"Ju-ud."

"Me-lo-dee," Jud mimicked in return. Then he turned to Stacy and mouthed, "Excuse me a minute."

"I really, really need a drink. I'm simply parched. What do you recommend? Something . . . tart." Melody fluttered her eyelashes and puckered her lips as if she wanted far more from Jud than a glass of wine. Which she probably did.

Stacy was glad for the interruption, except that Melody could be a trifle boring. Though close to thirty, the woman affected an annoying little-girl whimper when she wanted something. Pretty, with blue eyes, loads of blond hair, which Stacy was sure didn't come out of a bottle, she had a body that epitomized the current model-thin style. Except for her breasts. Melody had an immense chest that made men drool.

Polite to a fault when it came to his guests, Jud gave the blonde his attention. "How about a Campari and soda?"

She wrinkled her nose. "That's bitter, not tart." Then she pointed at Stacy's glass. "I want what she's having."

Jud shook his head. "You can't have what Serena's having. That's just for her."

He made peach champagne cocktails exclusively for her? Hmm, how sweet. She hadn't known that. She felt the ebb of her earlier coolness toward him.

"That's not fair," Melody whined.

"Life's not fair."

She pouted. Prettily. But Jud didn't give in.

"Then I want a Long Island iced tea. Make sure it kicks."

"Yes, ma'am. One kick coming up." And Jud moved down the length of the bar.

"He's *hot*," Melody whispered. "I wonder when he gets off?"

"Jud gets off exactly when he wants to," Stacy murmured.

Melody didn't so much as crack a smile at their dual double entendre. Though Melody had been to the club several times over the last year, maybe she didn't know that Jud was not an employee but the club's owner. Not everyone knew, not that Jud hid the fact, but he also didn't make a display of it.

Melody licked her lips. "I want another bite out of him."

Another? Stacy felt something inside her lurch. Jud had been with this . . . okay, she didn't want to think anything derogatory about Melody. Surely the girl was the sweetest thing since apple pie and maybe not a ditz at all. But Jud had bedded down with *her?* It was unthinkable. It was repulsive.

Jud returned with the prepared drink, sliding it across the counter on a coaster to sop up the condensation.

Stacy felt as sweaty as the mug. Surely Jud availed himself of the club's delights, but she'd never focused on the idea. Until now. She didn't like her thoughts at all, experiencing a proprietary feeling to which she had no right. Dammit, did Melody have a standing invitation, too?

"There you go." He smiled graciously, then turned back to Stacy. "Can I get you a refill?"

Her glass was only half-empty. Or was that half-full? "I'm fine, thanks." As possessive as it might be, she wanted to cut Melody out of the conversation. "So, what were we discussing?"

Then she remembered. They'd been talking about what Jud thought she needed. She certainly wasn't going to continue with darling Melody sitting beside her on the barstool.

"Oh, tell me, tell me, I love discussion," Melody clamored.

Stacy just wanted to tell her to get lost. She wasn't usually uncharitable, and she didn't allow jealous thoughts to gain a foothold.

She abhorred competing for a man's attention. It was beneath her. So she backed off, only to find it was almost voyeuristic watching Melody hit on Jud, her breasts brilliantly displayed as she leaned on the glass bar top, eyes roving over every inch of Jud's chest.

Jud merely smiled indulgently. "It was private. Sorry." The apology was added almost as a courteous afterthought.

That startled Melody, and the sparkle in her eyes dimmed. But only for a moment. "Let's start a new discussion. Are you boxers, briefs, or commando?"

God, she was *so* young. Stacy had her own immature moment of triumph realizing Melody didn't know the answer. Which meant Jud hadn't . . .

"That's private, too," he answered, still with a tolerant smile on his lips.

Melody trailed a finger along the back of his hand where it rested on the bar. "Oh, come on, you can tell me." She glanced slyly at Stacy. "I mean, you can tell us."

Pulling away from Melody, Jud held up his hands. "A man has to have some secrets."

Melody leaned on the bar, the outline of her breasts lit from below by the row of lights. "Then let's play another game. Which do you prefer, hand jobs or blow jobs?"

In the midst of a sip of champagne, Stacy almost spewed the fruity concoction across the counter.

Jud didn't flinch. "That's not a suitable topic, either."

It certainly was in a sex club, but Stacy didn't contradict him. She simply waited for Melody's next move. The show had now become amusing. Would Jud capitulate?

Melody fluttered her eyelashes. "Okay, we won't *discuss* it. We'll test it out. When are you off work for the evening?"

That was certainly bold. The woman didn't even seem to care that Stacy was sitting there. In fact, she eyed Stacy with a little gleam, as if to say, "I know you were talking to *her*, but I've got a better offer you can't refuse."

"I'm otherwise engaged for the rest of the evening." Then Jud turned to Stacy. "Right?"

Oh, the man was a devil, using her as an excuse. She merely affected a sultry, secretive smile for his benefit.

Melody gave a dainty huff, picked up her drink, and trotted off to a nearby table filled with men closer to her own age.

"What, not up for a little midnight nookie?" Stacy teased, just to rid herself of her own puzzling tension about the whole Melody exchange.

"Midnight nookie is exactly what I want, but not with her."

That was definitely another of his mysterious comments, and he'd been making a lot of them tonight. With any other man, she'd assume he was making a move on her, but this was Jud. In two years, he'd never made advances. That would spoil a nice friendship. Yet tonight, she was getting odd vibes from him. First when he'd asked her advice on how to handle Derek, then a brief foray into his past, now this.

She left the quandary alone in favor of teasing him again. "She's a fine, young feminine specimen. Why not go for it?"

Jud leaned on the bar. "One, she's had a boob job that is two sizes too large for her figure. Two, she's shallow. Three, I'm sure she doesn't have a clue how to give a proper blow job."

She tsked. "Ooh, that's mean." Jud wasn't generally mean, especially where his guests were concerned. "And I thought blow jobs weren't a topic of conversation."

"They aren't with Melody around." At the end of the bar, one of his waitresses signaled. "You asked a question, and I gave an honest answer. She's far too young to understand the full impact of a properly executed blow job."

Jud traced a finger along Stacy's arm before moving off to fill the latest drink order, leaving her to ponder where this was going. Her skin tingled at the lingering memory of his touch, and she was consumed with curiosity over his definition of a "properly executed blow job."

She should go home. This wasn't a discussion she should have with Jud, not when combined with how she'd felt watching Melody work her charms. Proprietary was putting it mildly. She'd felt downright victorious when he sent the woman away.

The rear view as he mixed drinks was just too damn good. The tailored tux fit him to perfection. The lights shone in his hair, flickering across the strands of gray mixed in. The flex of his shoulders as he moved riveted her gaze.

The situation was getting risky. Stacy saw, she wanted, she took, and she moved on. Possessive emotions didn't get involved. Really, she should leave . . .

Except that his gaze trapped her as he returned. He moved with the grace of a sleek panther, and her pulse raced simply watching him. It was strange how suddenly a man could attract your eye after years of knowing him, as if a switch suddenly flipped. It could be something as simple as a joke that made you laugh, or a look you'd never seen before. Or a topic of conversation that skated into territory that you'd never before visited with him. And suddenly, you saw him, really *saw* him.

However he'd done it, Jud had certainly flipped her switch. Surprise, surprise.

"So what's a properly executed blow job?" The question was out of her mouth before she consciously made the decision to continue the bizarre conversation.

He focused on her with a predatory gleam and smiled as if to say, *Gotcha*. Then he leaned on the bar, close enough for a faint whiff of his aftershave and something else. The scent of an aroused male animal.

She'd set the limits on their relationship in her own mind, preferring confidant status to sexual partner standing. Why she'd relegated him to that position she couldn't seem to recall in the rush of heat flooding her body. In a setting where just about anything was permissible, Jud had suddenly become her forbidden fruit.

And she wanted a taste of him. Badly.

"A PROPER BLOW job occurs when a woman so enjoys what she's doing that she comes just by the act of pleasuring the man."

Jud didn't touch Stacy. He simply waited for her reaction. And he got it. Her pupils dilated, and her chest rose and fell with rapid breaths. For once, she was absolutely speechless.

"And a woman like Melody is too self-oriented to understand that a man's pleasure enhances her pleasure." He had Stacy right where he wanted her. Breathless. Anticipating. "It works both ways. Most young men haven't discovered that a woman's orgasm can be as pleasurable as experiencing his own."

She recovered to arch one elegant eyebrow as if his speech had no effect on her. "So making a woman come gets you off?"

"Making a woman come is essential. Without it, a man can attain physical orgasm, but he can't achieve true pleasure. Another cocktail?" He prepared a new flute even as he asked.

She glanced at her glass, then up at him, and finally to the mirror behind the bar as if that would reveal something she needed to see. "Yes . . . no, I mean . . . Dammit, Jud."

He read her mind. She wanted, yet wasn't sure. She needed, but didn't know exactly what.

He pushed her second champagne into her fingers. "Let me show you what I mean."

She sipped. In her green eyes, indecision battled yearning. He wondered if she knew just how enlightening her gaze was.

He added one more line of inducement. "Consider it an invitation to passion the likes of which you've never known." He willed her to take him up on the offer.

At the end of the bar, a waitress signaled. He let her slip through the latch to get what she needed. A guest tapped his empty glass on the counter, requesting a refill. Jud ignored him until he went away. The bar chatter was like elevator music he tuned out. All that mattered was enticing this gorgeous woman.

"Jud, I really don't think—"

"Don't think, Serena," he said, using her club name to beguile her. "I want you. I have for quite some time."

She bit her lip, something he'd never seen her do except to lure a younger man upstairs with her. This was completely unconscious. He liked having her off balance.

"Quite some time? How long?"

"Months," he murmured, catching and holding her gaze. "I just didn't intend to act on it."

She thought a moment, then asked, "Why tell me tonight?"

"Why not?"

She obviously didn't have an answer, lifting the champagne flute instead.

"It will be the best orgasm you've ever experienced."

"Just one?" she quipped, and he knew she was trying to regain control.

Jud wasn't about to let her have it. "One will be all you need, all you can take. You'll sleep like a baby. Then you'll return begging for more."

Her nose tipped a haughty degree higher. "I don't beg."

And he knew he had her. Stacy Parrish loved a challenge.

"You will after tonight. You'll never go back to young meat." He took her hand, lacing her fingers with his. "Never."

She lifted her head, met his gaze, and smiled her amazing, sultry smile. "If anyone does the begging, it'll be you."

And the challenge was on.

GOOD LORD, WHAT had she agreed to?

Stacy didn't care. She'd been wishing for a man who would surprise her, and Jud had definitely done that. His desire was palpable, reaching out to touch her, his concentration on her unequivocal. Voices, laughter, soft strains of music, all faded into the background. There was nothing but Jud's attraction, like an elixir she craved. She might regret it tomorrow—only if she let herself—but for right now, damn the consequences.

Jud picked up the house phone and dialed. She couldn't hear the quiet conversation, but she knew he wasn't wasting a minute. Reaching into his pants pocket, he pulled out a gold key, turned her hand over and placed it in her palm.

"Top floor, last door."

"Is that where you live?" She fingered the gold filigree. That particular room had never been offered for her use in the entire time she'd been coming to the club.

"No. I'm not waiting long enough to take you to my home."

She cocked her head. "Afraid I'll change my mind?"

"Afraid, no, but convincing you all over again will waste precious time. I'll be up there in a minute."

Presumably after he'd found someone to fill in at the bar. Stacy closed her fingers around the key and rose from the barstool. She turned, then glanced back over her shoulder. "By the way, you didn't convince me. I decided. And I follow through on my decisions."

As if her heart weren't racing madly, she strolled through the tables on her way out. Melody glared, as if she'd seen the key exchange, then slugged back the dregs of her Long Island iced tea. Stacy didn't even look for her studs. Jud was too much in her blood. She couldn't understand how he'd managed that so quickly. Maybe her own attraction to him had been sizzling just below the surface all along.

At almost midnight, the club was hopping, music jamming the corridors from various rooms, people hugging tight to each other in gloomy corners. She liked to wander the hallways and some of the exotic chambers, enjoying the performances as much as she enjoyed actually doing the performing. But not tonight. It was as if she'd never had those earlier orgasms.

By the time she reached the third and top floor, she was almost running. The key slid into the door easily, and she pushed it open in a flutter to see the interior.

Jud was stamped all over it. Instead of the usual wall hangings and plush carpet, this room gleamed with hardwood. The walls were paneled except for one floor-to-ceiling mirror. Persian carpets decorated the polished floorboards. A brown leather sofa and chair sat before an ornate fireplace.

Stacy moved to the riser beside the high, sturdy, four-poster bed and confronted the reflection in the strategically placed mirror. Examining it, she discovered the glass was made of tiles placed so expertly the seams were almost invisible. Everything done on that bed could be viewed by the participants, but unlike the rooms she'd been in, this mirror wasn't a window affording someone else a vista of the bed. What took place in this room was for the pleasure of the occupants only.

Just the two of them. Somehow that put more importance on the whole episode. What did Jud expect from her?

"I've watched you."

She hadn't even heard him enter, but the door was closed behind him, and he'd crossed to the end of the bed.

"Watched me?" She could only repeat what he said.

He shrugged. "You asked why I chose tonight to tell you I want you. Because I was watching you and your young men, and you've got me so hard I can't ignore it anymore."

She'd always liked the awareness of being seen by an invisible lover. But knowing it was Jud who'd watched, Jud who got hot and hard? Her panties dampened, her breath caught in her throat, and a thrill skated down her spine.

But she couldn't let that sudden kick give him the upper hand. "You should have told me."

He angled his head, regarded her a moment. "Why?"

"It was an invasion of my privacy."

"You didn't ask for privacy. You asked for a room that had a two-way mirror." The corner of his mouth lifted slightly. "In fact, you've come alone to perform for whoever was behind the mirror. You never specified who it should be." He dropped his voice to a seductive whisper. "Three times, that man's been me."

Three times. Tonight and . . . when? She was dying to know.

Then he was behind her, the warmth of his body enveloping her, and he turned her to face the mirror. He grabbed her hand, dragging her fingers down the front of her dress to the hem. Then he tugged it up, the reflection revealing her inch by inch, and guided her to the crotch of her satin underwear. She was hot and very, very wet, her thong soaked. And it wasn't a residual leftover from her encounter earlier in the evening.

"Knowing it was me makes you hot and wet," he murmured against her hair, "and you like it. You like knowing how hard I got watching you."

He was so damn right. She always wondered about the men who watched her, who got hot and hard behind the glass. It added an extra dollop of pleasure. Knowing it was Jud gave her an immense power rush that made her squirm against him.

But the man was getting a little too arrogant. "If you were watching, then you know just how big an act you have to follow. Are you up—" she puckered her mouth around the word "—to it?"

His reflection smiled at her. "I did notice you had to tell your pupils what to do." He licked her ear, sending a shiver straight to her clit. "Wouldn't it be nice if someone figured out what you wanted all on his own?"

His husky voice and those hot hands were getting to her, but she liked having control, too. Pivoting, she put her palm to his pants. He was thick, hard, and she turned the tables on him. "Have you forgotten what we came up here for? I'm going to give you the most proper blow job you've ever gotten," she told him. She'd have him screaming and begging.

He cupped the back of her neck and dragged her close, his lips coming down on hers in a crushing kiss. She opened, gave him entry, and sucked his tongue. He tasted of malt, though she hadn't seen him drink, laced with the subtle flavor of her peach champagne. As if he'd already partaken of her. She rose to her toes, wrapped her arms around his neck.

God, he tasted good. He met every thrust, and did her one better. Her nipples peaked with nothing but the brush of his chest against hers and his tongue in her mouth. She was breathless by the time she eased back onto her heels.

"No kissing," she whispered. It wasn't a rule she had for the club, it was just something she didn't do. Somehow, kissing was more intimate than all the others things she'd done. And while she adored sex, she wasn't keen on total intimacy. That wasn't what she wanted from her visits to the club.

His eyes were dark as he searched her face, then dropped his gaze to her lips. "Oh yes, we're going to kiss."

He took her mouth and allowed no battle for control. He turned her knees to jelly, and she clutched his arms to steady herself. When he pulled back, her lips felt utterly devoured.

He was very good, and her body demanded more. Holding onto him, she angled herself so that she could see them together in the mirror. A flush had risen to her skin, making her glow. His dark hair was out of place where she'd run her fingers through it. Beneath the fitted tux, desire was written in every line of his body.

Then he bent his head again, capturing her with a barely there kiss, and eclipsing the sight in the mirror.

"Take off your panties," he murmured against her lips.

His words in the bar came back to her. A proper blow job was one in which a woman so enjoyed what she was doing that she came. Suddenly, she wanted that *proper* blow job more than she'd ever wanted anything. She wanted to bring Jud McCord to his knees. Raising her dress, she slipped her panties down her legs, never taking her eyes off him despite the mirror in the periphery of her vision.

When she straightened, he grabbed her chin, holding her gently. "Tell me you love knowing it was me who watched you."

She closed her eyes, seeing herself impaled by her two virile young lovers. Then she visualized Jud on the other side of the mirror, watching her every move, his whole focus on her. And God, yes, the image made her tremble. He wanted her. The knowledge seduced her completely.

"Yes, I like it."

Satisfaction flickered in that dark gaze of his; then he reached for his zipper.

Melody's question was answered. No boxers, no briefs. Commando. The head of his cock already glistened with moisture. Stacy dropped to her knees before him.

"You're beautiful." The words slipped from her with awe.

"And you're a thing of beauty down on your knees. In that position, a woman holds all the power."

So true. She held him in the palm of her hand, slowly wrapping her fingers around him. She took one last glance at the sexy image in the mirror before she bent to slip him into her mouth. His unique, salty flavor burst on her tongue. She drank, savoring the beads of come. His musky male scent rose to cloud her mind. This was Jud. God, it was *Jud*. His taste and scent seduced her in ways she'd never imagined. He cupped her face in both hands, his fingers deliciously rough on her cheeks, and guided her to take his full length. But he was too big. When she'd taken as much as she could, she let him glide from her lips, sucking on him as she drew back.

A purr welled up from her throat. He was so delicious, and her pussy creamed for him. She ran one hand down her dress from nipples to thighs. A pulse beat between her legs.

"Again," he urged.

She took him with her lips, over and over until he groaned and moved against her, thrusting his hips, forcing her to take more than she ever thought she could. And she loved it. She loved that it was *him*.

"I can't get enough of watching you."

She slid her tongue along the slit of his cock and felt his full-body shiver.

"Christ, I can't even think when you're doing that."

She opened her eyes to see him in the mirror. His head was thrown back, his neck corded, those long lashes of his dusting his cheeks. Then he looked down, tipping her chin away from the reflection. His gaze trapped her, a dark pool of need. His intensity had her skimming her hand between her thighs, compelled to touch herself. She gave herself up to the sheer, overwhelming pleasure of his taste, the feel of his hard flesh between her lips, the intoxicating scent of his skin. He plunged deeply, fucking her mouth as he held her head in his hands. All the while, she caressed herself in rhythm to his thrusts.

She squeezed his balls and felt his orgasm build against her throat. When the first wave of come filled her mouth, heat shot from deep inside her. With one last stroke across her clitoris, she came as hard as he did, flying off in an out-of-body experience where all that existed was the salt of his come in her mouth and the pulse of her pleasure sweeping through her limbs. Where the only person that existed for her was Jud.

JUD CAME TO himself with his back against the bed and Stacy in his arms, wrapped around him, her skirt up around her hips and her naked ass screaming for his touch.

She took a deep breath and let it out slowly, then lifted her chin. "So, was that proper?" she asked, something he couldn't quite gauge flickering in her gaze.

"I don't think I need to tell you. You already know."

"It was very proper." The words were right, but she gave him a smile he didn't believe.

Then she eased away from him, stretching, her breasts rippling beneath her bodice. Straightening her dress, she turned and fluffed her hair in the mirror. She smoothed two fingers beneath her eyes, fixing the mascara that had smudged.

"Look at that, my lipstick's all mussed."

He pulled her back against him. Reeling her in with a kiss, he tasted her tongue, still piquant with his essence, sucked at her mouth, then finally licked along her lower lip.

He rubbed a thumb over the lush jewel he'd just tasted. "Now it's gone, and you don't need to worry about fixing it."

Once more slipping from his grasp, she came to her hands and knees and arched like a cat. His cock leapt, and he wanted to take her in that position, with his balls slapping her ass and his cock reaching to her womb.

She grabbed her panties and slipped into them, her movements unconsciously graceful and seductive in the aftermath of a powerful orgasm, yet somehow . . . detached. "You were right, Jud, I'm going to sleep like a baby. Thanks." Even her words were uninvolved, something she'd give to any man.

He wasn't just any man. As his cock claimed her mouth, he'd claimed *her*. She just wasn't ready to admit it yet.

She flipped her skirt back into place. "My sincere apologies for doubting you." She raised a brow. "Though I did touch myself. Wasn't I supposed to come without touching?"

"Not necessarily." Jud rose, his pants undone, but his dick back in place. Instead of zipping, he shrugged out of the tux jacket and threw it on the nearby sofa.

"You had your finger on your sweet little button," he went on, "because you so enjoyed what you were doing to me, you *had* to touch yourself." He paused a moment to let that sink in. "And we're only just getting started."

"But," she spread her hands, "we both had an orgasm. What more is there?"

He smiled like the predator she made him. "A lot more."

She backed up. "It's late. I need to get going."

He wasn't about to let her brush him off like a pesky gnat. He was more than one of her club trysts. He took a step toward her, his hand out.

"Jud." It had the tone of a warning.

He gave her own name back to her. "Stacy."

Her eyes widened. "You're supposed to call me Serena."

"In here, you're Stacy. Whatever I do, I'll do it to Stacy. Serena is just a figment of your imagination."

His gut tightened, and God help him, for a moment he wanted to beg. But begging wouldn't gain him anything. He knew just how to get to her.

"I've got another challenge for you."

She narrowed her eyes, but she didn't head for the door. "What?"

"Every time I give you a better orgasm than the one before, you give me another night."

"Hmm." She tipped her head from one side to the other, her mind obviously working overtime on how she could possibly lose.

Because she knew him well enough to figure out there was a catch. "That *sounds* reasonable. But . . . ?"

"But you don't take anyone else in between."

Her eyes went wide. "You mean . . ." She trailed off as if the idea was too horrific to put into words.

"We'll be exclusive. Monogamous. Just the two of us. I won't take another. And neither will you."

"If I consider exclusivity," she said after a brief pause, "I'll do it after you prove yourself, not before."

He pulled her close, took her mouth, sucked her tongue until she trembled. "I don't share." His fingers fisting lightly in her hair, he pulled her head back. "And after tonight, you're not going to want to share either."

"You're way too sure of yourself."

"And you're dying to know if I can deliver the goods."

She swallowed. Her lips glistened with the moisture he'd put there. Against him, her nipples were hard, needy beads.

"Let me get this straight. As long as you give me the kind of orgasms I so clearly deserve, we're exclusive. But if you fail to deliver, I'm free to find someone who will."

"That's about it."

"Then I really can't lose."

He let a corner of his mouth rise in an undeniably triumphant smile. "Deal, sweetheart?"

She considered for half a heartbeat. "Deal."

Hooked. Neither of them was going to lose with this bet.

FOUR

SHE COULDN'T LOSE, right? If he didn't live up to his end of the bargain, it was adios. And really, how long could he keep it up? So to speak. The tediousness of being with one person would get to them both within . . . she gave it three sessions. Three sessions together, and he'd be as ready to call it quits as she was.

But what did that mean for their friendship? She wasn't sure. But most likely, that had been over the minute she took his cock in her mouth. No use crying over spilled milk, as her mother had been so fond of saying. She'd mourn the loss later.

She raised an imperious brow and flicked her wrist. "You better get cracking. Because while that orgasm was exceptional, I gave it to myself."

Jud grinned. "You wouldn't have had it if *my* cock wasn't in your mouth." She didn't miss the slight emphasis on the pronoun. Since it was true, she didn't bother to deny it.

He removed his tie and cummerbund, tossing them on the sofa, then loosened the top buttons of his dress shirt. Dark hair sprang from the opening. She wanted to test its softness.

"Your turn."

"I don't have very much to take off." She swept a hand down her cocktail dress. "Just panties and the dress."

"What about the shoes?" He pointed to her high heels.

"Oh, I forgot about them." She hadn't been doing much *thinking* at all.

"Do you know what it did to me looking down at you with my cock in your mouth and those shoes on your dainty feet?"

"No." But she wanted to hear.

"It blew my mind to the point where I couldn't think of anything else but having you swallow all of me. Over and over."

The deep timbre of his voice, the dark desire flashing in his eyes, and those words were nothing short of perfect. They left her speechless as he went on.

"This is exactly where I want to be. Here. With you. Nowhere else. With no one else."

If he kept the monologue up, she'd be a puddle of mush at his feet.

"Keep the high heels. Lose the panties and the dress."

The command made her heart beat faster. She didn't like to be told what to do. She did the telling. Jud's tone, however, with its edge of hunger, made her cream her thighs. She started with her thong, teasing him by revealing as little as possible when she reached for the waistband. Backing up, Jud watched with a long exhale as she tossed the flimsy garment.

She undid the back zip of the dress, the straps sliding off her shoulders while she held the front in place. Watching her on her knees, he would have seen all of her right down the neckline, but playing the tease now gave her a thrill.

He pointed. "Show me everything."

Dropping the dress, she kicked it aside and stood before him naked. An annoying question mark quivered in her belly.

"You're so beautiful you could make the sky weep."

She sucked in a breath. How did he know the perfect words to get her to do anything? "You're all talk and no action."

He reached behind and lifted a glass from the round end table. Preoccupied with the room, she'd missed that he'd brought the champagne she'd left on the bar downstairs.

After the few paces it took to reach her, he held the flute to her mouth. "Drink."

She sipped, then licked her lips, the champagne fizz going to her head. Holding her gaze, he raised the glass, taking from the very spot her mouth had rested. It was incredibly erotic, almost as if he were savoring her.

"Another," he murmured, "and don't suck it off this time."

The sizzle once again filled her mouth. Jud wrapped his arm around her neck, pulling her close to lick the libation from her lips. The ruffles of his shirt tantalized her nipples. His erection rubbed her belly. Then he let her go.

"Now that I've taken it from your mouth, I'll taste it everywhere else, just to discover how uniquely different each sample is."

He was a master at seduction. Owning a sex club, she was sure he'd had a wealth of experience at it. She pushed the thought of his other encounters aside.

"Talk, talk, talk," she whispered.

"You're a hard, demanding woman."

She palmed his cock. "I'd say you're the one who's hard."

"Uh-uh-uh." He shook his head and pulled her hand to the dusting of hair in the opening of his shirt. "Your turn."

"But it works both ways, right? That a man's pleasure enhances a woman's pleasure?"

He rubbed noses with her, the caress as intimate as his kisses. "You get the idea, but I want you mindless before you force me to come again."

"Force you?"

"Oh yeah. I won't be able to stop myself. Neither will you.

Spontaneous combustion, baby." He turned her, patting her butt before he whisked back the covers on the bed. "Get ready to combust."

She climbed the riser, landing first on her hands and knees to give a teasing view of her bare behind. Flopping down on her back, she propped a pillow beneath her head, turning slightly to see the line of her body in the mirror. She bent her knees, planting the heels of her stilettos firmly in the mattress.

Jud toed off his shoes, and otherwise still fully clothed, climbed up beside her, blocking any reflection. His first act was to drizzle champagne into the hollow of her throat, then lick it away before it dripped onto the bed, sucking her flesh into his mouth.

He looked at her. "Everything will taste like peaches."

"Maybe, maybe not. You've got a lot more to taste."

He tipped the glass to splatter her nipple. The cool liquid sent a jolt through her and made her realize how hot her skin was, how rosy and flushed.

"You have gorgeous, perfect breasts," he whispered, the warmth of his breath in sharp contrast to the cool champagne.

Then he did his best to clean her up, licking like a cat at a bowl of cream before he pulled her nipple into his mouth. He drew hard on her, almost to the point of pain, but so good her hips rose from the bed and moisture spilled through her body.

"Still peaches," he murmured against her breast.

"Try the other one."

He did, with the same result. This time her hands skimmed down her sides to meet the sensual roll of her hips.

He poured champagne into her belly button. She turned to the mirror to admire the sight of his dark head bent over her.

As if he felt her movement, he reached up to tap her cheek. "Close your eyes and just feel."

"But the mirror enhances everything."

He lapped at her belly button, then rested his chin lightly on her abdomen. "The brain is the biggest sex organ. Close your eyes and imagine the sight."

She did as he requested. Behind her eyelids, she visualized his long fingers lightly stroking her thigh, his sensuous mouth caressing her stomach, his tongue dipping into the crease of her belly. The sensations heightened with her imagination, a dual effect. Her tension soared, and her hips rotated against the bed. Almost as if she could anticipate his next move, her legs parted moments before his hand strolled to her curls.

The first touch on her pussy was electric, a shock rushing through that had her pushing up against his fingers. Then his hand was gone, though the tickle of his dress shirt still tantalized her skin as he shifted. Cold liquid hit her mound, then sizzled down her center, only moments later to be heated by the warmth of his tongue and his fingers parting her folds. He lapped, sucked, teased, and she shot out of herself, close to coming in a matter of seconds.

He read her body's reactions and whispered, "Not yet." Then he blew gently on her hot flesh.

She writhed against the touch, which wasn't really a touch at all. "More," she moaned. "Please don't stop." Her ears buzzed, her blood pressure climbing. She wanted to come, she needed it so badly, nothing else mattered.

He rose up above her, the rasp of his clothing against her like an electric current traveling her skin. Glass chinked on the side table, then the drawer slid in its track.

"Keep your eyes closed and roll onto your stomach."

She did, the bedclothes strumming her overheated skin. Without sight, her body's awareness of him enhanced each touch, each whisper of sound. She was beyond trying to figure out what he was doing, she only wanted it, whatever it was he planned.

With a few well-placed taps, he got her to rise to her knees and tucked a pillow beneath her belly. His fingers circled her clit, shooting her to the orgasmic plane once more, then he eased back to her rear.

"Open up for me."

The heat of his body melted her from the inside out. She pushed her ass higher and spread her legs. Warm lube caressed her anus. He smoothed it forward, teasing her clitoris only to slip away once more. She contracted deep inside, her body almost coming on its own.

Then he gave her the more she asked for. He entered her pussy with the thick head of a toy, gliding easily in all her moisture. Another rubbery head probed her rear entrance with a slow, gentle, inexorable penetration. Oh God. Yes, yes. He'd watched her tonight, seen what she liked, and he was giving it to her all over again, his own special rendition. He eased out, then farther in, expanding her, fitting her body to the tool.

"More, baby," he whispered, "you can take more."

And God, she wanted more. She pushed back, taking another micron of the dual dildo. She felt so full, one head storming her vagina, the other working its way deeper between her cheeks. She moaned and wrapped her arms around the pillow in front of her, giving him full rein of her ass and pussy.

"Fuck me with it, please fuck me."

He increased the pace, forcing her to accept more, pulling out, then in again, going deeper with each gentle thrust. Her body started to move on its own, rocking against him. He held her hip, working the double-headed toy inside her, deep, deeper, until the heat was so great she rose to her elbows for leverage to take everything he gave her. In, out, faster, higher, enhancing the pleasure with the edge of pain. She should have been sore from her previous workout, but Jud had prepared her so well and stoked her fire until she was dripping with need.

"Harder." She panted, and then she was actually ramming herself back on the thing. *So good. So hard.* Mindless. Filled. *More.*

Please. She wasn't sure if the pleas were in her mind or if they actually fell from her lips.

Then he covered her body with his, rocked with her, his hard cock straining against his clothes, found her aching clitoris, and took the nub in rhythm to his dual penetration. His body, his touch, his voice was everywhere. She screamed his name and exploded into the stars behind her eyelids, losing herself, losing awareness to everything but this man's touch, his passion for her, and the cry of his own release.

SHE WAS MAGNIFICENT in her passion. He'd never brought another woman to this room, but regardless, he kept it well stocked. The toy had come to him in a moment of genius when his head was between her thighs. Definitely one of his better ideas.

"Oh my God." She sighed deeply.

"The best? Or shall we try again?" He knew it was the best, far better than that earlier bout with her two studs. She'd screamed louder, longer, and he'd come when his name burst from her lips. He disposed of the dildo and pulled her snugly against him.

She drew in a breath, squirmed into the pillow, and let out a long exhale. "I never thought I'd say one orgasm was enough." Then she smiled, closed her eyes, and hummed her satisfaction.

"So I win the bet." He felt like a rooster ready to crow.

"I don't remember what you were supposed to win." She nestled again. Her skin was soft against his fingertips.

"I won the enjoyment of giving you pleasure." He would win more in the future. He would win *her*, the ultimate reward.

"I *am* going to sleep like a baby," she murmured. "That was better than tonight."

He knew exactly what she meant. "Better than your young, virile playthings. That's high praise indeed."

She opened one eye. "Don't let it go to your head."

"Which one?" He skimmed the front of his pants.

She laughed, yawned, then rolled, hugging the pillow. "Did I hear the unmistakable grunt of male orgasm when I came, or was that my imagination?"

He smiled. Now she was the one who wanted to crow. And he'd let her, all she wanted. "I came in my pants like a schoolboy." He tucked a curl behind her ear. "I warned you that your pleasure would force my pleasure."

"You're just saying that to make me feel good." Jud could hear sleep claiming her voice. She didn't move as he slipped off her heels and pulled the covers to her shoulders.

"I'd never lie about something so immense," he whispered, though he was sure she no longer heard him.

He undressed, cleaned up, then climbed in beside her, his cock finding a home in the crease of her ass. In all the time she'd been coming here, Stacy had never slept at the club. She would this time. She would sleep in his arms and awaken to his touch. Then he would come with his cock buried deep inside her, exactly where he wanted to be.

STACY WOKE FEELING marvelous, safe, and relaxed. So damn *good*. It was more than a mere bodily feeling, it was a mind thing, a sense of satisfaction as emotional as it was physical. Her pleasure rumbled in her throat like a cat's purr.

She wiggled her toes and encountered bare flesh covered with a fluff of hair. Then she became aware of arms around her, a warm body pressed close, and her cheek resting against a rising and falling chest. Opening one eye, she gazed across the expanse of naked man. His chest hair tickled her nose, and his warm scent teased her senses. The tang of clean male sweat, the musk of sex, and something uniquely him, something earthy and elemental, like a forest after a hard rain.

Jud. Her stomach clenched. Her lassitude fled like a rabbit with a coyote on its heels. She'd slept with him. Not just sex, but . . . sleeping. She didn't sleep with men. She left, went home to her apartment, showered, and slept in her own bed. She twisted to look at the nightstand. The lights were still on, and the sizzle in her remaining champagne had fizzled. There was no clock, so she couldn't know the time for sure, but she felt like she'd slept forever.

He'd given her the most extraordinary orgasms. How he'd managed to make the sex better than it had been with two men was beyond her, but he'd demonstrated he was an imaginative lover who focused on his partner's pleasure. Knowing he'd come without even being inside her was a huge boon. He'd said she'd sleep like a baby, and she had. She just hadn't intended to do it with his body wrapped around her. That was more like something monogamists did. And as much as she loved bringing people together, exclusivity was for *other* people.

She eased from his grasp, sliding across the big bed to the edge. He grabbed her hand before she could slip away.

"Where are you going?"

"Home. What time is it?"

He glanced at his watch. "Three a.m."

It wasn't dawn, at least. That felt a little better. What didn't feel good was that she'd woken in his arms and actually liked it. She needed more of him. She never *needed* more from a man. The thought unsettled her. It sounded like dependency.

He smiled, a lazy, sleepy, yet wholly sexy smile. "Get back in bed." He tugged on her arm.

"No. I'm leaving."

He propped himself up on his elbow, nothing sleepy or lazy in his gaze now. "Why?"

"Because I feel like it."

"I can make you feel something better."

"You already made me feel quite a lot of things, and that's enough for tonight." Irritation sparked through her words.

He stroked her hands. "What's wrong, sweetheart?"

Sweetheart? What's up with that? They'd had great sex, but they weren't sweethearts. "I don't want anything serious, Jud. We've got a nice little challenge going here, and you definitely won both rounds last night, but don't spoil it by making it more than it is."

He let go of her and rolled to his back, stacking his hands beneath his head. "You have no idea what *it* is. But believe me, I'll get a lot of pleasure out of showing you."

With yet another subtle, enigmatic remark, he was trying to entice her back to him. She was made of stronger stuff. "Not now, thanks."

Keeping her eyes on him as if he were a lion that wanted her for breakfast, she backed down the riser. The sheet lay at his waist, exposing the gorgeous pelt of hair on his chest. It tapered to a neat arrow pointing to his erection outlined by the cotton. As she watched, a bead of come soaked through.

She salivated, wanting a taste of him. Wanted to climb right back in that bed and have at him. Then she raised her gaze to the smug slant of his eyes and the knowing crease of his mouth. The cocky bastard knew exactly what he was doing to her. And she wasn't about to let him win this time.

The very thought relegated the situation to its proper place. A challenge. He'd won with the orgasm challenge, but she'd win this one. She was not getting back in that bed.

She grabbed her thong, put it on inside out and had to start all over again. Then she stepped into her dress, zipped it, and righted her shoes, which were at the foot of the bed. She found her small clutch purse containing the essentials on the coffee table.

"Don't forget, sweetheart. Since I won, you're mine."

"I never welch on a bet." She arched her eyebrow as cockily as he grinned. "But you're going to have work much harder next time."

He pushed the sheet aside and stroked his very hard cock from base to tip, then began a leisurely pump. "Believe me, hard won't be a problem."

* * *

SHE HADN'T BALKED when he said she was his. That was certainly a step in the right direction. Of course, he'd had the notion that he'd be spending the rest of the night and most of Sunday making love to her until she couldn't remember her own name, but he was an optimist. There was always next time.

Jud pumped his cock, closed his eyes, and imagined Stacy's elegant lips sucking him off. Her eyes had darkened, her nipples peaked beneath the material of her dress, and she'd swallowed like a woman dying of thirst. For his come.

He'd gotten under her skin, and she wouldn't be able to resist coming back, bet or no bet. It was just a matter of when.

Release came as he planned all the things he was going to do to her.

FIVE

BY THREE IN the afternoon, Stacy had vacuumed, dusted, scoured the bathroom, and fantasized about Jud a million times. Other than a few brief smiles to herself over an evening's escapades, she didn't allow her assignations at The Sex Club to preoccupy her thoughts. Why was this thing with Jud different?

There was the forbidden fruit thing, but they'd crossed that line, she'd tasted him, vice versa, yadda yadda, so why did she feel this compelling need to go back for more?

Something indefinable had made the things he did to her more acute. She'd taken two studs, and while the orgasm had been wonderful, Jud, alone, had given her something far better. Both with and without the sex toy. How could that be?

By six, she'd finished the laundry and changed the bed. Jud was still like the call of the wild. She never went to the club when she had to work the next day. She never went on consecutive nights. Yet she felt a irresistible tug to throw her usual pattern to the wind.

By eight, she'd eaten a light salad and half a sandwich, soaked in the tub, reread the first five pages of a novel three times and still couldn't remember what it said. Jud kept worming his way back into her mind. Dammit. Why was she analyzing the whole thing as if it were a problem that needed to be solved?

Her sex club trysts *had* taken on a certain routine. Two or three nights a month, the same kind of men, young, studly, and, if she were honest, unimaginative. Maybe *she* was becoming unimaginative by sticking to the same sexual blueprint. Jud challenged her and gave her the unexpected. She wanted his next surprise. And there was no reason she couldn't have it tonight.

By nine she was dressed in the hot red leather dress she'd picked up last week. A black bead choker circled her throat, and matching earrings dangled amid the locks of her hair. The fact that she was going commando—as Melody called the pantiless state—set her body on simmer.

She was ready for anything Jud dished out. She was ready to let him win the challenge at least one more time.

THE UPSTAIRS BAR was quieter than a Friday or Saturday night, a few of the tables empty and no one venturing onto the small dance floor yet. By club standards, it was early, and his guests hadn't gotten down to their business. Jud had been making his usual rounds, playing the good host, stopping to chat, assessing the moods of the clientele.

He saw her the moment she entered, and everything inside him stilled. Conversation faded, music tinkled on the edge of his hearing's reach, and the people standing about him could have been cardboard cutouts. He hadn't realized that he'd been stressing about when she'd show up again, but with the sight of her in that hot red dress, the tension eased from his neck like water bubbling in a brook. He knew the woman's habits like his own, and she didn't take her sport at the club two nights in a row.

Stacy had come for him, and the knowledge shot through his veins like fire.

She sauntered toward him, pressing past a couple engaged in heavy sexual negotiation. She was like a star shining in an otherwise dark sky. The red dress left her exquisite shoulders and legs equally bare, wrapping her in leather from the swell of her abundant breasts to midthigh. The zipper that ran from top to bottom begged a man to simply pull the tab and reveal the luscious prize that lay hidden beneath the leather. He wanted to chew on the choker that caressed her throat and bury his face in the silk of her hair.

"Jud, you didn't answer my question," said the blonde he'd been chatting with. Or maybe it was one of the brunettes.

He couldn't remember the woman's name, nor those of her two companions. They were all in their late twenties. Beyond their hair tint and the differing colors of their dresses, they were indistinguishable. He decided it was the blonde who'd spoken when she dragged a fingernail down his arm.

"What were you saying?" He stepped away, adding no apology for his inattention.

"We wanted to know what you're doing later tonight."

His heart beat faster as he glanced over her head to Stacy's approach. He knew exactly what he'd be doing, tonight and for a long, long time after that. All he had to do was keep winning the challenges between them.

"Working, ladies, always working."

He smelled Stacy's subtle perfume from three feet away as if she were the only woman in the room. He had it bad, and it felt damn good. She was finally within reach, both physically and metaphorically. Taking her arm, he pulled her into the circle of women, effectively steering the blonde to the side.

"Hi, Jud."

"Hi, sweetheart."

He felt Stacy tense at the endearment. *Get used to it, baby, there's a lot more where that came from.*

"How was your day?"

She tipped her head, her eyes widening. "Fine, thank you."

He could see her brain working. At the club, people didn't exchange the same greetings. They didn't call each other sweetheart, and they didn't ask about the day, mostly because nobody gave a damn. He put his arm around her bare shoulders, then curled her hair behind her ear.

"You'll be glad to know my conversation with Derek had the desired effect."

For a moment, her eyes glazed as if she couldn't follow what he was saying, then she glanced at the long bar where Derek was drying glasses.

"Oh. Great."

"Your advice was right on." He wasn't sure she even remembered her suggestion regarding Derek's erratic work habits. So much had happened in between.

But she smiled, a pasted-on, plastic smile. "Great."

She was repeating herself. He couldn't decide if she had no idea what he was talking about or she was suddenly the frightened doe in the headlights not knowing which way to run.

Recovering, she turned to politeness, her gaze encompassing the small group they stood amid. "Who are your friends?"

He was nonplussed for a moment. He never forgot names. Or faces. Yet tonight, he could care less who the new guests were.

He tucked her closer beneath his arm even as she squirmed unobtrusively against him. "This is Serena. Ladies, why don't you introduce yourselves?"

"Amethyst." Brunette number one.

"Glory." Brunette number two.

"Tiffany." The blonde waggled her plucked eyebrows at him.

He didn't respond to the sexual message in her eyes. She was hitting on an already taken man.

"Are you Jud's mother?" Tiffany smiled at Stacy like a ballplayer psyching out the other team.

He almost laughed, the remark was so ridiculous and the intent clearly feline. Stacy was a live wire beneath his arm, her tension riding his rib cage. She pulled away, and he let her go with a spurt of elation at the idea that she was about to enter battle. It had nothing to do with the desire to have women fight over him, which, at this stage of his life, was insignificant. He simply wanted Stacy to realize she *wanted* to fight for him.

When she answered, it was with her eyes on him, not the twenty-something beauty queen. "Jud doesn't have a mother. I think he was hatched."

Well, hell, so much for fighting for him. He smiled at his own idiocy. Stacy was not an easy conquest, but she did drive him to play childish games.

"Well, *darling*, I'll leave you to—" her gaze slashed Amethyst, Glory, Tiffany, and then him "—your triple fun dip. I have my own to find."

Rather than do battle, Stacy was the type to walk away with dignity, but like hell she'd have her fun without him. "I don't think so, *sweetheart*," he said with extra emphasis, then held her gaze, challenging her. "We have an agreement."

"Not when you're breaking it." She lifted her chin.

"I have no intention of dissolving our pact." But he liked the angry spark in her gaze. She was jealous.

Before she could object, he cupped her face in his hands and took her lips. Not a demanding, take-charge kiss, but a soft melding of his mouth to hers. Her lips parted, and he delved more deeply, tasting her, letting her taste him. Her fingers fisted in his lapels, her body leaned into his, and a low moan rose up from her throat. He kissed her until the sweet lushness of her mouth and the scent of her was all that mattered.

She smelled of hot woman and need. Sex. Arousal. The small group they'd been standing with had grown to a full-fledged, hungry audience expecting a down-and-dirty show.

When he released her, she stared up at him with dazed eyes. He steadied her in the light hold of his arms. Putting two fingers to her lips, her gaze flitted from his mouth to his eyes, then his hair. His heart thumped erratically in his chest, waiting for her words. He was never quite sure how the woman would react. Which was a big part of the delightful challenge.

"Oh, I think I'm going to swoon, that was so romantic," brunette number one, or maybe two, said. He couldn't be sure and didn't care. She'd pegged the nature of his kiss exactly.

Stacy shook her head, and some of focus returned to her eyes. She wriggled in his arms. He loosened his hold to a mere grasp of her arms, but he didn't let her go completely.

"That was a taste of what's to come," he leaned in to whisper, his mouth against the shell of her ear. "I promised you ecstasy, remember? I'm prepared to do anything to provide it."

She was silent for two beats of his heart. "Anything?"

And he knew he had her. "Oh, yeah."

Pushing lightly at his shoulders to gain a few scant inches of distance, her gaze once again mapped his face, her eyes a deep, thoughtful green. "All right. But *you* remember, you don't come through with the goods, I'm outta here."

"Deal, sweetheart." Then he grabbed her hand before she could change her mind and pulled her from amid their avaricious audience.

"And stop calling me sweetheart," she hissed for his ears alone.

"Yes, dear."

THAT KISS. STACY shivered as the full impact of it sizzled through her once more. She still felt drugged by it as Jud led her upstairs. He'd scrambled her brains. He'd melted her bones. And she had the feeling that though *he* was the one who promised *her* anything, she'd actually agreed to something completely different. Not to mention that wild spark of jealousy when she'd actually been thinking he was sizing up the three stooges for triple fun. She had to keep repeating in her head that this was *just* a sexual challenge, one she had no desire to turn down.

Jud unlocked the door to a room that wasn't a bedroom like most of the other private rooms. Instead, a large circular tub surrounded by gleaming marble tile sat at one end. Steam rose from the water and fogged the mirror behind it.

"We're going to do a little hot-tubbing?"

Jud smiled. "Nothing quite so mundane. I'm going to bathe you. And you're going to bathe me."

"But I just spent an evening preparing myself. Why do it all over again?" Though thinking about giving Jud an intimate water massage was extremely appealing.

"And I'm clean as a whistle, but bathing isn't just about getting clean."

To Jud, everything was a sensual adventure. She spun on her heel to survey the rest of the room. On the opposite end, piled atop plush cream-colored carpeting, lay a thick dark blue futon covered by a mountain of pillows. Along the wall between the tub and the makeshift pleasure bed was a cabinet filled with a smorgasbord of sexual toys running the gamut from vibrators and dildos to cock rings and specialty condoms.

"Gee, everything a girl could ask for."

"And more."

She tipped her head, eyeing him speculatively. And appreciatively. "Pretty sure of yourself, aren't you?" She raised her hands to encompass the room and all its apparent preparation. "What if I'd decided not to come tonight?"

He lowered his head, smiling as if he had some private thought. "With me or by yourself, I knew you'd come tonight." He loosened his tie a notch. "And I'm always prepared for any eventuality." He took her hand. "Now show me what you're wearing under all that leather." Husky command entered his voice, and his dark eyes melted to the color of cognac.

She'd done sexy stripteases for men, but something in Jud's look made her want to rip her clothes off her body. Though she didn't have much to strip off. Maybe she should have worn some frilly lingerie to entice him, but she'd dressed with easy access in mind.

She skimmed a finger along the bustier-style bodice. "Why don't you do the honors?"

Jud eyed the zipper running the length of her red leather dress. Reversible, it could be undone from either end. He leaned down and slowly zipped up until he revealed her neatly trimmed bush. His eyes on hers, he trailed a finger over her sex just short of slipping inside her folds. Her body reacted with a flow of warmth and moisture from deep inside.

"Naughty woman. If I'd known you were bare, I don't think I could have resisted your zipper down in the bar."

Which is what she'd had in mind when she chose the dress.

His mouth quirked up on one side. "And that's exactly what you were hoping for, wasn't it? Did I disappoint you?"

She'd wanted his hands on her, but somehow that kiss had been all the hotter for the fact that he'd only touched her lips. "You haven't disappointed me yet, Jud." She raised one brow, then shrugged. "But there's always a first time."

"Always keeping me on my toes."

"Or on yours knees," she said, hinting at what he could do for her now to make up for it.

"Sweetheart, I've been on my knees for you for months now. You just haven't noticed."

"Talk, talk, talk. Let's get to the main course."

"This *is* the main course. Everything we do is." He held a strip of the dress and zipped to the top with a flourish. The leather fell away and dropped to the floor, leaving her naked except for her red high heels and the choker at her throat. He leaned in, skimmed his lips along the beaded necklace, inhaling deeply. "Appetizer, main course, dessert," he whispered, the rush of his breath across her skin making her shiver.

God. All these years, maybe she'd been rushing things. She

hadn't gone straight to intercourse, but she hadn't taken time to enjoy sexy banter, kissing, or simple touches. The dance of attracting
a man had been her foreplay, but once she'd chosen a partner, she'd
jumped to the erogenous zones, which was nice indeed, but purely
physical. She'd missed the slow build of passion. She had a feeling
Jud could keep up the play until she screamed and begged for a fast,
hard fuck.

The way his gaze stroked her bare flesh was far more than an
appetizer. Her skin flushed, her breathing jumped a notch, and her
body slickened deep inside in anticipation.

"You have the most enticing breasts I've ever seen. Hold them
up for me."

She cupped herself, unable to resist a slight pinch on each nipple
to make them hard and rosy.

"Stop that, or I'll fuck you where you stand."

"Control yourself, Jud." But again, a thrill zoomed to her clitoris. Yes. Definitely. She'd missed something big. Long, slow foreplay. If nothing else, that's what she'd take away from this time
with Jud. Slow down. Enjoy the flirty touches, fingers roaming her
back, long hand strokes up her calves to her thighs, a deep kiss. Except that she didn't find the prospect of a sexy kiss so attractive
with say, Erik or Caesar, her boys of Saturday night. There wasn't a
man she'd been with in the last few months that she could say she
felt like kissing. Except Jud.

It must be that he had a magic tongue. Speaking of which, she
wanted it on her, in her, all over her. Soon.

He turned her, patted her bottom, and pushed her to the tub's
two steps. "Bend over and put your hands on the edge."

She still wore her shoes, and the stance had her butt in the air,
her pussy open for his view. The mirror behind the tub revealed him
squatting fully clothed by her side. His hand moved as if to caress,
but there was only his breath on her backside, nothing more. He
lifted one foot and removed her shoe, tossing it aside, then the
other.

He rose. "In you go."

Steadying herself on the tub's rim, she climbed in, then sank beneath the surface to let the bubbling water froth over her breasts. Steam rose, and she was glad she'd worn waterproof makeup.

Jud simply watched, a dark heat masking his thoughts and harshening the lines of his face.

She floated to the side, then flourished a hand at him. "Well, come on. Get those clothes off."

"Shall I do a striptease?"

She salivated, then laughed at the image that came to mind.

"The thought of me stripping makes you laugh? I'm offended."

He was no such thing. She didn't think Jud could be offended by anything. The owner of a sex club would have seen and done it all. "I'm not laughing *at* you. It just made me think of that movie, *Deuce Bigalow: Male Gigolo*, where the two guys do a strip dance wearing teeny tiny sequined Speedos. Very ridiculous and funny, but so not sexy."

"I've never seen the movie. But I think I could do better."

"Forget it; sequins don't suit you." Besides, she couldn't wait to get him naked in the water. "Just take it all off now."

"Whatever you desire."

Her desires were boundless, her appetite for him unlimited. And there wasn't a doubt in her mind that Jud would deliver everything he promised.

—————— S I X ——————

JUD THREW HIS suit jacket on a corner chair, then loosened the tie and undid the shirt buttons. A glimpse of dark chest hair tantalized her. She hadn't explored his body last night, but tonight, ah yes, she'd investigate every inch as she bathed him. That's what this whole scenario was for.

He'd gone commando again. With his pants undone, his cock sprang free. His magnificent cock. Stacy had sucked it, licked it, made it come, but she hadn't studied it, hadn't yet memorized its texture or its fit in her hand.

"You're making me want to get right to the fucking again when you look at me like that." He stroked himself, then pushed his pants to his ankles and toed off the whole shebang, including his shoes and socks.

Her mouth watered. Beneath the bubbling surface, her body wept for want of him. "How am I looking at you?"

"Like you can't wait to get me inside you." He pulled off the tie, but with the tails no longer confined in his slacks, the shirt covered his erection.

"So hurry up. I've never seen a man dillydally so long."

"That's your problem, sweetheart, rushing."

Which was very close to the thought she'd had a few minutes earlier. At last he'd tossed aside every stitch of clothing. His rigid cock bobbed as he climbed the steps and stepped down into the water beside her.

"I'm naked, and I'm yours. What do you want to do to me?"

Suck him. Fuck him. Make him come. But in answer, she perused the bottles of shampoo and body wash along the rim of the tub. "Which scent do you prefer I use on you?"

"I don't care what you use on me, but I get to use something fruity on you. Tangerine maybe. I want something that reminds me of eating." He bared his teeth.

"All you think about is eating." But then, so did she, as long as it was his body parts she was savoring. She chose cucumber for him. Not too unmanly, but then something from the men's counter wasn't an available choice. She pulled him to his knees in the water and lathered his chest.

"I like that you're hairy but not too hairy." She loved the texture, coarse on his chest, but getting softer as it arrowed down his abdomen. She washed off the soap, then sucked his taut nipple into her mouth.

He drew in a hiss of breath. "I like that you like. So tell me, what's your secret fantasy? The thing you haven't done yet that you're dying to do."

"Now that's cheating." She brushed up against him as she reached behind and washed the slope of his back down to his butt. And between. "If I tell you, then you'll provide it and automatically win the challenge."

"It's not cheating to want to know what goes on in that gorgeous mind of yours."

"Cheater, cheater," she taunted as she scouted round to his

front side and foamed his balls and the base of his cock. His lids drooped in lazy desire, and he rocked gently in her fist, doing all the cleaning work himself.

"Come on," he urged. "Let's do a little Q and A. I ask something, then you get to ask."

She didn't give a damn if he cheated. It could only be to her benefit. Imagine having all your fantasies acted out for and on you. She slithered down in the water and washed his powerful thighs. "All right. But I'll only answer what I feel like answering." It's not as if she could appear to give in easily.

"Have you ever thought about being with another woman?"

She tipped her head. "There's one major obstacle to that."

"What?"

"Women don't have cocks." She took his clean, slippery tool in her hand and pumped lightly, swirling a drop of come over his taut crown. Then she shuffled back and bent her head, taking him, tasting his salty desire. "I don't think I'd enjoy sex if I didn't get to taste this."

"Well then, how about a ménage with a man and another woman? You'd get the cock as well."

She laughed. "Then it becomes a competition. Which is not the same as a challenge." At least not *their* challenge.

"And you want everything to be about you."

"Yes. As it should be." She batted her eyelashes. "Isn't that what this *agreement* between us is all about?"

"Of course. My turn now." He plucked the bottle from her hand and grabbed the tangerine wash he'd wanted to use on her.

"What about you?" she asked, though a slight tremble traveled through her as he drew soap bubble sketches all over her body. "Have you ever thought about being with another man?"

"It doesn't hold any attraction. I love women. I love everything about them."

"Like what exactly?"

"I love the way a woman tastes. Her mouth." He kissed her,

taking her tongue as if he savored a fine wine. Then he backed off to soap her shoulders. "Her skin," he murmured as he sluiced the spot with water, then bent to the curve of her neck, licking along her choker, sucking her skin lightly, then finishing off with a gentle nip. She shuddered in response.

He buried his face in her hair, breathing her in. "I like the way she smells. All the lotions she uses, the shampoos, the concoctions, the perfumes that smell completely unique with each application."

"I like the way they feel." With soapy hands, he traced her breasts, flirted with her nipples, then trailed two fingers down her arm. "Their skin is soft, like silk and satin."

With another palm of liquid, he sudsed her bottom, slipping between her cheeks and making her quiver with desire. With the other hand, he tunneled between her legs. "I like the plump feel of their sex, how slippery they get." He nudged her legs farther apart and slid across her clitoris for the moisture he liked. She purred deep in her throat like a contented feline.

"I love the sounds they make when they're aroused." He put his damp fingers to his mouth. "And did I say I liked the way they taste and smell?" He sucked on his finger as if he relished her. "Hot, spicy, fragrant."

Pulling her over him, he rubbed his cock between her folds. "I love the way a woman's pussy squeezes me when she comes. I love her heat surrounding me." He pushed her hips down to hug his contours. "I love discovering what turns her on, what makes her scream. But mostly I love being the man who gives it all to her."

She felt herself melting beneath the onslaught of his well-placed touches and the litany of sexy descriptions. "So why on earth would you want to tie yourself down to one woman?" He should have been like her, loving the variety. "I mean, after a couple of times, it's been there, done that, on to something new and exciting."

"You need to open your mind to the enormous potential. A man can never know everything there is to know about a woman. She'll always have a fresh mystery for him to uncover. A man isn't worth much if he thinks he's discovered everything. The challenge is in figuring out new ways to please her." He tapped his temple. "The only limit is in the mind. The possibilities are boundless. If she likes *this*—" he stroked her clitoris in tight circles "—then why not try *that*?" He struck deep inside her and pushed his thumb up against the base of her clit. She gasped and held onto his arms, her nails digging into his flesh.

"Wouldn't that be even better?" he whispered. "There are so many variations. I'm surprised, Stacy; I thought you would have been more imaginative."

It wasn't as if she hadn't been imaginative, but then again, instead of choosing variety in technique, she'd chosen variety in partners. Which provided some procedural differences, but pretty much it *was* the same basic thing. However, she didn't want to admit that Jud had a point. "I still think you're limiting yourself if it's only one man and one woman."

"Don't women always say men can't multitask? You deserve every ounce of my total concentration."

True enough, she liked his total concentration on her pleasure, her body, her needs. "Then concentrate harder. I haven't had an orgasm yet."

He raised her higher out of the water and stroked deep into her slick channel. "But you're very, very wet."

And very, very hot. Sparring with Jud had become a big part of the pleasure. "We're in a bathtub. Of course I'm wet."

"You're one tough lady, you know. You're wet because you're excited. Unbearably. Which is why you want the orgasm now. But I'm not done figuring out what turns you on. Give me your hottest fantasy."

"I don't have fantasies. If I want something, I do it."

He leaned in, caressing her ear with just a puff of air. "Liar. Every woman has fantasies, even you." Two fingers pumped slowly inside her, hitting a delicious spot. "Tell me."

She shrugged. "Fine. I had a fantasy I didn't act on. But only because it wasn't appropriate at the time."

"Ah. Those are the best kind. Close your eyes—" he put his fingers to her eyelids, forcing them shut "—and tell me every hot detail of it."

He hitched her closer, splaying one hand along the base of her spine, and gently worked her body from the inside with the other. She wrapped her arms around his neck and gave in.

"I was speeding, and a cop pulled me over." A flash of heat spread through her chest, and her breath seemed harsher in her throat as she remembered each individual sensation she'd felt that afternoon. "He was a hottie. I think it was the sunglasses, because I couldn't see his eyes, yet his uniform was tight enough over his crotch to showcase the thick outline of his cock."

Stacy's nipples peaked to rosy buds. Her breath dropped to a shallow exhale and inhale, and a sweet rush of moisture made Jud's fingers inside her even more slippery than before. For this one moment, he knew he didn't even exist for her, and he loved that her mind could so easily take over her body. Only a woman who could create passion with a mere thought could experience the heights to which he wanted to take her.

"And he was giving me the speech—" her voice deepened in imitation "—'Ma'am, do you know how fast you were going?'" She sighed. "I knew how fast I wanted to go, right down on his cock."

Her words wove a spell around them, and right now, Jud was that cop with a hot, sexy woman eyeing his cock, and he wanted to drag her out of her vehicle and fuck her on the hood of her car. He leaned down and sucked on her throat, toying with the sexy choker, eliciting a needy moan. He wanted her kiss, but more, he wanted to hear her go mad with the telling of her fantasy.

"I kept looking at that nightstick on his belt the whole time he was talking and asking for my license. But his cock—" she groaned, her body gently riding his fingers inside her "—kept growing. Huge, long. I think I started to salivate."

Her head fell back, and she licked her lips, as if her mouth had gone dry. Or she imagined tasting the cop. "Then for some reason, he touched his nightstick. He wrapped his fist around it and adjusted it on his belt, almost as if what he really wanted to do was wrap his fist around his cock, and the nightstick was the next best thing. I had the most powerful image of him bending me over the trunk of his cop car and taking me with that nightstick. In and out, in and out, while I fingered my clit and screamed and begged. I was so damn hot sitting in my car that I almost came thinking about it. When he let me go with a warning, I had to stop at the next exit and get myself off in the gas station restroom. The whole time I kept hoping he'd burst through the door and take me."

Her body moved and undulated against him, in the throes of her imagination. Jud's cock was so hot and heavy, he wanted to fuck her now, while she was dreaming about the cop, but he merely added to her experience by giving her clit long, hard swipes.

Then she clung to his neck, panted in his hair, and rode his fingers as if they were the nightstick she'd fantasized about. "God, I wanted him to fuck me. With that nightstick. Over and over, on his car. My hand splayed wide on the hot metal, trying to hold on every time he shoved it inside me. His finger sliding over my clit with every pass. Oh God."

He felt her muscles start to contract, and he entered her with two fingers. Her pussy clamped down on him in a tight grip, and she came all over his hand, clinging, moaning, crying out, until finally she relaxed against him and her body slid beneath the water. He was hard as a billy club.

He pulled her into his arms, shuddering with his own need. He had so much more to give her and all night to do it.

THE STRENGTH OF her orgasm almost made her self-conscious, and the lassitude she felt in his arms for the long moments after set off a string of warning bells. There was something *too* good about

Jud. So Stacy laughed and glanced up at him. "I would have offered him a deal for not writing up a ticket, but I was afraid I might get arrested for trying to bribe a cop." She shrugged. "Then all he did was tell me to slow down and went on his merry way. It was rather anticlimactic."

"I'm sure he had to get the hell out of there before he came all over the side of your car. Honey, I bet he was in the men's room at that same gas station jerking himself off." He stroked a hand up and down the length of her body, keeping the contact.

"Doesn't it bother you that I just came thinking about another man?"

He gave her a typical Jud smile. "Not at all. It was my fingers buried inside you when you came. But tell me something. Was the experience hotter the day it happened? Or when I stroked your clit while you were thinking about it?"

She bit her lip, then tipped her head. "I—"

"Be honest, sweetheart. At least with yourself."

She'd been hot that day. She had stopped at the gas station, and she'd had a pretty darn good orgasm. But the truth was, telling Jud about it had fueled the excitement. She could actually feel the nightstick inside her, a roughened finger on her clit with each thrust, the hot metal of the trunk, the sun beating on her head. Her mouth had watered with the need for come on her tongue. And she wouldn't lie. She might enjoy the one-up game she and Jud had going, but she wouldn't outright lie.

"It was better tonight." Though that was putting it mildly. The sensations had been downright cataclysmic.

He smiled, a sexy, triumphant smile, then turned his mouth to hers for another long, drugging kiss that had her digging her fingers into his shoulders to maintain her equilibrium.

He withdrew enough to murmur against her heated lips, "And we've got so much more to accomplish before we're done tonight."

Rising, he held out his hand, helping her down the tile steps. Wrapping a towel around her, he dried her briskly, stimulating all sorts of skin cells. Then she dried him, lingering over his cock, pumping it a few times. She glanced at him through her lashes. "Just to make sure it's very, very dry."

"It's very something, and you're only making it wetter."

He threw both towels on the edge of the tub, then tugged her across the room. Easing open the glass door on the cabinet, he reached for a dildo. Angled at the head, it was a little shorter than a regular vibrator, and the shaft was a series of graduated ripples, smaller toward the top and larger down by the base. This one was definitely a toy meant for rear use.

"You're getting a bit dyed in the wool, Jud. You've already done that particular act on me."

He stroked the silicon tip down between her breasts. "This isn't for you."

She raised a brow. It wouldn't be the first time she'd employed a dildo on a man, but men could be so . . . touchy about their masculinity. For the most part, it wasn't worth trying to convince them how much fun it could be if they opened up a little. So to speak.

She waggled an eyebrow. "It's not every man that'll let a woman take him this way."

He laughed. "You've been doing men too young to broaden their horizons. And this happens to be a very masculine pleasure, believe me. The absolute fucking center of male pleasure." He waggled the thing in front of her. "Admit it, you'd love to use this on me."

He had a point. A very good point. She reached for the strap-on harness on the shelf, but he stilled her hand. "Not with that. Just your hand."

"Hmm. So you do have your limits."

"There are no limits. But I want access to your body at just the right moment." He leaned in. "If you're very nice to me, I might let you use the harness someday."

He was so cocky and sure of himself, as if there was never a doubt who would win this challenge between them.

"If you're very nice to me, I might let you use the nightstick. But only if you beg." She'd felt his cock beneath her as she came with her little fantasy. Jud would adore playing out that fantasy.

He grabbed a tube of lube, led her to the futon, and pushed her to her knees. "Consider me begging already."

She wondered why none of it bothered him. He was supremely masculine, yet he had no problem succumbing to her wiles. Maybe that was the ultimate state of maleness, where a man couldn't lose his virility in the quest for ultimate pleasure.

He handed her the tube, setting the dildo on the carpet at his feet. "The lube heats when it touches skin."

He stood in front of her, his legs spread, his cock hard, the skin stretched finely at the tip, yet he was so damn proud and unsubjugated. She could do anything to the man, and he'd still maintain that crooked smile and his absolute maleness.

She poured the lubricant onto her palm and indeed, the liquid buzzed with a pleasant warmth. Looking up at him, she slid her hand back through his legs, coating him between the cheeks. He stared down at her as she prepared him, his eyes dark, yet a hint of humor at the corner of his mouth.

She took his cock between her lips at the same moment she pushed lightly into his anus. He sucked in his breath. She glanced up to find his nostrils flared, even as he reached down to cup the back of her head and ease his cock deeper into her mouth. His knees bent slightly, whether by design or with need, and she slipped farther inside him to press against his inner wall and the center of all that masculinity.

"I knew you'd figure out how to make it good," he murmured, lightly pumping his hips, his buttocks clenching on the gentle probe of her finger. "Christ." He groaned, and his cock pulsed against her tongue.

She was the one on her knees, but he was all hers. She eased back and prepared the dildo with lube warmed in her hand. Stroking her hair, he watched with heated eyes. That look sent her body's own brand of liquid heat pooling to her center.

"Fuck me, sweetheart. I'm a man, I can take it."

"Oh, I will fuck you. Darling." When she was done with him, he'd be her slave instead of the other way around. "Hard and fast?" she whispered. "Or slow and easy?"

"Whatever makes you the hottest."

"Slow and easy, the better to enjoy every moment of this."

"Suck me while you do it."

She took his pulsing cock, and he curled over her a moment to help her fit the toy. The first ripple popped in, and he jerked against her, letting out a long breath that played across her flesh. Then he stood up to watch her suck him deeply into her mouth. He thrust lightly, she pushed, another graduation slipping inside him.

He grunted, closed his eyes a moment, and a flash of ecstasy crossed his features. His hips flexed and pumped, pulling the toy deeper and thrusting his cock to the back of her throat in a dual taking. Together they found a synchronous rhythm, and he threw his head back, letting loose a lusty groan that shimmered along her nerve endings. She wanted nothing more than to lay him down and fuck him. It was the sexiest, scariest, most intimate moment she'd ever known.

Increasing the pace, both of her mouth and her hand, she twisted to hit a new spot inside him that made him gasp. "Damn."

A stream of hot curse words fell from his lips. She grabbed his thigh with one hand to keep herself steady. The muscles bunched and flexed beneath her hold, and the action gave his thrusts full control of her mouth. Then he wrapped her hair in his fist and pulled her head back.

"On your back. Spread your legs."

He pushed, and she fell back. With grace and agility, he turned and straddled her with barely a break in their rhythm. His hard cock, still wet from her mouth, slid between her breasts, his balls dangled before her lips like a treat offered from a lover's hand.

He pulled her knees up, pushing them to the futon and opening her completely to his hungry gaze and his hot mouth. "Don't stop. This is the part where I get access to every inch of your sweet, hot, wet pussy."

She took the base of the dildo and worked him again, unable to resist licking the underside of his balls and pulling the sack into her mouth.

He buried his face against her. When he tongued her clitoris, she reacted with a thrust of the dildo. He grunted and attacked her ferociously, licking, sucking, nipping, his fingers everywhere. She bucked against his mouth, his touch pushing her so high so quickly that the most she could concentrate on was getting the dildo exactly where it would give him the most pleasure. Heat built inside, outside, at the spot he sucked, and straight up through her chest to her throat.

She twisted and moaned, tears leaking from between her squeezed lids. She could barely catch her breath, and the musky, salty scent of his arousal spiked in her head. She took him, loved the noises he made, harsh guttural sounds of pleasure and passion. The slap of her fist against his rump, the brush of his trimmed balls across her lips, the tightening of his muscles, the relentless beat of their bodies. She felt so powerful yet so needy, so in control of him, yet so out of control of herself. And she wanted him to scream for her. She wrapped her fingers around his cock and made him ride her fisted hand even as she pumped the dildo faster, harder. She sucked the whole of his package into her mouth, swirling his nuts until they tightened and strained and she knew he was close, so close. All hers.

He hitched her closer, rammed two fingers straight up to her womb, stabbing her clit with the tip of his tongue, and she took the dildo all the way home. He shouted, the hot spurt of his semen flashed across her belly, her fingernails sank into the flesh of his butt, and she flew off into orgasmic nirvana the likes of which she'd never known.

SEVEN

HE'D TOSSED THE toy in a nearby receptacle and returned to lavish her body with the attention it deserved. On his side next to her, his head resting on her thigh, the sweet scent of her explosion filled his head. Jud lapped gently around her pussy, not enough to drive her insane, but enough to make her body spasm in reaction before she settled again.

Christ, she tasted good.

"Oh my Gawd," she whispered.

He relished that off-key note of awe and amazement.

"You're a master of the dildo, sweetheart."

His body was replete, sated, and slightly weakened with the force of his orgasm, with the force of her passion. Yet she hadn't kissed him yet. He was waiting for it, knowing that somehow it would be a turning point for her. He could talk her into all manner of sexual things, but the kiss she had to give him on her own. In time. All he had to do was wait.

She idly swirled through the come he'd shot across her belly and brought the tip of one finger to her lips. Sucking the digit clean, she went back for more. He loved a woman who wasn't afraid to enjoy a man's come in her mouth. There was nothing more erotic than a woman swallowing a man's essence.

Her eyes closed, she stretched, a sensuous full-body twist, a throaty hum of pleasure escaping her, then relaxed back against the futon. "You win again." She raised her head just enough to eye him. "But don't let it go to your head."

He stroked the crown of his cock, proving to her that she'd already gone to his head. Again. "I can't help it. That's what you do to me with just a look."

Raising her arms, she tucked a pillow under her head. "I think you need a new challenge."

She would always be a challenge. He wouldn't have it any other way, but he raised a brow, indicating she should go on.

"I've noticed you have a predilection for toys."

He stroked through her curls, sliding in the sweet moisture still filming her sex. "It's apparent you have a predilection for them, too."

She wriggled her hips, settling deeper into the cushion. "I'm not saying I don't like them." Lowering her lashes to give him the once-over, she flashed a saucy smile. "They're wonderful, in fact. But it makes things too easy for you."

"You think that was easy? I've never worked so hard in my life. And it was worth every moment."

She tapped her chest, her breasts jiggling beneath the touch. "*I* did the work this time."

And what a workout it had been. Everything about her excited him, pleased him beyond measure, and gave him a cock hard enough to drill through walls even when he wasn't with her. "What do you have in mind?"

"Next time," she paused long enough for the thought of that next time to lengthen his cock another half inch, "no props. No dildos, no vibrators, no toys, no sexy bathtub play."

Ah, she'd liked that.

"No drinking champagne off my body." She twitched her lips, thinking. "No fantasy talk."

He allowed himself an inward smile. She'd loved everything he'd done to her. "What about mirrors?"

She took a bit longer to answer that one. "No mirrors. No watching or being watched by anyone else."

That was one helluva big step forward in their relationship. He thought better of pointing it out, though. "So, you think I can only bring you to the heights of passion if I use outside stimuli."

"It'll be more challenging for you without them." She fluttered her eyelashes at him like a young coquette testing a man's mettle. "And you do like a challenge, don't you, Jud?"

He bent to her luscious pussy and swept his tongue straight up from her moist center to her clitoris. Then he licked his lips and looked up at her. Her eyes had deepened to the color of a lush Amazon jungle. "I'm up for it." In more ways than one. "Any other limitations? Speak now or forever hold your peace."

"No further limitations. Just make sure you surprise me, Jud. I love surprises."

He started strategizing the moment the words left her mouth. As much as he wanted inside her body, he'd save the ultimate possession for the next time. Hedging his bets? Maybe. But he'd make sure she enjoyed every moment.

She rolled to nip his ankle. "But remember. It's not just an orgasm. But the *best* orgasm. You have to beat tonight as well. And all you get to use," she purred, "are your hands, your mouth, and your cock."

He snapped up her offer immediately. "Done."

They were the only weapons he needed.

DESPITE ARRIVING HOME long after midnight, the Monday workday was marvelous, a pleasant, sated buzz thrumming through her body right on into the afternoon. Stacy oozed energy. Her hormones were rushing. Which was a bit odd. She couldn't remember a night at the club doing quite that much for her before. Perhaps limiting her club visits to a couple of times a month wasn't the way to go. Lord knew, at her age, a woman could use all the hormones her body could manufacture. They helped reverse the aging process.

She knew Jud expected her back at the club the very next night. For that reason alone, Stacy decided to stay home. It wouldn't do to let him think she was becoming obsessed. Or rather, addicted to his growing knowledge of her body's hot spots. The man had cockily accepted her challenge, but she wasn't going to make it easy for him. Alone together in a room, even without the possibility of his delicious little props and mind games like that whole fantasy thing, she was sure she'd get a damn fine orgasm, at the very least. And Jud did have one very big advantage. He still hadn't fucked her, and she dearly wanted to feel him inside her. But topping what they'd created together last night? That wasn't going to be easy. He'd given her a sense of ultimate power over him when *she* took *him*. That had been three-quarters of the high.

The only question was, what did she get if she won the challenge? A hot session with one or two of his clients? She wasn't sure if she'd be winning something better than what Jud gave her. Was she cutting off her nose to spite her face, as the old saying went? But what the heck, she wouldn't think about that *now*. Letting him win carried its own orgasmic delight.

She bathed, scrubbed off her makeup, moisturized, and snuggled into her favorite blue flannel pajamas. The knees were worn thin and the material soft from so many washings. They were the antithesis of sexy, but when she spent an evening on her own, everything was about comfort. Now, for a good book or a good movie. She started to scan the shelves in her den, but the doorbell rang before she could decide.

Who on earth? She glanced at the clock on the DVR. Eight thirty. Her slippers scuffed over the carpet as she headed to the front door of her condo. And then she glanced through the peephole.

Jud. She whirled, flattening her back to the wood, her hands flying to her cheeks. Her makeup-free cheeks. Her hair was all over the place, and her damn pajamas had a tear in the crotch. She peeked through the peephole once more, his face round and un-Jud-like in the distorted image. What was he doing here? Well, hello! She knew exactly what he was here for, and she should have known he'd pull something like this.

What had he said last night? *"Any other limitations? Speak now or forever hold your peace."* Damn sneaky man, he'd already been planning how he could catch her off-guard and win the bet.

She didn't have to let him in. But what the hell. She was a woman, not a conglomeration of makeup, hair, and clothing. And Jud McCord wasn't going to get one up on her.

She turned, yanked the door open, and lost her breath. He wore a navy T-shirt beneath a black leather jacket. Jeans rode his hips, well-worn and molded to the magnificent package she'd learned every inch of over the past two nights. Dark hair, dark eyes, dark clothing, he looked the epitome of a motorcycle-riding bad boy, and so in contrast to the dressed-to-the-nines Jud she was used to at the club.

He was tempting in either incarnation.

"This wasn't quite the surprise I was imagining," she said.

"If it was, it wouldn't be a surprise, now would it."

"Well, the surprise is on you." She spread her hands, indicating her state of undress. "You've caught me au naturel."

He ran a finger along her nose, past her lips, over her chin, and down her throat to the top button on her pajamas. "I like you this way."

She shivered at his touch. He really did have a way about him. She thought about accusing him of being a stalker, of invading her privacy, of violating club rules by showing up at her house. She went by Serena at the club, but she'd never hidden who she was from him. She'd even had invitations sent to her home address. But that didn't give him the right . . .

Actually, once she'd accepted his challenge, she'd given him carte blanche. And he'd used that to up the stakes between them every chance he got. Especially tonight.

He damn well knew showing up on her doorstep would throw her off balance. And she damn well wasn't going to let him know it had worked. "So, why are you here?"

"I brought a movie." He pulled a DVD case from the inside pocket of his jacket.

A *movie*? She wanted to laugh. Really, the man was so full of surprises, she couldn't keep up. "What, like *The Story of O* or *Debbie Does Dallas*?" She tsked and shook her finger at him. "Porn movies are considered props."

He put his hand to his chest in mock offense. "It's not a porno." He flashed the case in her face.

She read and this time couldn't help the burst of laughter. "You're going to seduce me with *Deuce Bigalow: Male Gigolo*?"

"Are you maligning my movie choice?" He had such a seductive twinkle in his eye. He was so damn appealing, her heart actually beat faster.

"I just wanted to watch it," he explained almost plaintively, "after you said it was funny. I happen to like a good comedy."

This all felt very strange. The challenge had been about sex. This was beyond sex. She didn't feel completely comfortable with it. The thought almost made her laugh. She was fine having sex with men, but she wasn't at ease sitting with one while watching a movie. *Get a grip, Stace!* She had to admit it was definitely backward thinking.

She sighed. Then she chuckled and shook her head. He'd won this round. Honestly, what woman wouldn't be tantalized when pursued by a man of Jud's caliber?

"All right." She stepped back and waved him in with a flourish. "But I'm only letting you in because I'm intrigued." It might be her condo, but with Jud, she wasn't so sure that gave her the home field advantage.

SHE'D SLICKED HER hair back behind her ears, removed her makeup, and wore light blue pajamas. Flannel. He'd never have guessed she was a flannel woman. Satin, silk, or lace, yes, but not this. Fuzzy blue slippers encased her feet.

She made his heart race and stripped his ego down to bare-bones need.

He'd been ready to do heavy battle to get inside her door, but she'd acquiesced with only a mild reproof. Now, she took his jacket, hung it in the closet, and he stepped right into her life. Though she didn't know that yet.

Faux marble covered the entry floor. Red roses filled a vase on a half-round table, the mirror above it reflecting the brilliant color. He followed the vision in blue flannel into her sanctuary, not the main living room, but through the first door on the right past the kitchen. The difference between it and the glass-and-chrome elegance of her living room was startling. Floor-to-ceiling bookcases crammed with paperbacks and stacks of DVDs scattered over the top of an already jam-packed holder. An easy chair with its footrest up faced the flat-panel TV, a pair of reading glasses tossed haphazardly on the table beside it.

This was the real Stacy Parrish.

"Sorry." She shrugged, looking at the chair. "I never got around to buying a sofa."

Because this was *her* room, her sanctuary. He had the feeling she'd never invited a man into it before.

"You can sit in my lap." Squeezing her firm, shapely bottom, he pushed her toward the DVD player. "Why don't you put the movie in?"

He reached into his jeans pocket and tossed the condom he'd brought on the table next to her chair.

Returning, she glanced at it as she grabbed the remote and commented dryly, "At least we know where this night is headed."

"I wanted to be prepared for when you make your move." He wanted her to initiate that kiss she'd denied him last night.

She laughed. "Maybe I can resist temptation."

He realized they'd just issued each other another challenge. He was certainly up to the seduction. He sat, patting his lap. He wanted his hands on her, now.

She shook first one foot, then the other, dropping her slippers onto the carpet. The chair was large, and she settled against him, wrapping an arm around his neck as she pointed the remote. She smelled of some sweet floral scent like nothing she'd ever worn to the club. There, she was exotic, erotic Serena. Here, she was simply a woman, and he wanted her badly. As the opening credits rolled, she snuggled deeper into him, the soft shifting of her hips bringing his cock to attention.

The slight smile curving her lips said she knew exactly what she was doing to him, the little tease. But teasing worked both ways. Before the night was over, she'd be begging him to come inside her. And she *would* kiss him.

The movie made her laugh from the moment the pathetic Deuce went to the pet shop for sea snails. Jud felt the sexy sound deep in his vitals. Raising the flannel top to her waist, he petted her abdomen in slow, rhythmic strokes. Her skin was soft, fragrant. Without missing a beat, she pulled his hand from beneath the thin material and placed it on her knee. Like a teenage girl keeping her date in line. He stroked back up her leg, his thumb heading along the inside of her thigh. She clamped her legs. He punished her with a nip to the earlobe.

"You're supposed to be watching the movie."

"I am watching." He once more slipped beneath the soft flannel and headed straight for one of her full, luscious breasts. The nipple beaded before he even touched it.

She pursed her succulent lips. "What just happened?"

"Your nipple got hard, and it's begging me to suck it."

She sighed. "I meant in the movie."

"Deuce is going to become a gigolo."

"You know that just from reading the back of the DVD."

He grabbed the remote. "I think we should pause a moment."

Then he lifted her shirt and took that very ripe nipple in his mouth. She arched against him, putting her hand to the back of his head and holding him close. He flicked his tongue over her, then sucked her deep, and she moaned. For a second. Then she pushed him away and took control of the remote.

"That's enough for now. We'll never finish the movie this way, and it's really very funny."

"I can touch you and watch the movie at the same time."

"Yes, but you're distracting me."

And he'd bet that if he could get his hands between her legs, she'd be wet and wildly hot. He tried.

Stacy cupped his face in both her hands and put her nose down to his. "Stop that and watch the movie."

Jud didn't stop touching her, of course, but he did watch the movie. And laughed. Stacy snuggled in his lap, her arm around his neck, and his body touched her everywhere, set each nerve ending alight. It was the sexiest thing she'd ever done with a man. He kissed and petted her constantly, his hands all over, stroking, stoking her fire. Love bites on her neck, his tongue along the shell of her ear, kisses on her cheek, her eyelids, the corner of her mouth, her throat. He even caressed her feet. He skimmed up her leg from calf to thigh, smoothed over her hip, then followed the crease of her butt. He would have gone deeper, but she closed her legs. Which only served to make her hotter. She wriggled and fidgeted in his lap, continually riding that erection of his to further hardness. The condom was in sight on the table, and the game was who would grab for it first and who could hold off the longest.

And it was so damn much fun. It wasn't as if she didn't have fun in bed, but this was different in a way she couldn't explain. And she wanted more.

When the movie got to the part where the woman with Tourette's started hurling profanity at the couple in the next car, Jud grabbed her chin and kissed her soundly, his tongue deep in her mouth. "You have a raunchy sense of humor. I like it."

She started thinking of the other movies she could show him, some a tad raunchy, a few dark comedies. Then caught herself. What? She was contemplating watching *more* movies with Jud?

During the strip dance scene, he sneaked a hand down her pajama bottoms and whispered, "I *know* I can do better."

"No Speedos."

"Oh please, please, let me wear the sequined Speedo." His eyes sparkled with humor and little boy delight.

Her chest tightened, and her heart flipped over. It was like that moment in the bar when he'd offered her the lure of the proper blow job, and she'd suddenly seen him in a whole new light. Here was another side of Jud, another aspect, another piece of the man revealed in his laughter and his warm eyes. And she wanted it, wanted him, the feelings overwhelming, the man himself utterly captivating. It wasn't about sex or pleasure, it was about all the mysteries she'd uncovered and all the mysteries still to come. And she had to taste him.

She took his face in her hands and touched her mouth to his, opening to him, tonguing the ridge of his teeth. The kiss was sweet yet erotic, almost as if she were tasting him for the first time, and she was, because her eyes had been opened yet again. She slipped both arms around his neck and angled her head, making his mouth hers, plastering herself against the hard length of his body. He groaned, and the kiss deepened. He tasted of hot male, raunchy sex, and pure bliss. In all her experience, she'd never had this, at least not since she was in her twenties. But even then, it hadn't been like this.

Far more than pleasure, it was passion.

She pulled back, breathing hard, her heart racing, and chanced a look at his eyes, almost afraid of what she'd see there. He simply skimmed a finger down her cheek to let it rest at the corner of her mouth.

Something simmered in his gaze, but his words were light, teasing. "To what do I owe that pleasure?"

"You make me laugh." He made her heart beat faster and trapped her breath in her chest. There were other physical reactions, tight nipples, heat and wet gathering between her legs, but it was the racing heart that got to her, the warmth spreading through her chest and limbs. She shifted, bringing her legs up to straddle him.

Putting both hands on her behind, he tugged her body tight against him to cradle his cock, then he slid back up to grip her neck and tangle his fingers in her hair.

"If I make you laugh again, do I get another kiss?"

She nodded, but took his mouth before he even had a chance to try. She kissed him with her whole body, her thighs gripping his legs, her pussy making love to his cock through the layers of clothing, breasts to his chest, arms tight around his neck. She changed the angle of her mouth over and over, going deep, withdrawing, skimming his lips, then finally deep, deep once more. Her body purred, low, throaty sounds slipping from her mouth to his. His hands glided down her back and beneath her pajama bottoms to mold around her butt and intensify the pressure of his cock against her.

She hadn't given herself up totally to the passion of a kiss in so long, she'd forgotten how good it could be. Even the few times Jud had kissed her, she'd held something back.

"We're missing the end of the movie," he finally said between her assaults on his mouth.

"I've seen it. I'll tell you what happens." Reaching down between them, she cupped his cock, squeezing first, then rubbing him to increased hardness through his jeans.

"Get naked with me," she urged, trying to keep the tremor out of her voice, yet her fingers trembled with need.

"I thought you'd never ask."

They'd had a challenge between them. Who could seduce whom first. Who would succumb first. He'd played her body lightly all night, but in the end, she'd been seduced by a mere look, a playful smile, and his boyish laugh.

And she didn't give a damn that he'd won.

EIGHT

STACY PULLED JUD'S shirt over his head before she slid off his lap. He was quick to stand, unbuckle, unzip, and toe everything off into a heap on the floor.

"You are magnificent." Hard lines of muscle, dark hair arrowing down his abdomen, taut buttocks, and the most beautiful cock she'd ever touched. Where were the signs of age on his superb frame? She touched, sliding her fingers down the center of his chest to the tip of his penis, and found only firm flesh everywhere her hand traveled.

He tipped her chin. "I'm almost half a century old, and I'm not perfect."

Yet she couldn't find any flaws.

His spicy male scent filled her head, and the heat in his eyes brought an answering rush of moisture between her thighs. God, she loved to be wanted like this. Her mind and body craved it like water, food, sustenance. Her interludes at the club had never come close to the way his touch shuddered through her.

Even last night, as good as it had been, was a level below what he made her feel right now.

He pulled the tie on her pajama bottoms, and they fell to carpet. Even as she stepped out of them, he tugged on the buttons of her top.

"I want your breasts." They overflowed his big hands, and he stroked her nipples. Then he slid the sleeves off her arms. She was naked, no makeup, no hair gel, no clothing.

"Perfect," he whispered, and the tone of reverence beat deep inside her.

He skimmed a finger down into the folds of her pussy. "You're wet. And I've barely touched you."

Jud had taken her from zero to sixty with unbridled laughter, lingering touches, and hot kisses. And what a master of kissing he was. The man could suck the face off the *Mona Lisa* and leave behind just her smile. Stacy was wet and ready for him. He pulled her into the chair, helping her slide her legs along the side of his thighs but maintaining inches between the fit of their bodies. When he entered her with two fingers, she shivered and her body clamped down on him.

She tipped her head back and relished the mind and body sensations he created. "Fuck me with your fingers."

He smiled, the color of his eyes deepening to the warmth of earth. He started a slow, unyielding pump. Another finger eased in with the first two, grazing a spot inside that spiraled her into mindlessness. There was only his fingers taking her, his voice whispering to her, and the steady, unstoppable climb to the pinnacle of passion.

"Kiss me while I'm inside you," he murmured.

She would have done anything at that moment. She took his mouth, her tongue darting in rhythm to his touch inside her. He cupped the back of her neck, holding her steady, then he sucked her deep, taking her mouth, her lips, and her tongue the way his hand took her body. Completely. She let herself drown in his scent, in the sheer pleasure of his taste.

Then he withdrew from her, dragging a finger across her clitoris, and finally pulling his lips from hers. She felt dazed, needy, powerless. And impaled by his gaze.

She took a deep breath. "Fuck me, Jud. Please." All she wanted was the feel of him inside her.

He held out the condom he'd put on the side table earlier. "Put it on me."

She always employed condoms, and she often did the honors, yet the heat in Jud's eyes made her want to raise the simple act of donning a condom from a mere necessity to part of the main course. She took the package from his hand, "Hmm, flavored," then broke the seal and tossed aside the wrapper.

Scooting back on his lap, she stroked a hand down his cock. Heat seared her, his hardness in her soft palm, pulsing against her flesh. She went to place the latex, then backed off for a moment of consideration.

"You're not hard enough to put it on yet." He was a rigid staff in her hand and more than ready, but she needed a little play. Holding him tightly, she smoothed her thumb over the slit in his crown, smearing the tip with droplets of precome. He sucked in a breath. As she pumped him lightly in her fist, his hips surged upward, a curse seething through his lips.

"Hell, it's hard enough. Any harder and I can drive a fucking car with it."

"No," she sighed, shaking her head, "still not quite there yet." Her mouth watered for a taste of him, and she didn't deny herself, sliding his cock into the depths of her mouth and back out again, teasing another drop of come from the crown.

"Jesus, Stacy, you're killing me. Just put it on, dammit. Please." His plea broke in the middle with a groan.

The sound was so damn powerful, it made her heart stutter and miss a beat. He was every woman's wet dream, the fantasy of scores of women at The Sex Club, yet he'd chosen her, was begging her. She could get used to it, start to need it. In her current state, that didn't bother her one damn bit.

"Pushy, pushy," she whispered. Placing the condom, she unfurled it, following its progress with her mouth as she did so, the flavor faintly strawberry. His shudder traveled along her thighs, through her belly, and straight up into her heart.

"Fucking tease," he muttered, and she loved the harsh rasp of his voice. Then he wrapped his arms around her and pulled her forward on his lap. He slid into her pussy so easily, so perfectly, as if he was meant to be there. The triumph of making him beg faded in the devastating sensation.

It was the most gentle taking she'd ever known, and in that, it carried its own power. She clung to his neck, burrowing against the side of his throat, and let him control each movement. There was nothing frantic, yet it was somehow so elemental. He filled her to her womb, sealed every empty space inside her, made her feel beautiful and desirable. He moved her hips over him, his hands guiding her to a faster pace.

"Kiss me again," he demanded, and she took his mouth as deeply as his cock took her. Chest hair tantalized her nipples, warm breath puffed through her hair sending shivers along her scalp, and his cock inside her hit something deep and untouched.

She always stroked her clitoris during intercourse, or made the man do it. She needed outside stimulation. With Jud, there was only how he felt inside her, the glide of his penis, the grip of her pussy on him, the heat rushing through her body, the electricity in his touch, and his minty taste against her tongue.

She came from the inside out, shattering, moaning against his throat. When he pulsed in her, shoved up hard one last time, rotating her against him before the throb of his orgasm filled her, she came again, melting into his arms, holding onto him during the last moments of passion. Held onto the fleeting, once-in-a-lifetime feeling.

In her orgasmic bliss, it felt like making love.

* * *

JUD DIDN'T KNOWN how long they sat in the chair, his cock still inside her, her silky skin pressed against him, her delicate scent entering his mind and his heart. Her lips moved against his neck, the dampness of her tongue sending a spiral of warmth down to his gut. When he came, he'd given her a piece of himself, and he'd taken a piece of her.

She just didn't know that yet.

"Now *that* was the real thing," he murmured into her hair, nuzzling along her ear. She'd kissed him. Finally. It had been more than a concession on her part. It had been an expression of her need for him.

She pulled back and stared at him. "How do you do that?"

"Do what?"

She fluttered her hands. "I don't know. It was just ordinary sex, nothing kinky or off the wall. And yet—" she shrugged, searching for words "—it wasn't ordinary at all."

"Another best?"

She slapped at his arm playfully. "You are so cocky and full of yourself."

"Which means it was another best." He felt cocky. Sort of. When he was inside her, she was all he needed. It was a slightly terrifying feeling, and yet it was what he craved from her, what this whole challenge had been about. He'd set out to prove that he could be all she needed, too.

Only he couldn't explain to her why their relatively vanilla sex— no toys, no props, no fantasies, just his mouth, his hands, his cock, and most importantly his mind—had been the best. She had to discover the answer for herself. It was a mind and a heart thing in addition to physical attraction that transmuted pleasure into passion.

Since she hadn't answered him, he took her chin in his hand and forced her to look at him. "Good enough to remain exclusive?"

She chose a glib answer, revealing nothing, giving nothing more than she'd already given. "At some point, you're going to set an impossible goal for yourself. You can't keep on topping the last time *every* time."

Another irresistible challenge. "Try me, sweetheart."

She sat up, arching and raising her arms above her head, then twisted her body, a long sigh escaping her. The slide of her flesh around him and the sounds she made in her throat filled his balls and cock. She felt it and raised one brow.

"You're cocky *and* insatiable." Bracing her hands on the side of the chair, she rose and planted her feet on the carpet. Then she yawned. Pointedly.

His stomach sank as he removed the condom and threw it in the plastic-lined trash can beside the chair. She'd boot him out now. She was two steps forward and one step back. Sometimes two. Which put him at the exact spot he'd been before.

Except that she'd kissed him. He'd made her laugh. And she'd begun the escalation tonight.

He rose. Without her high heels, she was pleasantly petite next to him. "I'm tired, too. Let's go to bed."

Nothing like forcing the issue.

She stared at him, her hands on her hips, not one iota of self-consciousness about her nudity or his.

"All right."

The bottom dropped out of his stomach. And then he almost laughed. He'd been prepared for rejection, which was par for the course with Stacy. Instead she'd given him . . . What? He couldn't be sure. It could be another trick. Another tease. Whatever. He'd take the bonus.

He folded her beneath his arm and led her to the door. "Can I use your toothbrush? I didn't bring one."

"No, you cannot use mine. I've got another one in the drawer. You can use that."

And leave it behind for the next time. And the next time.

Because, in the end, even if took fricking years, he would win this challenge.

SHE HAD A digital clock, but still, Stacy could almost hear it ticking in the darkness. Jud had filled up her bathroom with his size and presence and now dominated her bed, wrapping himself around her like a big wooly bear rug.

His breathing evened out and deepened. If he wasn't asleep already, he would be soon. But though she'd said she was tired and followed it with that big yawn, she couldn't sleep.

Why on earth had she let him stay?

Because he felt good. It was as simple as that. Jud felt good. Being unsettled about the idea of letting him spend the night was like admitting he was somehow important to her. So she let him stay. His cock fit her perfectly, his taste tantalized her lips. And he made her laugh.

Sex was always fun. Well, of course, she wouldn't do it if it weren't. But Jud made it . . . more than fun. That was the best way to describe it. More than fun. No, no. That wasn't right. What they'd done was, quite simply, more than just sex. A mere rearranging of words gave the thought a whole new meaning.

She liked young men. She liked variety. Both things made her feel desirable, sexy, young, and vital. One more man conquered gave her one more opportunity to shake her fist at Time. She liked control. She liked telling men what to do. She liked feeling that she was teaching her lovers valuable lessons for future generations of lovers.

But she liked the way Jud made her feel on the inside. Oh God, she loved it. There were so many things, above and beyond just the physical act. When one of her interludes was over, she recalled a general replay of the event, but not every word, every breath, every look. With Jud, she remembered everything. In her mind right now, she could recite that whole speech about how much he loved women. Word for word. It made her feel ridiculously dreamy on the inside. It hadn't been about why he loved women in general; it was why he wanted her in particular. It was damn near a serenade.

She challenged him to give her the best orgasm without benefit of any props but his body. He'd done her one better. He'd made her laugh and revealed the mischievous little boy still lurking in the man's body.

He'd shown her the things she'd been missing in her quest for variety and youthfulness. She'd gone for quantity instead of quality. Did she feel any less afraid of growing old? No. Did she feel any more sated? No.

Did she really want another woman to touch him, have him, lick him, enjoy him? Hell no.

So why not give the man a chance? An exclusive chance. Why not give that chance to herself? She was sure the owner of a sex club had myriad ideas with which to tantalize her.

And if he smiled at her with that naughty little boy smile while he did it? She might never let him go.

She nudged him with her elbow. "Jud, we haven't tried phone sex."

He answered immediately, even though a moment before, she'd been sure he was asleep. "I'd love to do you with phone sex."

Phone sex would be really good. She'd engaged in it before, but Jud was . . . inventive. She figured he would add a few unexpected twists. What else? She'd done the romantic dinners overlooking a brilliant skyline, she'd done down-and-dirty sex in front of a crowd. But she hadn't just *been* with a man since she was in her twenties. Another thing she'd missed out on over the years.

"I want to see the pyramids in Egypt. Not just Giza, but all of them."

His chest rumbled against her back. She couldn't tell if he was laughing or having a heart attack. "We can do that."

"And I want to have a picnic on Machu Picchu."

"I never would have suspected a bunch of old ruins would interest you."

"They're not ruins, they're history, and they're vast."

"I agree. I just never would have guessed you'd care one way or the other. *Deuce Bigalow: Male Gigolo* and now Machu Picchu and the pyramids at Giza. You amaze me."

She laughed, burrowing deeper against him and the erection that was rising along the crease of her butt. "There's a lot you don't know about me."

"There's a lot I'm dying to learn."

"And there's so many things I don't know about you." Not sex things. But how he grew up. His so-called wild days that he'd promised to tell her about. The books he read. She didn't even know if he *liked* to read. She'd thought she knew him, but there was so much mystery she'd never even bothered to question before. "Teach me everything, Jud."

His arm tightened beneath her breasts. "You do realize that could take a long, long time."

She rolled to face him. "I do." And it felt right.

He raised a brow. "What about variety?"

"I'm sure you're up to the challenge of providing it." He'd proven that. Just as she'd proven to herself that the pattern she'd established needed some . . . improvement.

"Is this a standing invitation then?"

She shook her head. "No. You've got too many standing invitations out there as it is."

"Actually, that's not true, sweetheart." He tucked her hair behind her ear. "No one else but you ever received one."

"You're kidding." The idea turned over in her stomach, and settled. Wonderfully.

"Just you. I wanted to make sure you kept coming back."

Despite everything he'd said to her over the last few nights, it was only just now dawning on her that she'd been his obsession.

Yesterday, the idea would have been frightening, today, it felt irresistibly good.

And she wanted more, a lot more. "Well then, let me extend you an exclusive open invitation—" she put the tips of her fingers to her chest "—to me. All of me. With no expiration date." She traced his lips. "And no one else has ever received one of those, either."

He leaned his forehead against hers and let out a long sigh. "Does this mean I won?"

"You know, I don't remember you being so cocky during our late-night discussions. We're going to have to work on that." She nipped his bottom lip, thinking about all the ways she could bring him to his knees. "And incidentally, it means we both won."

"I was just waiting for you to see it my way." Then he kissed the tip of her nose. "Now, let's talk about the cop and his nightstick. I know a place I can rent—"

She clamped a hand over his mouth. "Surprise me."

ABOUT THE AUTHOR

For **Jasmine Haynes,** storytelling has always been a passion. With a bachelor's degree in accounting, she has worked in the high-tech Silicon Valley for the last twenty years. She and her husband live with their cat, Eddie Munster, and Star, the mighty moose-hunting dog. Jasmine's pastimes, when not writing her heart out, are hiking in the redwoods and taking long walks on the beach. Jasmine also writes as Jennifer Skully and J. B. Skully.

She loves to hear from her readers. Visit her Web site at *www. skullybuzz.com;* e-mail her at *skully@skullybuzz.com*: or write her at PO Box 66738, Scotts Valley, CA 95067. For info on upcoming releases, join her e-newsletter by sending an e-mail to *skullybuzz-subscriber@yahoogroups.com.*